THE CRIMSON FLAME

BEN WOLF

BLOOD MERCENARIES BOOK 1

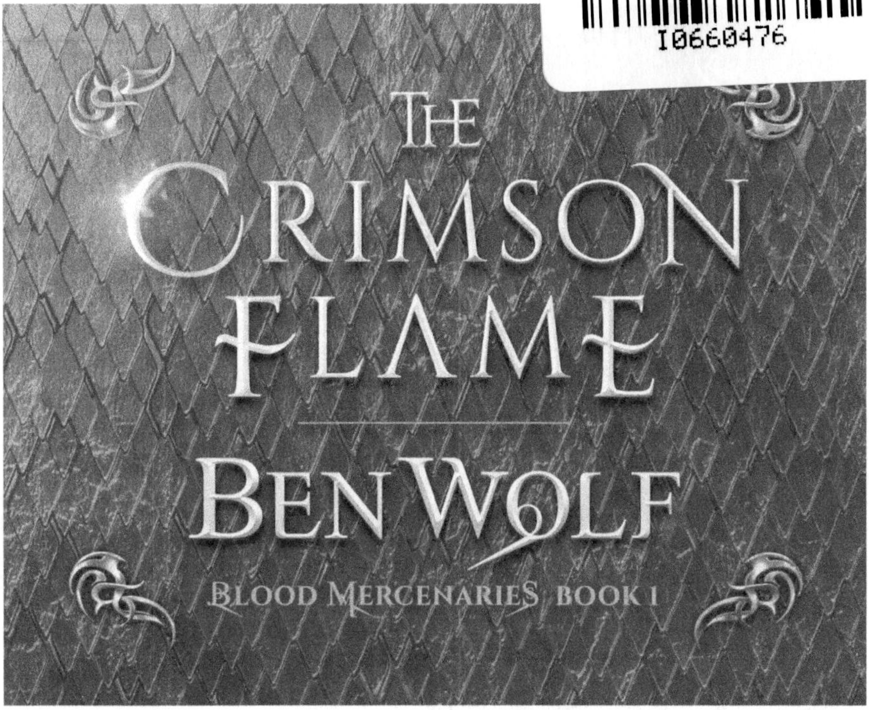

A SWORD & SORCERY DARK FANTASY NOVEL

PUBLISHED BY

SPL CKETY
PUBLISHING GROUP

WWW.SPLICKETY.COM

The Crimson Flame
Blood Mercenaries - Book One

Published by
Splickety Publishing Group, Inc.
www.splickety.com

ISBN 978-1-942462-26-2
Copyright © 2019 by Ben Wolf, Inc. All rights reserved.
www.benwolf.com

Cover design by Kirk DouPonce of DogEared Design
www.dogeareddesign.com

Available in print and ebook format on amazon.com.

Contact Ben Wolf directly at ben@benwolf.com for signed copies
and to schedule author appearances and speaking events.

Library of Congress Cataloging-in-Publication Data
Wolf, Ben
Crimson Flame, The/ Ben Wolf 1st ed.

Printed in the United States of America.

"In every story he tells, Ben Wolf has a way of drawing you into the world he's created. *The Crimson Flame* is no exception. It's a perfect blend of peril, death, and humor, and the cast of unique and interesting characters keep you turning pages till the end. A must read!"
   - **Daniel Kuhnley**, Author of *The Dark Heart Chronicles*

"These stories took me back to the days of the *Forgotten Realms* and *Dragonlance* novels, which I still regard very highly. I MUST know what happens next. Each story leaves you hanging like a season finale. I am certainly looking forward to the rest of this series!"
   - **Chris Hall**, Reader

"Ben Wolf's writing is unpretentious and easy to read; it has great flow, which is what I really enjoy to help me get lost in a story."
   - **Amelia Gieschen**, Reader

"Not only is Ben Wolf handsome, but he's a damn good writer as well!"
   - **Kirk DouPonce**, Reader & Cover Designer

"Mama Mia! This series is fantastic! Great writing, plot, characters, imagination, and world-building. I'm looking forward to seeing where this story goes. Ben Wolf has a winner here!"
   - **Peter Younghusband**, Reviewer at www.PerspectiveByPeter.com

*This book is dedicated to all the people who
have never stopped believing in me.*

*Thank you for your unending
support and encouragement.*

CONTENTS

Aletia

KUHNLEAS
OCEAN

THE THORNBACK MOUNTAINS

Mirstone

ETRIJAN

★ Sefera

The Cratered
Mountain

Valdis
Keep

XENTHAN

★ Tebaryx

URTHIA

TOSCA RIVER

LIPARULO RIVER

★ Stroeton

MUROTH

FROSTONG

ETHERIDGE

★ Drion

GOVALIA

Ranhold
Fortress

Dewmire
Fortress

Telyn

INOTH

Goldmoor

★ Govaliston

● Hachéron

● Osnal

ZINEHX
OCEAN

TAHN
SEA

Pashatan ★

CACLOS

BONAN
OCEAN

CHAPTER ONE

I t was supposed to be a quick, normal visit.

Aeron Ironglade hadn't seen his family for months, so when Mum scuttled out of the weatherworn house and trudged across the snowy street toward him, he couldn't help but smile.

He opened his arms to embrace her, but instead, she grabbed his wrist, turned back, and yanked him toward the house.

"Hurry," was all she said. "Hurry."

Aeron glanced back at Kent, his traveling companion and mercenary partner, who was already following. From the confusion on Kent's face, he had about as much idea what was going on as Aeron did.

As they went inside the door, a frantic Mum tried to shut Kent out.

"He's a friend, Mum." Aeron had to repeat it three times before she caved and let Kent inside as well.

"Upstairs." Mum tried to urge Aeron toward their rickety staircase made of old, gray pine, just like the rest of the house. "Hurry."

"Upstairs?" Aeron asked. "Mum, what's going on?"

"It's your sister," Mum replied. "We think she's dying."

Aeron couldn't have made it up the stairs faster if he'd been riding Wafer, his wyvern mount. When he reached the second floor, he threw open his sister's bedroom door.

A girl, twenty years of age with blonde hair, lay on the bed, pale and covered in perspiration, under a pile of blankets. Her lips had a sickly, purple hue to them, and the same color tainted the area around her closed eyes.

Were it not for the long, labored breaths she drew through her open mouth and the shuddering rise and fall of her chest, Aeron would've thought she was dead already.

It was his sister, Kallie, but he'd never seen her in such a state.

"What in the third hell are you doing here?" a gruff voice asked from Aeron's right.

He turned and saw Pa standing at a washbowl they'd set up on a small table in a corner. He held a dripping rag in his hands. Behind him, wintery sunlight streamed through the solitary window in Kallie's room.

"What's wrong with her?" Aeron asked. When he'd left, she'd been a perfectly healthy girl, barely over twenty years of age. Now...

"If we knew that, she'd be better by now," Pa grumbled.

Aeron went to Kallie's side and dug under the covers for her hand. He found it and gave it a slight squeeze. "Kallie, it's me. Aeron."

Her head lolled toward him, and her eyes cracked open. "Aeron?"

"Hey," he said. "How are you?"

Kallie moaned and tugged him down closer. She reeked of sweat.

At first, Aeron thought she was going to whisper something into his ear, but instead, she kissed his cheek.

Aeron smiled. She'd always kissed his cheek, ever since she was little.

He brushed a lock of blonde hair away from her face. "What's got you feeling ill?"

Kallie's eyes opened wider, and she stared up at him with a weak grin. "I'm so glad you're here."

Aeron touched her forehead. It felt hot, but not like she had a fever. It felt like a blacksmith's fire was raging inside her skull. "Gods, your head..."

Aeron turned back to face Pa and saw Mum standing in the doorway with Kent behind her. Both of them were watching.

He refocused on Pa. "Her fever is out of control."

"Why else would I be standing here with a wet rag in my hand?" Pa grunted.

"Oh." Aeron stepped aside, and Pa placed the rag on Kallie's forehead. "How long has she been like this?"

"A few days," Mum replied from behind. "But this isn't even the worst of it."

Her head felt like it was on fire, and that wasn't the worst of it? "What do you mean?"

Mum said, "She'd been gone with some friends in Urthia for a few days—"

"Nights, too," Pa added.

"—and when she came back, she was in a stupor," Mum continued. "I don't mean to be rude, but it was like when you would take your magic mushrooms."

"Worse than that," Pa interjected. He looked at Kent. "And that's saying something because he's all but worthless when he's high."

"You *know* I take those for my back pain." Aeron's voice flattened. "So thanks, Pa."

Pa blinked at Kent. "And just who in the third hell are you? And what are you doing in my house?"

Aeron could fault his father for plenty, but he understood how the sight of Kent must've been confusing to him. Clad in traveler's clothes, wearing a sword on his hip, and nearly twenty years older than Aeron, Kent occasionally got mistaken for Aeron's father while they were traveling together.

And given how his actual father behaved, Aeron wished that were the case.

"My name is Kent Etheridge. I am a fellow mercenary," Kent said. "How do you do?"

"Fine…" Pa glanced between Kent and Aeron. "Do you have to be here?"

"He can stay, Pa," Aeron said. "He's helped me out of plenty of jams over the last few months."

"Though it was you who saved me first," Kent countered.

"I don't give two coppers who saved who or when." Pa's voice started as gruff as usual, then it wavered. "I only care about saving my little girl."

Kallie laughed, and it caught them all off-guard. They looked at her.

"Little girl, little girl," she sang, "Show me your most precious pearl…"

"Is that supposed to mean something?" Kent asked.

"It's a Govalian nursery rhyme," Mum said. "She's not right in the head."

"Into the deep and under the swirl," Kallie continued her song, "Show me your most precious pearl…"

"That's enough, Kallie, dear." Mum walked over to her, picked up the wet rag, which had slipped off and onto the bed, and pressed it against Kallie's forehead again. "Rest. You need to conserve your strength."

Kallie's pale face took on a greenish pallor. "I feel sick."

"Get the bowl!" Pa snapped. "I'm not cleaning up any more of her lunch!"

Mum positioned the bowl, but Kallie batted it aside. "No… I need air."

"Can we open the window?" Aeron asked.

"It just snowed outside, and it's expensive enough to heat this house as it is," Pa growled. "We're *not* opening a window."

"Take me outside." Kallie reached for Mum and started to swing her legs out from under the blankets.

"Whoa!" Aeron rushed to her side and hooked his left arm around her back. "Easy, Kallie."

"I need air," she repeated.

As Pa got on Kallie's other side to help Aeron support her, Kent approached.

"May I be of assistance?" he asked.

Pa jabbed a finger at him. "If you dare to so much as *touch* a hair on my daughter's head..."

Kent backed away with his hands up.

"Pa, come on," Aeron moaned. "He's a friend."

"I know Govalia's emperor better than I know him, and I've never met the emperor," Pa fired back. "And if you think I'm gonna take *your* word for it, you'd better suck down another magic mushroom and go back to dancing with rainbows and unicorns."

"That's not—" Aeron released a sharp sigh. There was no sense in arguing this point with Pa. It had never worked before.

"Boys, boys." Kallie's head lolled back and forth and all around with each new step. "Always fighting over me."

"What's *that* supposed to mean?" Pa growled as they moved her toward the door.

"Pa, just help me get her downstairs," Aeron growled back.

It took a couple of minutes, and Kallie faded in and out of coherence, but they finally managed to get her to the front door.

"She needs boots!" Mum called from behind.

"Then go find some!" Pa hollered back.

Mum produced a pair of boots and slipped them onto Kallie's feet while Pa and Aeron held her upright. Kallie giggled and tried to kick them off, but Mum grabbed her ankles and forced them on.

"There. She's only wearing bedclothes," Mum said. "Should I get her a coat or a blanket?"

"She's hot as a volcano with a dragon on top," Pa said. "She'll be fine."

"Then take her outside." Mum motioned toward the door.

"Woo!" Kallie raised her fist, and Pa nearly dropped her amid a slur of curses and profanities.

Aeron didn't understand how she could go back and forth from deathly still to loud and loopy in such a short amount of time. But she'd wanted to be outside, so outside they would go.

He pulled the door open, and a cold breeze blew into the house.

Kallie inhaled a deep breath of the wintery air and exhaled it in a series of coughs.

"Easy, Kallie." It felt like the twelfth time Aeron had said it to her since they'd started heading toward the stairs. Maybe it *was* the twelfth time.

"I'm good, I'm good..." She tried to shrug out of their grasps, but neither Pa nor Aeron would let go of her. "Please, just give me some space?"

Pa sighed and released his hold. Aeron shot him a look, refusing to let go.

"What?" Pa asked. "She's been saying that to me all her life. I've learned by now it's better to just let her go her own way."

Kallie seemed content with having only half of her freedom restored to her, and she allowed Aeron to help her through the door and outside. She inhaled another deep breath, and this time she didn't cough when she exhaled it.

She opened her weary eyes wide, looked around at the snow- and slush-covered streets of Govaliston, and smiled her gigantic, crooked-toothed smile that Aeron loved seeing so much.

"Snow!" Kallie twisted free of Aeron's grasp and crouched down next to a mound of snow.

"Hey!" Aeron crouched down next to her and tried to pick her back up, but she'd already scooped up two handfuls of snow and smashed them against her face. "What's wrong with you?"

Kallie gave a contented moan as Aeron pulled her up and spun her toward him. The snow on her face was actually steaming as it melted.

"What in the third hell...?" Pa said it even as Aeron thought it.

"It feels so good..." Kallie uttered. "I'm gonna do it again."

"No, wait—"

She broke out of his grasp again and flopped onto her back, right onto the snow-covered street, and started trying to swim through the snow, moving her arms up and down and letting it wash over her. Steam rose from her body wherever the snow made contact with her skin.

Aeron marveled at the sight. *Hell of a fever.*

People walking by stared at her, wearing puzzled expressions, and then they shifted their stares to Aeron as if he were responsible for her behavior.

He was far more concerned with the prospect of them recognizing *him*. After all, he wasn't supposed to be in Govaliston—or anywhere in the entire country of Govalia at all.

Perhaps Kallie's behavior would distract people enough to keep the focus off of him, but he didn't want to risk standing around outside for any longer than he had to.

He pulled the hood of his cloak over his head. The cloak already covered his teal armor well enough, but people around his parents' house would sooner recognize his face before they'd care about his armor.

"For the gods' sakes, get her up, Aeron!" Pa yelled.

Aeron wanted to, but Kallie was clearly enjoying her snow bath. Then he noticed mud starting to form underneath her where the snow had melted, so he reached down and pulled her up once again.

More steam billowed up in her wake, and it quickly dissipated in the frigid air of early winter. That was *not* normal.

"Feel better?" Aeron asked her.

Kallie smiled up at him. "Much better."

"Let's get you back inside. By now, half the neighborhood's seen what you wear to sleep."

"Lucky them," she said with a wink.

"*Kallie!*" Mum and Pa snapped at the same time.

"I'm just kidding." She dismissed their concerns with a wave and a giggle. "You two can take a joke, yeah?"

"That *wasn't* funny," Pa countered. "Now get back inside."

In contrast to his parents, Aeron took comfort in her changed demeanor. The old Kallie was back, at least as far as he could tell. Maybe the cold and the snow had helped level her out.

Back inside the house, Mum tried to usher Kallie back upstairs, but Kallie refused to go.

"I'm better now, Mum." She shivered. "But I'm a bit chilly. I need to warm up by the fire."

"No surprise there," Pa grumbled.

Aeron helped her over to the hearth, and they stood there, together, letting the warmth of the fire wash over them.

"What's going on, Kallie?" he asked.

"You tell me, big brother," she replied. "What are you doing here?"

"A break between jobs." Aeron studied her blue eyes and her sweat-and-snow-matted blonde hair. "I can't stay long. Just wanted to swoop in and check on everyone. I'm glad I did."

"I'm glad you did, too." Kallie wrapped her arms around his torso and squeezed him into a hug.

Her embrace awakened the pain in his lower back, but at least the snow had reduced the smell of sweat she'd been giving off. Aeron hugged her in return. He could always take a shroom later, but who knew when he'd next have the chance to hug his baby sister?

Kallie released him and stood facing the fire again. "The last few days have been a blur. Longer than that, actually."

"She won't tell us what happened." Pa folded his arms and puffed out his chest, just like Kent was doing, only Kent pulled it off better. Pa even glanced at Kent a couple of times, but Kent didn't seem to have noticed. "Says she can't remember."

"I *can't* remember," Kallie said.

"That doesn't make a sliver of sense," Pa grunted. "How can you take a trip to Urthia and not remember what happened there?"

"She's sick, Pa," Aeron said. "Give her a break."

Pa's arms lowered, and he pointed at Aeron. "Keep talking to me like that, and I'll *break* something on you, boy."

Aeron rolled his eyes and refocused on Kallie. But she was lost in the flames in the hearth, staring at them, or perhaps past them, grinning slightly.

"Kallie?" he asked.

She didn't look away from the fire. "Hm?"

"You alright?"

"Mhmm." She nodded, still grinning.

"Sorry. You're just… being weird," Aeron said.

"Tell me about it," Pa muttered.

Aeron turned toward Pa, a retort cresting his tongue.

"Aeron, grab her!" Kent shouted and sprang forward.

But by the time Aeron had turned back, Kallie had already fallen headfirst into the flames and face-planted directly onto the molten center of the flaming logs.

Kent appeared right beside Aeron, grasping for her shoulders as Aeron grabbed a fistful of her hair with one hand and her biceps with his other.

A pained growl escaped Kent's lips as they yanked her up and out of the hearth, and they fell back onto the floor with her in between them.

Aeron registered Mum's shrieking and Pa's shouts, but they sounded tinny and distant. He smelled a hint of burning flesh and singed leather, and heat permeated his gauntlets.

He didn't feel burned, but he didn't care either way. He had to tend to Kallie's wounds before—

Aeron stopped short. Kallie lay there, on the floor, completely unscathed.

Her face looked the same as it had before she'd fallen, albeit smudged with ash now. But her hair wasn't singed, and she didn't have a single burn on her face, neck, shoulders…

Yet the collar of her bedclothes had burned and charred over. Scattered embers still puffed out little ringlets of smoke. Aeron patted them out with his leather-clad fingers, and the smoke quickly dissipated.

But Kallie was fine. Unconscious, or asleep, but totally fine.

How is this possible?

Then Aeron noticed Kent clutching his left wrist. Above it, his left hand bore telltale white blisters along his fingers, thumb, and palm.

How had the flames burned Kent, but Kallie's face was entirely fine?

Mum and Pa rushed over to Kallie, but Pa stopped short at the sight of his little girl's face *not* burnt to a crisp. Mum reached down and scooped Kallie into her arms and held her close, rocking her on the floor.

"What sorcery is this?" Pa uttered.

"Forgive my interruption," Kent forced out, "but if you happen to have any ointments for tending to burns, I would appreciate some aid."

Pa glanced at him, blinked, glanced at Kallie again, and said, "Yeah. Sorry. Hold on."

Then he headed into another room.

Aeron gawked at Kent. Had his magic somehow spared Kallie from harm?

"I would prefer if you did not stare at me," Kent said through gritted teeth. "I have no idea what is happening. I had nothing to do with the outcome, if that is what you are thinking."

So it wasn't Kent.

"But you're a mage. You saw what happened," Aeron said. "Is it magic?"

"Again, I have no idea," Kent replied. "I just know that I reached into that fire to save your sister's life. And in doing so, I have turned my left hand into a holiday roast."

"But why didn't she burn? Is *she* magic?"

Kent's mouth shut, and he closed his eyes and exhaled a long breath through his nose.

"Sorry," Aeron said. "I'm thinking aloud now, not asking you."

"It is not that. The pain is…" Kent opened his eyes. "I have not sustained a burn of this severity in decades. I had forgotten the depth of this kind of agony, though I imagine I will not soon forget it again."

"Here." Pa emerged from the other room with a vial of clear liquid plugged by a cork. "I'm a blacksmith. Get burns all the time. Molten metal, sparks, fire from the forge itself… you name it, I've probably been burned by it.

"This stuff won't outright fix it, but it'll help a lot. Aeron knows it helps. He used to work with me before he ran off to the Govalian Army sixteen years ago." Pa shot Aeron a glare.

Aeron ignored him. That was another topic that wasn't worth arguing about.

He handed it to Kent, who took it in his right hand. "You have my sincerest thanks, Mr. Ironglade."

"I should be thanking you… what'd you say your name was?"

"Kent."

"Mr. Kent…" Pa nodded to him. "I'm grateful, and we can be friends now, if you like."

Kent gave an agonized smirk. "I accept your offer. Now, as my friend, would you kindly help me by removing the cork from this vial? I fear my other hand will be of little use for quite some time."

"Of course, of course." Pa eased the cork out with a dull *pop*. "But you might be surprised. That stuff really helps."

Kent poured the entirety of the salve into his open palm and then handed the empty vial back to Pa. "I hope it does. Thank you."

"Like I said, I owe you far more than that for what you tried to do."

Aeron considered asking Pa what he was owed for *his* role in helping to pull Kallie out, but he kept his mouth shut. He already knew the response would've been *a swift kick in the rear* or *a smack across your smart mouth*, anyway.

Kent gingerly massaged the burn salve onto his blistered hand, and Aeron noticed the burns had traveled around the sides of his fingers as well, to some degree. He winced just looking at it, thankful he wore gauntlets with his armor. Kent couldn't because he used magic.

A thought occurred to Aeron. "Why didn't you use your magic to shield yourself from the fire?"

"I acted on impulse." Kent bared his teeth as he rubbed the salved deeper into the blisters. "I did not think to do it. Your sister's wellbeing was my only consideration."

"Magic?" Pa squinted at Kent. "Like a... a mage?"

Pa had been fetching the burn salve when Aeron had mentioned it. "Yes, Pa. He's a mage."

"Or *was*." Kent scoffed and held up his burned hand.

Pa eyed Kent, tense at first, but then he relaxed. "I suppose that's alright."

Aeron rolled his eyes. *Not much you could've done had you decided otherwise.* "Has she been behaving this way since she got back? In and out, and whatnot?"

"Yeah." Pa folded his arms again, but he didn't bother puffing out his chest this time. "But not this extreme. Today has been the strangest day so far."

"Have you taken her to see a physician or a healer or anything?"

Pa's neutral expression shifted to a glare. "No, we haven't, thanks to you."

Aeron recoiled. "What?"

"A lot's changed around here since you left." Pa's glare didn't waver. "Of course, I don't expect you to know that, since you don't see fit to visit."

"That's literally what I'm doing right now."

"You've been gone for months."

"Pa, I was in the army before that. I was gone for *sixteen years*, and now you're concerned about a few months?"

"Point is," Pa continued, unfazed, "your friend, the jackass commander in the gray armor, has been hounding me ever since you reclaimed your pet and took off."

"Wafer's *not* just a pet, and you know it." Aeron's anxiety was resurfacing. Pa had a knack for bringing it out of the depths of Aeron's soul at record speed.

"In any case, the Govalian Army canceled most of the blacksmithing contracts they had with me right after you pulled off your wyvern heist. They claim it's unrelated, and by law, I shouldn't be punished because of *your* wrongdoing—"

"It wasn't wrong to do," Aeron protested. "You gave me that secret gate key, after all."

"—but your commander nemesis has seen to it that I'm barely shoeing army stallions anymore, much less making armor or weapons," Pa said. "So coin's been tighter than usual. I'm fighting it in the imperial courts because a contract is a contract. I think I'll win, but they're bleeding me dry in the process."

Now guilt piled on top of Aeron's growing anxiety. Commander Brove was harassing his family because Aeron had taken Wafer back.

"I'm going to move you out of the city," Aeron blurted.

"What?" Pa squinted at him, and even Mum looked up from where she sat, still cradling Kallie.

"I said, I'm going to get you out of the city. I'll keep taking jobs, save up some coin, and I'll buy you a new home somewhere else."

"That's over-the-top." Pa shook his head. "The courts will—"

"And if they don't?" Aeron interrupted. "I know Commander Brove. He can't get to me, so he'll leech every last drop from you. He's the most vindictive person I've ever met."

Mum and Pa looked at each other.

"Trust me. He won't stop until you're dust under his boots."

"Where would we go?" Mum asked.

"Anywhere but this country. Pick a place, and I'll find a way to make it work. It won't be glamorous, but if you sell the forge, Pa, it could work out nicely for you."

"I don't *want* to sell the forge, Aeron."

"I didn't *want* to join the army, either, but I did what I had to do at the time," Aeron snapped.

Silence lingered in the small house.

"Look, Pa, don't argue with me about this." Aeron held up his hands. "You risked everything to help me save Wafer, and you'll never know how grateful I am to you for that. You can still be a blacksmith if you want, but you can't do it here. Commander Brove won't let you. So let me help you get a new start somewhere else."

Pa looked at Mum again, and she shrugged, then nodded. Pa nodded too. "Fine. But right now, Kallie's the bigger concern."

"Of course," Kent spoke up. He'd stopped rubbing the salve on his palm and used his right hand to push himself up to his feet. "You cannot afford to have her examined?"

Pa shook his head.

"Then take this." Kent untied the bag of gold he'd received from the last job he and Aeron had completed, and he held it out to Pa, who took it cautiously.

When Pa looked inside, his eyes widened. "I can't take this. I don't even know you."

Aeron couldn't believe it either. "Kent, you really don't have to do that."

"But we are friends now, are we not?" Kent asked them both. "Friends help each other."

Aeron did truly consider Kent to be a friend. Over the last several months, they'd been through a lot together. Kent was old enough to be his father, but Aeron had come to view Kent as a sort of big brother instead.

Even so, an offer like this, to help Kallie, went beyond the bounds of their friendship.

Pa shook his head. "We haven't been friends long enough for... *this.*"

"Take it," Kent said. "I insist."

"Don't you need it?" Mum asked.

"Not as much as she does," Kent replied. "Clearly."

Pa looked at Kent, who now held his left wrist in his right hand again. "You sure?"

Kent nodded. "Quite. She needs attention, and I am happy to do it."

"Then again, thank you," Pa said. "This is a huge help."

Aeron thought he noticed a glimmer of moisture in Pa's eyes, but he blinked, and it was gone.

"Farico," Mum said, her voice low with concern. "Look."

Pa turned toward her and then rushed over to Kallie. Aeron followed, but Kent stood back.

Mum lifted up Kallie's hair from the back of her neck, revealing some sort of mark Aeron had never seen before—or perhaps he'd just never noticed it.

"I know I haven't been here for awhile, but... has that always been there?" Aeron asked.

Mum and Pa both shook their heads.

Aeron leaned in closer and realized the mark wasn't just a mark; it was an imprint, almost like a tattoo, but sort of golden-bronze in color. If he weren't looking closely, he never would've been able to make out what it was.

Then again, up close, he still wasn't entirely sure what he was looking at.

The bottom of the mark was a single line that curved upward on both ends. Above it, another line formed three jagged peaks, with the one in the center being the longest. And a single, straight line extended from just above the bottom curve toward the center peak.

It wasn't a birthmark; its metallic sheen made that apparent. But if it was a tattoo, it was unlike any tattoo Aeron had ever seen.

And with Kallie's unexplained illness, her fall into the hearth, and the lack of damage to her body from the fire, it had to be something rooted in magic. Aeron didn't have the slightest idea what it was or why or how it got there, but he couldn't conceive of any other explanation for it.

By now, Kent was looking at it as well.

"Do you recognize it?" Aeron asked him.

Kent nodded. "Yes, I am afraid I do."

Aeron, Pa, and Mum stared at him, awaiting further detail.

"I have seen it before," Kent said. "It is a mark associated with the Crimson Flame."

✦

KENT ETHERIDGE HAD SEEN THAT SYMBOL ONLY ONCE BEFORE. HE HAD NEVER encountered any members of the Crimson Flame cult himself, but it had long been rumored that they operated in every country on the continent of Aletia, including Kent's homeland of Muroth.

Yet the symbol on Kallie's neck wasn't the cult's primary mark. The Crimson Flame emblem consisted of curling, swooping lines forming a tongue of fire, usually cast in gold or in crimson, as befitting their name.

Kallie's was a wholly different mark, but one of the cult's all the same.

"What does it mean?" Mum Ironglade trembled as she asked.

Kent didn't fault her for her fear.

What little he knew of the Crimson Flame came from legends and myths, tales of darkness spoken in hushed tones. No one really knew anything about them, but mystique had cast them as a religion of fire-worshiping phantoms capable of almost anything.

"I cannot say for certain," Kent said. "I saw it in a tome of fire magic techniques. The text mentioned the emblem's association with the Crimson Flame, nothing more. It is as much an enigma to me as the cult itself is."

"There's gotta be something to know about it," Aeron said. "Something we can find out."

"Tell me…" Kent fixed his attention on Pa Ironglade's weathered face and graying mustache. He was, perhaps, as much as a decade younger than Kent, though a life of hard manual labor had doubtless aged him. "…did any of Kallie's friends return home from their journey to Urthia?"

Pa shook his head. "Not a one, as far as I know."

"And that did not give you cause for concern?" Kent asked.

Pa's dark eyes narrowed. "The whole thing gives me *cause for concern.*"

"We figured they had stayed in Urthia," Mum clarified, still cradling Kallie in her arms. "When Kallie returned, she was so unwell, we could hardly get anything out of her."

"She was confused. Loopy. Like when you two got here. She couldn't tell a horseshoe from a halberd, and neither could her stomach, for that matter," Pa said. "And whenever she talked, she avoided answering our questions. You can't imagine how frustrating that was."

"You said it's Crimson Flame-related." Aeron turned to Kent. "And when she fell in the fire, she didn't get burned. And you said you saw the mark in a tome about fire magic. That has to mean something."

Aeron's mention of the fire incident reignited the pain in Kent's hand. The salve had already done him good, but it would be a long time before he'd feel comfortable trying to use magic with his left hand, nor could he hope to wield a weapon with it. If only he knew some healing magic as well.

But such thoughts invariably led to Aveyna, so he pushed them out of his mind. Now was not the time to focus on what he'd lost.

"I am certain it does, though I cannot speculate as to what," Kent said.

The Crimson Flame had thrived in obscurity for centuries. In Kent's old life, the officials and men of status around him had occasionally remarked how the cult may very well have already infiltrated countries' governmental structures, and no one would know it but them.

Of course, no one had any proof, so it was only conjecture to speak of such things. Yet a part of Kent had always believed it could be true—and that perhaps it actually *was* true.

But even so, what would powerful men in a secret religion want with a common girl? A mere blacksmith's daughter?

Kallie was certainly beautiful; Kent could imagine how pleasant she would look were she not gravely unwell, but there were countless beautiful young ladies scattered throughout Aletia.

Her lowborn parents weren't worth anything to nobles beyond the value of their labor, and even when Aeron had still been in the army, he didn't rank high enough to have any pull, so ransom and extortion made no sense.

As Kent considered the possibilities, a knock sounded from the door.

"Get the door, Aeron," Pa ordered more than asked. He'd taken a seat on an ancient wooden stool that looked ready to give out entirely.

Aeron didn't say anything, but he delivered a long glare to his father as he made his way over.

Meanwhile, Kent examined the puffy, burned skin on his left hand yet again. It hurt even to look at it, despite the salve's cooling effect.

But all of Kent's concerns regarding his hand evaporated when Aeron opened the door, only to have a ball of red flames slam into his armored chest.

CHAPTER TWO

The blast knocked Aeron across the house's small interior, and heat lashed at his face in whips of crimson fire, threatening to scorch him to a crisp.

His back collided with the small, wooden table where he'd taken his meals for the first sixteen years of his life, and it snapped apart under his weight. He landed on the floor among shards of the table and its legs.

Somewhere ahead of him, Mum shrieked.

His breastplate had saved his life. He looked down at it. The fire had burned away a chunk of the teal that had colored the steel breastplate, but the flames dispersed upon impact instead of igniting him. Even so, there was no mistaking the heat coming off of it, still slowly cooking his torso inside.

Better than being dead. He could survive some extra sweat and discomfort. If the fireball had hit his head instead, it would've all been over.

He blinked through the smoke trailing across the inside of his parents' house and saw wisps of red flames clinging to various spots: the corner of a stuffed chair by the hearth smoldered; an old crossbeam on the ceiling had caught fire at two separate points; several small fires dotted the floorboards between Aeron and the front door.

And in the open doorway stood a woman in crimson robes. Blonde hair poked out from under her hood, which covered the top half of her face. A golden insignia made of curled lines marked the hood at her forehead.

Until that moment, Aeron had never seen the sigil of the Crimson Flame, but he knew he was seeing it the moment he laid eyes on it.

Then again, the woman's hands were ablaze with red flames, and when she looked up at him, her charred eyes also burned—*literally burned*—with red fire as well. Who else could she be?

As the Crimson Flame woman stepped into his family home, Aeron struggled to get up to his feet, but the impact with the table and then the floor had aggravated his back pain, and it seized up on him. He gritted his teeth, adjusted his positioning quickly, and forced himself upright.

He reached over his shoulder for his spear, but then he remembered he'd left it with Wafer so as to appear less conspicuous while he and Kent snuck back through Govaliston to his parents' house. He'd considered leaving his armor behind as well, but thankfully he hadn't gone through with it. If he had, he'd be nothing but a blackened skeleton now.

As Aeron realized the exact blend of his fortune and misfortune, the woman looked at Kallie, who still lay across Mum's lap, and opened her mouth to speak.

Instead, a barrage of shards of wood launched at her, keeping her silent.

Kent stood to the side, glowering at the woman with the ferocity of a wyvern in battle. His hand gave off a faint, blue glow, and he held a piece of wood in his right hand. The wood that had careened toward the woman was the very kitchen table that had broken Aeron's fall.

Rather than speaking, the woman slashed her hands down in an X-shape and cast two slanted pillars of fire before herself. Instead of striking her, the broken table shards caught fire and incinerated to ash once they hit the flames.

While Kent and the woman traded magical blows, two men burst into the house from the back door. They wore comparable robes, but they were black instead of crimson, and their hoods were lowered, revealing their bald heads and scarred faces. Each of them held an iron sword.

More Crimson Flame cultists.

Mum gasped.

They had come for Kallie, along with the fiery blonde woman.

As the men stormed into the house, Pa shouted, "Grab the poker!"

Then he hurled his old, wooden chair at the two men. They batted it aside with their swords.

It only slowed them down for an instant, but that instant was all Aeron needed.

Aeron scrambled toward the hearth and grabbed the soot-covered poker from the rack next to it. Pa had probably forged it eons ago, but it had held up all these many years. Now it would finally see some real action.

He squared himself with the two men and held it in his gauntleted hands, ready to bash their faces in. If these bald-headed jackasses wanted Kallie, they'd have to go through him to get her.

"Pa, protect Kallie," Aeron yelled. "I'll handle these two."

The two cultists glanced at each other and smirked, then they started toward Aeron.

If he'd had his spear, he could've taken them out with a couple of quick blows at a distance. Normally the spear gave him a reach advantage over pretty much anyone he fought, whether riding Wafer or not. That was part of the reason he liked it so much.

But the poker was six inches shorter than their swords, so he'd have to get close to them to take them down. A *lot* closer.

The one on the left swung first, and Aeron matched him with a swing of his own. The iron poker held up nicely against the forged steel of the cultist's sword as they clanged together.

Fire blazed from somewhere behind Aeron, brightening the whole room with violent red light, but Aeron was fighting two men at once with a fireplace poker. He couldn't afford to look back.

Instead, Aeron whipped the poker down hard to his right side and parried a hack at his knee, then he dove and rolled past the cultists toward the back door.

He regretted it immediately because of his back, but he had better positioning now. With the cultists between him and his family, they'd be forced to contend with Pa, who had found another chair to throw while Aeron recovered his footing.

The chair smacked into the back of the cultist now on Aeron's left, and he reacted poorly. He didn't maintain his focus like Aeron had when the fire had flared behind him. Instead, the left-side cultist started to turn back toward Pa, as did the other cultist.

That's when Aeron made his move.

He hadn't trained with a sword since he'd transferred from the Govalian Army's cavalry division to the Wyvern Knight Corps twelve years ago, but swinging a chunk of metal hard enough to fell a man—especially a distracted man—was easy enough.

As the left-side cultist started to turn back toward Aeron, the poker bashed into his cheekbone, tearing his jaw halfway off of his face and leveling him to the floor. Blood flung across the room and splattered on the far wall, then more of it formed a pool under the downed cultist.

The other cultist roared and lashed his sword at Aeron's head, but Aeron's poker deflected the blow to the side. As Aeron tried to make a follow-up attack, a blast of crimson fire hit the cultist from behind, propelling his charring body toward Aeron, who dove to the side. the cultist screamed as the fire consumed him.

The flames easily killed the cultist and ignited most of the house's lower level in the process. Through his back pain, Aeron looked up and saw the blonde woman standing at the door, holding onto Kallie's wrist. A wicked smile adorned her face, and she continued to spray crimson fire from her free hand into the house.

Kallie just stood there, confused and wobbly while it happened.

To the side, Kent lay on the floor with his eyes closed, either unconscious or dead. Mum and Pa were still alive but cowering, trying to hide from the inferno blazing all around them.

Aeron wanted nothing more than to charge at the woman with his poker and run her through, but if he tried it, she would burn him to ash within seconds.

But she had Kallie. She had his only sister, whom he loved more than anyone else.

Whom Aeron would gladly die for.

So he jumped to his feet, forfeited his own life, and ran toward the woman.

Mum shrieked again.

Then the house collapsed on top of Aeron.

It hadn't killed him, perhaps thanks in part to his armor, the gods, or sheer luck, but the debris had pinned him to the floor, trapping him in place. Helpless, he watched through the rubble as the blonde woman escorted a dazed Kallie away from the wreckage of their childhood home.

"No! Kallie!" Aeron shouted. Why was she going with the blonde woman? Why wasn't she resisting? *"Kallie!"*

He struggled and strained, but he couldn't move. Around him, the old, dry pine that had made up his family home was catching fire rapidly. He needed to get out of there. He needed to get Mum and Pa and Kent out of there before the fire consumed them all.

No matter what he did, he couldn't free himself. The weight was too crushing.

But Aeron had one more dice to roll. He dug into his breastplate and pulled out the wyvern tooth necklace he always wore. It was hollowed out, and it acted as a whistle that Wafer could hear from miles, even though Aeron couldn't hear it.

He put the Wafer whistle to his dry lips and blew it hard and long.

By then, a crowd had gathered around the remains of the Ironglade house. Aeron could see them through the debris all around him, standing there like a bunch of do-nothing gawkers. His family's neighbors and friends. Fellow Govalians.

Were they refusing to help because of Aeron's history with the army? Did they hate his family because they thought he was a traitor? Or were they afraid to get involved because of the flames and the wreckage?

It didn't matter. He just needed to get out of there and chase after Kallie and the blonde woman who'd taken her. That was Aeron's only concern.

Amid the crackling of fire and the groaning of the wood and debris all around Aeron, he heard the steady, familiar flapping of wings against the air. With each wing beat, Aeron's bond with Wafer strengthened, and he sensed him drawing closer and closer.

"I'm here!" he yelled. "Wafer, hurry!"

A shadow loomed over him, and a huge, dark form dropped onto the debris between him and the crowd of people. Relief flooded Aeron's body, wiping out his anxiety and filling him with hope.

"Here!" Aeron called again.

Wafer's metallic, blue-green head bobbed down, and his golden eyes locked onto Aeron's. He tore at the rubble around Aeron with his teeth and talons, hurling huge chunks of wood to the side and clawing a path for Aeron to escape.

Others? Wafer sent to Aeron through their bond.

Mum, Pa, and Kent would have to wait. If Aeron didn't find Kallie and the blonde woman, he might never see his sister again.

"No. We're going after Kallie." Aeron climbed out of his parents' destroyed home and mounted Wafer. Then they bolted into the sky and began their search.

KENT WOKE UP WITH A POUNDING HEADACHE, COVERED IN DUST AND WOODEN boards. Despite the fires burning nearby him, he felt cold and exposed in the wintery air.

Movement flashed in the corner of his eye, and he turned his head as much as he could manage. He saw Wafer leap into the sky from the house with Aeron on his back.

Was he leaving Kent behind?

No. Kent's mind constructed the scene quickly enough.

The Crimson Flame woman had somehow rendered Kent unconscious. The last thing he remembered was a blast of fire heading for him. Using his magic, he'd erected a shield made of broken wooden furniture from inside the Ironglades' home.

The shield had saved Kent from being incinerated, but the overwhelming force of the blast had knocked him back. He couldn't remember anything else after that. Had his left hand not been so badly burned only minutes earlier, he might've stood a chance against the blonde woman and her magic.

Now the house had collapsed, and she'd disappeared. She'd taken Kallie with her, and Aeron and Wafer were pursuing her.

It hadn't been a heartless decision. It was the decision Aeron needed to make—the only one with any degree of certainty of finding his sister.

Aside from his head and his burned hand, Kent didn't feel injured anywhere else. Just buried. But he couldn't stay there. The fire was spreading throughout the old wooden home far too fast.

Kent's right hand grasped a shard of pine, and he let his magic flow into it. He concentrated his will, and the wooden debris around him began to tremble.

Gradually, the debris lifted off of him, and he managed to stand to his feet. Still holding the wood, he commanded the wreckage to continue to move. He wished he could've moved it all at once, but with his left hand unable to wield magic and his head still swimming from the blow he'd taken, he could barely use his magic at all.

The fire continued to spread. If Kent didn't find Aeron's parents soon, the fire would overtake them—if it hadn't already.

Even despite his fatigue, he forced his magic to move the smoldering boards and planks and logs aside until he found Aeron's mother and father, huddled together and trapped in the wreckage of their lives. Flames surrounded them on every side, drawing ever nearer.

Pa had shielded Mum with his own body, and he'd taken the worst of it. By the time Kent got him upright, Pa could barely walk due to all the bruises covering his body, but fortunately, he didn't seem to be wounded beyond that.

As Kent escorted them away from the fire, Pa asked, "Where's Kallie?"

"I do not know," Kent replied. "But Aeron and Wafer went after her."

He led them through the crowd gathered on the street. They'd gone silent as soon as Kent emerged with Mum and Pa Ironglade.

"What're you looking at?" Pa snapped at them. "Don't any of you have jobs? Doesn't anyone work anymore?"

The crowd slowly broke apart and dissipated, leaving only a few onlookers who would not be deterred.

"Wretched vultures," Pa muttered as Kent helped him and Mum sit against a stone building opposite of their burning home. "Waiting for us to pound off for the night so they can scavenge through the ruins for whatever's left behind." Pa raised his voice, "You'd better think twice! We're not going anywhere!"

A couple of the remaining onlookers turned back and glanced at Pa, but they kept standing there, watching as the fire continued to overtake the house.

"It wasn't much…" Mum's voice cracked with emotion, and tears streamed through the soot on her face. "…but it was our home. And Kallie…"

Kent didn't blame Pa for his anger or Mum for her sadness. He'd lost just as much as they had. He knew their pain.

He sat next to them, put his good hand on Pa's shoulder, and exhaled a sigh.

"Do you have somewhere else you can stay for the night?" Kent asked.

Mum buried her face in Pa's shoulder and wept. He looked on the verge of crying as well, but his jaw tensed as if he were trying to hold back his emotion.

"The forge, I suppose," he finally replied.

"Your blacksmith shop?" Kent asked. "Surely there is a better place. What about friends? Family?"

Pa shook his head. "No family to speak of. No friends thanks to *Aeron*." Disdain oozed from his voice.

Kent felt obligated to defend him, but now was not the time. "What about seeking shelter at the Temple of Laeri? In Goldmoor, the temple offered temporary housing for the homeless."

At that last word, Mum's weeping grew louder and more heart-wrenching.

Kent regretted saying it, but strictly speaking, it was the most accurate term for their predicament.

"I'm not staying with any fanatics. It was a fanatic who burned our house down and took our daughter. I won't accept charity from another," Pa growled. His sadness had shifted back to full-on anger. "We'll be fine at the forge. Won't be the most comfortable experience, but we'll make do."

Kent nodded. They would have to—that was for certain.

❧

BY THE TIME AERON LANDED ON THE SLUSH-COVERED STREET WITH WAFER, ALL that remained of the two-story Ironglade home was a pile of blackened, smoldering logs and ash. He dismounted and approached Kent and his parents, both of whom had long since given up their tears.

At the sight of Aeron, Pa noticeably tensed, and he slowly rose to his feet. His voice sounded more defeated than angry as he asked, "Well?"

Aeron shook his head. He felt just as defeated as Pa had sounded. "Not a trace of Kallie or the Crimson Flame woman."

Pa tilted his head skyward. His voice shook. "My little girl."

"I'll find her, Pa," Aeron promised. Nothing else mattered now. "I'll find her and bring her back."

Pa's eyes lowered to Aeron, as cold as always but now equally as sad. He didn't say anything. He just shook his head.

"I *will*," Aeron insisted.

"She's gone, Aeron," Pa finally said. "You heard what Kent said. These people are ghosts. She's gone…" His voice quaked. "…and we'll never see her again."

"I don't believe that." Aeron stepped toward Pa and stared him straight in his eyes. "We can find them."

For Aeron's whole life, Pa had never believed anything good about him. It was part of why he'd left to join the Govalian Army at age sixteen.

He'd thought it would prove his worth to Pa, once and for all, but it had done exactly the opposite. And getting discharged under accusations of treason hadn't helped anything either.

This was Aeron's chance to not only save his sister but also to make his father understand that he wasn't a waste. That he mattered.

That he had a purpose.

"She escaped from them once. That means we can find them," Aeron said.

Pa kept shaking his head.

"Look," Aeron snapped, "I don't care if you believe me or not. That's what I'm going to go do. I'll bring her back. I swear to you that I will."

"Swear all the oaths and make all the promises you like," Pa said, his voice flat. "I'll believe it when I see it."

Aeron resisted the urge to deck him right then and there. It was the same urge he'd been resisting since childhood.

"Aeron," Kent said. "We cannot linger much longer. I imagine city officials will be returning soon. A patrol of soldiers stopped and examined the burning house while you were searching for your sister."

Tension gripped Aeron's chest. Kent was right. If they stuck around too long, word of it would get back to the army soon enough, and then the entire Wyvern Knight Corps might come for them. After what Aeron had done, he wouldn't put it past them.

"I agree." He walked over to Mum and wrapped his arms around her. She began sobbing against his chest. "I'll find her, Mum. I'll scour the entire continent if I have to. I'll lay waste to the Crimson Flame wherever I find them until I get her back."

She just nodded and hugged him back, then she let him go.

Aeron did not hug his father. Instead, he said, "Take care of her."

"I have for the last thirty-five years. Don't intend to stop now."

There was nothing more to say. Nothing more to hear.

Aeron nodded to him and headed toward Wafer.

"We will find Kallie," Kent said to them both. "We will not rest until we do."

Pa didn't respond to Kent, either.

Aeron mounted Wafer and called, "Come on, Kent. We've got a fire-worshiping cult to destroy."

CHAPTER THREE

Lord Valdis doesn't give second chances.

As Garrick Shatterstone entered the throne room of Valdis Keep, the thought crossed his mind that he might never walk out.

Gray walls arched into the throne room's cathedral-like ceiling. Iron bowls of fire rested on stone slabs protruding from the charcoal-colored granite pillars evenly spaced down the length of the throne room. They barely cast enough light for Garrick to see the figure seated on the throne at the far end of the hall.

Lord Blayne Valdis, a sorcerer of incomparable power and wealth.

Garrick gulped. At nearly seven feet tall, close to 400 pounds, and with accelerated healing and durable skin thanks to troll blood in his ancestry, Garrick didn't fear much. Lord Valdis was one of few exceptions.

Ten feet from the throne, Garrick knelt and stared down at the dark-gray granite floor tiles.

"My lord…" Garrick stared up at Lord Valdis.

He'd imagined—and dreaded—this moment for weeks. He'd rehearsed these words hundreds of times on his journey back from Etrijan, but now he couldn't remember any of them. So he settled on the truth, direct and curt.

"I failed you." He looked at Lord Valdis. "I'm sorry."

Garrick didn't lower his eyes or bow his head. He stared up at Lord Valdis, conveying a boldness he didn't truly feel. But if he was going to die, he wanted to see it coming.

Even so, he hoped Lord Valdis's business sense would win out. Garrick had performed well for him many times before. Perhaps it would earn him a pardon.

Lord Valdis didn't move. He sat on his throne, a grand chair made of interwoven black bones twisted together long ago by some form of dark magic, staring down at Garrick. Somehow, even though his eyes were dark, they seemed to glow with an otherworldly energy.

Garrick couldn't help the chill that coursed through his body at the sight of Lord Valdis's eyes. They had always unnerved him, not solely because of how they looked, but because Garrick understood, at least on a basic level, what Lord Valdis had *done* to get eyes like those.

As little as Lord Valdis had moved since Garrick had entered the throne room, Garrick wondered if he was dead. Part of him secretly hoped he was. But as he watched, he noticed the faint rise and fall of Lord Valdis's chest.

An invisible pressure blanketed Garrick—not overwhelming, but oppressive all the same. His head felt heavier, and his shoulders threatened to sag. He fought to stay upright as his arms and legs quivered.

He'd been in Lord Valdis's presence before and never experienced anything like it. He couldn't identify what exactly was happening, but he knew it was Lord Valdis's doing. Or perhaps he just exuded it by virtue of being a sorcerer.

Whatever it was, it wouldn't kill Garrick, at least not at its current intensity. But the more it weighed on him, the more his calm diminished.

Lord Valdis shifted in his seat, leaning forward slowly. "I know."

Garrick's eyes widened. *He already knows? How?*

Lord Valdis stood, and the pressure on Garrick intensified. Sweat gathered on Garrick's brow and ran down the sides of his face.

He'd faced menacing opponents, battled monsters, and survived outright betrayal, but he'd never encountered anything like this before—because he'd never earned Lord Valdis's ire before. How could he resist something he could neither see nor identify?

He briefly considered drawing his snow steel sword and attacking Lord Valdis, but he doubted he could lift his arms for even a single swing. It took all of his focus and considerable strength just to keep from crumpling to the floor.

"It is my business to know."

Lord Valdis walked toward Garrick, and the pressure increased. His trembling limbs began to shake, and he bowed, unable to keep his head up anymore.

"The map is now in the hands of one of my rivals. Suffice it to say, I am thoroughly displeased."

Though Garrick tried with all his strength to remain on his knees, the unseen power flared, finally forcing him to the floor where he lay prone, unable to move. Still the pressure increased, as if someone had set a raiding ship on his back, squeezing the air from his lungs.

"After all you've done for me," Lord Valdis continued, "all the jobs you've completed… for you to fail now, when it matters most, is infuriating."

Garrick wheezed, dragging in a breath by sheer will. "I'm… sorry…"

Lord Valdis crouched beside him, and the boulder on Garrick's back became an ocean, slowly driving him into the floor, trying to bury him in the ground below, or perhaps down into the Underworld itself. He could barely draw breath at all anymore, and the pressure still didn't relent.

"Your apologies are worthless to me." Throughout the whole conversation, Lord Valdis had maintained an even tone with each new word. But now his voice lowered, more ominous. "I'll just have to find someone else."

With the last of his breath, Garrick uttered a single word, "Be…trayed…"

The pressure diminished slightly, and Garrick gasped precious air, but he still couldn't hope to get up to his feet.

"What did you say?" Lord Valdis asked.

Garrick marshaled his remaining strength and will. "I was… betrayed."

"By whom?"

Did he actually want names? Or did he just want to know what happened?

It was a risk, but Garrick had nothing to lose, so he fought back in the only way he could. "Can't… breathe…"

Lord Valid exhaled a harsh sigh, and the pressure lifted off Garrick entirely.

Air flooded Garrick's lungs, and he sucked it in greedily.

"Rise," Lord Valdis said.

Strength returned to Garrick's limbs, and he slowly pushed himself up to his knees and then to his feet. He stood tall, trying not to shudder, and looked down at Lord Valdis, who stood a foot and a half shorter than him.

"Tell me what happened," Lord Valdis said.

Unlike some other throne rooms Garrick had been in, the guards in this one loomed in the deep shadows behind the pillars rather than flanking their master's throne. He supposed that they weren't truly necessary, given Lord Valdis's immense power, and that they held their posts solely as a failsafe.

Whatever the case, the guards continued to hide in the shadows, unmoving yet ever-present while Garrick explained what had happened.

"What a tale of woe and misery," Lord Valdis mused. "These brigands murdered your comrades, took the map, and left you to die."

Garrick nodded. It was the truth.

He glanced up at the huge, black sigil of the three-horned ram hanging on the wall behind the throne—Lord Valdis's sigil. Looking at it had always made Garrick uneasy, though he didn't exactly know why. Perhaps the oddness of a ram with three horns creeped him out.

His arms remained slack at his sides. He didn't dare raise them for fear of Lord Valdis interpreting the action as a threat.

"Yet you miraculously survived a stab wound from a mage steel blade and escaped the dungeon, only to return to me to tell the tale."

Garrick nodded again, and he felt the handle of a knife pressing into his side from where he'd tucked it into his belt. It was the very knife Noraff had stabbed him with back in that dungeon.

One day, Garrick would return it to Noraff in the same manner.

"I tried to catch them, my lord, but they met a pair of wyvern riders wearing Govalian Army colors and flew off."

Lord Valdis's dark eyes narrowed. "The Govalian Army, you say?"

"Yes. It was unmistakably the Govalian Army's colors."

Lord Valdis stared at him but said nothing for a long moment. Finally, he said, "I find it hard to believe any of this is true."

Garrick swallowed the lump in his throat and hiked up his chest armor, revealing the scar on his side. "This is where Noraff stabbed me."

"Am I to document your scars now?" Lord Valdis asked. "Who's to say you didn't have that before you left?"

"I didn't have this sword and shield before I left," Garrick countered, referring to the snow steel blade and shield hanging from his back.

"Which only proves that you retrieved a sword and a shield at some point."

"And I knew it was a map you were after." Garrick eyed Lord Valdis. "You don't think I'm in on this, do you?"

Lord Valdis's expression remained neutral. "It has crossed my mind."

"My friends are *dead* because of those bastards," Garrick growled. "And I almost died. Why would I come back here if I were in on it? What more do I have to gain by risking my life and telling you a story like this?"

"*Calm yourself*," Lord Valdis's voice rose to match Garrick's. "You have proven both loyal and fruitful over the years, yet this outlandish story fills me with severe doubt in your word and your capabilities.

"Furthermore, you are well aware that I do not suffer fools, miscreants, or impotence. But in light of this failure, now I must question your loyalty to me."

"I have *always* been loyal to you, Lord Valdis," Garrick replied.

"Up until this point."

Garrick bristled. "I still *am* loyal. You hired me to do a job, and I failed. Let me prove myself to you again."

"And how do you intend to do that?"

"I'll find the map and bring it back."

It made all the sense in the world. Garrick already knew what he was looking for. He'd seen the map. He'd held it in his hands. And he needed to find Noraff and his treacherous friend, Phesnos, anyway to deliver the vengeance he'd promised them back in the dungeon.

"Why should I entrust such a task to you?" Lord Valdis clasped his hands together. "You failed to deliver, and the world is full of mercenaries. Some are already in my employ as we speak. Why shouldn't I use them instead?"

"You already paid me for my initial expenses."

Lord Valdis waved his hand. "The coin is the least of my concerns."

"Then believe me when I say that if I can't do this, I'll never work as a mercenary again. At least, not on anything important. No one else will trust me. I need to do this in order to reestablish my good name."

"And you want vengeance for your friends."

Garrick's jaw tensed. "Yes. That's part of it."

Lord Valdis stared at him. "So how can I trust you to put my interests above your own, should you find these brigands with the map? I can't allow your vendetta to taint my ambitions in the process."

"Look" Garrick started, "I'll figure out my end some other time. Your desires are my desires. You want the map, and I want to bring it to you. Nothing's gonna stop me this time."

Lord Valdis's stoic face showed the first indication of emotion thus far: his eyes narrowed slightly, and the corners of his mouth turned up in the faintest hint of a smile conceivable.

Garrick's heart thundered in his chest. He needed this job... and the coin.

"Very well," he said. "But let me make one thing perfectly apparent: I have given you a second chance to prove your worth. Do not squander it, as there will not be a third."

"I won't let you down, my lord." Garrick bowed, careful to keep his eyes on Lord Valdis as he did. If this were all just a ruse, and Lord Valdis meant to kill him anyway, Garrick still wanted to see it coming.

Instead, Lord Valdis took a seat on his throne once again, this time resting his palms atop two black skulls perched on the ends of the chair's arms.

One of the skulls was unquestionably human, but Garrick couldn't begin to identify the other one. Aside from its domed cranium and two sagging eyeholes, it was misshapen and twisted beyond recognition.

"Truthfully, I did not expect you to return at all. So when I learned of your failure, I sent word to my contacts in Aletia's various countries, calling for mercenaries. The message summoned them here, to Xenthan, so I might select a new team to retrieve the map for me.

"Now that you're here, I needn't worry about such trivialities," Lord Valdis said. "You can do it instead."

"Of course," Garrick replied, but the idea of recruiting another team after what had happened in Etrijan soured Garrick's mood.

At least you're not dead, he reminded himself.

"They were instructed to gather at the Gray Cauldron, a public house in town, by sundown today," Lord Valdis said. "If anyone has answered the call, that is where you can find them."

Garrick nodded. "I know the place."

Lord Valdis stared at him. "Then what are you waiting for?"

"You'd mentioned that one of your rivals has the map," Garrick started. "Any idea who it might be?"

"I have innumerable enemies and rivals across the continent." Lord Valdis tilted his head. "However, I have no doubt that the cult of the Crimson Flame is behind this. After all, it was their property you were to take. If you are certain that those brigands flew away with Govalian Wyvern Knights, then I suggest you begin your search there."

Garrick bowed again. *More of that wretched cult? One encounter was bad enough. Is there a Crimson Flame temple in Govalia, as well?*

He would soon find out.

"I will, my lord. Thank you." Garrick straightened up and was about to leave, but he stopped. "And thanks again for giving me—"

"You had better leave before I change my mind, Garrick," Lord Valdis cut him off. "And see my treasurer on your way out. He will provide you with enough gold to recruit a team and cover your travel expenses."

The familiar sense of pressure fell upon Garrick again—a final warning. He bowed once more, then he turned and headed for the exit, all the while expecting something to skewer him from behind as he walked.

Nothing did.

Instead, the throne room doors opened, and he entered a familiar gray hallway with gray, stone floors. The same gargoyles he'd seen when he'd entered stared down at him from their perches above, and the same soldiers in black armor watched his every step.

The architecture was designed to intimidate anyone entering the throne room, but none of it had that effect on Garrick anymore. Stone gargoyles didn't frighten him. He'd overcome the odds and snatched a second chance out of thin air—a second chance he didn't deserve.

But he'd gotten it nonetheless, and he intended to make the most of it. And when he finished, he'd find Noraff and Phesnos and tear them limb from limb.

CHAPTER FOUR

Nothing about the Gray Cauldron impressed Kent.

In his old life, he never would have entered such a dour place, much less sat in one of its creaking wooden chairs or shared a drink with a friend. But thanks to everything in his life going wrong during his forty-ninth year, that's exactly what he was doing now.

He looked across the ancient table at Aeron, the only other person in the small pub aside from the barkeep, and took the tankard of ale into his left hand. Thanks to the salve Aeron's father had given him weeks earlier, the burns had reduced to nothing, and his hand had healed as good as new.

"It is almost sundown. The notice said to meet here, at this establishment, today, did it not?"

"That's what it said, yeah."

After the Crimson Flame had taken Kallie, Kent and Aeron had set out in search of answers, starting in Urthia, the country due north of Govalia, where she'd gone with her friends before being captured.

Their initial search had led them to an abandoned temple outside of Stroeton, the capital city of Urthia. Based on the markings they'd found inside, it had been a Crimson Flame temple at one point, but by the time they'd gotten there, nothing of consequence remained.

Without anything else to go on, and low on funds after Kent gave his coin to Aeron's family, they'd resorted to searching for more mercenary work instead.

That's when another mercenary had referred them to a notice calling for sellswords who didn't fear the Crimson Flame.

If this panned out, it could be a job that would not only put the Crimson Flame directly in their path but would also pay them something. Regardless of the pay, if they got any closer to finding Aeron's sister, it would be worth it.

"Gods, these chairs are *murder* on my back. I think I need another shroom." Aeron yawned, then he rubbed his lower back.

Kent didn't entirely approve of Aeron's reliance on magic mushrooms to cope with his chronic back pain, but thus far, they hadn't diminished his effectiveness in searching or battling, so Kent had left the matter alone.

As Aeron dug into his satchel for a fix, the door to the Gray Cauldron groaned open. A lone figure, backlit by a dark red light from Xenthan's burgundy skies at dusk, ducked under the doorframe and entered the pub. Wind howled behind him, and thick snowflakes swirled into the pub around the man until he shut the door.

In spite of all the ruckus and hubbub of the man's entrance, Aeron continued digging in his pack, oblivious to it all.

When the man straightened to his full height, Kent almost adjusted his own posture in response, but instead he stayed put and studied the man before him.

He stood close to seven feet tall and probably weighed 400 pounds—all of it muscle, by the look of him. He had long, dark-blue hair, a strange pallor to his skin, and he wore unimpressive leather armor on his chest. When he pulled off his gray cloak, his gigantic arms, despite the cold weather, were bare up to his shoulders.

A white shield and a sheathed sword hung on his back. The sword's hilt was colored a vibrant blue and accented with white gemstones, and a crystalline spike protruded from the bottom of the pommel. Kent had never seen a sword like it before.

At first, Kent wondered if he was some sort of orc or another fell creature, but aside from his skin color, hair color, and his overwhelming size, he appeared completely human. He had a well-defined jawline, but otherwise nothing about his face looked disproportionate or off.

Not the kind of fellow who could get lost in a crowd, Kent mused.

Aeron pulled out a mushroom that glowed with a faint blue hue and was adorned with yellow spots. It was about half the size of Aeron's fist.

He grinned and popped it into his mouth, but his grin faded when he noticed the giant staring at them from near the door.

The big man eyed them both for a moment, then he headed over to the bar and ordered a tankard of ale.

Kent had already ascertained that the barkeep knew nothing of any meeting that was supposed to be taking place there, but he was glad for the coin all the same.

Perhaps the big man would have some answers. Or perhaps he was there to throw in his lot for the job as well.

The barkeep poured the ale into a tankard and passed it to the big man, who turned toward Aeron and Kent and motioned toward the third chair positioned at their table.

"Anyone sitting there?"

Aeron looked at Kent with wide blue eyes and kept chewing his magic mushroom.

Kent took the opportunity to straighten his posture and to adopt a more neutral position. If anything were to go wrong, he couldn't do much while leaning back against his chair.

Then he replied, "No. You are welcome to it."

The big man sat down, and Kent studied him anew. He was far bigger up close.

Kent had faced large foes before, but he'd never encountered anyone quite so perfectly designed for combat. If the day ever came when Kent would need to battle someone like this man, he resolved to throw honor out the window and just slay him with magic from afar.

"You got names?" The big man took a swig of his ale.

Aeron glanced at Kent again. Though Aeron had technically been a mercenary for longer than Kent, he continually deferred to Kent for decisions, both large and small.

"Kent Etheridge," Kent replied. "And this is my companion, Aeron Ironglade."

"Mercs?" the big man asked.

Aeron nodded. He picked up his own tankard of ale and gulped down the rest of its contents. He swayed a bit, but Kent suspected it was from the mushroom more than from the ale.

Kent said, "We are. And you?"

The big man nodded and put the tankard to his lips again. As he drank, the pub door opened again.

As before, snow and wind billowed inside, but this time, instead of dark red outlining the hooded figure who stood in the doorway, Kent only saw the silhouette of a man against the black night sky outside.

He shut the door behind him, and the flickering candlelight illuminated the lower half of his chin, just for an instant. Then the man receded into the shadows in the corner of the pub and took a seat facing them.

Something about him didn't sit right with Kent. Flaunting one's size and capabilities, like the big man with his unique sword and shield and his impressive size, was one thing. Kent didn't mind that because it gave him a pretty good idea of what to expect.

But concealing one's face with a hood, a flowing cloak, and melting into darkness set Kent on edge.

Then again, perhaps he was just another mercenary looking for a job.

"And your name is… ?" Aeron spoke for the first time since the big man had sat down.

"Garrick." The big man had noticed the hooded newcomer as well, and only at Aeron's question did he finally look away. "Garrick Shatterstone."

"Your last name is… *Shatterstone?*" Aeron blinked at him.

"That's right." Garrick's eyes narrowed. "You got a problem with my last name?"

Kent raised an eyebrow. Maybe a bit on-the-nose, given his appearance.

Wide-eyed, Aeron shook his head. "Nope. We're good."

"The summons for the job said we were to arrive here, at this pub, by sundown," Kent started.

He stole a glance at the cloaked man in the corner. He hadn't moved except to wave the barkeep away when he'd approached with a tankard of ale.

What kind of man enters a pub and refuses to drink?

Kent refocused on Garrick. "Do you know how much longer we can expect to wait?"

"Waiting's over. I'm your contact." Garrick drained the rest of his ale and wiped his mouth with his forearm. "And I'll be leading the job, too."

Kent didn't know what to make of Garrick's assertions. He certainly appeared capable of handling himself, but whether or not he could be trusted to lead was an entirely different question.

"The notice mentioned the Crimson Flame," Aeron said.

"Heard of 'em?" Garrick asked.

Aeron cleared his throat. "You could say that."

Prior to entering the pub, Kent and Aeron had agreed that revealing Aeron's personal connection to the Crimson Flame early on might not be beneficial. Kent was glad Aeron hadn't decided otherwise.

"What's the job?" Aeron asked.

"Find a map that's tied to their cult and bring it back here."

Aeron stared at him with a measure of dismay on his face. "That's it?"

"The wrong people have it," Garrick said. "So this might get messy. What kind of fighting experience do you have?"

Aeron perked up at that. "I'm ex-military, and I know my way around a spear."

Aeron nodded toward his spear, which leaned against the wall to the right of their table, easily within Aeron's reach if need be. It was a vicious weapon, with a three-pointed steel spearhead.

The sight of it made Kent wish he'd trained with spears more often over the years, but when it came down to it, he preferred swordplay and magic over any other forms of combat. And having seen what Aeron could do with it, Kent had no love-loss that they had different giftings.

"Also, I have a wyvern," Aeron added.

Kent said, "And I am trained in multiple forms of—"

"You've got a wyvern?" Garrick cut Kent off.

Kent tried not to let it bother him, but it did.

"Yeah."

"Where?" Garrick leaned back in his chair.

"He's elsewhere, awaiting my signal," Aeron replied. "Can't really bring him into a pub."

"Where'd you serve?"

"Govalia."

Garrick nodded, and he grinned. Then he looked at Kent again. "And you?"

Kent cleared his throat. "As I was saying, I am proficient in multiple forms of combat as well as strategy and tactics, but perhaps my greatest asset is my ability to wield and manipulate magic."

Garrick's grin vanished, and his voice flattened. "So you're a mage."

"Yes."

"I don't like mages."

Kent frowned at him. He could've just as easily dismissed Garrick for being a muscle-headed idiot, but he hadn't.

"He's really good," Aeron said. "You should see some of the things he can do."

"Some other time, kid." Garrick looked Kent up and down. "Even if I were to work with you, aren't you a little old for this type of work?"

"I assure you, I am capable of handling anything that comes my way."

"Sure you are," Garrick muttered.

Frustration flared at the base of Kent's neck, but he suppressed it. "I would be happy to demonstrate right here, right now, if you wish."

Garrick folded his arms. "Is that supposed to be some sort of threat?"

Kent kept his voice calm, but firm. "Consider it an open invitation."

Garrick started to lean forward, but Aeron spoke up.

"Tell us more about the job." Aeron leaned between them. "Where do we get this map? Does the Crimson Flame have it now?"

"Aeron, right?" Garrick asked. "I'm slow with names."

Aeron nodded.

"Well, Aeron, that's what we need to find out." Garrick leaned back again. "Like I said, where the Crimson Flame's involved, it's bound to get messy, so before we go any further, I need to lay down a couple of things."

Kent and Aeron exchanged glances.

"First off, I've encountered these Crimson Flame fanatics before. They're dangerous, good with weapons, and some of them can use magic. In Etrijan, I fought one blonde woman who burned down an entire pub trying to kill me."

A blonde woman wielding fire magic? Who was also a member of the Crimson Flame? Kent glanced at Aeron, but neither of them said anything about it.

Perhaps it was the same woman who'd taken Kallie, but perhaps it was just a coincidence. After all, Garrick had encountered her in Etrijan, and Kallie had been taken from Govalia, practically on the opposite side of the continent.

"When it comes down to it," Garrick continued, "any enemies we meet will want us dead. If you don't have the stomach to take them out first, then you'd best quit before we get started."

Kent continued staring at Garrick, unfazed. After what he and Aeron had endured at the hands of only three Crimson Flame cultists, nothing Garrick could say would surprise him.

Aeron's voice hardened. "I've got *no* problem fighting cultists."

"And you?" Garrick asked Kent.

"I am in agreement with Aeron," Kent replied.

"Good. Second, I don't know for sure what, exactly, we're walking into. Last time I faced these flamejobs, I ended up dungeon-diving into an ancient Aletian vault. Faced down some undead warriors, a swarm of dog-sized carnivorous insects, a golem, and a duotaur."

Aeron glanced at Kent. "A… what?"

"A duotaur. A minotaur, but with two heads. Nasty, huge, undead beast. Hard to kill." Garrick cracked his knuckles. "But I got it done in the end."

Aeron looked to Kent again.

"Look, if you can't handle taking on more than your average idiot with a sword…" Garrick started.

"No," Aeron held up his hand. "We can. We're good with all of that."

Kent asked, "What should we expect by way of payment terms from you?"

"Oh, I'm not the guy with the coin. Even though I'm leading the job, you're not working for me. We're all working for Lord Valdis."

Kent didn't know who Lord Valdis was, but it didn't matter as long as they found the Crimson Flame and received a fair payment for the job.

"How long do you expect this job to last?" Aeron asked. "If you don't know where the map is, it might take awhile."

If this job took too long and didn't lead them closer to finding Kallie, they would need to reevaluate their plans. Even if the pay was good, a long job that didn't bring them closer to finding her wasn't ideal.

"You'll know when I know, kid," Garrick said. "I've worked for Lord Valdis a bunch of times, and he's never misled me or tried to play it cheap once I delivered. He's loaded, so he can afford to pay for quality work. No matter how long it takes, you'll make plenty off of this."

"What is the map for?" Kent asked. "What does it lead to?"

"It shows the location of various Crimson Flame temples across the continent," Garrick replied. "I don't know why that's important, but Lord Valdis wants it, and I'm gonna get it for him."

Aeron glanced at Kent, a grin playing at his lips. A map like that was exactly what they needed to lead them to Kallie. This job was sounding better and better with each passing moment.

"If we're lucky, he'll blast the entire cult out of existence," Garrick added.

"He could do that?" Aeron asked.

"Oh, yeah. He's so powerful, it's stupid," Garrick said. "All the more reason why we need to get this right."

"What kind of power are you talking about?" Aeron leaned closer.

"Dark magic," Garrick replied.

"Whoa…" Aeron gawked at him. "I've never met a dark mage before."

Kent's stomach soured at the mention of dark magic. He'd only ever met two dark mages, and both of them had tried to kill him. Hopefully Lord Valdis would not be the third.

As Garrick and Aeron continued chatting about Lord Valdis, Kent noticed the man in the corner again. He still sat there, unmoving, watching them.

Was he just curious? Or did he have nefarious intentions?

Kent had no qualms about judging people by their appearances. It had kept him alive more times than he could count. Measuring a man's capabilities by his appearance ensured that Kent took the proper amount of caution in any given situation.

And nothing about the man in the shadows conveyed a sense of friendship, kindness, or anything positive. Ever since he'd entered the pub, he just sat there, lurking in the corner like a demon, a phantom haunting them, waiting to claim their souls.

But he wasn't a phantom. He was flesh and blood and bone, like anyone else.

Flesh could be bruised or torn. Blood could be spilled and splattered. Bones could be broken or crushed.

Whatever the case, Kent wanted answers. And he was about to get them.

"Pardon me, gentlemen," he interrupted Aeron and Garrick's conversation.

Then he stood up and started toward the man in the corner.

CHAPTER FIVE

As the man with short, graying hair approached, Mehta's body tensed under his cloak. His left hand clutched one of his knives, ready to draw it at the first sign of a threat, eager to satisfy the thirst that heightened with each step the man took toward him.

Sifting the man would be easy, as long as Mehta struck before the man could wield his magic. He wore no armor—only a thick gray cloak for the winter and what looked like a thick tunic underneath.

The wyvern rider, Aeron, still sat at the table. By contrast, he wore teal armor from head to toe, including armored gauntlets. Yet despite his armor, he didn't look imposing at all.

The gray-haired man's age meant he had experience, and his boldness meant he lacked fear, but Mehta was a trained assassin, and his knives were perfectly sharp. This man's blood called to him, begging to be spilled.

It had been weeks since he'd sifted anyone. Most of his travel from his home in the mountains separating Etrijan from Xenthan had taken him through the wilderness, along rough paths devoid of human life.

The solitude had done his soul good. He'd taken time to think, to assess, to reflect, to plan, to commune with nature and the goddess Laeri, even though he still wondered if she truly existed. Ferne certainly believed she did.

But the thirst had fluctuated within him throughout that journey. It had threatened to overwhelm him in the days prior to returning to his family's home, but with Ferne's help, and with the blood of the Xyonates pursuing them, he'd suppressed it.

Now his blade demanded blood yet again, and his body yearned to comply. It took every ounce of his control to remain in his seat, to not spring forward and sift the man as he approached mid-step.

This man is no one to me, he reminded himself.

Yet some dark part of Mehta hoped the man would make some sort of move, try to do Mehta harm. Then he'd have the excuse he needed.

The man stopped four feet from Mehta's table.

In that moment, Mehta recognized the table as providence: were it not there, between them, sifting the man would've proven much easier—so much so that he might not have been able to restrain his thirst.

"Is there a reason you keep staring at us?" the man asked.

Kent. That was the name Garrick, the big man, had called him.

"Pardon me, but I asked you a question." Kent's voice sounded pleasant enough but also firm.

Mehta lifted his head and stared into Kent's blue eyes. Behind him, both Garrick and Aeron watched intently.

Kent didn't say anything else. He just stood there, his hands at his sides, waiting for Mehta to answer.

Several leather pouches, each of them bulging, hung from Kent's belt. Mehta had heard him say he was a mage, and while he hadn't encountered many mages outside of Ferne's now-deceased parents, he gathered that those pouches must contain something suitable for use with magic.

Now that Kent had drawn nearer to him, Mehta realized that Kent's attire would let him move freely. And with the sword hanging from his belt, despite referring to himself as a mage, Kent could probably handle himself when fighting in close quarters.

Mehta's assessment shifted slightly—he expected he'd have the advantage of speed, but Kent would likely be stronger and, as a mage, perhaps unpredictable. Sifting him would prove challenging.

He blinked away those thoughts. He didn't need to sift Kent. He just needed to answer his question.

"No reason," Mehta replied.

"Were you ever taught that staring is impolite?" Kent asked.

Mehta granted himself a smirk. Ferne had once expressed that same sentiment to him. He replied, "I was taught the opposite, in fact."

Kent's eyes narrowed. "I do not follow your meaning."

Mehta hesitated. He didn't like talking to strangers... or anyone, really. "It's not important."

Kent stared at him, unmoving, unflinching, unfazed. "What do you want?"

Mehta had to quell the thirst rising within him yet again. "You approached me."

"You entered this pub, noticed us, sat down, and started watching," Kent said. "You are clearly not a spy or a bounty hunter. If you were, you would not be so foolish as to watch us in the open. Or perhaps you are, and you are extremely overconfident."

"I am neither," Mehta replied.

"Then what are you?"

"I'm here for the job."

Garrick perked up at that. "You're a merc?"

Mehta nodded. *I am now, anyway. Whatever gets me closer to my commission.*

"What kind?" Garrick stood and approached now as well, leaving Aeron alone at the table.

Did Mehta dare reveal his past to them? With Kent and now Garrick looking down at him, the pressure mounted. As he weighed his options, he concluded that the truth—or at least most of it—would best serve him here.

"I was a Xyonate."

Garrick's left eyebrow rose, and Kent's eyes narrowed again.

"I thought Xyonates were a myth," Garrick said.

"No," Kent replied, his voice still firm. "They are real."

"So you're an assassin?" Garrick asked. "Trained to kill in dozens of ways?"

"And he's a member of a *cult*." Kent added, "A death cult. We already have one cult to deal with. We do not need another."

"You do know this decision isn't up to you, right?" Garrick eyed Kent.

Kent said nothing in reply.

"I'm not a Xyonate anymore," Mehta said.

"Why not?" Garrick asked.

Flashes of blood and gleaming metal saturated Mehta's memory. "They tried to kill me."

Garrick squinted at Mehta. "And?"

"And now there are no more Xyonates in Sefera."

Silence filled the pub.

"You expect me to believe any of that?" Garrick folded his arms.

It was the truth. Why wouldn't Garrick believe it?

Mehta took in Garrick's imposing appearance. If it came to it, sifting him would prove difficult.

Kent spoke before Mehta could come up with a response. "Even if it is true, I do not want a cult assassin on this job."

Garrick turned toward him. "Like I said before, that's not your decision to make."

"It is if you want Aeron and me to help you."

"Who said I did?"

"We were negotiating terms just a moment ago," Kent replied.

Garrick pointed at his chest. "Then *you* walked away from the table and found me another mercenary. What makes you think I need you at all anymore?"

"He is an *assassin* from a *death cult*," Kent reiterated. "We cannot trust a person like that."

Garrick nodded. "I can. At least I know where he stands. I'm not so sure about you two."

Eagerness arose in Mehta's chest. Was this plan actually working?

In every fight he'd ever been in, he'd found at least one moment that changed the course of the conflict. The fights he'd won, he'd taken advantage of that pivotal moment. The ones he'd lost, he'd missed his opportunity to act.

Perhaps now was that moment in this conversation.

Though he would've preferred not to say anything at all, Mehta stood and faced Garrick. "So am I in?"

Garrick looked down at him. "Maybe."

Mehta didn't know how to respond to that.

"If you agree to this," Garrick said, "that means we're on the same side. I need to be able to rely on you, and you can bet you'll be able to rely on me. An agreement with me *means* something. Understand?"

Mehta nodded. Better to earn his trust and only betray it if he had to—only if Garrick stood between him and completing his final commission.

"What's your name?" Garrick asked.

"Mehta."

"That's it? Just 'Mehta?' No surname?"

His thirst screamed his Xyonate name in his mind: *Requiem*.

"Just Mehta," he replied.

"Alright. Easy enough to remember. As for you two…" Garrick turned back toward Kent and Aeron, away from Mehta.

If he'd wanted to sift Garrick, now would've been the perfect moment. His thirst begged him to try.

But he restrained himself.

"The Xyonate's with me now," Garrick continued.

"*Former* Xyonate," Mehta interjected.

Garrick looked back at him with his brow furrowed.

"It cost me everything to leave that world behind. And behind is where I intend to leave it."

"Fine. Whatever you want." Garrick faced Aeron and Kent again. "What's your decision? Are you in or not?"

MEHTA'S OMINOUS APPEARANCE FREAKED AERON OUT, AND HIS ADMISSION OF having been an assassin didn't help anything, but Aeron needed this job, whether Kent felt good about it or not.

They'd run into a dead end at the Crimson Flame temple in Urthia. The end was so dead that they couldn't even *find* any more Crimson Flame cultists.

So when they'd discovered the notice about this job, it made all the sense in the skies for Aeron to go for it. It was an easy choice, an obvious path to get closer to finding answers.

"I'm in," Aeron said.

Garrick nodded then turned to Kent. "And what about you?"

"Give us a moment to discuss this, please." Kent motioned for Aeron to follow him to the opposite end of the pub.

Aeron did, and he immediately noticed how much colder the other side of the pub was, being so far away from the hearth. He tried not to shiver.

The effects of the shroom he'd taken were still in play, and while his back felt better, it was harder to concentrate than usual. Even so, it frustrated Aeron that Kent even felt the need to talk about this.

"What is there to discuss?" Aeron frowned at him. "This is everything we've been hoping for."

"I do not like how this is transpiring," Kent said, his voice low.

"Because there's an assassin involved?"

"Because he is a former cultist and, specifically, a Xyonate," Kent replied. "What do you know about Xyonates?"

Aeron shook his head, and his vision swirled. He closed his eyes for a moment to quell the sensation.

"Does it matter?" he countered. "The only cult we need to be concerned about is the Crimson Flame. They're the ones who took Kallie. They're the ones who have answers."

"So you are willing to risk traveling with a confessed assassin in order to get closer to the Crimson Flame?"

"Kent," Aeron's determination broke through the haze of the shroom, "I'd risk far more than that to save my sister. I'd risk everything."

Kent didn't respond.

"Look, we don't have any other leads. This job is the only way forward, regardless of who comes along. Will you at least listen to his offer?" Aeron asked. "I still need to move my parents out of Govalia. If the coin is good, this could solve a lot of our problems all in one shot."

Kent exhaled a long, quiet breath, then he replied, "Very well. I will hear the offer."

Even as Kent said it, Aeron noticed him eyeing Mehta as they headed back across the pub.

By that point, Garrick and Mehta had taken a seat at the table once more. Garrick drained the rest of his ale, set the tankard on the table, and looked up at them. "Well?"

Kent pulled out a chair and sat, and Aeron sat in his chair as well.

"How much?" Kent asked.

"5,000 gold," Garrick replied.

Aeron fought to keep his eyes from widening.

"Each," Garrick added.

Aeron stopped fighting it and let his eyes expand to the size of dinner plates. They had never made that much coin, either together or apart. 5,000 gold was the better part of what Pa brought in through his forge in a *year*.

He looked at Kent, whose face remained stoic and calm, and Aeron tried to match him. After all, every job was a negotiation, and conveying too much excitement wouldn't play well for them.

"We want 7,500 each," Kent said. "Plus expenses."

Garrick blinked at him. "No."

They sat there, silent, for a long moment, until Kent asked, "You have nothing else to say? No counteroffer?"

"If I cared to offer something else, I would've offered it."

"Then just take us," Kent proposed. "Leave the assassin behind, pay us 7,500 gold each. It is simple arithmetic."

"Except I want him more than I want either of you," Garrick said. "So how about I pay *him* 10,000 gold and leave the two of you behind?"

Aeron's heart hammered. 5,000 gold would be more than enough to help him move his family out of Govalia, especially if Pa could sell the forge. He didn't need Kent to fight for any more than that.

And if Kent lost them this opportunity, they'd find themselves at yet another dead end with regard to the Crimson Flame. Finding that map would change everything for them.

"Can you complete the job with only two mercenaries?" Kent countered.

"Won't know until we try." Garrick nodded toward Mehta. "Right?"

Mehta just sat there, silent and still. Only his eyes moved, glancing between the three of them.

"How much do we receive up front?" Kent asked.

"Ten percent." Garrick sneered at Kent. "Is your *arithmetic* good enough to figure that number out?"

"Ten percent is low," Kent said. "Normally we require half down."

"And normally I wouldn't consider hiring a mage to help me," Garrick said. "So if you don't like it, you can leave any time you want to."

"My concern is that 500 may not be enough to cover our travel expenses."

"Then you need to learn to manage your coin better," Garrick muttered.

Fury filled Kent's eyes and began to contour his face. Garrick couldn't have known what he'd said, so Aeron interjected before Kent could reply. "We'll take the 5,000 and the 500 up front."

Kent's ire redirected to Aeron, but only briefly. Then it faded from his eyes along with his desire to continue negotiating.

"But we want to see the map once we recover it. We need to know where we're heading after we finish this job."

"I don't see any harm in that. Agreed." Garrick turned toward Kent. "So are you in?"

Kent stared at Garrick for a long moment, and then he nodded. "Yes."

"Looks like we've got an accord, then." Garrick shook Kent's hand and then approached Aeron, who extended his hand as well.

Combined with the low-key high Aeron still had from the shroom he'd taken earlier, the handshake sent Aeron's equilibrium spinning, and he thought Garrick might tear his arm from its socket.

"C'mon." Garrick let go of Aeron and started walking toward the pub door. "Lord Valdis likes quick results. We're leaving now."

Aeron didn't mind the quick departure in the least. The sooner they got going, the closer he'd get to finding Kallie. Once they got outside, he'd blow the Wafer whistle, and together they would take to the sky, where they belonged.

He snatched his spear from where it still leaned against the wall and then slung his pack over his shoulders again. "Where are we going first?"

Garrick grinned. "Govalia."

Aeron's eyes widened.

If Garrick had named any other location in all of Aletia, Aeron wouldn't have so much as blinked.

Outside the pub, clouds filled most of the dark skies in Xenthan, blocking the stars from shining. The four mercs stood amid the snow all around them.

With his spear in hand, Aeron finally spoke up. "Why... uh... why Govalia?"

"That's our first lead," Garrick replied. "I have information that suggests that the map was taken to Govalia, at least as a starting point."

"That's... gonna be a problem," Aeron said.

Garrick and the others looked at him, including Kent, who already knew why returning to Govalia was such a risk. Now it looked like Aeron didn't have a choice.

Garrick sighed and looked up at the night sky. "Why?"

Aeron swallowed. The high from his shroom was wearing off, and the pain in his back began to prickle anew. Must've been a dud. Normally they lasted longer. "It's sort of a long story."

"Let me stop you there." Garrick held up his hand. "I don't care what you have to say. The job starts in Govalia, and if we're lucky, it ends there, too. You told me you were in. We shook on it. So are you coming or not?"

"I'm a fugitive from the Govalian Army," Aeron blurted.

It felt good to get it off his chest, but he worried what Garrick and Mehta might do with that information. He fingered the hollowed-out wyvern tooth hanging from a cord around his neck, ready to use it if need be.

"If I go back, I'm putting us at risk of getting caught. If we're careful, it shouldn't be a big deal, but you have to know that there's a chance that me being there might attract unwanted attention."

Garrick studied him for a long moment. "Then you're out."

CHAPTER SIX

Aeron's mouth hung open as he gazed at Garrick. "No... I'm not saying I can't go. I'm just saying we'd have to be careful."

"And I'm saying that I don't need your help if you're only going to put us at more risk," Garrick countered. "Sorry, kid. I don't need you that badly."

Terror seized Aeron's chest. He was about to lose his best chance to find Kallie. "I—I can help in so many ways, though. I can scout, I can fight, I know the land, I know how the wyvern knights work, I—"

"The wyvern knights," Garrick cut him off. "What can you tell me about them?"

"Anything you want to know," Aeron held his arms out wide. "I used to be one. That's why I still have a wyvern now."

"Yet somehow you're still a fugitive."

Aeron hesitated. "Like I said, it's a long story."

Garrick shook his head. "Sorry. Can't have a fugitive with me on this journey."

Kent spoke up. "Then I cannot accompany you, either. I am a fugitive from Muroth..." Pain filled Kent's face, reminiscent of when Aeron had pulled him out of that fateful battle outside of Dewmire Fortress. "...and I am also a fugitive from Inoth."

Garrick tilted his head at them both. "Are you kidding?" He turned to Mehta. "Tell me you're not wanted, too."

A long pause lingered in the cold air between them.

Finally, Mehta confessed, "It would be unwise for me to return to the city of Sefera."

"What in the third hell is wrong with you people?" Garrick snapped.

"But no one is pursuing me," Mehta quickly added. "Not anymore."

"Right. Because you supposedly killed them all." Garrick sighed.

So Kent and Mehta had dark pasts, just like Aeron. He looked to Garrick.

"Don't look at me. I'm not a fugitive from *anywhere*." Garrick muttered, "Why is it so hard to find good help these days?"

Aeron asked, "What makes you think the map is in Govalia in the first place?"

Garrick's jaw tensed, and he frowned. It took him a moment to respond. "Some Govalian wyvern knights transported the map. At least, they were wearing Govalian Army colors. So it makes sense to start in Govalia."

"Then you definitely need me, fugitive or otherwise." Aeron might've found an opening. He needed this job, for Kallie's sake. "I can help you figure out what's going on."

"This happened in Govalia?" Kent asked.

"No. In Etrijan," Garrick replied.

Aeron's eyebrows rose. *What would Govalian wyvern knights be doing up in Etrijan?*

"Etrijan?" Kent pressed. "You saw this happen?"

Garrick exhaled a sharp sigh. "I led the first job to get the map. Two of my mercs betrayed me and took it with them. They met the Govalians on a cliff in north-central Etrijan, just outside of the Crimson Flame temple where we'd found the map, then they flew away."

"So this whole job is an attempt to rectify your own failure?" Kent folded his arms and stared at Garrick.

The frustration etched on Garrick's face shifted to anger, and he squared himself with Kent. They stood before each other, neither one willing to back down, separated by only five feet of empty, snow-powdered ground and several inches of height.

"I don't like your tone," Garrick warned.

"And why should that concern me?" Kent countered.

Mehta hadn't moved. He just stood there, his hands concealed within his cloak, watching them.

Kent lowered his hands to his sides, near the pouches where he kept the fodder for his magic.

Garrick's hands balled into fists, huge and hard.

Well, this is off to a rough start. Aeron drove the tip of his spear into the frigid ground and stepped between the two men with his hands up. He hadn't taken nearly enough shrooms to deal with this sort of conflict, and his anxiety was threatening to erupt over the whole situation.

"Easy, easy," he said as much to himself as to Kent and Garrick. "We're on the same side."

"I don't like insinuations that I don't know how to do my job," Garrick snarled. He casually pushed Aeron aside with the back of his hand against Aeron's chest. "I've crushed skulls for much less."

"'Insinuations' is an awfully big word for someone who failed to recover a simple map," Kent fired back.

Garrick's hand shot toward Kent faster than Aeron would've expected, and it grabbed him by the collar of his tunic and yanked him forward.

But Kent's hand had already slipped inside one of the pouches at his belt. A dozen shards of rock burst up from the snow, answering the call of Kent's magic. They swirled over Kent's shoulders like a flock of birds, each pointed at Garrick's face.

Aeron's anxiety spiked. Wafer, who was flying somewhere above the town, must've sensed it, too, because an impression filled Aeron's mind through their bond. While Wafer couldn't communicate to him with concrete language, the idea came across clearly enough:

Should I come?

Aeron told him to stay put for now. But he couldn't let this situation devolve into a fracas, and Mehta didn't look willing to intervene any time soon, either.

"Enough!" Aeron shouted. He levered his way between them once again and pulled on Garrick's wrist, but it didn't move at all. In that moment, Aeron realized it would never move unless Garrick wanted it to.

Garrick released his grip on Kent's tunic and stepped back. Kent backed up as well, and the rocks swirling near his head thumped back into the snow around him, and he pulled his hand out of the pouch on his hip.

Aeron caught movement out of the corner of his eye and noticed the glint of a blade in Mehta's right hand. It disappeared beneath his cloak just as quickly.

Too close. Waaaaay too close. Aeron rubbed his back. His pain was intensifying right along with his anxiety. "We're not going to accomplish anything if we can't even get out of Xenthan."

"I still haven't decided if you're even coming." Garrick eyed him.

"Alright." Aeron held up his hands and exhaled a vaporous breath into the cold night air. "Look... you said you saw two wyvern knights. How do you know they were Govalian wyvern knights? They could've just been wearing

Govalian armor. And other countries have some wyvern knights, too. Urthia, Caclos..."

"Govalia is where we're heading," Garrick interrupted. "That's the end of the discussion. Govalia has the most wyvern knights, by far. And we have to start somewhere. Why assume they weren't from Govalia when everything about them suggests they were?"

"As much as I am loath to admit it, his reasoning is sound," Kent said.

Garrick glanced at him, rolled his eyes, and then refocused on Aeron.

"Fine. What did the riders look like? Or their wyverns?" Aeron asked. "I know all of the current riders and their mounts and most of the Featherwings—the new recruits—as well. Maybe we can narrow it down further."

Garrick sighed. "We should already be heading south by now."

"Humor me, alright?" Aeron forced a desperate smile. He wasn't sure if he was making progress with Garrick or not, but for Kallie's sake, he wasn't going to give up any time soon. "I can help you with this if you let me."

Garrick folded his big, bare arms and grunted something unintelligible. Then his voice flat, he said, "One of them rode a green wyvern. Nothing special about him. Just a guy."

"The other rode an orange wyvern with purple striping. A female rider. I was far away and couldn't make out many details, but she had short hair," he motioned around them, but to nowhere in particular, "almost as white as all this snow."

Aeron's eyes widened. The man on the green wyvern could've been one of several knights he knew. Most wyverns were colored somewhere in the range of greens and grays.

But the orange wyvern with purple stripes and its female rider with blonde hair almost as white as snow—Aeron knew exactly who they were.

"You know them?" Garrick's tone took on some color.

Aeron nodded. "One of them, for sure."

And I'd give almost anything to see her again.

"Give me a name."

"Not unless you take me with you."

Garrick frowned at him. "I could beat it out of you instead."

"Paying me will be a lot easier on both of us," Aeron countered.

"I'll pay you the 500 for the info, and you can be on your way."

Aeron shook his head. "No deal. I'm coming along, and you're paying me the full amount. Otherwise, you get nothing."

Garrick stared at Aeron for a long time, and Aeron began to worry that Garrick might opt for the beating option instead.

But then Garrick grunted again. "Fine."

Relief flooded Aeron's senses. Maybe he'd figure out a way to check on his parents while they were searching for the map, too.

But his relief was short-lived. When he began to consider what Garrick had said about the situation, it made no sense. Why would the Govalian Army help two random mercenaries transport a map from Etrijan? Something was very off about that.

Faylen, the blonde rider, complying with the order to bring two mercenaries back from Etrijan struck Aeron as especially strange. She'd always followed orders, but she'd always maintained her own sense of independent thought, too. He couldn't imagine her going along with… whatever this was… without at least questioning it.

Aeron rubbed his forehead and squeezed his eyes shut. His thoughts of Faylen mingled with his anxiety about Kallie and impressions from Wafer overhead and his back pain and—

And he just needed some peace. And more shrooms.

"What's wrong with you?" Garrick asked.

Aeron looked at him. "Nothing. I'm fine."

Everyone was staring at him, including Mehta, who Aeron had almost forgotten was there in the first place.

"Seriously," he said. "I'm alright."

Garrick said, "Then call your wyvern so we can leave."

That, Aeron would gladly do. "Stand back, would you?"

Garrick eyed him, but when Kent backed up and nodded at him, Garrick complied. They formed a loose line with Mehta in the middle. Mehta glanced between them with a hint of panic on his face and abruptly stepped even farther back.

Aeron put the Wafer whistle to his lips and blew into a hole in one end. As with every other time he'd used it, no discernible sound came out, but through their bond, Aeron immediately sensed that Wafer had heard it.

Within seconds, the familiar, rhythmic beat of leathery wings sounded around them. A dark form dropped out of the night sky and landed before Aeron with a heavy thud that shook the ground and sent powdery snow billowing into the air.

Wafer released a low hiss as he scoured Kent, Garrick, and Mehta with his golden eyes, but relief and renewed confidence flooded Aeron's body.

Finally, Aeron no longer felt small. Garrick may have stood close to seven feet tall, but Wafer was easily thirty feet long from head to tail, with a twenty-foot wingspan. And with Aeron commanding Wafer through their bond, whether riding in the saddle or not, the remainder of his anxiety melted away.

Garrick and Mehta gawked at Wafer, and even Kent, who'd been traveling with Aeron and Wafer for the last several months, recoiled a bit. Then again, Kent had seen what Wafer could do in action.

With Wafer once again at Aeron's side, the only thing still bothering him was his back pain. He anchored his spear onto Wafer's saddle, then he reached into his pack, removed his two favorite shrooms—one with yellow spots and one with purple stripes—and scarfed them both down.

He didn't care if Garrick and Mehta saw him do it. They'd eventually find out anyway, so he might as well make it apparent to them early on that he took them. "I have chronic back pain."

They had all watched him do it, but no one said anything.

"Well, I've got my ride," Aeron said. "What about you guys?"

Garrick cleared his throat. "Lord Valdis will let us use some of his horses. There are some waiting for us outside of—"

Wafer snorted, leaned forward, and started sniffing Garrick's chest.

Garrick froze, and his face contorted with concern, anger, confusion, and then back to concern again. "You'd better get this thing away from me before I do something we'll all regret."

Wafer reared back and glowered down at Garrick. He clicked his teeth together, and it sounded like horse hooves clopping along the ground.

"He understands when we talk, just so you know," Aeron said. "So I wouldn't threaten him unless you're prepared to back it up."

Garrick straightened his back and puffed out his chest. "I just don't need to be that close to his teeth. That's all."

Aeron chuckled. "Believe me, I understand. You were saying something about horses?"

"They're waiting for us outside of town," Garrick finished. "And we need to get moving."

"Fine with us," Aeron said.

Wafer opened his mouth and chomped it closed several times.

"Yes, once we get out of here, we'll find you something to eat, too," Aeron said.

Kent and Mehta kept staring at Wafer until Garrick led them away from the town.

TWO WEEKS LATER

Kent rode between his new companions, with Garrick leading and Mehta bringing up the rear.

He would've preferred to ride in the back, but Mehta had taken the spot before Kent could do anything about it. And every time Kent slowed his horse, Mehta's horse slowed as well, matching Kent's step for step, regardless of how wide the road was.

But over the last two weeks, Mehta hadn't yet stabbed him in the back, so Kent had resolved to just keep riding.

As they crossed the border from Urthia into Govalia, the terrain shifted from peaks and valleys to rolling hills and forests. The road in Xenthan had taken them southeast, through Tebaryx, Xenthan's capital city, and then down through Urthia along the Liparulo River, which they still followed.

The weather had grown milder as they'd progressed farther south. They'd gone from plodding through snow to clopping along cold, hard ground instead, but winter's bite still hung in the air, especially at nighttime. Now, at nearly midday in a forest, Kent's breath still came out as vapor, just not as thick as it had back in Xenthan.

They reached the forest's tree line and proceeded into the farmlands beyond, all barren and brown thanks to harvest's end a month before. As they rode into the open air, a shadow passed over them.

Initially, Kent thought nothing of it. Somewhere overhead, Aeron and Wafer soared through the skies, scouting the terrain ahead of them and around them in wide arcs.

Their presence had proven even more useful given the size of their traveling party, as Wafer had a knack for hunting deer and other large prey from the air. Suffice it to say, they hadn't gone without meat for more than two days since they'd left Xenthan.

Every now and then, Kent caught a flash of Wafer's blue-green scales glinting in the winter sunlight, but for the most part, the distance and the persistent cloud cover kept them concealed from sight. At other times, particularly when the sun loomed high in the sky, their shadows streaked across the ground as they flew over the trio of horses.

But when a second shadow chased the first, and then a third, and then several more after that, Kent's demeanor changed from apathy to concern. He looked to the skies, shielding his eyes with his hand.

Garrick and Mehta had seen the shadows as well, and like Kent, they now searched above. They didn't have to search for long.

A squad of six wyvern knights clad in the telltale forest green armor of the Govalian Army landed on the road in front of them.

As the wyverns beat their wings to slow their descents, Kent urged his horse forward next to Garrick, and Mehta stopped his horse beside them as well, once again putting Kent in the middle, but side-by-side instead of front-to-back.

"Watch what you say," Kent muttered to Garrick without taking his eyes off the Govalians. "If they find out about our friend above, we are all in trouble."

"I know," Garrick snapped. "I'm not an imbecile."

Kent held his tongue. In the two weeks they'd been traveling together, Garrick still hadn't shown any reason why Kent should trust him to lead well.

The wyvern knight in the front wore the same armor as the others, but the emblem of a steel-colored wyvern wing stamped on his left shoulder denoted him as the leader. He rode a brown wyvern with a tan underbelly. It studied them with curious red eyes.

"Greetings, travelers," he said with artificial regality. "What brings you to Govalia?"

"Just passing through," Garrick replied.

"My, you're a big one, aren't you?" the leader said. "I don't envy your horse."

To his credit, Garrick didn't respond. He just waited. It's exactly what Kent would've done if he were the group's mouthpiece.

"From where do you hail?" the leader asked.

"Etrijan, but we've come by way of Xenthan and Urthia." Garrick added, "We're heading south to the Tahn Sea to charter a ship. We're going to winter in Caclos this year."

The leader squinted at them. "A little late to be journeying to Caclos for the winter. We're almost a third of the way through."

Kent didn't like the yarn Garrick was weaving. He preferred to err on the side of providing less information rather than more.

Kent also would've preferred that Garrick didn't respond to the leader's statement, but Garrick did anyway.

"It's a long journey from Etrijan, and we had to wait until the harvest concluded," Garrick said.

"So you're farmers, then?"

That was a trap. Garrick's appearance and the snow steel weapons on his back were more than enough to rule that out as an occupation. Before Garrick could reply, Kent spoke up.

"Mercenaries, actually." Kent felt Garrick's heavy gaze shift to him, but he ignored it and continued to spin Garrick's story. "About a month back, we finished a sizable contract with a lord who had enlisted our aid in dealing with a band of brigands. They had been harassing the families working the lord's farmlands."

The leader glanced at each of them in turn, then he looked at a couple of his fellow wyvern knights. "Mercenaries? Sellswords?"

"That is correct," Kent continued.

Garrick cleared his throat as if trying to signal Kent to shut up. But the sooner they could move on, the better, and Kent believed he could expedite the process more efficiently than Garrick.

The longer they lingered around these wyvern knights, the more likely they would inadvertently expose Aeron to them—and that would spell disaster for them all.

"I see." The leader's hand rested on the shaft of his spear, which was anchored to his wyvern's saddle. "Why didn't you travel through Muroth and Inoth instead?"

Kent had an answer prepared, but Garrick spoke louder.

"We stopped in Xenthan to meet with a potential employer, but it didn't pan out." Then Garrick asked, "Tell me, do you always ask travelers so many questions?"

Kent bit his lip. Garrick shouldn't have taken the conversation that direction.

Kent had performed more than his fair share of interrogations during his time overseeing Muroth's southern defenses, and he'd successfully rooted out dozens of Inothian spies and infiltrators. One of the telltale giveaways was resistance when answering even simple questions.

Garrick was headstrong—Kent had recognized that the moment they'd met. The sense of urgency to move past these wyvern knights for Aeron's sake no doubt weighed on him as it did on Kent, but pushing too hard could incline the knights to ask even more questions.

"It's customary for Govalia to defend her borders from encroaching enemies," the leader quipped. "And the only way we can determine whether you're friends or foes is by asking you these types of questions—especially since you're so heavily armed."

"'Heavily armed?'" Garrick parroted back. "We're not 'heavily armed.'"

"There's no mistaking your snow steel shield and the blade on your back," the leader said. "Those are rare weapons, forged with the aid of magic. Who's to say what you intend to do with them?"

"They're family heirlooms. I inherited them from my father," Garrick said. "Are you trying to tell me I can't carry my family's legacy with me while I travel?"

Now it was Kent's turn to clear his throat. *Too far, Garrick.*

Garrick shot him a glare.

"They're unusual and unique. Certainly worth a conversation," the leader said. "Why are you getting so defensive?"

Kent interjected, "It is a sensitive subject for him. His father passed away recently and bequeathed it to him. We do not mean any offense. We are just eager to be on our way."

The leader fixed his attention on Mehta. "You're a quiet one. Got anything to add?"

In true Mehta fashion, he simply replied, "No."

The leader frowned again. "And there are only three of you traveling together?"

"How many do you see?" Garrick asked.

Kent cursed Garrick under his breath.

"Just answer the question."

Garrick pointed to Mehta, then to Kent, and himself. "Looks like there are three of us, yeah."

"You do understand that by the laws of Govalia, I can arrest you for being insolent. Foreigners' rights are restricted."

Garrick started to say, "Try it and—"

"We mean no disrespect," Kent blurted. "We ask your forgiveness. We have endured a long journey and still have several more days of travel ahead of us. My companion is fatigued and grouchy. Please pay him no mind."

"I don't need you to speak for me," Garrick growled.

"Clearly you do," Kent snapped. "These soldiers are merely performing their duties, and you are creating more problems than you are solving. Perhaps we would already be on our way if you had cooperated."

"I said, I don't need you to speak for me," Garrick repeated, his voice low and ominous. He glared at Kent with a ferocity unlike anything Kent had ever seen. "And I sure as hell don't need you to *correct* me."

"You ought to heed your comrade's words," the leader said. "We would much rather be patrolling the skies right now instead of talking to you, but you've given us ample cause for concern."

Garrick's jaw tensed, and he looked between Kent and the leader. He looked at Mehta, too, but Mehta continued to wear the neutral expression he always wore.

Kent took Garrick's silence as an admission of defeat, but it could've just as easily been frustration. Either way, Kent was right.

"You are certain there are only three of you?" the leader asked.

"Only three," Kent replied before Garrick said anything else that might dig them deeper into this hole.

The last thing he wanted was for the conversation to escalate into an actual conflict. They couldn't afford to be arrested, but he preferred not to fight, either. If he could talk them out of the situation, he would.

"What other questions may we address for you?" Kent asked with a smile.

AERON NEVER GREW TIRED OF RECONNAISSANCE WHILE RIDING WAFER. IT MADE for some incredible views and plenty of quality time with his best friend—not to mention the occasional thrill whenever Wafer would plummet toward the ground and pull up at the last instant. They both got a kick out of that.

Add in some of Aeron's magic mushrooms, and the sensations got even better. Though he used them primarily for pain, the brilliant displays of swirling colors that happened as side effects were pretty great, too. Flying atop a wyvern already made him feel a degree of weightlessness, but the shrooms enhanced the effect even more, and he loved it.

But today, the reconnaissance had taken on a somber, cautious feel, for both Wafer and Aeron. They'd entered Govalian territory several hours earlier, so Aeron and Wafer were on high alert as they flew.

It helped that Aeron understood the patrolling patterns and methods employed by the Govalian Wyvern Knight Corps, and he doubted much had changed since he'd left. Things in the army rarely changed at all, and when they did, it didn't happen fast.

Years ago, they'd actually flown the patrol routes up here in northern Govalia for about six months. Then, as the army tended to do, they reassigned Aeron and Wafer to a different post.

As they flew, Aeron's head swiveled back and forth, searching for threats. Urthia had wyvern riders, too, but the riders in Urthia weren't looking for him. The ones in Govalia were, and Govalia had nearly triple the number of wyvern knights.

They dipped underneath a thick, white cloud. Aeron didn't want his vision obscured at any point, so he'd avoided it for that reason alone. But as soon as they passed under it, Wafer sent Aeron an impression through their bond: *Danger.*

Aeron glanced back and saw a pair of dark, winged forms descend from within the cloud.

Govalian wyvern knights. His former comrades.

Aeron cursed. Wafer must've smelled the wyverns, but the cloud's vapor had masked their scent until it was already too late.

It was a tactic the wyvern knights rarely employed, so Aeron hadn't thought to consider it. But it didn't matter now. They'd spotted him, and with Wafer being the only blue-green wyvern anyone had ever seen in the corps, they would know exactly who he was.

Patrols ranged from a minimum of six wyvern knights up to twelve or, occasionally in wartime, twenty.

As far as Aeron knew, Govalia wasn't at war with any of her neighboring countries, but several more wyvern knights were undoubtedly nearby and could soon converge on their position.

The screeches and roars of the two wyverns sounded behind him—they were already raising the alarm to the other wyvern knights nearby.

Aeron cursed again. He could either flee, or he could fight.

He didn't want to fight his former comrades, so he told Wafer to dive. Together, they plunged toward the ground thousands of feet below. When Aeron looked back, the two wyvern knights were pursuing him.

The thing about aerial battle was that hiding wasn't really an option, especially on a mostly clear day. So unless Aeron and Wafer could outrun them, or unless they landed somewhere and took cover, they could only flee for so long.

Some wyverns trained for speed. Others were trained for combat and maneuvering during battles. Wafer was one of the latter types. He could twist and loop and execute acrobatic aerial moves, but he wasn't an exceptionally fast flyer, except in occasional quick bursts.

As such, the wyvern knights behind him were getting steadily closer.

It didn't take long for Aeron to realize the truth—he was going to have to fight them. He hadn't recognized either of their wyverns, and he hadn't been close enough to see if he knew the knights' faces, but he still might know them.

Was he really prepared to face down his fellow wyvern knights?

For Kallie, yes. Without question. He was doing all of this to find her, to save her. He would do anything for her.

Now he was being forced to prove it. If these wyvern knights took him down, Kallie would be lost to the Crimson Flame forever. He couldn't allow that to happen.

Taking on two of his old comrades would prove challenging, but he'd once defeated Commander Brove in aerial combat, and he was a Silverwing. He could handle these two Leatherwings, but if the rest of the patrol arrived before he defeated them, he and Wafer were as good as dead.

So he looped Wafer around, pulled his spear from the anchor on Wafer's saddle, and careened toward the wyvern knights.

CHAPTER SEVEN

M ehta had kept silent while Garrick and Kent jockeyed for control over the situation with the soldiers. He was out of his element and wary of the wyvern knights, mostly because he couldn't conceive of how he could ever get close enough to sift them.

Getting past the wyverns' jaws was the real challenge. The Xyonates had trained Mehta to deal with men in armor and men with spears, but they'd never addressed combating wyverns.

The closest training he'd had was in dealing with cavalry. He could bring down riders on horseback easily enough, but horses only grew to a certain size. Even the smallest of these wyverns was double the height of a standard military horse.

And they had teeth. And talons. And they could fly.

Mehta was *definitely* out of his element.

Kent had taken the reins in answering the lead wyvern knight's questions, and Garrick still sat atop his horse, sulking. Between the two of them, it seemed as though Kent had a better grasp on how to handle the situation.

Then again, Mehta's default response to potential conflicts was to sift anyone who dared to stand in his path. It was the Xyonate way.

And though he'd left the Xyonates and Xyon, the God of the Underworld, behind, much of their influence still lingered within him—including his thirst.

Now, presented with the possibility of a fight, the thirst swelled within his chest. A huge part of him wished the wyvern knights would attack just so he had the chance to spill their blood—even if he wasn't totally sure how to go about doing it.

And if a fight did break out, he wouldn't have to try to control his thirst—he would only have to direct it.

But Kent had calmed the situation with his keen words and smooth personality. Mehta envied him for it, to some extent. He'd never developed such abilities, and he'd never had a knack for personal interaction in the first place.

Perhaps seeing his parents murdered while still only a child had played a role in that.

Even so, Xyonates didn't value communication skills. Why bother charming someone he was just going to sift anyway? And extracting information was simple enough with the proper application of pain.

Yet now that Mehta lived in the real world, apart from the cult, he needed to develop real-world abilities. So he watched Kent and listened to his every word, trying to absorb his tone, his inflection, his nuanced speech—all while suppressing the thirst raging within.

Then a two-toned cry ripped through the skies, half screech, half roar.

Mehta's horse whinnied and stomped its front hooves, and Mehta almost fell off from the shock of the sound, as did Garrick and Kent. What horrific thing had made that noise?

The wyvern knights reacted totally differently. Rather than showing surprise, their demeanors shifted to resolve as the leader, his knights, and their wyverns launched from the ground in a burst of frantic energy and hurtled into the sky with their weapons drawn.

Mehta looked at Garrick and Kent for answers, but they both scanned the sky with their hands shielding their eyes.

"It's Aeron." Garrick pointed. "They've found him."

Mehta followed Garrick's gaze and saw a blue-green wyvern clashing with two other wyverns, both of them darker in color than Wafer.

"What do we do?" Mehta asked.

Kent shook his head. "Nothing we can do now. They are too high. I do not know any magic that could hit them from so far away."

Out of my element, Mehta thought. *Literally.*

"If he can get them back down here, to us, then we can help," Garrick said.

"Does he know where we are?" Kent said.

"He's the scout. He's supposed to keep track of our position as well as let us know about incoming threats." Garrick muttered, "He's doing a miserable job on both fronts."

Mehta noticed a solitary pine tree in the middle of a field, perhaps a half-mile away. Instead of a rich, dark green, it was the telltale gray color of dead foliage.

Mehta turned to Kent and pointed at the distant tree. "Can your magic light that tree on fire?"

Kent glanced at Garrick, then he looked back at Mehta. "It can."

"Good idea, kid." Garrick whipped his reins, and his horse sped off toward the dead tree, and Kent followed.

Mehta brought up the rear, as usual.

Kid?

Mehta certainly didn't feel like a kid. He hadn't since the day the soldiers killed his parents and sold him to the Xyonates.

He chose to ignore the comment as just a reflection about his age. He figured he was around twenty-seven years old, but he'd lost track along the way. The Xyonates hadn't cared about his age; they'd only cared about whether or not he could fulfill the commissions they gave him.

Moments later, Mehta arrived at the tree behind Kent and Garrick. Kent had already dismounted about five feet from the tree and was trying to strike a flint against a knife, but then Garrick dismounted and started rummaging in his pack for something.

Kent's flint sparked, and his hand flared with blue light, but the sparks disappeared before anything else happened. He cursed and struck the flint again.

"Here, let me." Garrick held up a vial of red liquid and rushed over to the tree.

"What are you doing?" Kent shouted.

"You're too slow with that flint," Garrick hollered back. "Watch this."

Now at the tree, Garrick uncorked the top of the vial and splashed a few drops of the red liquid onto the lowest branch. The liquid ignited the instant it touched the dried wood, even in spite of the cold winter air.

Garrick stepped back toward Kent. "Now light it up."

Kent hurried over to the tree with his hands covered in blue light. He reached into the dwindling fire Garrick had set.

His magic shielded him from the flames, and he somehow took the fire into his hands, which started swirling with orange and blue fire at the same time. Then he retreated a few steps and hurled a fireball at the center of the tree.

Garrick's fire might've spread if given enough time, but Kent's fireball kindled the whole tree into a pine-scented inferno that raged with towering flames and sent a column of thick, black smoke into the air—a perfect signal to Aeron.

And even if it failed to catch his attention, it would certainly attract the other wyvern knights.

Mehta grinned. One way or another, his thirst would be quenched today.

AERON'S SPEAR PLUNGED INTO THE BASE OF THE TWO-TONED GRAY WYVERN'S wing. It roared, and dark red blood oozed out of the wound.

Quickly, Aeron wrenched his spear free from the wyvern's wing joint. It shouldn't have been a fatal blow, but it was enough to knock them from the sky.

The wyvern dropped, furiously flapping his one good wing and trying to use the other to slow their descent. Its rider shouted and yelled, but with the wyvern's wing joint damaged, they couldn't stay airborne.

He'd recognized the Leatherwing and his wyvern, but he didn't know their names. It made Aeron sick, having to harm a fellow knight's mount.

Only a few months ago, he'd been separated from Wafer for several weeks. He remembered the toll it had taken on him and how incredible it had felt once they were finally reunited. After having endured that period, the idea of being separated from Wafer forever wasn't something Aeron ever wanted to experience.

The only comfort Aeron took from downing the two-toned gray wyvern was that he hadn't permanently separated the knight from his wyvern. Perhaps one day it would even recover well enough to fly again.

But he couldn't focus on any of that now. Not with another wyvern knight coming at him.

This one, Aeron didn't recognize. The wyvern, brown with splotches of black along its hide, screeched as it drew nearer, and the knight on its back raised his long sword for a strike at one of Wafer's wings.

Aeron only had time to react. As Wafer closed the distance to their foes, Aeron drew the spear over his shoulder, lined it up with the wyvern knight's flight path, and hurled it into the open air.

As the wyvern knight began his swing, Aeron's spear pierced through his breastplate, knocking him clean off his saddle.

Aeron conveyed a command through their bond, and Wafer dove after the falling knight. Behind and above them, the brown-and-black wyvern screeched again. Aeron stole a glance to see it following them toward its knight.

Faster.

Wafer's wings tucked back against his sides, and he went rigid. They streaked toward the falling knight like an arrow until they came up alongside him.

Aeron's aim had been true. The knight was already dead.

As the ground rushed up to meet them, Aeron grasped the shaft of his spear and held it firmly.

Pull up!

Wafer's wings snapped open, and as they curved away from the ground and back into the sky, the spear tore from the dead knight's body, once again in Aeron's possession.

Such a beastly weapon. Its head was divided into three points, but all on the same blade, making it especially useful for piercing armor.

When he'd stolen Wafer back from the army, he'd taken the spear as well. It had belonged to Commander Brove, the man responsible for getting him kicked out of the army, so Aeron felt no guilt about taking it.

Wafer's wings pounded against the air, and they steadily climbed in altitude as the other wyvern landed next to its knight, whose body had splattered against the grassy terrain upon impact.

The wyvern bellowed and roared, heartbroken over the loss of its rider. Its cries were worse than those of the first knight's.

Aeron's remorse over it didn't last long, though, because as Wafer's wings elevated them back among the clouds, six distinctly wyvern shapes loomed in the sky before him.

He glanced over his shoulder to check for others, but he didn't see any. It didn't mean others weren't out there, but even if they weren't, Aeron and Wafer couldn't hope to take on six trained wyvern knights on their own.

But he noticed something else over his shoulder, too—a column of smoke rising from a burning tree in the middle of a field.

It made no sense at first, that a tree would just spontaneously burn in frigid winter weather.

Then he realized what it was. It had to be Kent and the others signaling him.

Well, they'd signaled him a little late.

Still, the prospect of facing down the six remaining wyvern knights alone didn't appeal to him at all. He got a comparable impression from Wafer, too: *No thanks.*

So he directed Wafer to veer hard to the left. The wyvern knights were still far enough away that Aeron had ample time to make the turn and get back to his friends with room to spare.

Friends? Wafer asked through their bond.

I don't know. Partners, I guess? Aeron sent back.

He considered Kent a friend by now; they'd developed a measure of trust that Aeron didn't share with Garrick and Mehta yet.

As Wafer flew toward the burning tree, Aeron stole a look backward. Sure enough, all six of the wyvern knights pursued him. From that distance, he couldn't make out any of their faces, but he'd encounter them soon enough anyway.

Wafer circled around the burning tree and came in for a landing beside Kent, whose horse spooked and trotted away with Kent still riding her. Kent reined her in with his left hand—tongues of blue and orange fire still burned from his right hand.

Kent shook his head. His mare still hadn't adjusted to Wafer, even after traveling together over the last two weeks.

Then again, Aeron couldn't blame her; horses *should* fear wyverns, one of the few natural predators in Aletia that could pursue them in the wild for prey.

But now wasn't the time to consider wyvern eating habits or horses' defense mechanisms. The approaching wyvern knights demanded their full attention.

"I took down two of them already," Aeron said as Wafer settled on the ground. "Are there only six more?"

"We've only seen six total." Garrick eyed Aeron. "You got two on your own?"

Aeron nodded. "Yep. So there were eight overall on patrol. I told you, I used to be one of these guys. I know what to expect."

"Then what should we expect?" Kent asked.

"Coordination," Aeron replied. "We're outnumbered, so they'll try to double-team us or isolate us and take us down individually. Try to stay close to each other. They'll want me more than anything since Wafer and I are known fugitives, so we can try to use that to our advantage."

"How?" Garrick asked.

"As a distraction. If they want me the most, they'll come at me the most," Aeron said. "You know how a clothesline works, right?"

Kent, Garrick, and Mehta all looked at each other.

"Yes...?" Kent replied.

"You... hang clothes on it?" Garrick said.

"No." Aeron shook his head. "I mean, yes, you do, but that's not what I'm saying. Imagine if you hold a clothesline taut across someone's path while they're walking. What happens?"

Garrick tilted his head. "They run into your clothes?"

"No!" Aeron rubbed his forehead. "Look—I'll set 'em up, you knock 'em down. When I'm flying toward you, they'll be right behind me. Take them out however you can."

As Aeron said it, the six wyvern knights converged on their position and formed nearly a complete circle around them, with the burning tree at their backs. The horses bucked and went wild, and their riders fought to restrain them.

"Don't let your horses run!" Aeron shouted. "They'll surround you and take you down one at a time."

The others struggled to control their horses as the wyvern knights landed around them amid the thundering of wings. Aeron wondered if he should've already taken to the sky instead of staying there, but it was too late now. He'd just have to work with it.

His thoughts regarding battle strategy stopped when he saw the squad's leader, identified by the steel wyvern wing stamped on the left shoulder of his green armor—a recent addition.

He'd sided with Commander Brove to get Aeron kicked out of the army, and the sight of him washed away the remainder of Aeron's remorse over fighting his comrades.

❦

GARRICK DIDN'T LIKE THIS SITUATION.

He didn't know much about Govalia's corps of wyvern knights, but wyvern jaws could crush some types of boulders and rocks. Even if the knights' spears couldn't penetrate Garrick's hardened skin, their wyverns could kill him easily enough.

His horse had calmed, so he drew his snow steel sword and shield from his back. The runes marking the weapons glowed with bright teal and blue light as soon as he took hold of them—an effect of the snow steel reacting to the cold air and to his touch.

They'd done the same thing outside the temple in Etrijan after he'd taken them. The warmer the air, the less the runes glowed.

Garrick hadn't used a shield in ages, and he'd only wielded this one once before, so it felt unnatural to him. Thanks to his durable skin and accelerated healing abilities, he'd never really *needed* a shield.

But it matched the sword, and snow steel was rare, so he'd snagged them both when he'd had the chance.

Part of him still missed his old battle-axe, though.

"Aeron Ironglade," the leader of the wyvern knights said. "I'd say it's good to see you again, but I'd be lying."

"Porgus Darleton," Aeron said to him. "I'm surprised they promoted you to Steelwing, especially after you fell asleep while trying to keep me from escaping with Wafer."

"That's—" Porgus's countenance darkened. "You used treachery to put me —and everyone else at the roost—to sleep. It doesn't mean I'm unworthy of the promotion."

"If you say so. My opinion never mattered to you anyway."

It amazed Garrick the level of confidence Aeron exhibited while atop his wyvern. Without Wafer, he behaved more like a mouse than a man.

But while riding Wafer, Aeron became the king of the air.

"Commander Brove wants Aeron alive." Porgus glanced at Garrick and the others. "The others are enemy combatants. Kill them."

While Garrick didn't mind a good scrap every now and then, he would've preferred not to make enemies of Govalia's army within the first few hours of crossing the border. Quietly advancing until they'd obtained the information they needed would've been easier.

But thanks to them discovering Aeron and Wafer, it hadn't played out that way. He knew he'd regret bringing Aeron along, but he'd done it anyway. Garrick should've just choked the name out of him instead.

Now he'd have to carve through these idiots.

Porgus motioned to the wyvern knights, and each of them raised their weapons. Four of them held spears, including Porgus, while another wielded a long sword. The sixth wyvern knight held a poleaxe that looked to be about a foot longer than the old battle-axe Garrick had left in the dungeon in Etrijan.

As Garrick surveyed the field, he noticed Mehta removing his cloak. He tossed it aside, donned a wide grin, and drew two curved knives from the sheaths in his belt.

The sight of Mehta's grin struck Garrick as strange and a bit creepy. He was about to say something, but the wyvern knights blasted toward them from every angle.

Garrick raised his sword and his shield, and then he grinned as well.

CHAPTER EIGHT

Aeron and Wafer vaulted into the sky, barely escaping the wyvern knights' advance. As he'd expected, some of them followed him specifically—three of them, including Porgus and his wyvern.

Kent could handle himself, and Garrick looked and seemed plenty capable, but Aeron still had no concept of what Mehta could actually do.

But he couldn't think about that now—Aeron couldn't fight three at once, but he *could* lure the other three away from the battle. Maybe that way he could buy the others some time.

❦

Kent had kept his right hand burning the entire time in anticipation for this moment. He'd also removed a small piece of wood from one of his pouches and held it in the other hand. Why not make use of the gigantic, burning tree behind him?

So when the wyvern knights lurched forward, Kent was ready. One of them launched right at him.

He pumped more magic into his hands and targeted the tree. As he'd intended, several burning branches snapped off of the tree, rushed past him toward the wyvern knight, and formed a fiery barrier. Then Kent dumped magic into the fire in his right hand, and the flames on the branches burned hotter and brighter.

The wyvern tried to slow its approach, but it couldn't, and it crashed through the wall of flaming branches. The fire scorched the wyvern and its knight, and they spiraled to the ground, dazed but not dead.

Another wyvern flew toward them from the side. Only a few of the branches remained, thanks to the extra heat from the expanded fire, and Kent redirected them toward the wyvern as flaming spears.

They flew past Mehta, who'd hopped up and now stood, precariously, on his horse's saddle. The branches swerved to avoid hitting Mehta and pummeled the wyvern in midair. They failed to pierce through the wyvern's scales, but they stymied him well enough.

Then, to Kent's utter amazement, Mehta leaped off his horse with his knives raised high and drove them into the wyvern's scaly head.

It screeched and shrieked and then dropped to the ground, motionless. The knight riding it rolled off to the side, gasping.

Mehta yanked his knives free of the wyvern's head and stood there, as calm as an ocean breeze.

Kent couldn't believe his eyes. He had access to magic and an endless supply of natural fodder through which to channel his power, yet Mehta had felled a full-grown wyvern with nothing but two knives and impeccable timing.

Unbelievable.

The knight rose to his feet, dismay and rage written on his tear-streaked face as he charged toward Mehta with his spear in his hands.

Mehta just stood there, watching him approach.

The knight jabbed his spear at Mehta's face. But Mehta slipped away from the spearhead, which missed his cheek by inches, and then lunged forward faster than any human Kent had ever seen.

His knives moved in a blur of dark gray steel, slashing open the knight's exposed throat and severing the tendons behind his right knee.

Then he buried both blades in the knight's torso—one in his right armpit where there was no armor and another in the unarmored section of his gut where his forest green breastplate met his belt.

The knight was probably dead before he hit the ground, and Mehta pulled his knives free, flinging blood several feet across the farmland on which he stood. More blood streaked across his face and torso, but none of it was his.

Kent marveled at him again. *Unbelievable.*

Kent's horse whinnied, and he whirled back to face the wyvern he'd stymied with his wall of fiery branches—a wall that no longer existed. The wyvern, covered in burn marks and charred scales along its front had gotten back up, and its knight was urging it forward once more.

The wood in Kent's hand had worn down to sawdust, so he pulled a stone out of one of his pouches. He could immediately sense rocks buried within the ground, and he called them forth.

Boulders erupted around them and hurtled toward the wyvern and pounded it out of the air from the side. It screeched and hit the ground once again, and a boulder struck the knight's helmet. He toppled off his wyvern's saddle, unconscious.

As the wyvern struggled to recover, Kent let the fire in his right hand die, and he grabbed a handful of leaves from another pouch instead. He shifted his magic into the leaves, and green light emanated from his closed fist.

Tree roots from the now-dead pine tree burst forth from the lifeless terrain and coiled around the wyvern's wings and hind legs and neck, mooring it to the ground. It roared and hissed and strained, but the roots held it in place.

Meanwhile, the leaves in Kent's hand, now brown and crinkly, withered to dust in the frigid air.

On Kent's other side, Garrick, now dismounted from his horse, continued to engage the third wyvern and its knight. From the deep, red slits on the wyvern's chest, Garrick looked to be winning the fight. The runes on his weapons glowed with teal and blue light and gave off a faint hum whenever he swung them.

Kent had never seen snow steel in action, but it appeared to cut better than the finest steel any Murothian smith could've forged.

Evidently, Garrick didn't know how to retreat—nor did he need to. Any time the wyvern's teeth snapped toward him or the knight's spear stabbed in his direction, he blocked with his shield, batted the attack away with his sword, or landed blows on his opponent.

And instead of backing up, Garrick forced the wyvern knight to recoil.

Kent considered helping, but Garrick didn't need any assistance. Instead, he chose to watch, all the while marveling at Garrick's prowess. He might not be as diplomatic as Kent, but he was unquestionably unique. A phenomenon. An anomaly.

Kent found himself hoping—planning to never end up on the wrong side of Garrick's wrath. Nor did he wish to face Mehta's inhuman speed and precision. And Aeron had already taken out not one but *two* of the wyvern knights on his own.

Who are these people?

§

MEHTA HAD BEEN IMPRESSED WHEN KENT HAD SHOWN OFF HIS MAGIC AGAINST

Garrick back in Xenthan. The only magic he'd encountered prior to that had come in the form of light magic from Ferne's father, who had used the last of his strength to heal Mehta in a time of dire need. And it had made all the difference.

But watching Kent manipulate fire and stones and plants simply by holding such elements in his hands was a marvel to behold. Not only could he speak with confidence, but he could also fight without so much as breaking a sweat.

And Garrick was relentless. Constantly attacking, berserking. Singlehandedly dueling a wyvern knight with nothing but a sword, a shield, and pure rage, all while on his feet instead of on horseback. And he was *advancing*.

Mehta had sifted the wyvern and the knight who'd attacked him, but only after Kent had pelted them with rocks and distracted them. He could've found a way to sift the wyvern and the knight without Kent's rocks, but they'd made it far easier.

And now Aeron streaked through the sky, leading the other three wyverns on a wild, looping chase without any concern for his own wellbeing.

The odds had been weighted against them, yet they were winning. If any of these men stood against him at any point in his final commission, he had to be ready to handle such an obstacle.

But if they *all* stood against him...

What would Mehta do then?

❧

THE TIP OF GARRICK'S SNOW STEEL SWORD NICKED THE WYVERN'S THICK HIDE once again, slicing a red line through its scales. Then the wound froze over with ice, one of the benefits of the weapon that Garrick hadn't realized.

The sword hadn't done that when he'd used it inside the cultists' temple in Etrijan, though it had cut down the fire-wielding cultists in his path easily enough. It must've been another effect of using snow steel weapons in cold environments, or perhaps the flamejobs just ran too hot.

The wyvern wailed and recoiled, and its knight's spear failed to even reach Garrick's position. Then they took to the sky and looped away from him in a wide arc.

Garrick glanced back at Mehta and Kent. So far, they hadn't died, and for now, that was good enough for Garrick.

A reptilian screech sounded from the wyvern, and Garrick whirled back to face him. The wyvern's head lowered again, creating room for the knight to attack with his spear. Garrick had seen it before—and defended it before.

If the knight's spear hit Garrick's skin straight on, it could pierce through and do serious damage. But thus far, the knight hadn't even managed to get close to stabbing him.

The guy just didn't have any good moves. And whenever he tried to get his wyvern to do the fighting, he only subjected the beast to more torment from Garrick's snow steel sword.

The one thing the knight did well was keeping a decent distance between himself and Garrick's sword. Garrick hadn't hit him yet, and while the wounds on the wyvern continued to mount, he still hadn't inflicted anything close to fatal.

But Garrick didn't want to keep playing tag. It was time to end their spat.

So when the wyvern's head lowered as it flew forward, opening the knight up for an attack, Garrick made his move.

In order for the knight to have any chance of hitting Garrick, the wyvern had to fly low to the ground, essentially gliding just above the terrain. So as it approached, Garrick ran forward and leaped.

He soared over the wyvern's head and toward the knight's spear, leading with his shield. If the wyvern had raised its head, Garrick's shield would've slammed into its face and probably been knocked aside thanks to its thick, muscular neck. But it didn't.

Instead, the knight's spear glanced off Garrick's shield and failed to slow his advance whatsoever. His shield collided with the knight's torso and helmet, knocking him off the wyvern's saddle.

The knight dropped his spear and tumbled heels-over-head down the wyvern's back and onto the ground below. His armor clanked as he skidded to a stop on the frozen terrain. Then Garrick landed nearby the knight.

When the knight looked up, a thick coating of frost covered his face shield and breastplate. Had Garrick's snow steel shield done that? It must've. Nothing else could have caused it.

Now weaponless, the knight called to his wyvern for help and struggled to get to his feet. He made it up to one knee by the time Garrick got to him.

With a mighty underhand swing, Garrick's sword sliced through the underside of the knight's jaw, through his skull, and through his helmet.

The blow knocked the knight onto his back, and a bit of blood spattered out, but the sword left behind a red gash, crystallized with ice and frozen blood, in what remained of the knight's head. Stranger still, his helmet's face-mask shattered upon impact.

Garrick had seen plenty of metal shatter under extreme cold before—it was a routine frustration in the islands off the northern coast of Etrijan where he'd grown up. But exactly how it had happened here confused him.

Had his shield frozen the metal, and the force of Garrick's blow then broke the facemask?

The knight's breastplate had taken the brunt of Garrick's shield and still bore frost. Garrick stomped on it, and the forest green metal crunched and crumbled into shards under his boot.

Incredible. Now he regretted leaving his battle-axe behind a little less.

The wyvern howled and launched at Garrick, back toward its knight. Garrick whirled around to face it, but it batted him aside and loomed over the knight's body as if protecting it.

Garrick recovered his footing, ready to finish the fight, but the wyvern didn't advance. It just stayed with the knight, nudging him with its muzzle and groaning.

Perhaps the humane thing to do would be to put the wyvern out of its misery, but it didn't seem interested in attacking Garrick anymore. He decided to let it be. A beast like that should never be taken lightly, especially in such a confused and desperate state.

Careful to keep the wyvern in his periphery, Garrick backed toward Mehta and Kent, both of whom had mounted their horses again.

Ahead of Kent, a wyvern strained against a network of tree roots that had somehow ensnared it and pinned it to the ground. Its corresponding knight lay nearby, unmoving, either unconscious or dead.

Beyond Mehta, another wyvern and his knight lay motionless on the ground, definitely dead and surrounded by blood, which gave off faint steam in the winter air. Garrick started to say something to them, but a series of screeches and roars from the sky turned his attention away.

When he looked up, Garrick saw Aeron headed straight for them with the three other wyverns close behind.

✥

THUS FAR, AERON HAD AVOIDED CLASHING WITH ANY OF THE THREE WYVERN knights pursuing him.

They'd tried to box Wafer in a few times, but thanks to some crafty flying and some daring moves, they'd avoided combat in the process. The very same training that made Wafer a great combat wyvern also enabled him to avoid fighting if he had to.

But abrupt maneuvers and flying near top speeds were taking their toll on Wafer. He was, after all, a living beast with a finite amount of energy, not some legendary creature loaded with magic powers and unlimited fury.

Aeron sensed Wafer's fatigue through their bond, and it wore on him as well. For all the great benefits of bonding with a wyvern, including connecting on a deep emotional level, one of the drawbacks was *connecting on a deep emotional level.*

So Aeron and Wafer shared emotions, feelings, and even sensations, to a degree, both good and bad. That included shared exhaustion as well.

They dove toward the burning tree and their fellow mercs.

I'll set 'em up, you knock 'em down, Aeron had told them. *Clothesline.*

He just hoped they wouldn't screw it up.

As Aeron and Wafer descended, the carnage around the other mercs clarified. All three knights were down. One wyvern was dead. Another was restrained by a network of something sticking out of the ground—which had to be Kent's doing—and the other lingered over the body of its slain knight.

Whatever they'd done, it had worked. And it meant Aeron and Wafer had bought them enough time to make it happen.

They flew straight toward the burning tree, and at the last moment, Wafer dodged to the right and zoomed over Kent and Mehta's heads. Aeron glanced back in time to see—

Nothing.

Neither Kent nor Mehta had done anything to attack the wyverns chasing after Aeron and Wafer. All three of them still pursued him.

What in the third hell? Why hadn't they attacked the wyvern knights?

Wafer groaned, and Aeron empathized with him. This could've already been over if their fellow mercs had done what he'd wanted them to do.

Maybe they still didn't understand?

But how do you not understand the concept of a clothesline?

Or maybe the other wyverns hadn't flown low enough. Maybe they knew what Aeron was trying to do, and maybe they'd ascended out of range to avoid Aeron's scheme.

Even though Wafer protested, Aeron opted to give it one more pass. Hopefully it would work this time.

They curled around, back toward the burning tree, and the three wyverns followed, now closer than ever.

Wafer's wings beat furiously against the air. If this didn't work, Aeron would have to land with Wafer to give him a break. Wafer would've kept flying until he literally fell out of the sky; such was his dedication to Aeron, so Aeron had to be the one to set limits.

They dropped altitude again and raced toward the burning tree. This time, Garrick, Kent, and Mehta had spread out in front of it.

Garrick stood on the ground, while Kent and Mehta sat on their horses. Rocks orbited Kent's form like a swarm of giant insects. He was ready, at least.

Aeron and Wafer flew even lower this time. The membranes in Wafer's wings rippled with the force of the air whooshing under them, crackling like heavy sheets of fabric in high winds.

Wafer's whole body quaked, sending tremors into Aeron and intensifying his back pain. He'd need another shroom soon.

They shot over the other mercs' heads once again, this time far lower, and again they avoided the burning tree, but this time they flew close enough that Aeron could feel the heat from the flames on his face as they passed it.

He looked back. Kent's rocks launched into the air, but the three wyverns had ascended once again, and they avoided getting hit.

Aeron cursed. The wyvern knights understood his strategy, and he couldn't force Wafer to keep flying with abandon. The clothesline wasn't going to work.

We just have to get back to our friends. Then we can land, he sent to Wafer.

A sense of more fatigue, but with a hint of relief, came to Aeron from Wafer.

But as Wafer started his turn, his wings faltered. They weren't slowing fast enough, and the ground was rushing up to meet them.

Aeron cursed again. He'd pushed Wafer too hard. But maybe he could still keep them from disaster.

Wafer grunted, and Aeron issued commands to slow down and turn, but it didn't change Wafer's descent.

Nope. Disaster it is.

Wafer pulled his wings tight against his body in a defensive shield around himself and Aeron, retracted his neck, and careened into the frozen ground.

CHAPTER NINE

W hen Kent saw Aeron and Wafer go down, he didn't hesitate. He lashed his horse's reins and charged toward their position, away from the warmth of the burning tree.

He didn't care if Mehta and Garrick were following or not. He needed to get over there to help, and the three remaining wyvern knights were already closing in on Aeron and Wafer.

As Kent approached, the wyvern knights landed near the fringes of the cloud of dust Wafer had kicked up upon his crash-landing. Between the wyverns' wings and the dust, Kent could no longer see Aeron and Wafer.

He still held the stone in his hand. Instead of hoping the fields around Aeron and Wafer had enough rocks for him to draw to the surface, Kent pumped magic into the stone.

He could sense more rocks beneath the soil. Careful to make sure he wouldn't ruin his horse's path straight to Aeron, he summoned the rocks to him. They began to burst from the ground at random spots and chased behind Kent as he rode.

The wyverns closed in around Aeron and Wafer, whom Kent could now see on the ground. Aeron had gotten to his feet and stood before Wafer, his spear extended, his face and teal armor caked with dirt.

Wafer looked worse. Also covered with dirt, he was up and moving, albeit slowly, but the membranes of one of his wings were pocked with holes.

Without both of them at their best, they didn't stand a chance. Kent cracked his horse's reins again, willing it to run faster. He was Aeron's only hope now.

❧

MEHTA HAD TURNED HIS HORSE TOWARD AERON AND WAFER'S CRASH AS WELL, but he hadn't immediately bolted toward them like Kent had. As soon as Kent took off, though, Mehta kicked the sides of his horse, and it sped after Kent.

He glanced back at Garrick, who moved with equal urgency, but he had to get back to his horse before he could follow.

Mehta was no expert rider. With his horse at full gallop, he struggled to stay in the saddle and found himself clinging to it just to stay put.

To further complicate matters, Kent's magic had somehow ripped dozens of rocks and boulders from the farmland all around him, so dirt sprayed Mehta and his horse as they dodged all the new holes in the ground.

Mehta didn't like barreling into the unknown, but his only other choice was taking no action. And of all of the mercs, he'd grown to like Aeron the most.

Not to mention, Aeron was their only link to finding the next step in recovering the map, and recovering the map meant Mehta could finally fulfill his final commission.

So he didn't really have a choice after all.

Mehta held on for dear life and raced after Kent.

❧

WYVERNS SNAPPED AT AERON FROM THREE DIFFERENT ANGLES, AND ONLY HIS spear and desperation kept them at bay.

Wafer was hurt. Aeron didn't know how badly yet, but he could feel through their bond that Wafer wasn't right. In any case, Aeron couldn't count on him to help fight these last three wyvern knights.

To make matters worse, Aeron's back was threatening to seize up on him entirely, thanks to their crash-landing. He needed a shroom now more than ever to counteract the pain, but grabbing one and taking it with three wyverns knights circling him like vultures wasn't an option.

Porgus and his wyvern, Lash, a brown beast with a tan underbelly and red eyes, towered over Aeron. Porgus yelled, "Surrender!"

And go to my execution? And lose Wafer all over again? Never. He wouldn't give Commander Brove the satisfaction of humiliating him yet again.

Aeron shouted back, "Go to hell, Porgus!"

"Then in the name of Emperor Taçin Ubardo, I sentence you to death."

As Porgus and Lash tensed, ready to lunge, dozens of boulders pelted them and the other two wyverns from the side. One of the rocks knocked Porgus from his saddle, and another slammed into the side of Lash's head, dropping him to the ground.

Kent rode into the fray with a swarm of rocks still whipping around his body. His magic continued to hurl them at the wyverns and their knights in a relentless barrage.

Of the two functional wyvern knights remaining, the one farthest from Kent recovered, took to the air, and flew due south without so much as turning or looking back. With his commanding officer down, and now outnumbered, he was retreating to report on what had happened.

Aeron would've given chase if Wafer were able. The escaping wyvern knight was a loose end they couldn't afford to leave lingering, but he didn't have a choice. After that crash, he didn't know how long it would be until Wafer could fly again—if he could even fly at all.

Aeron prayed to the gods that that wouldn't be the case, but all he got in response were impressions of pain and frustration from Wafer, which mingled with his own tremendous back pain.

He started backing toward Wafer. If he could down a shroom or two, he could return to the fight to help. Without them, his lower back pain would soon overwhelm him, and then he'd be close to useless.

The wyvern knight nearest to Kent lifted his poleaxe and urged his wyvern forward. It launched toward Kent with its jaws wide open.

Wide-eyed, Kent raised his hands, and the remaining rocks rained down on the wyvern and his knight, pinning both of them to the ground. A cloud of dust puffed out of Kent's fist, and he dismounted his horse.

As Mehta approached on horseback from behind Kent, Aeron turned fully back toward Wafer. With two of his friends close enough to engage in the fight, and with the remaining two wyvern knights downed, Aeron could focus on Wafer instead—and on the piercing pain in his lower back.

As Mehta closed the distance to the new field of battle, he watched Kent dismount, draw his sword, and stride toward the wyvern and the knight he'd just buried under a mound of rubble. Along the way, he bent down and scooped another rock into his left hand.

Mehta dismounted once he reached Kent's horse, and he stalked after Kent with his knives in his hands.

Ahead of them, the knight had pushed through the rubble and started pulling rocks away from his wyvern, but he stopped when he saw Kent drawing near. Instead, he grabbed his poleaxe and held it at the ready.

Mehta increased his pace. The knight had a reach advantage over Kent, but fending off two foes instead of just one would negate some of that advantage.

But as Mehta approached, Kent charged forward to engage the knight on his own.

The knight swung his poleaxe, timed perfectly. If Kent didn't block the blow or duck under it, he would die.

Kent extended the rock he'd picked up in his left hand instead, and it flashed with blue light. Then rocks from all over the field sprung up to Kent's arm, covering it in a layer of stone up to his shoulder.

Kent raised his stone-covered left arm, and the poleaxe clanged against it harmlessly. Then Kent lurched forward and drove his sword into the knight's stomach.

The knight gasped and dropped his poleaxe. He clutched at Kent's sword with his gauntleted hands as if trying to pull it out.

In one clean motion, Kent drew the sword out of the knight's gut and slashed it down at his head. The sword cleaved through the man's neck and lodged in his upper chest.

Kent stepped forward and kicked the man's chest, freeing his sword once again, and the knight fell back and hit the ground, saturating it with his blood.

From under the rubble, the wyvern roared, and it thrashed against the rocks. It was beginning to break free.

But Kent turned his stone-covered arm toward the pile. The stones on his arm shot off and joined the rest of the rubble, which started rolling and grinding against the wyvern, hard and fast, from every direction.

The wyvern shrieked and tried to escape, but the rocks continued churning against it, snapping its bones and pulverizing its flesh. A moment later, its shrieking stopped, and the rocks buried its crushed carcass anew.

Mehta marveled at Kent. Was there anything this man couldn't do with his magic?

Garrick rode up to the field next, and as he dismounted his horse, he cursed. "Did I miss the end?"

Only then did Kent turn away from the wyvern and the knight. He tossed away the rock he'd been holding, now just a small, smooth stone, but he didn't sheathe his sword.

He noticed Mehta standing there. "I did not hear you approach. A warning would have been appropriate. I would hate for you to get caught in my wrath by mistake."

"I wouldn't have," Mehta replied, though based on what he'd seen, he couldn't be certain whether or not that was true. But it was more important to convey certainty and confidence instead, so that's what he'd done.

"Still, next time, please announce yourself. I do not prefer to have to look over my shoulder in every battle to ensure I do not accidentally harm you."

Mehta gave a reluctant and insincere nod. He thrived on quietness and quickness, and Kent was asking him to abandon half of his approach to fighting.

"Come," Kent said to Garrick and Mehta. "We must check on Aeron and Wafer."

He led them over, and they found Aeron examining the wings of a perturbed, snarling Wafer. From what Mehta could tell of their behavior and appearance, the damage was evident, but not considerable.

"How does he fare?" Kent asked. "And how are you?"

Aeron shook his head. "His wing bones aren't broken, I don't think. But the membranes in one of his wings are pretty messed up. When we get some time to breathe, I can patch him up, and his body should take care of the rest, but he won't be flying any time soon. Beyond that, he's bruised and sore, and so am I."

Aeron's eyes had a glazed look to them. He must've taken more magic mushrooms. The crash couldn't have helped his back any.

Kent said, "I hope he makes a full recovery."

"What happened?" Garrick asked.

"It's my fault," Aeron replied. "I pushed him too hard. I knew he was reaching his limit. We were about to set down so he could rest, but I wanted him to loop back to you guys so we could all fight together. After all that evasive flying, he didn't have the energy to make the turn, and we went down hard."

"No... no!" a voice shouted from behind them.

Mehta whirled around first, his knives ready, followed by the others.

The leader of the wyvern knights, Porgus, knelt in front of his brown wyvern. The beast lay before him, twitching, its red eyes glassy and vacant. A bloody gash on the side of its head completed the story for Mehta.

He'd seen it before. The wyvern was brain-dead, or very near it. It happened sometimes when a person—or in this case, a wyvern—got bludgeoned hard, but not hard enough to yield immediately fatal results.

"Lash, wake up!" Porgus begged. His hands nudged the wyvern's neck and jaw as if trying to jar it awake. "Lash!"

They were both suffering, and Mehta's thirst had not yet been sated. And even though he *couldn't* sate his thirst, no matter how many people he sifted, he started toward them anyway.

A hand clamped on his shoulder.

Mehta's reflexes told him to whirl around and skewer whoever had grabbed him, but his better judgment gave him pause. Instead, he just stopped and turned back.

"Wait," Aeron said.

Mehta complied, but waiting out his thirst had always proven a losing strategy. The thirst always outlasted him.

He could always lock it away in the box he'd crafted in the back of his mind, just as Ferne had taught him to do, but he didn't want to do that until he was certain he could not sift anymore today. Forcing the thirst away stretched the bounds of his self-control, and having to do it twice in a short period of time would make everything worse.

So Mehta stood still and offered a silent prayer to Laeri to ask for her help in controlling his thirst. All the while, he tried not to think about sifting the fellow mercs standing beside him.

AERON TOOK UP HIS SPEAR AND APPROACHED PORGUS WITH CAUTION. PORGUS'S own spear lay in the dirt nearby, well within reach if he decided to grab it.

Tears streaked through the dirt and grime on Porgus's round face, and he stared at his wyvern with hollow eyes. Aeron doubted he'd try anything, given his state of mind and the overwhelming odds against him.

Then again, Aeron had been in a similar situation when the army had discharged him and separated him from Wafer. Aeron had gone to extreme lengths to get Wafer back. Considering that, he decided not to take Porgus's loss lightly.

As Aeron approached, Porgus shook his head and said, "He can't be gone."

"Stand up, Porgus," Aeron ordered.

Porgus didn't move. He just touched Lash's muzzle and repeated, "He can't be gone."

"I said, stand up." This time, Aeron's voice was firmer.

"We've been together for twelve years." Porgus ran his finger across the scales on the ridge of bone that housed Lash's eye. "He's my best friend."

Aeron knew the sentiment all too well. When Wafer had crashed, Aeron's first concern had been Wafer's wellbeing. The impact had sent Aeron tumbling across the cold, hard ground, but he'd rushed over to Wafer as soon as he made it back up to his feet.

He couldn't lose Wafer again, and he'd do everything in his power to make sure he didn't.

But it was too late for Porgus to save Lash.

"He's dead, Porgus." Aeron had never liked Porgus to begin with, and he'd outright hated him when he'd chosen to side with Commander Brove against Aeron. But he understood what Porgus was enduring now, and he actually felt sorry for him. "Let him go."

"No!" Porgus snapped.

He snatched up his spear.

Before Porgus could do anything else, Aeron slammed the blunt end of his spear into Porgus's opposite arm with all of his strength. Aeron had been aiming for his elbow, but his swing had gone high.

Porgus yelped, but he managed to get to his feet. He still clutched the spear, albeit against his opposite arm where Aeron had struck him. Spears like these were too heavy for single-handed combat on the ground, so, for good measure, Aeron swung at him a second time.

The butt of his spear cracked against Porgus's arm again. His armor had doubtless deadened the blow, but two hits in the same spot, and as hard as Aeron could swing, had to have hurt.

"Drop the spear," Aeron ordered.

Porgus complied, but the anger in his eyes didn't subside. He rubbed his arm. "You're a traitorous wretch. You deserve to burn in Xyon's furnace for this."

"I'm *not* a traitor."

Porgus spat at Aeron's feet, but his saliva landed in the dirt in front of Aeron's boots. If he had dared to spit on Aeron instead, Aeron probably would've skewered him right then and there.

"I lost my best friend because of you," Porgus growled. "And without him, I've got nothing left to live for. So go ahead. Kill me."

By now, Garrick, Kent, and Mehta had joined Aeron in standing around Porgus.

"Kill me!" Porgus shouted.

Mehta's knives moved, just slightly. Aeron watched him. He wouldn't hesitate if given the chance.

"No," Aeron said.

Porgus snarled at him and jerked forward, but Aeron smacked the side of his head with the butt of his spear. It clanked hard against his helmet, and

Porgus went down equally as hard.

This time, he didn't get back up. He lay on the ground, whimpering. "Please… please, just kill me."

"We need to go." Kent sheathed his sword. "One of the wyvern knights escaped. He will no doubt bring reinforcements."

"We need to head east. The terrain is harder to navigate thanks to the mountains and the hills as we head toward the coast," Aeron suggested. "More hiding places."

Garrick asked, "Why would we—"

"Trust me on this," Aeron interrupted. He didn't actually mean to take them east, but he needed Porgus to think that. He stared into Garrick's dark blue eyes and then pointed at Porgus. "This is my home country. I know how to make sure we avoid getting detected."

Garrick squinted at him, then he nodded. He'd gotten the message. "Alright. East it is."

"Wafer can't fly, so I'll need to travel on foot with you until I can repair his wing and give it time to heal."

"Suit yourself," Garrick said. "Everyone else, mount up."

"What about him?" Mehta nodded toward Porgus. He still held his knives in a death grip.

"Leave him." Aeron placed his hand on Mehta's shoulder. "Let's go."

Without making eye contact with Aeron, Mehta shrank away from his touch, sheathed his knives, and headed back to his horse. Aeron made a mental note to not touch Mehta anymore.

Then they left Porgus behind to lament the death of his best friend.

🐉

Garrick led the group east, but only at first. Once they'd traveled out of Porgus's line of sight, Aeron had redirected them south, the direction they actually needed to go.

It wasn't a particularly clever ruse. If it had been Garrick's idea, he would've had them fleeing the country to the north, back to Urthia.

They'd been traveling on the main road south toward Govaliston, but the Govalian Army's main fortress was north of the city, along that same road, between them and Govaliston. Specifically, Aeron was leading them toward a town nestled between the fortress and Govaliston called Dreynoth.

Aeron had said it would be the best place to find one of the two wyvern riders Garrick had seen, and then they wouldn't have to try to find a way into

82

the fortress. Apparently, Dreynoth was some dinky little town that catered to off-duty soldiers who took leave there.

Several hours later, and several miles southeast of where they'd encountered the wyvern knights, they discovered a cave among the hills and retired there for the evening.

Garrick was dubious at first, given his experience with the scorpers and the other horrors he'd encountered in the dungeon under the temple in Etrijan. This cave had a high ceiling like that dungeon, though not quite as high, and the cave floor didn't stretch nearly as far, either.

It seemed safe enough, and they could light a fire inside without smoking themselves out, but Garrick kept a watchful eye on every nook and cranny in the space nonetheless.

Most importantly, it had a wide enough opening for Wafer to fit through, and that meant Aeron had a safe place to tend to his torn wing membranes. Under other circumstances, Garrick might've suggested they leave Wafer behind, but Aeron wasn't much good without him.

As dusk overtook the landscape, Mehta took a seat against a rock in a shadowy part of the cave and started sharpening his knives. Aeron stayed near the fire and began mending Wafer's torn wings with a sizable needle and thick, wool thread. Meanwhile, Garrick and Kent left the cave to gather more firewood from a nearby copse of trees.

Kent had offered to go alone, but Garrick had insisted that he come along just in case Kent got ambushed. In truth, Garrick had something else in mind.

If this arrangement was going to work, Garrick was going to have to lay some more ground rules. He couldn't have Kent undermining him whenever they encountered a threat or whenever a tough decision needed to be made.

So Garrick had to make clear how things were going to go from now on.

The moon shone in the sky like a silver general among an army of twinkling stars.

"Today could have been far worse," Kent said as they walked side-by-side. "But I fear the repercussions of that battle will haunt us for quite some time."

"Mmm." It was exactly what Garrick wanted to discuss, but he needed the conversation to go a certain way, so he didn't reply.

They reached the copse and started gathering firewood. Garrick's breath came out in thick, white vapor, and the icy air made him wish he'd sent someone else to gather firewood instead. But he might not have another chance to get Kent alone.

As usual, he'd brought his snow steel sword and shield along. They hung on his back, there for when he needed them. Kent was a mage, and Garrick had no idea what kinds of tricks he could muster on short notice, so he wanted to be as prepared as possible.

Kent continued gathering firewood, one stick or fallen tree branch at a time, checking each one for dryness. Garrick saw his opportunity, glanced around to ensure no one else was around, and made his move.

CHAPTER TEN

The rhythmic sound of the whetstone scraping against steel, the cave's long shadows cloaking him from the light of the fire, and the steady breaths he'd been taking had finally enabled Mehta to lock away his thirst —for now.

Coupled with prayers to Laeri, he was getting better at controlling it and resisting the impulses it sparked in his mind. Then again, he still wondered if Laeri was even listening.

Ferne had told him she was, but Ferne was just a nine-year-old child who'd been raised by a Laerian priest and priestess. Of course she believed Laeri was listening. It's what she'd been taught all of her short life.

By contrast, the Xyonates had taught Mehta that Xyon demanded blood and souls—a *lot* of blood and souls—on a regular basis. So Xyonates sifted widely, spilling blood to honor Xyon and commending souls to the Gates of Hell, where Xyon himself would welcome them into eternity in the Underworld.

Xyon would have been displeased with Mehta's performance today. They'd been confronted by six wyvern knights—eight, if he counted the ones Aeron had dealt with before the fight actually broke out—and Mehta had only sifted one knight and his wyvern.

A distinct failure. He hadn't even sifted his fair share of the enemies. Even if he'd abandoned the title of Xyonate, how could he call himself an assassin if he couldn't carry his weight in a battle?

The wyvern knight who'd flown away, fleeing from the fight—he should've been Mehta's to sift, along with his wyvern. He blamed himself for letting them escape, even though he couldn't conceive of any way to have stopped them.

Still, there might've been a way. Had he not hesitated for that brief moment after Aeron and Wafer crashed, or had he hurled a spear at them after they took flight, or...

Mehta shook his head to knock the thoughts out of his mind. He'd been in a cult, and he'd carved his way through them to escape. He didn't have to think like them anymore. He had overcome them.

So why did so much of the Xyonate way continue to dwell in his mind?

He stopped sharpening his knife and dug into his garments at his neckline. He pulled the triangle pendant necklace free from his tunic and held it high enough that the orange light from the campfire shined on its silver surface.

This was who he was now—a follower of Laeri. Even if he wasn't sure she was real, better to follow a false goddess of light and peace than a god of darkness and death.

Mehta exhaled a quiet sigh and closed his eyes.

It would be a long road to finally fulfilling his final commission and thus ransoming his family and their village from oppression, but he would walk it nonetheless. He had to, for his family and for Ferne. And for his parents, slain so many years ago.

He opened his eyes again, tucked the pendant necklace back into his tunic, and continued to sharpen his knife.

In due time, Lord Valdis would pay for what he'd done.

🔥

KENT HAD EXPECTED A CONFRONTATION OF SOME SORT WHEN GARRICK HAD insisted that he join Kent's quest for firewood, but he hadn't anticipated an outright attack. Once it happened, he chastised himself for not having seen it coming. It was potentially a fatal oversight.

Now Garrick had him pinned against the base of a thick tree, elevated to Garrick's height so that Kent's boots weren't touching the ground. Worse yet, Garrick's snow steel sword lingered mere inches away from Kent's neck.

Even in the frigid winter air, Kent could feel the sword radiating bitter, unnatural cold. All Garrick had to do was press it against Kent's neck, and it would all end.

"Listen to me, you pompous jackass," Garrick uttered, his voice deliberate and fierce. "I don't like you. I don't trust you. And I sure as hell don't need you to 'help' me, *ever*. So if we're going to continue working together, you're gonna play by my rules and follow my lead. Crystal?"

Kent stared steel at Garrick. There was no question in Kent's mind that Garrick was the stronger of the two. Were they to face off in physical combat, Garrick's size and strength advantages, coupled with his thick skin and quick healing properties—two traits Kent still did not fully understand—would make him a nightmare to bring down.

But Kent had magic and intelligence. Strategic planning. Tactical prowess. Critical thinking. A clever tongue. And above all else, an ironclad will to overcome. Whether or not Garrick possessed any of those qualities remained to be seen.

Garrick shook Kent. "I asked you a question. Are we crystal?"

"Clear," Kent replied, his voice flat. He'd been taken off-guard, and no amount of magic or cunning on his part would free him from Garrick's grasp as quickly as that one simple word would, so he'd said it.

Garrick released him and stepped back, but he continued to hold the sword in his hand. "We won't be having a conversation like this again."

"You can count on that," Kent replied. His own sword hung at his side, but against Garrick's snow steel, it couldn't do anything.

But magic could.

Kent pressed his hand against the tree behind him and flooded it with magic.

Tree roots erupted from the ground and snared Garrick's left leg, then his right. He gawked at them but reacted fast, hacking at the roots with his sword and severing some of them cleanly. Yet still more continued to grab him, coiling up his torso and grasping at his arms.

Garrick didn't give up. He swung his sword with abandon, trailing teal and blue light from the runes along the flat of the blade with each chop. Frozen chunks of wood fell to the turf, and other roots snapped against Garrick's strength.

Kent pumped more magic into the tree, but Garrick kept breaking through the attack. How strong was he?

It reminded Kent of the time a young mage had tried to restrain him with a network of flimsy vines in a back alley in Goldmoor. Kent had simply torn them from his limbs and stepped forward.

These roots were far thicker and more relentless, yet Garrick continued to overpower them, albeit with great strain.

Garrick cursed and swore, but Kent didn't stop. Instead, he turned toward the tree and pressed both hands against it, all while looking over his shoulder.

He poured every ounce of his magic into the tree, and twice the number of roots burst from the ground.

They snagged Garrick's arms and legs like lashing whips and forced him to his knees before Kent, but still Garrick resisted, still hacked at them, still snapped them with his inhuman strength.

"Your strength is impressive," Kent said over his shoulder. The fatigue from expending so much of his magic was hitting him. He couldn't keep this up much longer. "What are you?"

A root curled around Garrick's neck and tried to pull him back. He resisted it and pulled forward, but it only tightened further. Garrick started to cough, and he tried to reach up to grab the root with his free hand, but other roots yanked it back down by his wrist.

Then, finally, the roots pulled him flat on the ground, with his arms and legs spread apart, anchored to the earth. Another root had wrenched the snow steel sword from Garrick's hand and pulled it out of reach. Garrick continued to cough and wheeze as the root around his neck constricted.

But Garrick hadn't killed Kent when he'd had the chance. He hadn't really even tried, so Kent wouldn't kill him now. He redirected his magic, and the roots around Garrick's neck loosened.

When Kent pulled his hands away from the tree, a huge section of it had turned gray and brittle with death, and its bark flaked and crumbled off. It would probably die entirely now, thanks to Kent's magic draining its essence away.

Kent walked toward Garrick, who grunted and jerked against the tree roots which no longer moved in the absence of Kent's magic manipulating them. Along the way, he pulled the snow steel sword free from the curled, motionless root that held it out toward him.

He looked it over. When the root had taken it from Garrick, the teal and blue light emanating from the sword's runes had faded away, but as soon as Kent's hand closed around the hilt, the runes lit up again.

Kent had studied the ancient Aletian language for about half a year while training to use his magic in Inoth so he could read ancient texts on magical techniques. But he hadn't devoted enough study to master his understanding of Aletian runes, so he didn't know what they symbolized.

He knew even less about snow steel itself—only that it was steel forged with magic, somehow, and that ice or snow or cold played a role in creating it. Perhaps the runes were a part of the process.

"This is truly a magnificent blade." Kent studied its edges, its ornate, deep blue pommel, its clean lines. Despite being a bit oversized for a one-handed sword, its weight felt close to perfect in his hands. "I cannot imagine what you must have endured to obtain it."

When he moved it around, the blade hummed. *Interesting. I wonder if—*

"Release me," Garrick growled from the ground.

"I do not think that would be wise at this point," Kent said. "You and I did not conclude our conversation."

"I'll *kill* you," Garrick warned. "I'll snap your neck like a twig."

"From the ground? While I am standing over you?" Kent grinned. "If you can manage that, then I will be most impressed."

Garrick glared up at him. "Let. Me. *Go.*"

Kent ignored him. He held up the sword. He'd never held a weapon forged with magic before. If he tried to use its essence, what would happen?

There was only one way to find out.

He cycled a little magic into the hilt and drew it back into himself, as he would do with any other source object.

A blue-white beam flashed out of the blade and hit a nearby tree branch, encasing it in a branch-shaped block of ice. At the same time, pain flared in Kent's hand, and he dropped the sword with a yelp.

"What in the third hell?" Garrick asked. "What did you just do?"

Kent looked down at his hand. Frost covered his palm, and he could barely move his fingers. First, he'd burned one hand to a crisp saving Aeron's sister, and now he'd nearly frozen his other hand off. *What in the third hell, indeed.*

He tucked it between his legs, near his crotch. He knew it looked stupid, but it was one of the warmest parts of the human body, and he had to do something to combat the cold before frostbite could set in.

"What did you do?" Garrick repeated. "Let me up!"

Kent could play with snow steel some other time. He'd captured Garrick for a reason, and he needed to speak his mind and get back to the campfire in the cave for the sake of his hand.

"Look, you held me up against a tree and threatened to end my life if I failed to cooperate with you," Kent started. "And then I used that same tree to put you into your current predicament."

Garrick grumbled something, but Kent couldn't make out what he'd said.

"My point is, you have some incredible attributes. They no doubt make you a spectacular fighter and a top-notch mercenary," Kent said. "But I am not to be trifled with, either. I, too, have much to offer, and I would prefer if we could work out our differences in ways that do not involve violence.

"If you insist on using violence as your primary means of resolving conflict," Kent continued, "I assure you, I am capable of violence on a scale you have never seen."

Garrick glowered at him but remained silent.

"So if you truly desire to work with me," Kent concluded, "I can provide a wide range of talents, skills, and knowledge to your cause. But I will not be talked down to, and I will not be threatened. Is that 'crystal' enough for you?"

Garrick huffed. "Take away your magic, and you're nothing special."

Kent's eyebrow rose. "Take away your strength and durable skin, and you are nothing special, either."

"My strength and skin are a gift from the gods."

"As is my magic."

Garrick had no retort for that. "Cut me loose, and we can have a fair fight."

"A fair fight could never transpire between us, ever. Unless you can shed your skin and remove your strength, you will always have a substantial physical advantage over me," Kent said. "In any case, I do not wish to fight you. I would have no quarrel with you if it were not for you initiating one."

"Because you're afraid of what I'd do to you." Garrick yanked on the roots again, but they still didn't move. His face contorted with strain as he continued to pull on them.

"If you are trying to make a case to get me to release you, I recommend ceasing your threats." Kent's hand had started to tingle between his legs. Some of the feeling was coming back. "I do not want to be your enemy, and now that you have seen what I am capable of, I suspect—"

Garrick roared, and the roots around his arms and wrists tore from the ground. He grabbed the snow steel sword and severed the bonds around his waist and legs.

Kent contemplated recoiling or wielding more magic, but with his hand just now starting to warm up, and given Garrick's rageful display, he elected to stand still. Perhaps Garrick would see it as a show of good faith.

Now on his feet, Garrick stormed over to Kent, covered in lingering roots and clumps of dirt. Fury burned in his dark blue eyes.

Kent stood his ground.

"I should kill you right now."

"Then you would forfeit my expertise and magic."

"I know that!" Garrick snapped.

"You held me captive, and I held you captive," Kent said. "We are even."

Garrick pointed his finger at Kent's chest. "Except I *escaped*, and you didn't. I let you go."

"And I simply stood by, watching in utter helplessness as you broke free, without interfering, without compelling the roots to continue holding you down." Kent stared up into Garrick's eyes. "But yes, you *escaped*."

Garrick's scowl deepened.

"We both want the same thing, do we not?" Kent asked. "Respect. And to find that map and earn our coin. In both cases, we must work together to achieve what we desire."

Garrick said nothing.

"Do you agree?"

Garrick leaned in close to him. "You work for me. Respect is implicit."

An impulse to shove Garrick back filled Kent's chest, but he ignored it. "It is, if it is returned in kind. Of that, I can assure you."

The frown on Garrick's face didn't change.

"Have we reached an understanding?" Kent asked.

"Yeah. We're done." With that, Garrick snatched up his sword and headed back toward the cave.

"What about the firewood?" Kent called.

"I respect your ability to carry it yourself," Garrick answered back.

Kent frowned, but... *Perhaps this is a start.*

AERON HAD JUST FINISHED PATCHING UP WAFER'S WINGS BY THE TIME GARRICK and Kent returned. He'd been wondering what was taking so long.

At first, only Garrick walked in, carrying his sword instead of firewood.

Shock and worry filled Aeron, but then Kent traipsed into the cave soon after, carrying an armful of branches and sticks. Aeron breathed easy once again.

"How's Wafer?" Kent dropped the stack of wood near the fire.

Miserable—that was the impression Aeron got from Wafer.

"He's fine. Sore all over, but his wings are patched." Aeron tucked the robust sewing needle and thread into his pack. Then he pulled out a trio of shrooms—two for his back and one to intensify some of their more interesting side effects.

"Where'd you learn how to sew, kid?" Garrick sheathed his sword, laid it against a rock next to his shield, and settled next to the fire. "Your ma teach you that?"

Wafer growled at Garrick, and Aeron rubbed his muzzle to calm him.

"The army, actually," Aeron replied. "I spent my early years performing mindless tasks for the Wyvern Knight Corps before Wafer hatched. Mending wyverns' wings was one of them.

"Their membranes don't rip on their own," he continued, "but against a sword or rocks or anything else sharp, they can get damaged. So we sew them up when we have to."

Garrick nodded. "How long until he flies again? Part of the reason I brought you along was because you two make a pretty good scouting team."

"It'll be a couple of days, at least. Wyverns heal fast, but their wings are delicate."

"Well, in that case, welcome back to the ground level with the rest of us." Garrick stared at Aeron for a long moment, and it made him uneasy. "I'm starting to regret bringing you two along."

Only starting to? Aeron didn't know whether to be relieved or worried. He stood there, uncertain. "I'm sorry about the wyvern knights."

"I should've listened to my instincts," Garrick said.

"I'm glad you let us come along."

"Why is this job so important to you, anyway?" Garrick asked.

Aeron hesitated, and he glanced at Kent, who gave him a small nod and a shrug.

"My sister was kidnapped by the Crimson Flame. I need to find them so I can rescue her and bring her back."

"Kidnapped?" Garrick tilted his head. "Why?"

"I don't know. We didn't exactly have time to ask when it was happening."

"They took her while you were there?" Garrick gawked at Aeron.

Aeron nodded, and shame that he hadn't done more—that he *couldn't* have done more—filled his chest. "Kent and I both were."

"These flamejobs are insane. How do you know she's not already dead?" Garrick asked.

"I don't. But I'm not going to stop until I know for sure, or until I save her," Aeron stated.

Garrick shook his head. "I knew bringing you to Govalia would be a bad idea."

"Every other time I've snuck back into the country, I haven't had any problems," Aeron said. "This was a fluke."

"It's not a fluke anymore," Garrick muttered. "We're all targets now."

Thanks to me, Aeron thought. "I'm sorry. If I could take it back, I would."

Garrick stared at him again. "I wouldn't worry about it. If they kill us, all our problems will come to an end, right?"

Aeron didn't agree with that sentiment at all. Maybe Garrick had nothing to live for but his problems, but Aeron had Kallie and his parents to consider. Whatever the Crimson Flame had done to her, and wherever they'd taken her, Aeron couldn't just give up if it got too hard to find answers.

"But it's time for you to tell me what you know about these two wyvern knights I saw."

Aeron hesitated. If he revealed what he knew about Faylen, what would keep Garrick from proceeding without him? And with Wafer's damaged wings, if they left him behind, he might not be able to keep up—or escape from Govalia safely afterward.

"I need your word that you won't leave Wafer and me here alone."

"Kid, we're way past that point," Garrick said. "When I shook your hand, I gave you my word that we'd see this through. Are you suggesting I'm not a man of my word?"

Aeron swallowed. The truth was, he didn't know Garrick well enough yet to make that kind of call, and though he didn't know it, Garrick was essentially asking Aeron to wager Kallie's life on his supposed trustworthiness. "I'd like to believe you are."

"Then tell me what you know. I'm not going to leave you behind. You're a part of this now, and we're gonna need you—and Wafer—to help us get out of it."

"Alright," Aeron said. Garrick seemed sincere enough, so Aeron ignored his reservations. "I don't know for sure who the male rider was, but Faylen Uridi was the female rider. Based on your description of her hair and her mount, there's no one else it could be."

"And?" Garrick asked.

"And, what? That's her name."

"Where do we find her?"

"Outside of the fortress, the best spot is Dreynoth. It's a small town due south of the fortress. It caters to soldiers. If she's got leave, she'll be there. It would be our best chance to find her, short of breaking into the fortress itself."

"Alright. Now we've got something to work with." Garrick glanced around the cave. "Where's the other kid?"

Kid? Aeron was grateful for the change in conversation, but he couldn't help but feel like Garrick was talking down to him. "Neither of us are kids, you know."

"You are to me. I know I don't look it, but I'm seventy-four years old. One of the benefits of having some troll blood in my ancestry."

"That explains your strength and durability." Kent fed a branch to the fire.

"And your hair," Aeron added.

Garrick's stare turned into a glare.

Aeron resolved not to mention Garrick's hair anymore. Instead, he nodded toward Mehta's hiding spot. "Anyway, Mehta's back there, in the shadows."

"Where?" Garrick looked back.

The back of a brown hand poked out of the darkness and waved a knife. Its blade glinted in the campfire.

"Oh." Garrick leaned forward and lowered his voice. "It's weird how he just goes off and sits by himself in the dark. He's been doing that ever since we left Xenthan."

As Garrick said it, Mehta approached him from behind, perfectly silent. Aeron kept quiet, just watching them both.

Now standing directly behind Garrick, Mehta said, "I enjoy my time alone."

Garrick jumped and reached for his sword. "By the gods..." He stopped when he saw it was Mehta. "How did you...? *Don't do that.* I could've killed you."

Mehta gave a slight grin and shook his head. "No."

Aeron chuckled and stuffed the first shroom in his mouth—one of the painkilling ones with the yellow spots. It tasted earthy and weird, as usual, but it would do wonders for his back pain.

As Aeron chewed, Mehta joined the others around the fire, but instead of leaning against a rock like Kent and Garrick were doing, he squatted in front of the fire and held up his hands.

Wafer lay near the fire as well, but not as close as any of the humans. Wyverns usually ran hot, which was part of the reason they could survive in colder climates.

Aeron took a seat and then rested his head against Wafer's scale-covered neck. His right hand rested on Wafer's head, between his horns, and Wafer's chin lay flat on the cave floor.

It was a position they often assumed while at rest. It helped Aeron feel close to Wafer, and vice versa, without having to ride on his back.

He'd finished the first shroom by now, so he popped the next one in his mouth—the purple-striped one. It both helped with his anxiety and served as a muscle relaxant.

With Wafer nearby all the time, Aeron's anxiety hadn't really bothered him since they'd left Xenthan, but after the crash today, his back felt extra miserable, so he'd taken the purple one anyway. If nothing else, he'd sleep well tonight.

"So today went to hell pretty fast," Garrick said.

...unless Garrick wants to talk all night.

"That it did," Kent agreed. "I cannot help but wonder if it could have been avoided."

Garrick turned his head toward Kent. "What's that supposed to mean?"

"It means what I said," Kent replied and said nothing more.

The campfire crackled and snapped as Aeron and Mehta watched the two of them. Whatever was happening wasn't good.

But by that point, the shrooms had kicked in, casting Aeron's vision in orange hues. The cave walls around him began to glow with fiery colors like the campfire itself, and they started to slowly spiral.

"You think you could've done better?" Garrick asked. "Is that it?"

"As you and I discussed only minutes ago," Kent started, "we each have certain skills that make us better suited to do different things. I believe we could have avoided the entire conflict if I had been afforded the opportunity to guide the narrative regarding our presence in Govalia."

Aeron felt weightless, a routine side effect of mixing those two shrooms together, and the conversation at hand grew harder to care about. So he just reclined against Wafer and watched it play out.

"Maybe it never would've happened if we'd left Aeron behind. Maybe if we would've just stayed in the woods, we could've avoided them even seeing us," Garrick quipped. "Or maybe we should've stayed in Urthia an extra day. Or maybe we should've just stayed in Xenthan and hoped the map would find its way to us instead."

Kent shook his head and poked at the fire with a stick. "Now you are being willfully obtuse."

"Am I?" Garrick snapped. "You know what else we discussed a few minutes ago? Respect. And I'm still not getting any."

Kent's jaw tensed. He set his stick down and replied, "I respect your position as the leader of this group. I respect your size, your strength, and your prowess as a fighter. I respect your knowledge of our employer, Lord Valdis, and your knowledge of the quarry we seek.

"I can even respect the fact that you have weaknesses, as do we all. But what I cannot respect is your outright failure to recognize your shortcomings as liabilities in our quest to recover this map," Kent concluded.

Garrick rose to his feet, his fists clenched. "Do we need to finish what we started outside?"

Kent stayed seated and looked up at him. "I believe we established that you would win in a physical altercation, did we not?"

Garrick's mouth clamped shut, and his eyebrows arched up. He finally replied, "Yes."

"Then that matter is settled." Kent reclined against his rock.

Aeron blinked, and the fiery colors in his vision evolved into vibrant purples and pinks. The high from the shrooms was hitting him squarely now. He could no longer feel any back pain whatsoever, and his other sore spots from the crash had faded to nothing as well.

But what had just happened in that conversation? Aeron couldn't tell Kent and Garrick had come to an understanding or if they were about to start a fight right here in the cave.

"However," Kent continued, "I see value in establishing a plan for how we might deal with the next group of soldiers or other authority figures who wish to question us about our journey and intentions."

Garrick cleared his throat but didn't sit back down. "What do you propose?"

"Normally, Aeron would be the ideal choice to represent us," Kent replied.

Aeron's eyes widened. "*Me?*"

The colors changed again, transforming from purples and pinks into vivid reds and robust browns, signifying the height of his high.

This was the moment he would normally take the third shroom, but if he did that, he definitely wouldn't be able to focus on the conversation. He could barely keep track of what Kent was saying now.

Kent smiled at him. "You are young and intelligent, well-mannered, and thoughtful. I cannot think of any reason why you would not be the ideal choice under normal circumstances. However..."

"The entire Govalian Army is looking for me and wants me dead." That much, Aeron had been able to follow, in spite of his high.

But even so, what was Kent saying? Aeron didn't consider himself remotely charming or capable of swaying anyone with his words.

"I still don't think you're making any sense," Aeron said. He wondered if he should've postponed taking the shrooms. But then again, he hadn't known this conversation would be as important as it was—nor did he know it was going to happen at all.

Kent blinked at him. "Regardless, in light of Aeron's relative notoriety around here, I think that perhaps I ought to speak for the group going forward."

The final shroom, with its light green cap and white gills underneath, called to Aeron, but if he took it now, tomorrow morning he'd undoubtedly be asking the others what he'd missed.

The yellow and purple shrooms did wonders for his back, but they pushed him beyond the cusp of comprehension at times. Adding in the light green one would wreck him completely.

He set it aside for now. Maybe the high would linger until the conversation ended, and he could take it then.

"You don't trust me to talk?" Garrick asked.

"I trust myself more," Kent replied. "I have been formally educated in business and economics, as well as strategy and tactics. The art of negotiation and the ability to communicate with people is inherent in each of those areas of study."

"Not doing a great job of it now," Garrick muttered as he sat back down.

"Whether I am or not, I am the only viable choice," Kent said. "We have already established that Aeron cannot."

"Right," Aeron said through the colors swirling in his vision. They wavered, and he wondered if he'd said it too loudly, but no one reacted as if he had.

Kent motioned toward Garrick. "Your skin has a greenish tint to it, and you have blue hair—both unmistakable identifiers going forward since at least one of the wyvern knights escaped."

Garrick grumbled something Aeron couldn't understand and folded his arms.

Kent nodded at Mehta, who still crouched in front of the fire. "And I sincerely doubt you have any interest in speaking to strangers about our plans."

Mehta's eyes doubled in size, and he shook his head.

"Meanwhile, I am a normal-looking man with the aforementioned well-developed communication skills," Kent continued. "So regardless of your opinion on my negotiation, I am both the best option and the *only* option."

Garrick scowled at him.

Mehta spoke up, "I think he's right."

Everyone looked at him. Through his haze, Aeron had forgotten what Mehta's voice sounded like, so it surprised him to hear words come from his mouth.

"He is the best choice," Mehta added.

Garrick sighed and rubbed his forehead. "Fine. Have it your way."

"Thank you." Kent turned back to Aeron. "What do you expect will happen next on the Govalian Army's end?"

Aeron tried to blink away some of the colors and the confusion that accompanied them, but it didn't work. They kept swirling, and the confusion continued to slow his brain. He blinked again, harder this time, and then forced himself to reply.

"More patrols, for sure," he said, trying not to slur his words. "Definitely more wyvern knights. Maybe infantry, too. We Govalians get pissed when people mess with us, and killing a bunch of wyvern knights qualifies. If I were still in the corps, I'd want blood."

"So they'll kill us on sight?" Garrick asked.

Aeron shrugged. It wasn't that complicated of a question, but... shrooms. "Probably, yeah."

"So we must proceed with extreme caution," Kent said. "And without a functional scout at this time, perhaps we should consider staying here for an extra day or so."

"No." Garrick shook his head. "We move forward. We'll stay off the main roads until we absolutely have to use them. Forests can provide enough cover to keep us out of sight, even with a wyvern crawling alongside us."

Wafer growled, and Aeron patted his head to calm him. "Easy, boy. Don't take it personally."

Green man stupid, came the impression from Wafer.

Aeron struggled not to laugh. Then he noticed Mehta staring at him, and his mirth dissipated, replaced by concern. After what felt like an eternity, Mehta finally looked away, and Aeron could relax again.

That was weird. And creepy.

"If that is what you wish to do, then that is what we shall do," Kent said.

"Get some rest," Garrick said. "Breakfast is at daybreak, and we're leaving right afterward."

§

GARRICK HAD BEEN RIGHT ABOUT LEAVING THE NEXT MORNING, AND HE'D BEEN right about traveling through the trees as well.

While they rode through the woods, he'd spotted two patrols—or maybe the same patrol twice—of wyvern knights flying high overhead. But the patrols hadn't noticed them, and their journey south, toward Dreynoth, continued.

They rode their horses, and Aeron still rode Wafer, who walked on all fours with the knuckles of his wings supporting his front half. They weren't traveling at a fast pace, but Garrick wondered if Wafer could've kept up if they'd had to rush.

As they traversed the woods, Garrick scanned the tree branches far and near for signs of movement. He wasn't looking for Govalians, though.

Onni, a sentient species of tree-climbing mammals with long, lanky limbs, occupied such forests. They weren't particularly dangerous, so Garrick wasn't watching out of concern.

He was watching with the hopes of spotting one Onni in particular: Noraff, the scum who'd betrayed Garrick back in the dungeon in Etrijan.

But Garrick didn't see any Onni, much less the specific one he'd vowed to kill once he got ahold of him again.

As they reached a clearing toward the afternoon, they dismounted and ate a modest lunch. Garrick checked the green-handled knife in his belt. It was a mage steel blade that Noraff had stabbed him with before leaving him for dead, locked in an ancient Aletian vault.

Noraff would never believe that Garrick could've gotten out of there. Not in a millennium.

But he *had* gotten out.

And the best part was that Noraff had no idea Garrick was still alive.

The thought made Garrick grin. After failing to deliver the map to Lord Valdis in the first place, the idea of driving the very same mage steel blade into Noraff's gut—right where Noraff had stabbed Garrick—was one of the few things that brought Garrick happiness these days.

A few hours later, Aeron pointed to a town in the distance. "That's Dreynoth."

"Doesn't look like much," Garrick said.

"That's because there isn't much there," Aeron replied. "A few boarding houses. A pub. An apothecary. A stable for soldiers' horses. A brothel."

Garrick eyed him.

Aeron stammered, "I—I've never been to it, of course. It has a reputation for—"

"No judgment here, kid," Garrick said. "What you do with your coin is your business."

"That's not—I didn't—"

"He is just antagonizing you," Kent said. "Ignore him."

Aeron's face turned red, and his mouth closed tight.

Garrick had to admit, he enjoyed seeing Aeron squirm. "You know the town's layout, right?"

Aeron nodded. "Yes. Been there dozens of times. Maybe hundreds. I was in the army for sixteen years, and we had leave on a regular basis."

"Then you'll know the best place to ambush your friend."

"Is that what we're doing?" Aeron glanced between Garrick and Kent. "That's the plan?"

"What did you expect?" Garrick asked.

"I don't want her getting hurt. I didn't agree to that."

"If she cooperates, she won't be hurt."

"You're not getting what I'm saying." Aeron squared his body with Garrick and looked up at him. "She will *not* be hurt, period. I won't allow it."

"There are plenty of ways to ensure her cooperation without resorting to the use of force," Kent said. "But getting her attention initially may prove challenging."

"I have an idea," Mehta said.

Garrick turned to him and looked him up and down. "I guess I shouldn't be surprised that the assassin knows about ambushing women."

Mehta stared at him, his face expressionless. "I have done it many times. And men, also."

"Of course you have." Garrick closed his eyes for a long moment and sighed. Either it took a lot to offend Mehta or he genuinely hadn't caught the sarcasm in Garrick's voice. "Alright. Let's hear it."

"We need a secure place to talk with her," Mehta said. "And a place for an ambush. At nightfall, I will handle the rest."

⸎

AERON WATCHED AS FAYLEN URIDI STEPPED OUT OF THE PUB AND INTO THE SIDE alley. She wore a dark cloak, but her short, unmistakable blonde hair still glowed almost white under the moonlight.

Waiting and watching had finally paid off, just as Mehta had said. Even so, the thought of lurking in an alley and hiding in the shadow of the tannery building next door didn't appeal to Aeron.

He would've preferred to ride Wafer over the town and just drop down and snag Faylen that way, but any number of complications prevented that, not the least of which was Wafer's recovering wings. So they'd left Wafer in the trees outside the town and done everything Mehta's way instead.

This had better work.

As she approached Aeron's position, he emerged from his hiding spot in the tannery's side doorway. "Faylen."

She stopped, and her hand went to the dagger at her hip, but she didn't draw it. "Who are you? What do you want?"

Gods, she looks great.

Aeron shook his cognition back into place. He lowered the hood of his cloak, revealing his face. "It's me. Aeron."

Her eyes widened, and she tensed.

Aeron imagined the shock she must've been feeling, to see him again after everything that had happened.

But the other mercs had insisted that seeing a friendly face—even one that belonged to a traitor—in a back alley in the dark of night was better than being ambushed by a stranger. The last thing Aeron wanted to do was scare her.

If Aeron were honest with himself, he'd always regretted not telling Faylen how he felt. But in hindsight, he'd been wise to keep his mouth shut. Who knew what kind of trouble she would've landed in because of his actions?

Yet a part of him still hoped for something more, perhaps some sort of future in which they could be together.

He envisioned them flying their wyverns side-by-side, floating on the clouds. And then a smaller wyvern joined them in the center, ridden by a child who looked like Aeron but who had Faylen's dramatic white-blonde hair and—

The *shing* of steel drawing from a scabbard severed Aeron's fantasy as Faylen brandished her dagger and stormed toward him.

So much for the "friendly face" theory.

"Faylen, wait..." he started.

But before he could say any more, a dark form stepped out from the shadows behind her and rendered her unconscious.

CHAPTER ELEVEN

Kent sat in a chair across from Faylen, who was still unconscious, in the small room they'd rented for the night in one of Dreynoth's boarding houses. Now up close, Kent could see why Aeron liked Faylen, even though he hadn't said as much aloud.

She had distinct, remarkable features. High cheekbones. Pointed, elf-like ears, but not as pronounced. And that blonde hair—short and nearly white. Kent normally preferred longer hair on women, but the length suited Faylen's face.

Altogether, she rivaled Aveyna in beauty, albeit a different kind. But Kent didn't want to think about Aveyna. Even though it had been months since her death—murdered at the hand of her own son—the pain was still too fresh for Kent.

Faylen, who was tied to a chair, began to stir. Her head lolled a few times, but then she jolted awake, blinking her wide blue eyes and looking around the room.

There wasn't much to see—just a bed and the chair she sat on, and a chamber pot next to it—so her survey didn't take long. Her eyes finally landed on Kent, who sat before her with his hands folded.

"Good evening," he said.

Faylen stared at him for a long moment. Kent had expected she would be less even-tempered about this, but she wasn't squirming or shouting. She finally asked, "Who are you? Where am I? What do you want?"

"I am afraid I cannot give you my name right now, but I can assure you that I mean you no harm."

"We."

Kent tilted his head. "Pardon?"

"You mean *we*, not I," Faylen said. "Aeron Ironglade is around here somewhere, too. I saw him in the alley."

"That is correct."

Faylen tried to move, but the ropes around her arms and the chair kept her in place. "If you mean me no harm, then why tie me up?"

"I hope you can forgive that measure." Kent gave her a sad grin. "I need to ask you some questions, and after you approached Aeron with your dagger, I could not risk further attempts at violence on your end."

She cocked her head and studied him up and down. "What are you, Murothian? On second thought, forget it. Just ask your questions and get it over with." Faylen shook her head. "But know that I'm just a wyvern knight. I don't know anything about the army's plans for Muroth, or even if there are any."

"I am not here to inquire about Muroth or any other country," Kent said. "I want to know about a recent trip you made to Etrijan. Specifically, your return trip.

"You and a fellow wyvern knight picked up two mercenaries outside some sort of temple in northern Etrijan," Kent continued. "I just need to know where and to whom you took them, and then you are free to go."

Faylen shook her head again and scoffed. "Yeah, no. I can't tell you that. How do you even know about that?"

"Someone asked me to look into it."

"Aeron? How does he know about it?"

"Someone else, actually."

"So there are three of you, then?" Faylen probed.

Kent smirked. She had some tenacity. Probably another reason Aeron liked her.

"No," he said. "But all you need concern yourself with is answering my inquiry. I need to find something those mercenaries took from my friend and return it to him."

"So you're a mercenary?" she asked.

She was smart, too. Trying to get information from him even though she was the one being interrogated.

"I need you to answer the question, Faylen."

She shook her head a third time. "I can't do that."

"Why not?"

"I can't tell you that, either."

Kent leaned back in his chair. "Then it appears we are at an impasse."

"I guess so. Or you could just let me go."

"Not until you tell me what I need to know."

"Then settle in, old man, because we're going to be here for awhile."

Kent frowned at her. Sure, he was forty-nine years old now, but he didn't think of himself as being old. He awoke with the same aches and pains in his body that any man his age might, but he could still contend with all manner of foes.

He leaned forward. "Faylen, you need to tell me."

She leaned forward, almost as if mocking him. "I can't."

"Look." Kent clasped his hands together. "I am being direct with you out of respect for your history with Aeron and—"

"I don't *have* a history with Aeron," she said. "We flew together in the corps. That's it."

Kent nodded. "Then out of respect for that camaraderie, I am being direct with you so we can all move on."

Faylen didn't say anything else.

"I need you to tell me where you took the mercenaries, and then you can go."

"How many times do I need to say that I can't tell you?" Faylen snapped.

"If you do not tell me, I will be forced to consider other measures."

Faylen's distress shifted to anger. "You're a wretched person, whoever you are."

"On the contrary, I have given you ample opportunity to provide the information I need. I do not want to resort to other means of extracting the truth from you, but I will if I must."

"It doesn't matter what you do. I'm not going to say a word."

AERON HEARD EVERY WORD THROUGH THE DOOR, AS DID MEHTA AND GARRICK.

"This isn't going well," Garrick muttered.

"Give Kent more time. He's good at this sort of thing," Aeron said.

"I don't want to linger here any longer than necessary. We're already at risk just by being in this miserable little town."

Aeron hadn't ever thought of Dreynoth as miserable. He'd had some good times there, in fact.

The pub was a regular hangout for Govalian Army soldiers, including wyvern knights, infantry, cavalry, and more. Even officers sometimes visited Dreynoth for leave—if they couldn't get all the way down to Govaliston.

"And what if her wyvern comes back and makes a fuss?" Garrick suggested. "I don't want to have to contend with a dragon crashing through the roof and ruining all of this."

"Unlikely," Aeron said. "Wyvern knights almost always leave their wyverns at the roost in the fortress whenever they're not on duty."

Aeron thought about how he could barely sense Wafer from this far away. As far away as the roost was from Dreynoth, Faylen couldn't possibly feel her wyvern at all.

"I hope you're right," Garrick mumbled.

As they continued to listen, Garrick's frustration grew more and more apparent. His gigantic hands would clench into fists and then release, then they'd do it again. His breaths, usually long and slow, had quickened, and the expression on his face hardened more with each passing moment.

It worried Aeron. If Kent couldn't get any information out of Faylen, Aeron didn't know what would happen next. They hadn't really discussed it as a group. Faylen was their only link to finding the mercenaries who'd taken the map.

Finally, Garrick said, "Enough of this. I'm done waiting." He turned to Mehta. "You were an assassin. Did you ever have to extract information from anyone, or did you just kill them?"

"Some of both," Mehta replied. "But mostly the latter."

"Whoa, whoa…" Aeron held up his hands. "We're not torturing Faylen. I told you I wouldn't allow her to be hurt."

"There are ways to torture someone that don't cause permanent damage," Garrick said. "I was hoping our friend with the knives knew some of them."

Mehta shook his head. "Not specifically. But I know plenty of ways to cause pain."

"No," Aeron reasserted. His anxiety was growing. "We're not having this conversation again."

"Then what else can we do?" Garrick asked.

Aeron held his breath for a moment. It was a harebrained idea, but… "Let me talk to her."

"After she tried to attack you in the alley?" Garrick said, "No chance."

"I can convince her. I'm sure of it."

"She came at you with a dagger. Bad idea."

"She's tied up now. She can't attack me."

"Apparently you haven't been around many women."

Aeron frowned at him. "What's that supposed to mean?"

"I don't understand either," Mehta said. "Female Xyonates have equal potential to be dangerous whether they're tied up or not."

Garrick glanced between them. "You've got to be kidding me."

"I'm going in." Aeron yanked the door open.

"Wait!" Garrick said, but Aeron was already inside the room.

Kent sat before him in his chair, looking up at Aeron with a neutral expression tinged with a bit of surprise.

Faylen sat with her back to him, and she tried to look back, but she couldn't see him because of his position in relation to the chair. "Who is that?"

"It's me." Aeron rounded the chair and stood next to Kent.

Faylen glowered at him, her eyes full of rage.

"Faylen was just telling me how she hoped she would never see you again," Kent said. "So your timing is ironic, to say the least."

"Would you excuse us?" Aeron asked Kent.

Kent hesitated, but then he stood and nodded. "I will be right outside."

"Thank you." Aeron waited for Kent to leave the room. Once the door shut, Aeron sat in front of Faylen. "Are you alright? Do you need anything? Water?"

"I need you to leave me alone, *traitor*." Venom dripped from her accusation.

"I'm *not* a traitor." Aeron leaned forward. He'd been called that far too many times in recent months. "You know General Cadimus ruled that I wasn't guilty."

"And then you stole the army's wyvern from the roost and fled the country," she countered. "Even if you weren't a traitor then, you are now."

"Do you know why I did that?" Aeron asked.

"Because you're bonded to Wafer and can't be without him. I know how it works, Aeron."

"That was part of it, but that wasn't the only reason."

Faylen shook her head. "No reason you could give me will change my opinion."

"Well, you're tied to a chair, so I'm going to give it to you anyway." Aeron wished he hadn't taken such a sarcastic tone with her, but she needed to know the truth. "You know the army tried to sell Wafer at an auction, right?"

Faylen wasn't even looking at him anymore. Instead, her eyes scanned the room, focusing everywhere except at him.

"Well, they did. And you know who bought Wafer?"

Again, he got no response and no eye contact.

"Commander Brove."

She glanced at him, then she looked away.

"Don't you think it's unusual that the army would sell a wyvern, only for one of its officers to buy him right back?" Aeron continued, "Because that's exactly what happened. I was at the auction. I tried to buy Wafer back, legally and true. But Commander Brove outbid me on purpose, knowing it was me."

Faylen squirmed in her chair but still refused to look at Aeron.

"I was prepared to let Wafer go after that. I didn't want to, and I knew I'd be miserable forever as a result, but I didn't think I had any other choice. I also didn't know it was Commander Brove outbidding us at the time. We couldn't see who was bidding because of the crowd.

"But he came to my pa's forge the next day and told me what he'd done. He told me he'd bought Wafer, and he made it clear it was just to spite me." Aeron seethed at the memory of that conversation. "And the worst part was, he told me he'd bought Wafer so he could cut him up and *feed him* to the other wyverns. Yours included."

That got Faylen's attention. She stared at Aeron with her striking blue eyes, looking as beautiful as he'd ever seen her, even though anger arched her eyebrows down.

"Do you know what Brove spent on Wafer at that auction?" Before Faylen could give a response, whether she was going to or not, Aeron kept talking. "Ten *thousand* gold coins. For a wyvern. A wyvern he was just going to butcher to feed to the other wyverns at the roost.

"My mum and my sister were pitching in to help me buy Wafer because I barely had any coin. My pa, who's never spent a coin in his life that he didn't have to, got the bid up to 4,500 gold. Even if he'd sold his house and his forge, Pa isn't worth that much.

"And Commander Brove swept in and offered more than double that, just to ruin my life further. *That's* why I came and took Wafer away," Aeron said. "Even if I could've found a way to live without him, I couldn't have lived knowing what Brove was going to do to him."

Faylen's mouth puckered into a tight frown. After a long moment, she said, "How do I know you're not just making this up?"

"The army keeps records of those auctions somewhere. I don't know where, but they have to be in the fortress. You can look up Wafer's purchaser and the purchase price."

Faylen said nothing.

"But even if you never do," Aeron continued, "ask yourself whether it seems like Commander Brove would ever do something like that. Then ask yourself if I've *ever* lied to you about *anything* since you've known me."

Another long moment passed between them. Finally, Faylen said, "Why didn't you tell me?"

"Would you have believed me? Would it have changed anything?"

"I would've viewed you differently."

"But would you have done anything differently?" Aeron pressed. "Or would you have done your duty, like always?"

Faylen sighed. "You know I would've done my duty."

That had never been more apparent than when she'd come at him with the dagger in the alley.

"And that's why I couldn't tell you," Aeron said. "That, and I had to flee the country pretty quickly after that."

Faylen stared at him. Aeron knew he hadn't won her over, but at least she understood his reasons for doing what he'd done.

"So while I'm a traitor on paper, now you know the truth behind it." Aeron had her attention, finally, so he decided to press his luck. "If Commander Brove has been that treacherous with me, a nobody Leatherwing who just happened to beat him in practice combat a few times, what is he doing behind *your* back?"

Faylen's jaw tensed, but she didn't reply.

"Do you remember my sister?" Aeron asked. "You met her once."

Faylen nodded but didn't make eye contact with him.

"A couple of months back, she was taken by a member of the Crimson Flame, who then burned down my parents' house with them inside of it."

Faylen looked at him again, this time with shock on her face.

"Kent helped them escape in time, but Kallie is gone. The Crimson Flame cult has her."

"Why?" Faylen studied him. She probably thought he was making it up.

"I don't know," he replied. "But the map those mercenaries brought from Etrijan is connected to the Crimson Flame. Why would Commander Brove order you to fly to Etrijan to retrieve a couple of mercenaries? How does that help Govalia in any way?"

"It's not my job to question the orders he gives us," Faylen replied.

"But I know you're wondering about it. Because you *know* it doesn't make any sense." Aeron was on a roll. It felt great. "And you and I both know it wasn't an official mission. It couldn't have been, even if my info about the map being related to the Crimson Flame is wrong. So he must be getting something in return. The question is what, and from whom?"

"That's not my concern."

"No, but you know it's wrong of him to use army resources for personal gain. That's part of the oath we all swore when we enlisted."

"Everyone breaks that oath at some point," Faylen said. "We're soldiers. We can influence regular people whether we mean to or not."

"I'm not talking about getting a free drink at the pub or boarding in a citizen's house when we travel throughout Govalia."

Aeron leaned toward her again, now only a few inches from her pretty face. Being so close to her sent shudders through his very soul—both good and bad shudders. But mostly good ones.

"I'm talking about something much more considerable. Something more obvious."

"Like what?"

Aeron shrugged. "Can't say for sure. Depends on where he ordered you to drop off those mercenaries."

Faylen's mouth closed again.

"Come on, Faylen. You know this isn't right, whatever it is," Aeron said. "And you know he's a jackass, too. Don't you think he ought to get what he deserves?"

Faylen remained silent for a long moment, just staring at Aeron, searching his eyes as he searched hers in return. Then she exhaled a long sigh. "Here's how this is going to go—how it *has* to go."

"I'm listening."

"I'll tell you what I know, but when I'm done, I have to go back and tell Commander Brove everything I told you. I was due back at the fortress an hour ago, so he'll be wondering where I am. That's why I left the pub when I did—so I'd have enough time to make the trek back home."

"Why can't you just make up an excuse?"

"Because everyone already knows you're back. And he knows…" She hesitated. With her voice lowered, she said, "…he knows that we were… close. If he starts asking around, my story will unravel quickly."

Aeron shook his head. "I really don't like this."

"I won't be telling him anything he doesn't already know. Look, I want to help you, but I can't get caught in the crossfire, alright? It's not something I'm willing to do. I like my career, and I like having Nilla around. I'm not about to let your vendetta separate me from her."

Aeron frowned. "I can understand that."

"I know you do." Faylen added, "And I need you to untie me before I tell you anything."

Aeron hesitated.

"It's not negotiable, Aeron. You're asking me to trust that your story, as wild as it may be, is true. Now you need to trust me before I tell you mine." Faylen watched him intently, her stare unwavering.

Before Aeron could respond, the door opened, and he looked up.

Kent, Mehta, and Garrick entered the room, but only Kent came forward. Meanwhile, Garrick shut the room door, sealing them all inside.

At first, Aeron didn't understand why Garrick and Mehta had entered the room at all. It seemed like an unnecessary risk.

But when he considered that the Govalian Army already knew they were looking for a group of four, he supposed it didn't matter if Faylen saw them or not.

Faylen's focus shifted to Kent's approach once he walked out from behind her. "You again."

"Hello, Faylen," Kent said. "I have considered the terms that you proposed to Aeron, and I believe we can come to an agreement. You may tell your commander of what transpired, but aside from Aeron's name, you will not learn our names. In exchange for that discretion on your part, I will loose your bonds now. Deal?"

Faylen nodded. "Deal."

Kent motioned with his hand, and Mehta stepped forward and untied Faylen.

Now free, Faylen rubbed her wrists, stood up slowly, and turned to face Garrick and Mehta. Her eyes widened at the sight of Garrick, probably more at his size than at his slightly green skin tone and blue hair.

Kent said. "Will you please divulge the information that we seek?"

Faylen sighed. "Yes. The mage rode with me, and I hated every second of it. Whenever I'd look back, he'd just stare at me with cold, dead eyes. He was a total creep-job."

"Phesnos," Garrick muttered.

"Sounds familiar," Faylen said. "We took them to Osnal and dropped them at the manse of Lord Arasmus Glavan.

"He's a former Govalian Navy Admiral, and he was based down there. Retired a few years back. I'd heard of him before. He was pretty great as a naval commander, from what I understand.

"When we arrived, he invited all of us into his house. The place was more like a palace. I had wanted to get going, but he convinced us to stick around for a hot meal. We obliged, and he had our wyverns fed, too.

"After dinner, the furry mercenary—I forget his name—handed a parchment tube of some sort to Lord Glavan," she continued. "He mentioned something about locking it away in a vault, then he took it into his study."

"Anything else?" Kent asked.

Faylen shook her head. "After that, he commended us and sent us on our way. The whole situation felt off. I had just figured that, at the time, he wasn't really retired, and so the job might've been legit. Maybe he was still secretly working for the emperor or something."

"And the two mercs?" Garrick asked. "Did they stay there?"

"They stayed longer. We left first, so I can't say what happened after that."

"Where in Osnal is his estate?" Kent asked.

"It's to the east of town. If you have a map of Govalia, I can show you."

Garrick produced one from his pack and spread it out on the bed.

"Here." She pointed to an unmarked piece of land to the east of Osnal, along the coast. "It's an incredible estate. Right on the water. He had a few boats in the back of the house tied along a dock."

"How far from the city do you figure it is?" Garrick asked.

"Maybe ten miles. Could be more. It's hard to tell when you're riding a wyvern. It passes pretty quickly while airborne."

"Thank you, Faylen," Kent said.

"Yeah," Aeron added. "Thanks."

"You won't be thanking me when I go back and tell Commander Brove everything I know about you," she said. "And you'd better leave now. That's about all the head start you're going to get."

"We were hoping you could be persuaded to grant us a little more time." Kent smiled at her. "I doubt your commander will know the difference between a couple of hours delayed and several more beyond that. Missing is missing, and when you return in good shape, he will be pleased that you came back at all."

Faylen looked at Aeron. "I suppose I can give you more time. I guess maybe another twelve hours, at most."

"Twelve hours is ample time," Kent said. "Thank you."

Aeron wished she could've given them more time. They were heading south, and they'd pass Govaliston along the way.

He'd hoped to check on his parents, but with only half a day's head start, they'd need every second to put distance between them and Commander Brove's inevitable response.

"But there's one other thing," Faylen said. "I can't go back there unscathed. If I show up fresh-faced and unharmed, they won't believe you forced the information out of me."

"And you will appear to either be a traitor yourself or weak because you offered up the information too willingly," Kent said. "And in either case, you are subject to more scrutiny as a result."

"Exactly," Faylen said.

Aeron glanced between them. He hoped they weren't considering what he thought they were considering. "What are you asking?"

"I need you to hurt me," Faylen stared right at him, "and I need it to be bad enough that it looks convincing."

Aeron couldn't believe his ears. "No. Absolutely not."

"Aeron, you have to," Faylen said. "Or they'll do the same thing to me that they did to you."

"No." No way could Aeron ever do such a thing to Faylen. "Even before we grabbed you in the alley, I told these guys that under no circumstances were you to be harmed."

"I'll be harmed worse if you don't do it."

"Faylen…" Aeron's words faltered.

How else could Aeron express his complete disdain for even the *idea* of hurting her, much less actually doing it or allowing it to happen?

For the gods' sakes, she was the reason he had back pain in the first place. He'd risked his life to save her from a horrible end back when he was still in the corps, and he'd paid for it in more ways than one. And she knew that, too.

And now she wanted him to hurt her?

"Aeron, this has to happen," she insisted. "If you can't do it, then someone else will have to."

She was right, of course. If Commander Brove suspected her of treachery, he'd make sure she suffered all the more since it had involved Aeron.

Commander Brove had nearly succeeded in getting Aeron executed over a decidedly non-treasonous letter to his parents. Aeron couldn't risk anything even close to that happening to Faylen. But…

"I can't do it. I won't. Even if you're right about Brove, I can't hurt you."

"Someone has to," Faylen said. "I'd do it myself, but it has to look convincing."

"I'll do it," Mehta said. "I have sifted several women in my time. If she must be harmed, I can do it without leaving her permanently scarred."

The idea of Mehta, a trained assassin, harming Faylen horrified and enraged Aeron. But the thought of doing it himself was worse, and he couldn't imagine Kent doing it, either. And Aeron doubted Garrick could show enough restraint, given his strength.

So Mehta, it seemed, was the best choice to give Faylen what she wanted.

Everyone was looking at Aeron—Faylen included—for permission.

He cupped his face with his hands and closed his eyes. "Fine. But please don't make me watch. I'd be too inclined to stop it."

"You couldn't stop me." Mehta's voice conveyed absolute certainty yet not even a hint of ego. It wasn't a boast or a challenge—just a statement of fact.

Aeron realized he believed him.

"Just… I'm going for a walk," Aeron said. "Let me know when it's done."

As the door shut behind him, a loud smack sounded from the other side, followed by a sharp gasp from Faylen.

Aeron shuddered and forced himself to ignore it as he walked away.

CHAPTER TWELVE

Several minutes later, Kent retrieved Aeron, and they returned to the room. Aeron almost refused to go back in. He didn't want to see the end result of Faylen's request.

But he did venture inside, mostly out of concern for her wellbeing. He wanted to make sure Mehta hadn't killed her or overdone it. He was an assassin, after all.

When the door opened, Aeron saw Garrick standing over Faylen, who sat on the chair facing the door with her head bowed. He held a bloody rag in his hand. Meanwhile, Mehta sat on the bed with his hands folded as if nothing had even happened.

When Faylen looked up, the sight of her face filled Aeron's chest with rage.

He noticed her split lip and her black eye, first. Then, as Aeron drew nearer, he noticed her bruised, puffy cheeks and jaw.

He shot Mehta a glare, but Mehta stared back at him with a neutral, emotionless expression. Had it even fazed him? Was his soul black? Did he even have a soul at all?

"I'm fine, Aeron," she said through it all. Her lip oozed a bit of blood. "It's not that bad."

Gods, he wanted to kill Mehta. But without Wafer at his side, he didn't stand a chance.

It was necessary, he rationalized. *A little pain now to save her life later.*

"Are you sure?" Aeron managed to ask.

Faylen nodded, but Aeron still didn't believe her. He never should've agreed to this.

"You all need to get going." Her voice had a new, bitter edge to it. "Your twelve hours has started."

All business, all the time. That's how Faylen was. Aeron admired her resolve—except when it put her at risk. But she was smart and capable and could handle herself. Perhaps he shouldn't worry so much.

But he did anyway.

They'd entered the early hours of the morning by that point. Twelve hours would put them in Osnal around mid-afternoon. Aeron figured they could squeeze another hour or so out of the time limit, as it would take Commander Brove time to muster a sufficient response—perhaps even longer if he had to get approval from General Cadimus.

"I also need to be clear on one other thing." She looked straight at Aeron. "This doesn't change anything between us. I'm still a member of the royal army, and as such, pride, honor, and loyalty dictate that if I encounter you again—any of you—I'll have to fight you."

Aeron nodded. She had no other choice. "I understand."

"Now get out of here. Twelve hours."

Aeron wanted to say something else to her, to tell her how he felt, but he couldn't bring himself to say it in front of the others. So instead, he wished her well and left the room first.

KENT FELT RIGHT AT HOME OUTSIDE LORD GLAVAN'S ESTATE. IT REMINDED HIM of the world he'd left behind in Muroth, but instead of farmland and forests of robust trees, the estate featured sprawling plantations and tropical plants of all sizes. The main house rested along the coastline, and the Tahn Sea stretched south as far as the eye could see.

By the time they reached Osnal, the afternoon sun hung low in the sky, warming everything despite the chill of winter in the air. The twelve hours had nearly elapsed. Whether they wanted to or not, they needed to get into the manse, retrieve the map, and get out with whiplash speed.

As the sun continued to sink toward the horizon, Garrick gathered the group under a cluster of trees about a half-mile from the manse. With the sunset behind him, and given his size, Garrick reminded Kent of Trag, a half-orc numbskull he'd scuffled with when he'd first arrived in Goldmoor several months ago.

But unlike Trag, Garrick wasn't some homeless bum in need of a shelter for the night. Garrick was formidable, and he wasn't the idiot Kent had assumed he would be.

"So how do we want to do this?" Garrick asked.

Kent spoke up first. "Considering our assets, skillsets, and manpower, I have an idea."

"Why am I not surprised?" Garrick muttered.

Kent looked at him. "If you have a plan formulated, I would be happy to hear it."

Garrick waved at him. "Go ahead."

"If he is agreeable to it, I suggest that Mehta enter the manse to clear a path for the rest of us, so to speak," Kent said. "Then he can get us inside via an entrance of his choosing—preferably something along the back, if possible.

"From there, we will progress through the manse as quietly as possible until we reach the study. I imagine it is on the third floor since the manse is three stories tall.

"Once we are there, I should be able to access the vault via my magic, one way or another." Kent concluded, "Perhaps that way, we will not encounter Lord Glavan at all."

"I can do my part," Mehta said. He almost looked eager, but he showed so little emotion normally that Kent couldn't be sure.

"I think it's wise for me to scout around the area to watch for signs of incoming soldiers," Aeron said. "Wafer's not totally better, but he's well enough that we should be able to glide around. I wouldn't count on him to do much aerial fighting, though. His wings would tear too easily."

"I agree. That is a prudent idea," Kent said.

"And how do we escape?" Garrick asked.

"Hopefully the way we came. Then we will make for our horses and head north once again toward Xenthan."

Garrick started shaking his head even before Kent finished explaining. "They're expecting us to ride north. Seems like we'd be riding into a disaster."

"Then what do you propose?"

"The house is on the coast. Faylen said it had a bunch of boats and a dock in the back, which makes sense since the guy was an admiral," Garrick said. "I say we steal one."

"And then pick a rendezvous spot where Wafer and I can meet up with you?" Aeron nodded. "Sounds great. And perhaps we can leave the horses there, too."

"Lord Valdis doesn't care about getting three horses back," Garrick said. "He has an army. He just wants the map."

Aeron held up his hands. "I just figured you wouldn't want to walk the rest of the way back to Xenthan."

"We'll buy new horses if we have to," Garrick said. "In any case, those boats are probably our best bet."

"I grew up inland in Muroth. I have scarcely been on any boats, much less do I know how to pilot one," Kent said. "Who will guide us?"

Mehta shook his head.

"I will," Garrick said. "I grew up in the islands off of northern Etrijan. My clan used to raid the coastal towns along the mainland up there. I learned plenty about seamanship along the way. Did that for nearly ten years of my life."

"Are we certain there will be a boat docked there that you will be able to captain?" Kent asked.

"If it has sails and a rudder, I can steer it," Garrick said. "And if not, the three of us can row something smaller."

No one voiced any further questions or concerns.

"Then it appears we all agree about our approach?" Kent asked.

"What happens if we get inside and you can't get the vault open?" Mehta asked.

"We'll improvise," Garrick said.

Kent didn't love the sound of that, but it was the best they could hope for. At least they'd worked *something* out, and it hadn't devolved into another argument. Perhaps Kent's heated conversation with Garrick had established some measure of cooperation between them after all.

"What kind of defenses do you think he's got in there?" Aeron asked.

"For an estate of that size, and given Lord Glavan's status as a retired military official," Kent said, "I would anticipate a robust, well-trained contingent of personal guards. Furthermore, Lord Glavan himself is also a considerable threat, unless he is so old that he can no longer fight."

Given the similarities between Lord Glavan's manse and his family's estate, Kent thought it wise to base his predictions off of his own experience. The main exception was their geographic positioning and how it affected their respective defenses.

Kent's family estate in Muroth was in the southern province of Etheridge, which bordered the nation of Inoth, the sworn enemy of Muroth. As such, fortresses lined both sides of the border, including one crucial fortress south of the Etheridge estate.

Due to the constant threat of attack from Inoth, far more Murothian soldiers guarded House Etheridge than would be guarding Lord Glavan's estate, so Kent had factored all of that into his assessment.

"I don't mind a good scrap," Garrick said, "but we need to be quick about this. I want to avoid the Govalian Army at all costs. That's a fight we can't win."

As they all turned their eyes toward the manse, the bottom of the sun touched the watery horizon in the distance.

It was nearly time.

GETTING INTO THE MANSE WAS EASY FOR MEHTA.

As the last rays of sun filtered over the horizon, he crept along the rear of the structure, slinking through shadows to avoid the handful of guards patrolling the estate, and entered a darkened window.

Inside he found a bedchamber filled with ornate furniture and simple, yet elegant decorations on the walls. His enhanced vision outlined everything in faint green lines, and it also told him he was alone in the room.

To his eyes, the construction of the manse appeared new, especially compared to the homes of other lords he'd visited on past commissions. Perhaps this wasn't an ancestral home but rather Lord Glavan had built the manse while still employed by the Govalian Navy.

Even so, furniture, decorations, and architecture didn't concern him. He headed for the door.

It felt amazing to be able to use this aspect of Xyonate training again. Much of the last two months, he'd spent traveling out in the open rather than sneaking around, hiding in dark places, and sifting commissioned targets.

He'd given up the Xyonate way, which meant no more commissions outside of bringing an end to Lord Valdis, but that didn't mean he had to give up the sneaking and hiding. Especially when he enjoyed them both so much.

With a light touch, he eased open the door, and golden light from torches mounted in the corridor streamed into the room. A form blocked out the light for an instant, and Mehta recoiled away from the opening, his knife instantly in his right hand.

But the shadow passed as quickly as it had appeared. Whoever it was, they hadn't noticed Mehta cracking the door open.

Even so, he waited another moment before he took hold of the bronze door handle again. Normally he would've waited even longer, but with some portion of the Govalian Army on their way, he couldn't afford the delay.

Still holding his knife, Mehta inched the door open farther and peered into the corridor beyond. He saw nothing, so he pulled the door open further, careful to keep perfectly silent.

He couldn't do anything about the torches themselves. Snuffing them would create darkness, and while he could use the darkness to his advantage, doing so risked unnecessary attention. Instead, he opted for speed.

He could've gone to the right or to the left. This early into the excursion, it didn't matter since he didn't know the layout of the manse. But the door opened to the left, and he could see a clear path down the corridor, so he elected to go that way.

Mehta checked to the right to ensure no one would see him, then he darted through the spacious hall. His footsteps barely created any sound whatsoever, thanks to his training and the decadent woven rugs that lined most of the floor.

But as he rounded a corner, he came face to face with a pair of green eyes set into a pale, freckled face.

His knife leaped to the girl's throat, and he pinned her against the nearest wall in one quick, jarring motion. She yelped, but his hand clamped over her open mouth and cut off the sound.

The thirst billowed in his gut, and it cried out for her blood. She was his now, to do with as he pleased.

But something about her eyes, stricken with terror as she inhaled and exhaled sharp, shaky breaths through her nose, reminded Mehta of Ferne.

His knife touched the skin on her throat, eager to open it and spill her life on the wooden floor. The thirst begged him to do it, commanded him, screamed at him to sift her.

It would be easy.

She wore fine linen clothes, but they were dirty—the elbows of her blouse and the knees of her skirt, especially. A tan headscarf tied her reddish-brown hair back and out of her face. Some sort of apron hung from her waist, draping down the front of her legs.

A servant girl.

She was pretty in a plain sort of way, and probably sixteen years old. Or maybe twenty. Mehta had never been good at guessing ages, but she was several years older than Ferne and at least a few years younger than him—or what he guessed his age was.

Xyonates lived short lifespans, so they hadn't bothered to help him keep track of his age. He'd have to ask Grandfather about it when he returned home.

Desperate for blood, the thirst threatened to overpower him and sift her. His knife blade pressed into her throat, and she inhaled a tense breath.

Mehta couldn't do it. He *refused* to do it.

He pulled the knife away to keep himself from giving in to the dark desires in his soul, and he prayed a silent prayer to Laeri. He tried to force his thirst back into the box in his mind.

She didn't deserve to die. She was just a servant girl, or perhaps a slave.

With his hand still clamped over her mouth, Mehta whispered, "Be silent."

Harmless as the girl was, a shriek would carry throughout much of the house and expose him to more trouble than he needed. If she cried out, he would silence her, but he still wouldn't sift her. Now, looking at her, all he could see was a green-eyed Ferne with dark hair, just a few years older.

Tears streamed from the girl's terrified eyes and onto Mehta's fingers, but she gave a slight nod.

Mehta slowly pulled his hand away from her mouth. His palm and fingers had left her face red and white from the pressure, but it quickly regained its normal color.

She didn't make a sound. Even her ragged breaths came quietly.

"I'm sorry I startled you," Mehta said. The thirst raged at him, still focused on making her body forever cold. "If you help me, I'll let you live. Do you understand?"

She nodded again.

Mehta didn't like threatening her, especially since he had no intention of sifting her anyway, but he had to get her to cooperate somehow. Since he'd already established himself as a dangerous presence, asking nicely would only confuse her.

And with the Govalian Army coming after them, he didn't have time for confusion.

"What's your name?" He stepped back to give her some space, but only a little.

"Mayri," she replied. Her voice was so quiet, he wasn't sure he'd heard her right.

"On which floor is Lord Glavan's study?"

She trembled, and her mouth opened, but nothing came out.

Mehta closed the distance between them again. He made his voice firm. "Mayri."

"This floor," she whispered, still shaking. "Down the west wing of the manse."

"Is there a servants' entrance?"

She nodded. "You—you're not going to hurt—"

"I'm not here to harm servants," Mehta said.

Relief filled her eyes, albeit temporary. "It's along the back of the manse."

"Take me there, quietly."

He turned her around and took hold of the waistband of her skirt. She shuddered.

"Quietly," he reminded her. "Go."

She led him down the corridor, the same way he'd already been heading when he'd rounded the corner and encountered her. They were heading into the east wing of the house, which was the wrong side for accessing the study, but Mehta could most easily let Kent and Garrick in through the servants' entrance.

They stopped at a wooden door on the left side, and Mayri opened it. Mehta peered over her shoulder, searching for any other servants who might be in the vicinity.

"Where is everyone?" he asked.

"The kitchen," she replied. "Or the dining hall."

The sun had set, so perhaps Lord Glavan was taking his evening meal. And with him being retirement age, he likely took his meals earlier.

Mehta had noticed that about older-aged commissions during his Xyonate days—they all tended to eat and go to bed earlier. It had meant less waiting for Mehta. Sifting people while they slept made for easy fulfillment of his commissions and generally less suffering, too.

"Are you expected back soon?"

"No. I'm supposed to scrub the floors," she replied as they entered an entryway beyond the door. Another door lay ahead, larger than the ones they'd passed in the corridors. Probably the external door Mehta was looking for.

"On which level?"

"All of them. All I do, every day, is scrub floors. Sometimes I dust off furniture and polish silver, but it's mostly just the floors," she stammered.

"Alright. Open that door, and keep quiet."

She complied, and Mehta stood beside her in the doorway and waved his knife, trying to catch a glint of moonlight on it. He searched the lawn with his enhanced vision and saw two green-outlined shapes emerge from their cover.

They took the forms of two tall men—Garrick and Kent. The signal had worked.

They darted across the lawn—well, Kent darted, and Garrick lumbered—and hurried inside the servants' entrance. Garrick pulled the door shut behind them and looked down at Mayri, who stared up at him with renewed terror and no small amount of awe.

"Who's this?" he asked.

"Mayri," Mehta replied. "She's a servant here. She says the study is on this floor, in the west wing."

"Guards?" Kent asked.

Mehta turned to Mayri. "How many?"

Mayri stood with her back against the wall and her hands at her sides. Her voice shook as she replied, "I've—I've never counted them."

"Roughly?" Kent asked. "Ten? Twenty? More?"

She shook her head. "Maybe ten. Maybe fifteen including guards outside. Lord Glavan doesn't have much to worry about these days, now that he no longer serves in Govalia's navy. The Septerran Pirates left him alone years ago, and the guards inside stay nearby him."

"What about kids?" Garrick asked. "Any heirs running around?"

Mayri shuddered again. "No. I mean, yes, but they aren't here."

Mehta looked at the others. Resolve shone in both Kent's and Garrick's eyes. If they could take on six wyvern knights in the open air, facing down ten or fifteen guards and an old soldier in close quarters would be a walk through the forest.

Garrick stepped toward Mayri, towering over her. "So what do we do with her?"

Mehta wasn't tall, but he stood taller than Mayri by a few inches. Next to Garrick, Mayri might as well have been standing next to the manse itself.

"Please," she whispered. Tears formed in her eyes again. "Please, I want to help you. Lord Glavan is... evil."

"What do you mean?" Kent asked.

Mayri shook her head. "I—I can't talk about it. It's too painful. He just is."

Mehta had heard of masters abusing their slaves and servants before. Why they didn't just fight back, he didn't know. Then again, he'd had years of training. Mayri did not.

"We don't have time to play house," Garrick said. "We have to keep moving."

"We are not here to harm anyone if we can help it," Kent said.

Mayri perked up. "So you're here for the vault?"

Mehta, Kent, and Garrick exchanged glances.

"What can you tell us about it?" Kent asked.

"I can get you inside," Mayri said, "if you promise to get me out of here afterward."

Garrick eyed her. "How does a servant get access to the vault of her master?"

"As servants, we're trained to be unseen. Silent. Sometimes, our masters forget we're even here," she replied. "Took me awhile to piece it together, but I know the vault combination. I was waiting for a secret moment to open it and take something for myself so I could get away from this place."

"If you cross us, it will end badly for you," Kent warned.

Mayri shook her head, trembling. "I won't. I need to get out of here."

Kent nodded. "Very well. Then lead us to the study."

Mayri nodded again and turned toward the door leading back into the hallway. This time she waited until Mehta took hold of the waistband of her skirt, and only then did she start walking.

For once, Mehta led the party, but he wasn't truly in the lead thanks to Mayri. He preferred it that way. While he had no intention of sifting her, he'd rather follow her into potential danger instead of walking into it head-on himself.

Kent followed behind Mehta, and Garrick brought up the rear, both holding their swords.

Mayri halted at the intersection of two corridors, to the right of the room where Mehta had entered the manse. With her hands at her sides, she waved at them to stop.

Metal clanked, and Mehta saw a pair of armored guards heading toward the direction of the study at a casual, unsynchronized pace. By their gait, they hadn't been alerted.

Mayri motioned them forward again.

She crept down the hall, past torch-lit tapestries, and then she stopped again, this time before a large set of double-doors housed under an archway. With their dark wood and shiny ornamentations, the doors looked like the entrance to some fine room, including, perhaps, a study.

"Open it," Mehta whispered.

Mayri reached for the gleaming bronze doorknob and pulled the door open.

Mehta urged her inside, and Kent and Garrick hurried in after them. Garrick shut the door as silently as Mayri had opened it and lowered a wooden crossbar to lock them inside.

Mehta could've seen well enough without the dwindling fire burning in the hearth, but Kent and Garrick would need it to access the vault.

The study had a lofted ceiling that took up all three stories of the manse instead of just one floor. Wood paneling adorned the walls, and several rows of towering bookshelves occupied the eastern half of the space.

Wooden slats made up the floor, patterned in a shape Mehta couldn't make out, but they looked like some sort of Govalian symbol.

A large, wooden table sat before a window, and a stuffed chair butted up against the window. Two additional stuffed chairs sat before the hearth, facing each other with a small end table situated between them.

A grand tapestry made of red fabric hung above the hearth. It bore some black design woven into the red, but due to its position above the room's only light source, Mehta couldn't make out what was on it. Whatever it was, it didn't matter.

Adjacent to the hearth, on either side, were more bookshelves set into the wall. But instead of books, they held miscellaneous objects in a variety of shapes and sizes.

Mehta couldn't tell what they all were, but some of them were skulls. Some looked animal-like, some were clearly human, and others—he had no idea what they could've come from.

"So where's the vault?" Garrick asked.

The sound of snapping wood cracked throughout the room, and the study doors flung open and slammed against the inside walls.

Mehta's instincts kicked in. He clasped Mayri's wrist in his hand and hauled her deep into the heavy shadows near the freestanding bookshelves on the eastern end of the room. She knew where the vault was and how to get inside it, so keeping her hidden was of the utmost importance.

As Mehta and Mayri disappeared into the darkness, a half-dozen armored guards stormed into the study, each one holding a torch and a weapon—most of them swords.

Mehta didn't stop moving. He chased the shadows with Mayri in tow, thankful she wasn't protesting, and ended up along the farthest wall to the east, shrouded in darkness.

Then he gripped her by her shoulders. "Stay low. Stay quiet. It will keep you safe from the coming savagery."

Before she could respond, Mehta abandoned her to the darkness and crept around the bookshelves toward the guards. He still held one of his knives, but now he drew the other.

And he waited.

§

GARRICK WATCHED AS THE SIX GUARDS PARTED DOWN THE CENTER, AND THEN A silver-haired man clad in dark robes walked between them toward Garrick and Kent. A golden medallion hung from a matching chain around his neck.

Behind him, six more guards entered the study. Each carried a spear and a long shield while the first six lit torches and candelabras spread throughout the western half of the room.

Mehta had done well to hide the girl while he still had the chance. Were she not their best chance to get the vault open, she would've made for a good human shield, or at least a distraction, in the fight to come. For as small as she was, maybe Garrick could have just tossed her at the guards.

Hopefully, she'd stay hidden. Her wandering around wasn't something Garrick wanted to deal with while taking on twelve armed guards.

He shot a glance at Kent, who stood there with his sword at his side, as if unconcerned at the sight of the guards. Perhaps he had some magic brewing, but it was too dark for Garrick to tell. Kent's focus remained fixed on the old man in the center.

"Greetings, interlopers," the old man said in a calm, cool voice. "I am Arasmus Glavan, lord of this house. It appears you are lost. Had you wanted a tour of the premises, you had but to ask."

Garrick rolled his eyes. Over the years, he'd hear some version of that line countless times, and he'd grown sick of his enemies offering to be exceptionally accommodating after it was already too late.

"Nonetheless, you've found your way into my most holy place," Lord Glavan said. "If you're scouring for coin, you should have broken into my treasury instead."

"Then kindly point us in that direction, and we will head there immediately," Kent said.

Lord Glavan grinned at him, but it was a grin oozing with power, and his dark eyes conveyed the confidence of a man confident in his advantage. "Well spoken, sir. You've had some measure of education, haven't you?"

"You may consider me a lifelong learner," Kent replied. "In fact, under different circumstances, I would have welcomed the opportunity to study some of the fine works in this room."

"Put down your weapons, and I will fill your prison cell with any books you desire to read."

"I fear I cannot oblige you, Lord Glavan," Kent said. "You see, we have come for one very specific reason."

"Which is?"

Kent looked to Garrick. Up until that point, Garrick had been content to let him talk—as much as he hated to admit it, Kent *was* better at it—but now it was Garrick's turn to decide how much they revealed.

Upon a quick reflection, Garrick decided there was no sense in making up lies. They were already here, and they would either succeed or die trying. "We need the map you stole from Lord Blayne Valdis of Xenthan."

Lord Glavan's grin twisted into a scowl. "If you understood what you have been charged to do, you would not have come to this place."

Garrick was about to respond, but then he noticed the icon emblazoned on Lord Glavan's medallion. He recognized it, but it was all gold, instead of the colors he'd seen before.

Then Garrick glanced up at the red tapestry hanging above the hearth. He'd seen it when he'd entered the study, but he'd paid it no mind because he couldn't see all of it.

Now, with the light from the soldiers' torches added to the space, the image on the tapestry was apparent. It was the same familiar, haunting symbol that decorated the temple in Etrijan—a black fireball set on a dark-red background. A symbol of death, fanaticism, and fiery evil.

It was the symbol of the Crimson Flame.

The familiar sensation of berserker rage ignited in Garrick's chest. It flowed through his arms and legs, and it spiked along his spine, up to the base of his skull.

Lord Glavan was a member of the Crimson Flame. That meant he'd hired Noraff and Phesnos as a safeguard against Garrick succeeding in finding and getting the map, even though it was already safely stored under a Crimson Flame temple.

What was Lord Glavan trying to hide? A map showing the cult's various temple sites and secret locations had some value, but why would Lord Glavan go to such great lengths to keep it out of Lord Valdis's hands?

Garrick's anger boiled. None of it mattered as long as he got the map back.

"I don't give two hoots about anything you say," Garrick said. "You're Crimson Flame scum, a twisted cultist, and a fiend. And because of you and your meddling, the only two men I could call friends on this continent are now dead—killed by the betrayers you hired to keep me from getting the map."

"Your friends' deaths are regrettable, but you have no concept of the importance of this map," Lord Glavan said. "Or what will happen if it falls into the wrong hands."

"At least you admit to being behind it," Garrick said. "At least you're not hiding behind cowardice. Now we can resolve this like men rather than you begging for your life."

Lord Glavan's dark countenance vanished as he grinned again. "If there is to be blood, then so be it."

CHAPTER THIRTEEN

Kent drew his sword, but before he could so much as raise it against the guards approaching him, Garrick launched toward the three guards headed in his direction and battered them with his sword and shield.

If Kent could've just watched Garrick the whole time, he would have; the sight of him thrashing those guards was extraordinary.

But he had three of his own guards to deal with.

The first guard slashed at Kent's legs—a nice change of pace, considering most men tended to swing their weapons directly at his head.

Kent brought his sword down hard to intercept the blow. Their swords clanged together and rang with fury in the aftermath of their connection.

But Kent also held a chunk of wood in his free hand, rough to his touch. He pumped his magic into it.

Once he'd started training his magic, it had taken Kent some time to master the process of flooding the object in one hand but not the other—otherwise he'd be taking the essence of his own sword.

But he'd mastered the technique and could now fight with both his body and magic in fluid harmony.

Through the wood in his hand, his magic tore up the wooden floorboards from their stone base, right under the first guard. The movement swept the guard off his feet, and the back of his armor clanked hard against the floor.

The second guard stormed forward, followed closely by the third, each of them holding swords. Their blades glinted yellow-orange from the torches spread around the room and the burning hearth.

Kent directed the floorboards, now hovering before him, toward the two other guards, and flung them forward. The floorboards collided with their arms, legs, chests, and heads, even as the guards tried to parry them with their swords.

With the two guards occupied, Kent refocused his attention on the first guard, who'd started to recover his footing.

Kent didn't give him the chance. He lunged forward with his sword, hoping to pierce the guard's armor with its tip.

The guard managed a pitiful block as he stood up, and he started to back away from Kent with a shocked look on his face—a valiant attempt at retreat, but ultimately worthless.

Kent summoned more of the floorboards to his cause, and they tore from the floor behind the retreating guard. They slammed into his back, splaying out his arms and forcing him back toward Kent, who was ready for him.

Kent's sword drove through the guard's armor, into his gut, and out his back.

The guard gasped, then he dropped to one side, nearly taking Kent's sword with him. But Kent yanked the blade out of his body before it could interrupt his flow.

He faced the two other guards coming at him once again.

The chunk of wood in his hand felt small and smooth, worn down from his magic stealing its essence. He wouldn't get much more out of it, but he needed one last action.

The wood obeyed his magic, and one of the downed floorboards lifted into the air and started rotating on its center point. It spun faster and faster, parallel to the floor, as the two guards rushed toward him.

Kent gave his final command, and the floorboard shot toward the guard on the left. The guard tried to block it with his sword, but it slammed into his helmet instead, knocking him to the floor, out cold. Chalky, wooden dust dropped from Kent's hand, useless.

As Kent shifted his focus from the second guard to the third, Garrick's snow steel blade sliced down along the third guard's back. He'd already taken down his three guards and apparently felt obliged to help Kent, whether Kent wanted the help or not.

But as a result, the first six guards were down. Six guards remained, plus Lord Glavan himself.

When Kent looked at Lord Glavan, he no longer saw a confident old man, sure of himself and the guards who outnumbered the intruders in his house. Instead, he saw the haunting image of a man overcome by some sinister influence.

Lord Glavan's head had tilted to the side at an awkward angle, and he stared at them with unnaturally wide, black eyes, like those of an insect. He began to levitate off the ground with his arms held out to his sides, almost casually.

His robes flowed behind him as if carried by some faint wind, and red light emanated from his palms as he reached toward his fallen guards.

Not only was Lord Glavan a member of the Crimson Flame—he was also a dark mage.

Kent cursed under his breath.

The first guard who'd attacked Kent was still alive, but only barely, thanks to Kent's sword. Or at least he was until Lord Glavan's magic took hold of him.

The guard lay on his side, clutching his wounded gut until an unseen force lifted his body into the air. Now he was hovering three feet off the ground, like Lord Glavan himself, and blood spattered on the floor beneath him from the hole Kent had put in his stomach.

The five other downed guards began to hover as well, some alive, some dead. In unison, the living guards screamed, their voices wretched and dissonant as their bodies contorted wildly.

Their screams gave way to a chorus of tearing noises, then came the smacking of blood splattering across the walls and the floors as dark magic ripped their bones from their flesh. The bones of the six men spiraled into a cluster and formed into a swirling mass of death that floated in front of Lord Glavan's chest.

Kent had seen the horrors that accompanied war, torture, and combat. He'd watched as Eusephus, a dark mage, killed Inothian soldiers and drained their essences with violet weapons born of dark runes.

But he'd never seen anything so dastardly and repulsive as what he'd just witnessed. His stomach threatened to upturn itself, but he managed to quell the sensation before it overtook him.

"Your presence in my home ends *now*." Lord Glavan's voice seemed to have intermingled with darkness itself. He stopped levitating and landed gently on his feet.

A series of loud cracks sounded as the bones snapped into smaller, pointed fragments and turned toward Garrick and Kent.

AT FIRST, MEHTA HAD TROUBLE COMPREHENDING WHAT HE'D JUST SEEN. THEN, when he heard Lord Glavan's hideous voice and saw the bones snapping on their own, it all made sense: Lord Glavan was a dark lord, presumably like Lord Valdis was.

The amount of blood and gore that spilled on the floor from Lord Glavan's deadly harvest astounded Mehta, and he'd grown up in a death cult where blood and trauma were normal parts of everyday life.

It wasn't that he found it horrifying; it just surprised him how powerful Lord Glavan was.

The sight of it sent his thirst into a frenzy. Would it ever be possible for Mehta to obtain power like that? To sift his foes that efficiently?

More imminently, if Mehta could sift Lord Glavan, a dark lord, then it meant he could sift Lord Valdis, too.

He'd been hiding among the bookshelves, biding his time, waiting for his moment to enter the fray. But Kent and Garrick had handled the first batch of guards without incident, so Mehta had maintained his position and continued to watch.

With the revelation of Lord Glavan's immense power, Mehta realized the true wisdom of his patience thus far. If Lord Glavan were to overcome Kent and Garrick, Mehta would be the last remaining hope for winning the battle, retrieving the map, and getting it to Lord Valdis—whom Mehta would then have the opportunity to sift.

But as the swarm of jagged, broken bones pointed at Mehta's comrades, Kent ducked low and grabbed one of the loose wooden floorboards.

The bones shot forward at random intervals and from multiple angles, but a husk of wooden floorboards slammed together around Kent and Garrick, bending and warping to shield them from harm.

Bones thudded against and dug into the floorboards, and some of the wood cracked apart and splintered, but more boards came to their aid, further cocooning them on one side. Upon impact, each of the bones disintegrated, unable to be used a second time.

While Kent maintained their defenses, Garrick hurried toward the grand table near the window, flipped it on its side, and hefted it toward Kent's magic wall. Together, they positioned it to reinforce Kent's boards, and they crouched behind it, out of Mehta's line of sight.

Soon after, the magic wall crumbled to the floor in a heap of shredded boards. About half of the mass of swirling bones in front of Lord Glavan remained, and now his other six guards, each wielding a spear and a shield, had started toward Kent and Garrick's position.

Mehta's knives wouldn't do much to aid Kent and Garrick against spears and shields. Yes, he was faster and stealthier, but he didn't need to intervene on their behalfs—especially given the clean shot he now had on Lord Glavan.

Mehta glanced back into the shadows behind him. His enhanced vision revealed that Mayri still lay there, curled up into a ball, clutching her hands over her ears and whimpering in the darkness.

She had been right in saying Lord Glavan was evil.

But she was safe. Out of the way.

And now Mehta could end this fight permanently.

He stepped away from the bookshelves, removed his cloak, and crept toward Lord Glavan.

§

KENT HUDDLED BEHIND THE OVERTURNED TABLE, SURPRISED AND ALARMED AT the overwhelming violence around them. His wall of wooden boards had shattered, and shards of bone thudded into the table now instead—just not as quickly.

Lord Glavan was keeping them at bay, but the table was thick enough to protect them from his attacks... for now.

Kent hissed at Garrick, "I thought he was just a navy commander!"

"Don't blame me. I didn't know," Garrick fired back. "Lord Valdis said the map was taken by a rival. I didn't know it meant a rival *dark lord.*"

"Clearly not."

Unlike anima magic, the discipline Kent practiced, dark magic fed off the essence of living beings—primarily animals and sentient races. Dark mages harvested essence from their quarry and then repurposed it in a variety of ways. Kent had encountered several types of dark magic before.

Prince Kymil of Inoth had kept a bag of living mice on his person so he could create blood arrows for each one. Then he'd sling them as fast as any real arrow, and with wicked precision.

Just before Aeron had pulled Kent out of his final battle in Inoth, Prince Kymil had managed to hit Kent with some sort of green, venomous arrow, perhaps derived from the essence of a viper. Were it not for Aveyna's light magic intervening, the arrow would've killed Kent.

Eusephus had constructed barriers, thrown red, serpentine blasts, and created violet, essence-draining weapons using dark runes. He'd used them to stymie and even kill some of the Inothian soldiers trying to bring him down.

And now Lord Glavan was ripping the bones out of his slain guards and using them as weapons. It all served to reinforce how repulsive and brutal dark magic was, and it repelled Kent from ever wanting to try to use it.

But Kent could examine the morality of dark magic some other time. For now, killing the dark lord in the room was absolutely the right and moral decision, and that was good enough.

Kent peered over the edge of the table, and he saw all six of the remaining guards moving to flank them on both sides. Then a bone launched at Kent's face from Lord Glavan's position.

He ducked down just in time to avoid it, and it struck the window behind him and shattered one of its panes.

Too close.

"We cannot stay here," Kent said. "The other guards are flanking us."

"Then let's handle it." Garrick started to stand, but Kent pulled him back down. "What?"

Two more bones zipped over their heads and smacked into the windowsill behind them. Then the tips of three others pierced through the table between them. They all dissolved immediately afterward.

"*That* is what," Kent replied. "I have an idea. Keep watch. See that I am not killed, please."

Kent touched the exposed stone foundation under the floor with his bare hands. He hadn't done this since Aveyna had tried to have him killed in her throne room, but it had worked then. Perhaps it would work now, also.

He poured magic into the foundation and cycled it, along with the stone's essence, back into himself. He could feel his body getting cold and solidifying, becoming like the stone itself.

It was working.

"What in the third hell are you doing?" Garrick snapped. "Your face... it's..."

Kent looked down at his hands. They matched the stone foundation's pale gray color. They had turned to stone, along with the rest of his body. But the effect wouldn't last long.

Kent bolted upright, only to be struck by an onslaught of bone spikes, but they clinked off him harmlessly. He shifted to one side, drawing Lord Glavan's attention away from Garrick, who, to his credit, reacted well and engaged half of the approaching guards right away.

Still cycling the stone essence and his magic, but now only within his body, Kent faced the other half of the guards and let them come for him.

As Mehta approached Lord Glavan from the side, he saw Kent rise from behind the table.

At first, the sight of Lord Glavan hurling a dozen bones at Kent startled

Mehta. They should have shredded him, but instead, they bounced off him or burst apart upon impact.

Then Mehta noticed Kent's face. Even in the low light, he could tell something had changed. Kent had somehow transformed into a walking, stone statue of himself.

The three guards that attacked Kent jabbed at him with their spears, but their spearheads pinged off his body with no effect.

Garrick exploded toward the other three guards, engaging them with his snow steel sword and matching shield, both aglow with blue and teal runes.

Meanwhile, a snarling Lord Glavan continued to fling bones at Kent. None of them did any damage, and he was running out of bones to throw.

This was Mehta's chance. He could close the distance in a few long, quick strides and deliver a killing stroke to Lord Glavan.

He darted out of the shadows in a silent ambush with his blades ready.

Lord Glavan immediately turned toward him and hurled a spike-shaped bone at him.

How had he known about Mehta's approach?

Mehta didn't grant the question so much as a second thought. It didn't matter. Mehta had trained for nearly two decades to anticipate attacks before their inception, and he'd trained to slow his mind down to adapt and adjust to anything that came at him.

So he watched the bone spike flying toward him, and he adapted. He adjusted.

He lashed his knife down without slowing his pace, and the bone ricocheted off its blade and hit the floor. A few more steps and he'd be digging his other knife into one of Lord Glavan's lifeless, blackened eyes.

But Lord Glavan launched more bones at Mehta. They would be enough to keep him from reaching Lord Glavan.

So he improvised.

He leaped off one foot and soared over the spiked bones, missing them by mere inches. Mehta's jump would land him well short of reaching Lord Glavan, who'd backed up a step in the process.

But Mehta's knife could still close the remainder of the distance.

While still in the air, he whipped the knife at the center of Lord Glavan's chest, aiming just below the golden amulet he wore around his neck.

Just before Mehta tucked his head to roll back up to his feet, he saw the knife embed itself in Lord Glavan's body, right where he'd been aiming. Then Mehta hit the ground, rolled up into a standing position, and lunged toward Lord Glavan with his other knife.

The tip of Mehta's knife struck something hard and invisible, followed by his forearm, elbow, and then his torso and face.

Brilliant red flames ignited at the tip of his knife and billowed out from there along Mehta's body. It hurled him back into a huge bookshelf so hard that it toppled over, spilling its contents onto the floor.

Pain lit up the front of Mehta's body first, then as it faded, a different, more lasting pain afflicted his back where he'd struck the bookshelf. He recovered his footing quickly, fighting through the pain as he had so many other times before.

He glanced down to see how badly the red fire had seared his flesh, but to his surprise, the bare skin on his arms looked normal, and as far as he could tell, the fire hadn't singed his clothing, either. What had happened?

As Mehta acclimated himself to the strangeness throughout the room, Lord Glavan cried out. His voice sounded normal again, not warped and hellish anymore.

At Lord Glavan's call, two of the guards pulled away from fighting Kent and Garrick and hurried back to him.

Mehta didn't know what good they could hope to do for him. His knife had landed true, an unquestionably fatal blow, even if it didn't kill Lord Glavan right away. But on the off chance one of the guards knew something Mehta didn't, he decided not to take any chances.

The pain in his back still hurt, but he would live. He bolted forward once again, shifted his other knife to his right hand, and engaged the first guard.

The guard's spearhead jabbed at Mehta's chest, and Mehta's knife batted it away. He spun with the block and jumped high into the air off his right leg. Mehta followed the spin and drove his right knee into the guard's shield, knocking him against the wall adjacent to the door. Without the shield, the blow might've cracked his skull.

As Mehta landed, he caught a glimpse of Lord Glavan reaching up toward the guard trying to attend to him. Then Mehta charged toward the guard against the wall.

The spearhead stabbed at him again, but Mehta dodged it and slammed his shoulder into the guard's shield with all of his momentum. The wall kept the guard from moving anywhere, and the force from Mehta's shoulder smashed the shield into him.

Mehta had learned long ago that if someone insisted on using a long weapon, the best way to triumph was to draw nearer to them so they couldn't use the range to their advantage. In many cases, their ranged weapon would then become a disadvantage.

Once he'd passed the guard's spear, he'd gained the upper hand. Time to make use of it.

Mehta grabbed the top of the shield, jerked it forward, and plunged his knife into the side of the guard's neck. He fell immediately, sputtering, and took Mehta's knife down with him.

Mehta wrenched the guard's spear from his dying hands and turned back toward Lord Glavan just as a piercing shriek filled the study.

The guard who'd been reaching down to help Lord Glavan up stood there, upright, with his back and head arched at a horrific angle. His mouth gaped open, and his wide eyes clouded over as he wailed.

Lord Glavan still sat on the floor, now against the wall, gripping the guard's hand in his own. Violet light glowed from Lord Glavan's hand and blazed up his arm toward his torso.

As the guard screamed, the skin on his face contorted and shriveled, and the healthy texture of his facial features melted away. His eyes turned perfectly white, then they shrank to nothing and sank into his skull, leaving two empty holes gaping at Mehta.

Then his neck constricted, and the skin tore away, revealing red muscles and white tendons and bluish veins. It all withered away to nothing as the violet light overtook Lord Glavan's entire body and rushed toward the knife protruding from his chest.

Mehta realized what was happening. He raised his spear and hurled it at Lord Glavan, but another burst of red fire knocked it from the air. The flames spread across an invisible wall for a few feet, then they dissipated. The spear clattered to the floor.

Lord Glavan's body levitated once more, and he released his grip on his guard's hand.

The guard fell to the floor, his skull crusted with slick, blackened blood, baring crooked yellow teeth up at Mehta. His remains no longer filled out his armor, and it slumped against his corpse, nearly as misshapen and twisted as the skeleton it contained.

The knife in Lord Glavan's chest popped out and hit the floor beneath him. Due to Lord Glavan's black robes, Mehta didn't know if the stab wound had healed as well, but he saw no signs of pain or suffering on Lord Glavan's face.

Stranger still, Lord Glavan somehow looked younger than he had when he'd entered the study. Mehta couldn't be sure because of the low light, but Lord Glavan's aged face bore fewer wrinkles than before, and his silver hair had darkened.

As Mehta retrieved his other knife from the guard he'd sifted, Garrick and

Kent joined him. They'd finished off the other guards, and now only Lord Glavan remained.

"At least now we outnumber him," Kent said as the last hint of stone vanished from his face.

Garrick scoffed. "We outnumbered him even with his idiot guards."

"My knife went straight into his chest," Mehta said, "and it didn't kill him."

"We will find a way," Kent said. "We must."

Lord Glavan's hand reached into a nearby torch, and the fire filled his hand. Then he clapped his hands together, and the fire burning in all of the torches throughout the room extinguished, as did the fire in the hearth.

The room plummeted into darkness except for the faint shine of moonlight through the windows. It didn't bother Mehta because of his enhanced vision—he could still see Lord Glavan's faint green outline.

Then red flames erupted from Lord Glavan's hands. He spread them wide and sent twin blasts of fire at the mercs.

Mehta dove out of the way and rolled to his feet once again as the fire licked at his heels and chased him toward the overturned table. He vaulted over it and took cover.

The flames scorched over his head, knocking out the remainder of the window and setting part of the lawn ablaze. Then it stopped, and the next instant, he felt the fire slam against the table once again.

Behind him, the table heated up against his back while the cold winter air blew onto his face from outside. It wouldn't be long until the fire burned through it and reached him, so he scrambled to his feet and darted into the freestanding bookshelves, toward where he'd left Mayri.

The fire didn't follow him, though he didn't know why at first.

Then he shifted his position and saw Garrick and Kent pushing forward. Garrick's snow steel shield negated some of the fire, and Kent's magic had ripped wooden paneling from the walls and stacked them on top of each other in an ever-thickening shield against the fire.

Lord Glavan had refocused both of his hands on streaming fire at Kent and Garrick, leaving Mehta alone. But instead of pushing them back, Lord Glavan was steadily retreating.

Kent continued to call more wooden panels and floorboards to his aid, Garrick continued to use his shield to resist the overwhelming heat, and Lord Glavan continued to blast it all with fire, but the flames weren't burning through fast enough.

But none of it would matter if they couldn't find a way to get past the shield of intermittent flames protecting Lord Glavan.

Mehta's knife had made it through once, but his two attacks after that had failed. So why had the first one worked?

He'd thrown the knife right when Lord Glavan had thrown bone spikes at him. Perhaps his shield lowered when Lord Glavan sent attacks out and then went back up afterward? Or maybe when Mehta's knife struck Lord Glavan's chest, the shield had triggered? Or was it something else entirely?

Mehta couldn't be sure. And backing Lord Glavan against the wall wouldn't be enough to win this fight.

As Mehta considered his options, he caught motion out of the corner of his eye. One of the dead spear guards had begun to levitate, just as the others had before their skeletons tore from their bodies to become fodder for Lord Glavan's attacks.

Then Mehta got an idea. A crazy, stupid, reckless idea.

He ran toward the guard's body and jumped on its back as it continued to ascend. The flesh beneath the guard's armor shredded, and blood splattered out in every direction, including all over Mehta.

But as the guard's spinal column began to tear from his neck, Mehta took hold of it with his free hand. It wobbled and curved like a spine should, and Mehta squeezed his legs around the bones to help keep from falling off.

Then the bones shot toward Lord Glavan, carrying Mehta along with them.

He readied his knife.

CHAPTER FOURTEEN

Garrick had worried his snow steel shield wouldn't hold up against Lord Glavan's incessant fire, but it had performed admirably. He didn't know how or why it could withstand the blasts, but it was doing its job, and for now, that was good enough.

Then the horrific rending of flesh tore into Garrick's ears, even louder than the red flames roaring against his shield. But the tearing sound put Garrick on edge. Could he and Kent contend against fire and bone at the same time?

But when he saw Mehta riding a bloody spinal column across the study, toward Lord Glavan, stark confusion usurped his worries.

By the time Lord Glavan realized it, it was already too late.

Mehta leaped from the bones and plunged his knife deep into Lord Glavan's chest, and they both dropped from the air. Mehta shifted his position in midair as they fell, and he landed on top of Lord Glavan with a satisfying *crunch*.

The flames ceased, the bones dropped, and the room descended into perfect quiet until the moan of the winter wind carried in through the destroyed window.

They'd won. Now they had to get inside the vault and get the map.

Garrick and Kent started toward Mehta and Lord Glavan's body.

AERON AND WAFER HAD DONE THEIR JOB SCOUTING, BUT THE SIGHTS AND sounds raging from the manse below gave him ample cause for concern.

The first indication that anything was wrong was when Aeron noticed about two dozen servants scurrying out of the back of the manse and running for the trees. That alone wouldn't have worried Aeron, but the subsequent blast of fire that shot through one of the front windows and ignited a sizable portion of the lawn wasn't a good sign.

He'd ventured low enough at times that he could hear hellish, tortured screams and the clanging of metal, but shortly after that blast of fire, it had all gone quiet. Whether that meant his friends were alive or dead, he didn't know.

Finally, he couldn't take it anymore. He directed Wafer to fly lower, toward the patch of embers that still lingered on the front lawn. He'd intended to land Wafer near there, in view of the window so he could peer inside, but as they descended, Wafer sent him a sense of alarm.

Aeron scanned the skies and the moonlit clouds above them. He didn't see anything at first, but then the silhouettes of at least two dozen wyverns flew into view along the northern horizon. They were flying toward the manse.

Wafer's alert hit him again, and Aeron looked back to see about a half-dozen warships approaching on the Tahn Sea from the south and southeast. And to the west, a contingent of infantry and cavalry numbering close to a hundred soldiers advanced toward the manse as well.

Aeron cursed. The Govalian Army had found them.

❦

MEHTA STOOD OVER LORD GLAVAN'S BODY ALONG WITH KENT AND GARRICK. Though the knife had embedded deep in his chest—again—he still wasn't dead. Because of that, Mehta stood far enough away to make sure Lord Glavan couldn't touch him and steal his life as he'd done to the guard.

The wound was fatal, just not immediately fatal. Still, it gave Mehta hope. He'd managed to sift a dark lord, and although it had been incredibly hard, he now knew it was possible.

And he'd be prepared for when the time came to sift Lord Valdis.

❦

GARRICK WAS SO CLOSE TO FINISHING THE JOB. HE JUST NEEDED TO BEND THE dying Lord Glavan to his will, and then he'd have the map in his hands once again. And when he returned it to Lord Valdis, his reputation would be restored.

"Where's the vault?" Garrick asked.

Lord Glavan laughed and wheezed. "Come closer, and I'll tell you."

"Not a chance," Kent said. "Give us the map, and we will hasten your death."

"If you knew the significance of that map, you wouldn't—"

"Yeah, I know. We wouldn't be so eager to send it back to Lord Valdis," Garrick said. "Pretend we don't care, and hand it over."

Lord Glavan coughed, and blood dribbled down his chin. "I would rather die knowing I have prevented a calamity than willingly contribute to one with my final breath."

He coughed again, lay back, and closed his eyes. Lord Glavan exhaled one last ragged breath, and then he died.

Garrick grunted and cursed. Mehta had been too effective, too quickly. If he'd stayed alive longer, perhaps Garrick could've gotten a line on where to find Noraff and Phesnos. He hadn't even had time to ask.

He regretted putting Lord Valdis's interests above his own, and even though he'd promised Lord Valdis that he'd do exactly that, it gave him no solace. The green-handled knife in Garrick's belt would have to wait a bit longer to be returned to its rightful owner.

"Kent, you stay here. Make sure he doesn't somehow wake back up." Garrick turned to Mehta, who was covered in blood and gore from head to toe. "Is the girl alive?"

"Yes," Mehta replied.

Given Mehta's appearance, Garrick considered sending someone else to retrieve her, but only Mehta knew where he'd stashed her. "Then go get her."

As Mehta threaded his way into the bookshelves, the rhythmic thunder of wing beats sounded outside the broken window. Wafer landed in the grass amid the dying embers leftover from Lord Glavan's fire.

From atop Wafer's back, Aeron shouted, "Army's coming soon! The dock is blocked by six warships!"

Garrick cursed again. They were out of time. If they didn't find that map now, they never would.

"Meet at the rendezvous point!" Garrick yelled back.

As Aeron and Wafer took to the sky again, Mehta returned with a quivering Mayri in tow.

She looked at Lord Glavan's body on the demolished floor and the blood underneath him, and her quivering stilled. She exhaled a long breath, and relief filled her face.

"He's dead?" she asked.

"Yes," Kent replied.

"He wasn't unkind to me." Mayri's face contorted with anger. "But his sons were. They..." She paused. "He knew, yet he did nothing to intervene."

Garrick didn't really care what she had to say. He just needed to get into that vault, or they were all dead. No amount of magic, durable skin, or killing prowess would save them from an army.

"Can you get us inside the vault or not?" he asked as calmly as he could manage.

Mayri nodded.

She showed them a hidden lever in one of the bookshelves lined with the skulls of various creatures and other weird artifacts. Each one probably had value to some rich person somewhere, but Garrick didn't have time to consider what to do with them.

In any case, the real payday would come when he delivered the map.

Kent pulled the lever, and the bookshelf to the right of the now-dark hearth moved. Together, Kent and Garrick hauled it back, and it swung outward toward the destroyed window. Behind it lay a vault with a huge metal door.

The door to the vault didn't have keyholes like the one under the Crimson Flame temple in Etrijan had. This one had some sort of locking mechanism on the front with a series of dials marked with symbols and a metal handle in the center.

Garrick stepped aside and motioned Mayri toward it. "Move quickly. The army's on its way."

Mayri gave him a wide-eyed glance, then she set to work. As she turned the first dial, Garrick didn't bother keeping track of what symbols she lined up. They were runes from a language he didn't know anyway, and once the vault was open, he'd never need to get inside it again.

Instead, he scanned the desolated study, complete with books, floorboards, and wall panels strewn about, along with furniture and bookshelves. An ocean of blood tainted the floor and splattered the walls as well.

They'd made quite a mess, but that wasn't his problem. He didn't have to clean it up.

A metallic click sounded from behind Garrick, and he turned back. "Did you get it?"

Mayri yanked on the handle, but it didn't budge. "I think so, but I can't..."

"Allow me," Kent said as he reached for it, but Garrick reached for it at the same time. Kent stopped and yielded to Garrick. "All yours."

Garrick had no time to be polite. He wedged his thick fingers into the handle, and pulled.

CLANK.

The vault door swung open, and the interior yawned at them like the mouth of a hungry metal dragon.

"Light," Garrick said. "I need light."

Kent retrieved a pair of floorboards smoldering at their edges, ignited them with fire anew, and tossed them into the vault. They burned brightly, illuminating the cramped space well enough for Garrick to see its contents.

As with the vault under the Crimson Flame temple in Etrijan, this one was stuffed with gold, jewels, and other junk that Garrick assumed must be valuable, but he couldn't identify any of it. Yet unlike the scattered nature of the vault under the temple, this one was organized with rows of shelves lining the walls.

In any case, he was only looking for one thing.

He was about to step in, but memories of Noraff and Phesnos's betrayal stopped him. Had he learned nothing?

Yes, they had to move quickly, but he couldn't risk getting locked inside yet another vault. This time, he wouldn't be able to break out.

"We're looking for a parchment tube," he said. "I'll stay out here with Mayri to make sure the door doesn't shut."

Kent and Mehta glanced at each other, and then Mehta went into the vault. Kent hesitated at first.

"I'm not gonna lock you in," Garrick said.

Kent eyed him. "Then I wish you had refrained from bringing it up as a possibility."

"Let me know if you see anything else worth taking in there." Garrick looked down at Mayri. "You can take whatever you want once they bring me the map."

She nodded. "Thank you."

It took longer than Garrick would have liked, but Mehta came out with a long, leather tube in his hand, followed by Kent, who'd filled a small sack of gold for himself in the process. Strangely, Mehta wasn't holding anything else.

"You know, you can take some gold or something else, if you want," Garrick told him.

Mehta blinked at him with dark eyes set into a face splattered with blood. He handed Garrick the parchment tube. "I have what I need. I just need to retrieve my knives, and I'll be content."

Garrick squinted at him. Who *wouldn't* raid a treasure trove like this if given the chance? Once Mayri finished taking her cut, he would claim some for himself as well.

But first, he had to make sure they actually had the map. He wasn't about to have come all this way only to return to Xenthan with an empty parchment tube, so he opened the fastener on the top of the tube and pulled out its contents.

Sure enough, he removed a rolled-up parchment from inside. He unrolled it and held it up to the light.

It was a map of the entire continent of Aletia. Familiar Aletian runes— runes he still couldn't read—lined its perimeter.

He recognized a large X near the center of Xenthan and several smaller X's that marked other locations across the continent in Muroth, Inoth, Govalia, and Urthia.

Garrick rolled it back up and slid it back into the parchment tube, fastened the top shut, and slung it onto his back. He smiled.

"We've got it." He turned to Mayri again. "Go ahead. Take anything you want."

As Mayri bounded into the vault and started rifling through the treasures contained within, Garrick noticed a stack of parchment on a shelf in the corner, just inside the door. He grabbed the stack and started to page through it.

The handwriting was delicate, like that of a woman's, so Garrick had to stare at it long and hard to make sure he could comprehend everything.

Then he saw it—a receipt for an order of payment directed to the Central Bank of Caclos. It was for 12,500 gold, and it was written out to Noraff.

12,500 gold. A solid amount of coin, but not enough to make it worth betraying and murdering Garrick. It irked him that Noraff thought his life was worth so little.

It wasn't much to go on, but it gave Garrick a country and a bank name. He committed the information to memory and set the stack of parchment back on the shelf.

Mayri emerged from the vault with a sack slung over her shoulder, nearly as large as her person, and she strained under its weight.

"Here," Kent said. "Allow me."

She passed it to him, and he shouldered it for her.

The thunder of wing beats sounded through the broken window again, this time farther away. Garrick peered out and saw a trio of wyvern knights landing in the distance. Beyond them, in the moonlight, he saw infantry and cavalry approaching the manse.

Garrick had tried to get them in and out as fast as possible, but the battle with Lord Glavan and his men had sucked up too much time. He cursed. "We're too late."

"We have a relatively fortified position," Kent said. "We can wait them out, force them to come to us. Their numbers will matter less if we can lure them into close quarters."

Mehta raised his knives. "I don't mind close quarters."

"We don't have to do any of that," Mayri said.

They all looked at her.

"This place has an escape tunnel underneath. Lord Glavan had it constructed once he made the rank of admiral. I was just a child, but I remember my parents telling me he'd dug them out because of the Septerran."

"I suppose it would make sense that a Govalian admiral would be a target of theirs," Kent said.

Mayri nodded. "Govalia had trouble with raids along the coastline for many years. My uncle even got killed in one before I was born.

"Lord Glavan rose through the ranks so quickly because he was good at defeating the Septerran," Mayri continued. "But the pirates figured out who he was and put a bounty on his head—"

"So he had the tunnels dug as a failsafe if they were to come here," Garrick finished for her. If Mayri was right, then maybe they could actually get out of there unscathed.

"Just one tunnel," Mayri corrected him.

Garrick eyed her. She'd certainly found her voice in the aftermath of Lord Glavan's death.

"Where does it lead?" Kent asked.

"To the road heading north to Govaliston," Mayri replied. "But it's a long journey. About two hours start to finish. It's how I was planning to escape. I heard it cost a fortune to build, but it should take us beyond the army's reach."

"Us?" Garrick asked.

"I'm going with you," Mayri said. "I can't stay. If they find out I helped you, I'm dead. I'm going to take this bag of gold and jewels and start a new life somewhere. Maybe Caclos. It's supposed to be beautiful down there."

Garrick frowned at her, but as long as she didn't try to accompany them to Xenthan, she wouldn't hurt anything. Either way, he didn't have time to argue. The army might try to enter the manse at any moment.

Speaking of which, a good diversion might buy them some time.

"Fine," Garrick said. "But first, I need you to do something for me."

Mayri's confidence shriveled. "What do you need me to do?"

Kent had to admit it: Garrick's last request of Mayri had been an incredibly good one.

Once the Govalian Army fully surrounded the manse, some Urthian-accented voice had called out to them from the distance, ordering them to surrender.

Instead of responding with his own voice, Garrick had told Mayri to answer instead.

"They have Lord Glavan!" she shrieked through the broken study window. "They're holding him hostage, and they're going to kill—"

Then Garrick had clapped his hand over her mouth and jerked her away from the window.

It was all planned, and Mayri had executed her role perfectly. Most importantly, it stalled the army from advancing.

The Urthian voice continued to speak, albeit more frantic now, demanding more information.

Neither Garrick nor Mayri said anything else. Instead, Kent and the others followed Mayri deeper into the manse, toward the wine cellar under the kitchen. There, they entered the tunnel and left the Govalian Army behind, confused and uncertain how to respond.

Around two hours later, they reached the end of the tunnel, doused their torches, and emerged into the night surrounded by trees. They headed north, to the road.

In the distance, Kent spotted torchlights from the Govalian Army still outside of the manse.

He smirked. They might not even try to enter the manse until sunrise when they could more easily see inside. In any case, Kent, Garrick, Mehta, Aeron, and Mayri would be long gone by then—perhaps even out of the country.

Instead of traveling north with them to Govaliston, Mayri opted to head east toward a port city called Hachéron.

"I have distant relatives there," she'd told them. "But when they see me with my bag of gold, they'll be much closer relatives, I'm sure."

Kent had expressed concern about her traveling alone, at night, overloaded with gold and jewels, but she'd waved away his worries.

"If the gods see fit to harm me now, after having escaped that household, then they are cruel and unjust, and I will perish all the same."

With that, she said her goodbyes, thanked them once again, and turned east through the trees with her bag of treasure on her back.

It took another couple of hours for them to get back to the rendezvous point along the road north to Govalia, but they'd made it. As a bonus, their horses were still tied there, right where they'd left them.

The long journey from the manse back to that point hadn't been too arduous, but Kent was glad he'd convinced Garrick to let them stash the horses there. They would need them for the ride back to Xenthan.

Once they arrived, Aeron and Wafer landed soon after, and the horses whinnied and pranced in protest until Garrick, Mehta, and Kent could calm them down.

"You made it!" Aeron said. "Gods, I thought you'd been captured. I was considering just abandoning Govalia altogether. Did you get the map?"

Garrick held up the tube. "We got it."

Aeron pumped his fist, and Wafer bobbed his head. "So what's next? We're done, right?"

"We head back north." Garrick started untying his horse. "I know everyone's tired, but we need to put as much distance between us and the Govalian Army as possible. They'll look for us around the manse for awhile, but it won't last forever."

"Are we planning to stop in Govaliston?" A tinge of hope lined Aeron's voice.

"No. I know we're all tired, but with the army after us, we can't rest easy 'til we're out of the country. Govaliston's too dangerous, so we'll stay off the roads and make our way through the trees until we can find some shelter." Garrick mounted his horse. "Let's go."

A FEW WEEKS LATER

Mehta had to stifle a grin when he saw the black spires of Valdis Keep scraping Xenthan's crimson skies. Due to foul winter weather, the return trip had taken longer than their initial journey south, to Govalia, but they'd made it nonetheless.

A few more miles, perhaps a few flights of stairs, and potentially a few dead soldiers, and he would soon complete his final commission to sift Lord Valdis. Then he'd go back to his home in the mountains to be with his family and Ferne and live in peace.

If he could finally learn to control his thirst.

He could. He knew he could.

Praying to Laeri and relegating the thirst to its box in his mind had almost always helped keep it at bay. And though it continued harassing him at a near constant pace, he'd learned to ignore it just as constantly and to actively subdue it when he had to.

Hours later, after their horses had trudged down the winding, narrow mountainside path and through the snow, they reached the courtyard gate. Now Valdis Keep towered overhead as if beckoning Mehta to test its strength.

But it would not taunt him for much longer. He was about to be invited inside.

Even so, Mehta had to restrain himself from sifting the soldiers at the gate. Each of them wore the sigil of Lord Valdis's three-horned ram on their breastplates, a constant reminder of that black, brutal day when Lord Valdis's men had slain Mehta's parents.

Soon his parents' memories would know justice, and Mehta would deliver that justice on a river of Lord Valdis's blood.

"You boys ready to get paid?" Garrick asked.

No one replied. They were all cold, tired, and miserable from their journey. And Mehta worried he might betray his intentions regarding Lord Valdis if he said anything.

As the soldiers at the gate approached, Aeron and Wafer landed next to them and sent the soldiers staggering backward. One of them even fell back into a snowdrift.

"Sorry!" Aeron called. "Sorry—didn't mean to startle you."

The soldiers lowered their weapons when they realized Aeron and Wafer weren't a threat, and they helped pull their comrade out of the snow.

"We're here to see Lord Valdis." Garrick held up the parchment tube. "He's expecting us."

"He's expecting *you*," one of the soldiers said. A scar ran from one side of his forehead to the other on a diagonal. He motioned to Mehta and the others. "Not anyone else."

Garrick glanced around. "It's cold out here. Just let us in."

"Can't. Orders from Lord Valdis himself," replied the soldier with the scar. "He doesn't know any of them, and neither do we. He knows *you*, so *you* get to go in."

Mehta's thirst screeched at him from inside his head. If they weren't going to let him in, he couldn't sift Lord Valdis. It didn't mean he'd never get inside, but it did mean he couldn't sift Lord Valdis today.

But he'd waited long enough. It *had* to be today.

"Are you serious?" Garrick asked.

"Give me a break, here." The scarred soldier held out his arms. "You know how he can be."

Garrick stared down at the scarred soldier for a long moment. Finally, he looked back at the others and said, "Go to the Gray Cauldron, the pub where we met. I'll bring the coin to you there."

Mehta's heart hummed in his chest. This couldn't be happening. He was right there, at the castle's front gates, and now he was being refused entrance? If they weren't going to let him enter, he could've found his own way inside and sifted Lord Valdis weeks ago.

"No offense, but how do we know you'll actually come back with the coin?" Aeron asked.

Garrick squared his body with Aeron and Wafer. "Have I misled you thus far?"

"No, but it's pretty shady that right here, at the end, we can't collect what you promised us," Aeron said.

"It's not up to me, clearly," Garrick countered. "So unless you want to storm the castle, this is the only way to get paid."

Mehta was ready to start storming right then and there, starting with the scarred soldier talking to Garrick. Despite the snow, he could easily sift the handful of other soldiers posted at the gate, obtain a set of keys to the castle doors, and get inside.

From there, he'd have to improvise, but he'd find a way. He'd overcome an entire sect of Xyonates virtually on his own. Handling a few dozen soldiers, or perhaps even more, wouldn't prove too difficult if he could sift them on his terms, in his timing.

His thirst begged him to do it. What better way to satiate its urges than by bringing down an entire castle full of the soldiers who'd killed his parents?

Under his cloak, Mehta's hands gripped the knife hilts protruding from his belt. It wouldn't take any effort to draw them and carve a new set of scars into the soldier.

But even if Mehta did make it inside, he didn't truly know what he'd be up against. If Valdis Keep held hundreds of soldiers instead of dozens, he might not make it out of there alive. And, for once in his life, he truly cared about getting out and returning to his family home in the mountains.

And if he started sifting soldiers here in the snow, he'd have to contend with Garrick, Aeron, and Kent as well. Sifting them would prove more difficult, more so for their prowess than because he'd grown to enjoy their company, though the latter was also somewhat true.

Mehta loosened his grip on his knives. As much as the thirst demanded he act, and as much as he hated to admit it, his head insisted that he hold back.

"Come," Kent said. "We will wait in the pub until Garrick returns."

The wind howled around them, sending biting cold through Mehta's cloak and clothing and prickling his face with tiny flecks of snow. North of the mountains separating Urthia from Xenthan, the temperature had dropped considerably, and here, even farther north than Tebaryx, it was even colder.

But Mehta welcomed the frigid air. It would give him something else to focus on instead of his thirst. And he would need all the help he could get.

⚶

GARRICK WATCHED AS KENT LED MEHTA AND AERON TOWARD THE PUB WHILE Wafer launched into the crimson sky and disappeared above the clouds. He didn't envy their concern, but they didn't have to worry. He would make sure they got paid.

With the parchment tube still in his hand, he followed the soldiers through the gate and into Valdis Keep. Warmth from the fires burning around the perimeter of the entry hall washed over him the moment the doors shut behind him, and he lowered the hood on his cloak.

Garrick walked through grand, familiar halls with gray floors, gray walls, and obsidian gargoyles ogling him from above until he reached the throne room's black double-doors.

When last he'd approached these doors, he'd done so as a failure, prepared for the end of his life. But Lord Valdis had granted him another chance, and Garrick had succeeded.

Now he would deliver the map and hopefully earn back Lord Valdis's complete trust. The soldiers opened the doors for him, and he entered the palatial throne room with his head held high.

He strode past the granite pillars and the iron bowls of fire toward the throne of twisted, black bones. Lord Valdis sat there, as Garrick had expected, stoic-faced and staring at him with his dark eyes—eyes that still glowed with insidious energy.

Garrick thought back to Lord Glavan's eyes, which had turned black and insect-like during the battle, but they'd had no glow to them. Perhaps he and Lord Valdis were different types of dark lords, or they had just manifested different powers.

Garrick didn't really care. The only thing that mattered was the map.

"Look what I found." He held it up for Lord Valdis to see. "You were right about the Crimson Flame having it. Lord Glavan, a former admiral from Govalia, had it. He was a member of the Crimson Flame, too."

"Yes," was all Lord Valdis said in response.

Did he already know all of that? Or was he just unimpressed?

Garrick stopped ten feet from the throne. He didn't feel the invisible pressure that had driven him to the floor the last time he'd been in Lord Valdis's presence, but that realization did very little to calm his nerves.

Crazy fears spiked in his mind. What if he'd grabbed the wrong map? What if someone had taken it out of the tube while he'd slept? What if water had somehow gotten inside and wrecked the parchment?

No. He'd been extra cautious. He couldn't afford to fail again. He'd made sure everything was in order.

"Remove it from the tube and bring it to me," Lord Valdis said.

Either way, Garrick was about to find out whether his concerns were valid.

He pulled the map out of the tube and placed it into Lord Valdis's hands.

Lord Valdis spread it open and studied it for a long moment. His finger ignited with crimson flames, and he ran it from the top of the map down to the bottom, but the map didn't catch fire.

Finally, Lord Valdis rolled it back up and handed it to Garrick. "Well done."

Garrick took it from him with a massive, silent sigh of relief, but confusion quickly usurped the sensation. Why was Lord Valdis giving back the map?

"Pay him," Lord Valdis said to no one in particular.

Two guards in black robes, both wearing gleaming scimitars on their belts, emerged from the shadows behind the pillars carrying a chest made of dark wood and edged with brass. They set it down next to Garrick and opened it.

Neatly stacked columns of gold coins filled the chest to its brim. Garrick ran a quick, rough count—it looked to be 25,000 gold—the full amount Lord Valdis had promised him *before* he'd failed to deliver the map.

"Lord Valdis," Garrick started, "I can't accept this. I failed my first attempt. No one pays the full rate for a second try."

"I do," Lord Valdis replied. "For this, I do."

Lord Valdis should've killed him for failing the first time. Now he was paying the full rate on a half-blown job.

Why?

"But I'm afraid I can't release you from your contract quite yet."

Lord Valdis waved his hand, and two more guards from the opposite side of the room produced another chest identical to the first. They set it down on the opposite side of the throne and opened it, revealing another 25,000 in gold.

"What's this?" Garrick stared at it. He'd only seen that much coin in one place a handful of times, and something had always kept him from getting his hands on it. Now it was just lying in front of him, there for the taking.

But for what?

"Another job," Lord Valdis said. "One that only a man of your talents can hope to accomplish—you and your new team of mercenaries, that is."

Garrick waited for Lord Valdis to elaborate. When he didn't, Garrick looked down at the map in his hands. He unrolled it.

It looked the same as it had before, except that one of the X marks on the map, located in Muroth, now glowed with crimson light.

Garrick looked up at Lord Valdis. He must've done something to the map when he'd traced his finger down the front of it.

"You will go to the Crimson Flame temple in Muroth," Lord Valdis said. "And within the dungeon beneath it, you will retrieve that which I desire."

"You gonna tell me what it is this time?" Garrick asked.

Lord Valdis smirked.

"A dragon egg."

CHAPTER FIFTEEN

Garrick blinked. He couldn't have heard right. "What did you just say?"

"A dragon egg," Lord Valdis repeated.

"Dragons haven't existed for hundreds of years," Garrick said.

"Millennia, actually," Lord Valdis corrected him. "But wyverns are considered to be a type of dragon, as are certain sea-dwelling beasts and a handful of land-dwelling creatures."

Garrick shrugged. "Sure. I'm not a historian. My point is, the type you're talking about, the kind that breathe fire and destroy cities, those are long gone. So how could a dragon egg still exist after that long?"

"As you said, you are not a historian," Lord Valdis said. "Trust me. It's there."

"And if it's not?"

"You'll be paid anyway."

Garrick blinked again. He couldn't believe his ears. It didn't make any sense. Why would Lord Valdis pay him either way?

But as strange as Lord Valdis's request was, the weirdness of it wasn't Garrick's main hang-up. Once he'd completed this job, he'd planned to put his earnings directly into finding Noraff and Phesnos. The payment order to the Central Bank of Caclos was a solid lead.

Yet even if it didn't pan out, it didn't matter how much coin Garrick spent or how much time he'd have to invest to find them. He would burn through every last piece of gold to find them and make them pay for what they'd done.

"I also require a certain ancient text that will accompany the egg. It is a tome of rituals."

Garrick nodded. *A tome of rituals and a dragon egg?*

"So, Garrick…" Lord Valdis stared at him with those dark, unnerving eyes. "Will you help me recover a piece of history?"

Garrick hesitated. "Lord Valdis, I—"

Lord Valdis waved his hand again, and four more guards with two more chests emerged from the darkness.

Garrick's eyes widened.

"Think carefully, Garrick," Lord Valdis warned. "If you do not accept, I can make this offer to someone else."

§

KENT HAD FINALLY STARTED TO GET WARM BY THE FIRE WHEN THE PUB'S DOOR opened and let in a rush of frigid air. Granules of snow swarmed into the pub and swirled around until Garrick, who carried a gigantic wooden chest under one arm, managed to pull the door shut behind him with the other.

A shiver traced from Kent's neck down through his spine. Even the coldest of winters in Muroth hadn't been *this* cold.

Aeron stood next to him. He shivered as well, despite wrapping his arms around his torso and wearing a thick cloak over his armor

"How does Wafer manage in this unspeakable weather?" Kent asked.

"He flaps his wings more," Aeron replied.

Kent eyed Aeron as Garrick approached, still holding the chest in one arm. Kent noticed the parchment tube slung around his other shoulder. Perhaps Lord Valdis had taken the map but allowed Garrick to keep the tube for some reason?

"Where's Mehta?" Garrick looked around the pub.

"Where he usually is," Kent pointed over his shoulder at a heavy shadow beyond the bar, "concealed in darkness."

Garrick raised his voice. "If he wants his coin, he'd better come and claim it."

Kent looked back as Mehta emerged from the shadows.

Aeron pulled a weathered gray table closer to the fire, and Garrick set the chest onto it with a heavy *thunk*, accompanied by the clinking of something inside. The table groaned in protest.

Garrick opened it up, began pulling out stacks of gold coins, and set them into four separate piles on the table.

"I told you I'd make sure you got paid." When he finished dividing the coins up, Garrick said, "4,500 apiece, plus the 500 I already gave you is 5,000. Go ahead."

Each of them produced a large sack and dropped the gold into it.

Kent wondered how Mehta intended to get around quietly with a bulging bag of gold jingling on his hip. Then he wondered how he himself would fight with so much gold on his hip if he had to.

He reasoned he wouldn't be able to; he'd have to deposit some of it at a bank. Perhaps the Royal Bank of Urthia would suffice. Kent didn't trust Xenthanian banks, mostly because he didn't trust the country of Xenthan in general, and Urthia was on the way back to Xenthan.

Kent noticed that the amount remaining in the chest was about equal to each of the four piles on the table. "And what is to become of the remaining coin?"

Garrick said, "It's for each of us."

Aeron's expression brightened. "Like... a bonus?"

"No." Garrick pulled the parchment tube off his shoulder and set it on the table. He extracted the remaining coin from the chest and created four new piles, each of them much smaller than the 4,500 Garrick had already paid them.

Then he picked up the empty chest and headed toward the fire as if to toss it in.

"Wait!" a voice called from across the pub.

They all turned back.

The barkeep, a round, short man with a beard and wearing an apron over his grimy clothes, waddled toward them. He rasped, "If you're going to just throw that into the fire, do you mind if I keep it instead?"

Before Garrick could answer, Kent said, "For a round of ales, it's yours."

"Deal," the barkeep said. "I need something to put my stockings in back at home."

Kent tilted his head. *How many stockings does this fellow have?*

Garrick abandoned his plan to toss the chest into the flames and instead set it on the table again.

The barkeep returned with four tankards of ale, two in each hand, and exchanged them for the chest. He waddled away with the chest in his thick arms and a grin on his face.

"Have a seat," Garrick said.

They each pulled up chairs and sat down around the table. The remaining gold gleamed up at them.

Garrick took a swig of his ale. "Lord Valdis has another job for us if we want it. The coin is the down payment."

Kent and Aeron looked at each other. Aeron spoke first. "I need to get back to Govalia to relocate my parents, and then I need to get back to searching for my sister."

Garrick had allowed Kent and Aeron to study the map in great detail while they journeyed back to Xenthan, and together they'd determined to search for the Crimson Flame temple in Inoth first, and then in Muroth, if they had to, to find Kallie.

"He's offering to pay a lot more than this time," Garrick said. "Triple the amount for each of us."

Kent's eyebrows rose. It was too good to be true.

"*Triple?*" Aeron's eyes were threatening to jump out of his head. "With that much coin, I could move my family to *Caclos*."

"So you're in?" Garrick asked.

Aeron started to nod, then he stopped. "What about my sister?"

"You want to find her? This job pits us against the Crimson Flame yet again."

"It does?" Aeron looked down at the parchment tube.

"*Directly* against them," Garrick said. "We're heading for a Crimson Flame temple."

Aeron gawked at Garrick. "Seriously?"

Kent folded his arms across his chest. After facing down Lord Glavan, he wasn't certain he wanted to directly accost the Crimson Flame so soon. He had hoped to employ a more strategic approach to dealing with them going forward.

"What is the job?" Kent asked.

Garrick looked at him across the table. "A dungeon raid."

"To retrieve what?" Aeron asked.

Garrick chuckled and took a drink of his ale. "You won't believe me when I tell you."

That made Kent all the more dubious. His voice came out firmer than he'd expected. "What is it?"

Garrick scowled at him, his face stoic once again. "Lord Valdis thinks there's a dragon egg down there. He wants us to get it and bring it back, along with some sort of ancient ritual tome."

Now Kent chuckled. "You have to be joking."

"Swear on my mother's soul, I'm not."

Kent shook his head, still smiling. "Dragons have been extinct for millennia."

"That's what Lord Valdis said. He thinks there's a way an egg could have been preserved, and he thinks this map—" Garrick patted the parchment tube with his hand. "—shows its location."

"Wait. Back up." Aeron held up one of his hands. With the other, he grabbed his tankard and raised it to his lips. "What happens if he's wrong and there's no egg?"

"We get to tear apart a Crimson Flame temple looking for it—and for your sister—and still get paid anyway."

Aeron had started to take a drink and almost choked at Garrick's words. He coughed and wiped his mouth on his forearm. *"What?"*

"Lord Valdis wants the egg. If it isn't there, we'll still get paid."

Aeron glanced at Kent, then he refocused on Garrick. "Why?"

"He didn't say."

"How does he know we will not simply report its absence and take his coin anyway?" Kent asked.

"Lord Valdis knows the weight of my word." Garrick glowered at Kent and pointed at the pub door. "And if you're gonna try something like that, then you can spare me the trouble and send yourself to the Underworld right now."

"I am merely trying to understand our employer's reasoning," Kent said. "There is no cause for alarm."

"So all we have to do is get into some dungeon, see if there's an egg, and bring it back if it's real?" Aeron asked. "And it's under a Crimson Flame temple?"

"Yes," Garrick said. "The one where I got the map was a miserable place. I don't expect this one to be any nicer."

"I remember," Aeron said. "You mentioned something about undead warriors, carnivorous insects, a golem, and... what was the last thing?"

"A duotaur," Garrick replied.

"Oh, right. A minotaur with two heads." Aeron cracked a grin.

"Smile all you want, but it was a nasty beast. Brutal."

"What does Lord Valdis plan to do with a dragon egg once he has it in his possession?" Kent leaned forward, staring at Garrick. "And what kind of ritual tome are we recovering?"

Garrick leaned forward, too, to match him. "He didn't say."

Kent took a drink from his tankard and watched Garrick's eyes. Did he, in fact, know more than he was letting on?

"When I was a small child, my mother would tell me legends of dragonfire ravaging entire *countries*," Kent said. "If there is even a hint of truth to those myths, and if we do recover a dragon egg, then are we certain we want it in the hands of a dark lord? Especially after our battle with Lord Glavan?"

"You think that's why he was trying to keep the map from us?" Aeron asked. "He's worried about dragons coming back?"

"Perhaps," Kent said. "Think about how powerful and dangerous Lord Glavan was, and that was *without* the aid of a dragon. It took a berserker, an assassin, and a mage to bring him down—one man."

"And if he and Lord Valdis were rivals…" Aeron started. "But Lord Glavan was a Crimson Flame cultist, and these jobs are keeping us fighting against them. I'm inclined to side with Lord Valdis anyway just because of that."

"What he does with his property is no business of ours," Garrick said. "And it's not like we're going to end up on his bad side, anyway. *We're* the ones bringing him the egg—if it's even there in the first place. And if it is, it's probably a thousand years old. It won't hatch."

"If it will not hatch, then what does he want it for?" Kent asked. "Mages use the essence of the world around them to direct and shape their magic. When I hold a rock in my hand, I can compel rocks around me to do my bidding. If Lord Valdis gets ahold of a dragon egg, what will happen?"

Garrick shrugged. "You're the mage. You tell me."

"I have no idea what he could do with it, and that gives me pause. As does your mention of a tome of ritual magic."

"So you're scared." Garrick took another drink of his ale.

"I said it gives me pause. Not every job is the right job, and not every employer is the right employer," Kent said. "To give you some added perspective, I have met three dark mages in my lifetime, and each of them has tried to kill me."

"Sounds like you're the common element, not them," Garrick said.

"That is a fair consideration, but it is hardly the complete story."

"Moral questions aside, do you want to make triple what you made on our last job or not?" Garrick asked.

Back in Muroth, in his old life, Kent hadn't wanted for anything—ever. At least, not until his magic awakened and everything went wrong several years later.

An additional 15,000 gold would make him quite comfortable. He might even be able to buy a small home somewhere and live out the remainder of his years in peace.

At least, he could once he resolved his unfinished business in Muroth and Inoth.

In either case, such a considerable influx of additional gold would better equip him to do that, and facing the Crimson Flame head-on might yield answers to help Aeron find Kallie.

"I require more details before agreeing to anything, but you have my interest," Kent replied. "Where is this dungeon?"

"It's under a Crimson Flame temple, like the one where I found this map in the first place," Garrick said. "Probably put there by the Aletians, who knows how many thousands of years ago. Probably loaded with more nasty traps and things that want to kill us. So it won't be the easiest coin to earn, but we'll be paid well—not to mention we can keep anything we find inside."

Garrick pointed over his shoulder at the vivid blue hilt of his snow steel sword. "I found these stashed in a dungeon vault next to the map. The room leading into that one was filled with gold and jewels. It would've taken two dozen strong men to carry it all out in one trip."

"The spoils are the least of my concerns," Kent said. "You still haven't told us where the dungeon is—what country?"

Garrick pulled the map out of the parchment tube and spread it across the table. He pointed at an X, glowing with crimson light, marked near the center of the continent. It was near where the borders of Govalia and Urthia met—but the X was on the wrong side of their borders.

It was in Muroth.

Kent's stomach dropped. Ever since he'd fled his home country, he'd done everything he could to avoid returning. So far, he'd succeeded.

He fully intended to return someday, once he was powerful enough to eliminate the fiend who'd stolen his birthright, but he wasn't ready. Not yet.

"I know you're a fugitive from Muroth," Garrick said, "but this is just barely inside Muroth's borders. Aeron went to Govalia, even though they wanted to kill him. If you do this, you'll earn more coin than you've ever seen."

"It is not more coin than I have ever seen." Kent continued to stare at the map, at the red X burning on it.

"Fine. More than you've ever owned," Garrick corrected himself.

"Still wrong." Kent finally looked up at him.

Garrick tilted his head, studying Kent with narrowed eyes. "Who are you?"

Kent didn't immediately answer, partly because he wasn't sure if he ought to reveal the information to Garrick. If there was any sort of bounty out on Kent's head, he didn't want to give Garrick a reason to try to claim it.

But in the end, Kent decided to follow his instincts. Garrick was more concerned about serving Lord Valdis than collecting bounties on his fellow mercenaries. If the latter had been the case, he could have reported Aeron to the army multiple times in Govalia, but he hadn't.

So Kent replied, "I am the firstborn son of Lord Oswin Etheridge and rightful heir to House Etheridge in Muroth. Or I was, anyway."

Garrick just stared at him.

"My brother, Fane, killed my father and framed me for it," Kent continued. "He stole my birthright and is now Lord of House Etheridge. But he won't be for much longer."

Kent took a drink of his ale, but not for courage. Enough time had passed that he no longer felt a strong sadness over what had happened. Instead, a desire for revenge and a heavy burden of regret had filled the void in his soul.

Garrick continued to stare at Kent. Aside from the winter wind howling outside, as it had since they'd arrived, silence saturated the small pub.

Finally, Garrick said, "You and I have more in common than I thought."

"I think we all want revenge on some level." Aeron looked to Mehta, who'd been quiet the whole conversation, just listening and observing. Kent respected that about him, even though it set him somewhat on edge. Aeron continued, "Except maybe you."

"I had my revenge back in Sefera," Mehta said.

"Think of what this coin will do to fight your bastard brother," Garrick said to Kent. "You could hire a small army and retake what's yours."

"Only to have it ripped away shortly thereafter." Kent shook his head. "Muroth's emperor is a zealot when it comes to eradicating magic from his country. Even if I managed to kill Fane and retake House Etheridge, I could not stand against all of Muroth. Our—*their* army is too formidable. No... my inheritance is truly lost."

"I want you with us, Kent," Garrick said. "You know how to fight, and you're smart."

When they'd met, Garrick had expressed nothing but disdain for Kent, particularly his status as a mage. Now, when he needed Kent's help, Garrick had nothing but praise and pleasantness for him.

But Kent pushed all of that aside. Garrick's opinion of him didn't matter in light of the prospect of returning to Muroth.

Kent's mind swirled with possible scenarios and concerns. The Govalian Army had caught their scent, and were it not for Mayri's provision of a convenient escape route at the eleventh hour, they may not have escaped. Traveling to Muroth would mean Kent would risk much more without any certainty of success.

For all of Muroth's bigotry when it came to magic and mages, they still had arguably the continent's finest army. It was certainly one of the better-trained armies of any country, and it was probably the largest as well, though reports from Murothian spies in Urthia routinely came back mixed as to their military capabilities.

If the army realized Kent's presence in Muroth, they might not stop their pursuit of him at the Murothian border. Unlike the mercenaries who'd betrayed Garrick, who didn't know he'd survived, Fane knew all too well that Kent was alive and well, thanks to Prince Kymil's stunt in northern Inoth a few months back.

Fane would be watching. For all of his personal faults, Fane was a sound strategist and a careful planner. He would have taken additional precautions in light of what he'd seen Kent do in that final battle against Prince Kymil and his men. That could mean additional danger for Kent—real, potent, palpable danger.

"If I agree to this," Kent fixed his gaze on Garrick, "then I need assurances from you that you will follow my lead once we arrive in Muroth. That means I guide the party, I speak with the locals—if we should happen to encounter any—and all decisions pass through me. This is not a request to bolster my ego. It is a necessity for survival. Crystal?"

"Clear," Garrick replied. "I wouldn't have it any other way."

No one said anything for a long moment.

"So are you in?" Garrick asked.

Kent stared at the map again with a sense of foreboding looming over his head. He exhaled a long breath and looked up at Garrick.

"Yes," Kent replied. He hoped he wasn't torching his future chances to avenge his father. "Count me in."

Garrick nodded and turned to Aeron. "With the army hunting you, Govalia's not a good place for you now anyway. So what's your decision?"

Aeron placed his palms flat on the table. "It's more coin than I could've ever hoped for, and it's a solid chance to find Kallie. Yes, I'm in."

Garrick faced Mehta. "You've hardly said a word this whole time. You in?"

❧

MEHTA HAD FOUND THE PROSPECT OF PURSUING A DRAGON EGG APPEALING FOR its novelty, but he also wanted to know if such a thing really existed in the first place.

But he'd also been brooding over his failure to get to Lord Valdis. And he'd been weighing the question of whether he should try to get into the castle on his own or if he should sign up for another mercenary adventure with the hope of earning a face-to-face with Lord Valdis afterward.

The way he looked at it, the scenarios he was considering measured up about equal: either way, he'd be walking into unknown danger to ultimately reach Lord Valdis and sift him. The types of danger and the time difference between them also came into play, but one defining factor separated the two options...

Gold. A lot of gold.

He'd be trading his time for it, and he wasn't guaranteed an audience with Lord Valdis even if they did manage to succeed, but he would have enough coin to care for his family and Ferne indefinitely.

Gold had never been a motivating factor for Mehta when he was a Xyonate. He'd spent it when they'd given it to him, and that had been the extent of it. Since then, he'd recognized the role gold could play in bettering his family's life.

Back at Lord Glavan's estate, Mehta hadn't taken any gold from the vault because he wasn't certain the fighting had truly ended. He didn't want coins jingling and announcing his proximity to everyone he approached.

In general, though, having gold made life easier. By that measurement, especially when combined with the other factors, it made sense to take the job.

"I'm in," he replied.

The thirst raged in his chest and mind, furious that he hadn't chosen the more expedient route to sifting Lord Valdis, but he subdued it as he always did. If they were indeed heading to a dungeon, he would have ample opportunity to let it run rampant among whatever foes lurked within.

"Good." Garrick raised his tankard. "Then it's settled. We're back in the game."

Aeron and Kent raised their tankards as well, and they all looked at Mehta.

"Aren't you going to join the toast?" Aeron nodded toward Mehta's tankard.

"No," Mehta said. "I prefer to stay alert."

They all kept staring at him.

The pressure of their stares bothered Mehta, so he pulled out one of his knives and held it out in place of his tankard.

"Good enough," Garrick said, and they all clinked their implements together.

"If you're not going to drink yours," Aeron said, "can I have it?"

Mehta sheathed his knife and slid the tankard across the table to him.

"Yes!" Aeron downed the rest of his ale and then picked up Mehta's tankard. "So when do we leave?"

CHAPTER SIXTEEN

Two weeks later

As Aeron and Wafer were about to cross from the southwestern corner of Urthia into Govalia, they veered to the west instead to scout possible paths into Muroth. They had again traveled from Xenthan down to Urthia, only they'd taken a more westerly route this time.

It had taken them south along the Tosca River, which started in southern Xenthan and served as the de facto dividing line between the eastern and western half of Aletia. It also formed a natural border between the countries on the eastern side—Urthia and Govalia—and the countries to the west—Muroth and Inoth.

Aeron and Wafer could just fly over the border without issue, but Kent, Garrick, and Mehta would have to cross at a bridge due to the river's depth, flow, and its icy, winter temperature. But according to Kent, Muroth guarded some of the bridges more heavily than others.

As they flew, Aeron considered how little progress he'd made in finding Kallie thus far. This whole journey was supposed to get him closer to finding answers about what had happened to her as well as putting the Crimson Flame squarely in his path.

But he'd learned nothing new about Kallie's location, and they'd only encountered one Crimson Flame member thus far, and Mehta had killed him well before Aeron would've had a chance to ask him questions.

Based on what the others had told him about the fight, he couldn't blame them for taking Lord Glavan out so quickly, but it still irked him that he'd missed an opportunity to dig for the truth about his sister's whereabouts.

Even so, he took solace in the thought that he'd soon be raiding a Crimson Flame temple and the dungeon beneath it. One of the kooks in that temple was bound to know *something* about what had happened to Kallie. Or maybe they'd at least know about the mark on her neck.

Staying optimistic about it was hard, especially after the months that had passed since she'd been taken. He often wondered if she was dead, or if they'd hidden her so well that he'd never find her again.

But every time thoughts like that ascended into his head, he skewered them with a thousand spears and banished them.

Having Wafer around helped with that. Their two minds together could support each other through their bond, and whenever Aeron began to worry about Kallie, Wafer sent him reassuring impressions.

I'd be lost without you, bud, Aeron sent to him.

Same, Wafer sent back.

Aeron noticed a small bridge below, and he took Wafer in low for a closer look. He didn't see any soldiers in the vicinity, so he and Wafer looped back toward the others, who'd lingered behind until Aeron finished scouting.

He found them and brought Wafer in for a landing, this time far enough away from the horses that they didn't spook, and he let the others ride over to his position.

"What did you see?" Kent asked through the frigid night air.

"It's like you said," Aeron replied. "Several bridges cross the river, but they're not all guarded."

"The prevailing theory is that the river prevents most unwelcome guests on its own," Kent said. "The ones that are unguarded are not connected to main roads. Lord Frostsong, the steward of the Murothian province on the other side, is more interested in the flow of commerce than the security of his eastern borders."

"Sounds perfect to me," Garrick said. "No one snooping when we're trying to cross over."

"Precisely," Kent said. "But even so, I suggest we wait until nightfall, just to be safe. It should be safe now, but the Frostsong province's defenses tend to grow laxer after sunset. And it is all thanks to the protection the province of Etheridge affords them from Inoth to the south."

"It's your decision," Garrick said. "This is your world."

"It was, anyway." Kent stared to the west, toward Muroth. "Come. We should find some place to rest until we are ready to cross over."

IT WAS GARRICK'S TURN TO KEEP WATCH WHILE THE OTHERS SLEPT. WELL, THE others except for Mehta, who barely seemed to sleep at all. He was awake as well, keeping watch along with Garrick.

Garrick had been traveling with Mehta for awhile now, but they'd barely exchanged any conversation outside of planning or in the throes of battle. The life of an assassin intrigued Garrick, so he wanted to know more about Mehta.

Especially since Mehta was the kind of man who would turn down the chance to take free coin, like he had at Lord Glavan's manse. Stranger still, Mehta had then sent away the majority of his earnings from the map job via a courier, even though the rest of them had deposited their earnings at a bank in Urthia.

There had to be a reason for it, but Garrick knew so little about him, he couldn't just start with that question.

"Tell me," Garrick said to Mehta, "how did you come to find yourself in Xenthan when we first met?"

"I saw the notice," Mehta said, his voice even as always. He had his whetstone out again and was sharpening one of his knives. He didn't look up. "Like the others."

"Where did you see it?" Garrick asked.

"On the ground."

Garrick studied him. "Yes, but where? What country? What city?"

"Etrijan. In Sefera." Mehta looked up. "Why?"

"Just curious," Garrick lied. "After my blunder, when I heard that Lord Valdis had sent the notice out, I was worried he would replace me permanently."

"Why?" Mehta repeated.

"He doesn't suffer failure."

"Without failure, growth is stunted." Mehta went back to sharpening his knives. "Where would you be now if you had only ever succeeded?"

Garrick scoffed. "Rich, retired, and drinking my fill of ale every waking hour. Living in a paradise, surrounded by servants who attend to my every need and want. Relaxing under golden sunshine by the ocean."

"But would you be any better for it?"

Garrick opened his mouth to answer, but as he thought about it, perhaps Mehta had a point. "Define 'better.'"

"I can't define what 'better' means to you. Only you can decide that," Mehta replied.

How had this turned into a mentoring lesson? Garrick was mining for information, but Mehta had somehow turned it around.

But Garrick knew one thing for sure: his version of "better" included killing Noraff and Phesnos for betraying him, Coburn, and Irwin back in that dungeon. Their blood would make everything much, much better.

Instead, Garrick said, "Being rich, living in paradise, and having servants attend to me would be 'better' than being in this dump."

"I've encountered many men who had fine clothes and jewelry, opulent homes, mountains of coin, and plenty of servants," Mehta said. "In the end, they were all the same."

Mehta's words chilled Garrick's bones. "You mean they all died the same."

"Everyone dies. It's how we live that matters."

"Says the Xyonate assassin."

Mehta looked up at Garrick again. "*Former* Xyonate."

Garrick considered pushing back on that point, but the quiet anger in Mehta's dark eyes made him think twice.

But then again, who was he to be afraid of a kid like Mehta, less than half Garrick's weight and a fraction of his age? Garrick could crush his skull in a heartbeat if he wanted to.

He resolved not to let Mehta's past and his creepy behavior bother him anymore.

"Were you born in Sefera?" Garrick asked. "You're a bit dark-skinned for the region."

Mehta wiped his knife blade on the fabric of his trousers, then he set it down on the bed and drew his other one from the sheath on his belt.

"I was born in the mountains to the east of Sefera. The Xyonates took me as a child." Mehta began sharpening the other knife. "I prefer not to talk about it."

"Why not?"

Mehta's jaw tensed, then it relaxed, but he didn't stop drawing the knife across the whetstone. "My childhood wasn't pleasant. It was a time of pain and longing."

"But are you 'better' for it?" Garrick prodded.

Mehta smirked and looked directly into Garrick's eyes. "Without question."

§

TWO HOURS AFTER NIGHTFALL, KENT WOKE EVERYONE. THEY FOLLOWED AERON and Wafer south until they reached the bridge. Anticipation filled Kent's chest at the thought of re-entering Muroth.

As they approached, Garrick asked, "You said this is the Frost-something province?"

"Frostsong," Kent replied.

"So if Lord Etheridge runs the province of Etheridge, then the guy running Frostsong is Lord Frostsong?"

Kent nodded. "Correct. Lord Aurelius Frostsong. He was a contemporary of my father, and they were dear friends. He was like family to me—at least up until my brother betrayed me. Now I suspect he is less interested in friendship given the lies Fane has inevitably spread about what transpired."

"Family members can be dicks," Garrick said.

"You have had similar experiences?"

Garrick nodded. "My father. He was the king of the dicks."

Kent huffed. "You have not met my brother."

"If I ever do, I'll hold him down for you."

"I believe you would, and you certainly could. He is not strong."

"I'll look forward to it, then." Garrick cracked his knuckles. "It's fun to pick on small, weak people. Especially when they deserve it."

"Everyone is smaller than you."

"Almost." Garrick nodded. "You should've seen the duotaur we had to fight in the last dungeon. I wasn't bigger than him."

Kent eyed him. "He was that formidable?"

Garrick sighed. "If that thing was guarding the map to a dragon egg then I don't want to think about what might be waiting for us in the dungeon that actually *holds* the dragon egg."

As they reached the bridge, Kent couldn't tell if Garrick was being serious or not. They hadn't joked much since they'd joined forces, so Kent didn't have a baseline for Garrick's sense of humor.

Stranger still, it seemed as though Kent and Garrick were actually starting to get along.

Three pillars of stone jutted out from the river at regular intervals to support the bridge itself, which was made of old wooden planks and rails. They could only ride across one horse at a time, so Kent went across first, followed by Garrick, and Mehta brought up the rear, as usual.

The Tosca River roared beneath them, cold and aggressive in the winter weather, and Kent wondered how anyone had managed to build a bridge over this section in the first place. Then he considered his magical abilities. Magic wasn't banned in Urthia or Govalia, so perhaps someone on that side had erected the bridge.

Or perhaps someone fleeing oppression in Muroth had done it.

Once they all made it across, Kent exhaled a deep breath. He'd done it. He'd returned to Muroth, the land of his birth—and the land of the death of his old life.

It looked the same as Urthia had on the other side of the river: snow-covered farmland, with low hills in the distance and plenty of trees to the north and south.

Under the cover of night, they passed through the Frostsong province without incident, though that did little to calm Kent's nerves. Dozens of miles south of their location, his brother slept in their father's bed, comfortable, safe, and happy.

Meanwhile, Kent's horse trudged through six-inch snow, carving a path for the others to follow as they headed toward unknown danger. But he took solace in knowing that someday Fane would get what he deserved. And Kent would deliver it to him personally.

They camped for the night in a cave secluded within the rows of mid-height pine trees planted by the Frostsongs a decade before. The trees in that area wouldn't be logged until they reached their full height in another decade or two, so Kent guessed that the locals had few reasons to venture into that part of the forest.

They waited until nightfall the next day and set out southwest, toward the supposed location of the Crimson Flame temple.

"Aside from the fiend who took Kallie, I have only ever encountered one member of the Crimson Flame," Kent said to Garrick. "That being Lord Glavan."

Aeron noticeably bristled at the mention of the woman who'd taken Kallie.

"But you had mentioned the map came from a dungeon under the Crimson Flame temple in Etrijan. What more can you tell me about them? Do they serve a particular god or goddess?"

"I don't know. Maybe Dheveri, but I didn't see any shrines to her. The mages I encountered all used fire with their magic, like the woman who showed up at Aeron's parents' house," Garrick replied. "Not sure if it's a requirement for joining or if it's a point of focus afterward."

It would make sense for the Crimson Flame to worship Dheveri, the Goddess of Fire, but Kent found it strange that Garrick hadn't seen any evidence of that in the first Crimson Flame temple.

"If there are mages here, in Muroth, they are in direct violation of Muroth's laws," Kent said. "I would be surprised if Lord Frostsong knew of their presence and had refused to take action. He was always emphatic about enforcing Muroth's laws."

"They're a hidden cult. Maybe he doesn't know about them," Garrick said. "And besides, you said he cared more about commerce than letter-of-the-law enforcement. If he does know about them, perhaps they're good for business somehow."

"Even if they were, a temple full of mages, unaddressed, is either a massive political risk for Lord Frostsong or a sign of weakness on his part. Muroth is a militant country; if the temple is known, any of the other provinces could use its existence as a reason to remove Lord Frostsong from power and seize his timber trade for themselves."

"Or they're in on it, like Lord Glavan was," Garrick suggested. "By the time we're done with the temple, there won't be any mages left either way."

"Perhaps," Kent said. "Or perhaps the temple is not there in the first place."

"We'll see."

They rode for another three hours until Aeron and Wafer landed several yards ahead of them.

"I think we found it," he called. "But you're not gonna like it."

⟡

GARRICK FROWNED AT THE SIGHT OF THE CRIMSON FLAME TEMPLE. IT HAD BEEN miserable enough to try to reach the one nestled high up in the mountains of northern Etrijan, but this one was worse.

He stood at the snowy shoreline of a wide lake, glassy and black under the stars and patches of clouds above. Near the center of the lake stood a solitary protrusion of stone, almost tower-like in its appearance but wider at its base.

And from what Garrick could tell, given that the only light was moonlight, the temple looked to be carved into the protrusion itself.

He cursed the Aletians, or the Crimson Flame cultists, or both—whoever had constructed all of these hard-to-reach temples and concealed ancient treasures in hidden dungeons had done too good of a job.

"Did you see any way across?" Kent asked Aeron.

"Nope." Aeron shook his head. "There are some old boats tied to a small dock on the far side of the tower, but I didn't see any boats along the lake's perimeter."

"Great," Garrick muttered. "I have no intention of swimming across. Can you and Wafer manage to bring one of them over here so we can get across?"

"Yeah, I think so," Aeron said. "Give me a few minutes."

Ten minutes later, Aeron and Wafer returned, towing a small boat along the surface of the water by a rope clutched in Wafer's talons.

The sight made Garrick wonder why he'd never recruited a wyvern knight for any of his past jobs. Having someone who could fly would've come in handy more times than he could count.

Wafer pulled the boat all the way onshore, and then Aeron landed him near the shoreline. The others tied up their horses and boarded the boat.

Then Garrick pushed it into the water and jumped in before the water could get too deep. The icy water seeped into his boots and stung his skin with chills, but he ignored it.

As Kent and Mehta picked up oars and began to row, Garrick waved at Aeron.

"Fly in closer," he called. "See if you can find a way up."

Then Garrick picked up a third oar and started rowing as well, alternating sides since his powerful strokes outdid those of Mehta and Kent combined. Aeron and Wafer flew over them, blotting out the moon and the stars for an instant.

Some of the clouds had cleared away, and the night sky and the boat reminded Garrick of his home in the islands off of northern Etrijan. He'd sailed across large stretches of water under comparable night skies many times.

He recognized the winter constellation of Senros, the God of Love and Romance, hurling his lasso due south across the sky. Beyond the lasso, other stars formed the sword of Lyrena, the Goddess of War, who always resisted Senros's advances—sometimes violently, depending on the stories.

Now grown up and approaching seventy-five years of age—though he neither looked nor felt it, thanks to the troll blood in his veins—Garrick no longer believed those stories like he had when he was a child.

The man who'd told them to him had been a charming, charismatic soul, but he'd also been a violent, hateful drunk.

Garrick exhaled a breath. He'd killed his father almost forty years ago, but some memories still haunted him nonetheless. Perhaps they always would.

It took nearly half an hour of consistent rowing to reach the center of the lake. After another five minutes, they curled around to the opposite side of the rock where Aeron had said the other boats were docked.

When they got there, Mehta tied the boat to the shore with a knot that would've made any real sailor cringe, but Garrick didn't bring it up. Perhaps knot-tying wasn't a focus of his Xyonate training.

A leathery flapping sounded, and Aeron swooped down and landed Wafer next to them. Wafer struggled to find purchase on the small dock and had to flap his wings a few more times to get his balance.

He finally lowered his front half down and braced the knuckles of his wings on the dock's surface. It creaked and groaned under his weight.

"The only way up appears to be an enclosed basket with a rope-and-pulley system," Aeron said. "Looks clunky, but if there's anyone actually up there, it has probably seen plenty of use. I think it's the only way in or out. Whatever the case, Wafer can fly two up at a time, including me. So if you'd rather do that…?"

"You're sure he can handle it?" Garrick asked. "His wings are fully healed?"

"Yes," Aeron replied.

"Then yeah. Definitely." Garrick had nearly fallen to his death a couple of times while trying to get inside the Crimson Flame temple in Etrijan.

The idea of flying up with Wafer didn't thrill him, but the thought of either climbing up the protrusion or being pulled up in some sort of basket had zero appeal to him.

"Come on, Kent," Aeron said. "You've already ridden Wafer with me. He knows you best, so he can get used to flying with two with someone familiar on his back first."

Kent took hold of Aeron's extended hand and climbed onto Wafer behind Aeron, and then Wafer carefully raised his wings and burst into the sky. A few heavy, labored flaps later, and they started to gain significant altitude.

Garrick turned to Mehta. Something about him still set Garrick on edge, but he couldn't put his finger on it. He decided to be more direct this time.

"I noticed you sent your coin north with a courier instead of bringing it along," Garrick said. "I didn't figure there'd be someone waiting at home for a former assassin. Or that you even had a home."

Mehta stared at Garrick for a long moment. "When I escaped the Xyonates, they followed me and tried to sift me. A priest of the goddess Laeri came to my aid when I needed it the most."

Garrick waited, but Mehta didn't say anything else right away. After another moment, he continued.

"The priest and his wife paid for it with their lives at the hands of the Xyonates. I could not protect them," Mehta said. "But I saved their daughter, a young girl with blonde hair and blue eyes named Ferne.

"I took her to my hometown in the mountains between Etrijan and Xenthan. I sent my earnings up to my grandfather and sister who are caring for her.

"They don't have much, and I'm sure the coin I left for them has nearly run out, so I decided it was better to send some now, even though it was expensive to do so."

A young girl with blonde hair and blue eyes? In the mountains separating Etrijan from Xenthan? Garrick had *seen* her on his return trip to Xenthan from the Crimson Flame temple in Etrijan. He'd passed through a village of brown-faced mountain people—people colored like Mehta—and the girl had stuck out like a gash in an apple.

"What is it?" Mehta asked. "Do you doubt my sincerity?"

Garrick shook his head. He must've been gawking. "Not at all."

"Then what is it?"

Garrick didn't want to say anything else. He decided to keep his information to himself. "Nothing. It's just interesting that an assassin would care for anyone other than himself."

Mehta's concerned expression shifted back to a neutral one. "Growing up in a cult taught me a lot, but it did not teach me right from wrong. I'm still learning that, and I'm still learning not to sift anyone and everyone that I meet. Ferne was the first person I chose not to sift.

"Her parents died because they chose to help me. With her dying breath, Ferne's mother cursed me and Xyon, the god I once served. I didn't hold it against her; she was right to say it.

"But I knew in that moment that I had three options: kill Ferne, too, leave her behind, or take her with me. The right thing to do was to get her to safety, so I did."

Garrick nodded. Mehta's past sounded even worse than his. "I'd agree with you on that point."

Leathery flaps sounded again, and Aeron and Wafer landed on the dock once again.

Garrick motioned for Mehta to go next, but Aeron waved him back.

"Mehta's way lighter than you," Aeron said. "Let me take you next. Then Wafer won't have to work as hard when he brings Mehta up."

Garrick gave a moment's consideration to whether or not Aeron had just insulted him, then he gave in and started down the dock, which creaked with his every step.

As Garrick approached, Wafer began to growl. Aeron shushed him, and then Wafer snorted and huffed.

"I don't think he likes me," Garrick said.

"He's not enthusiastic about having to try to carry you," Aeron said. "But if he can manage it, that will mean he can probably carry Kent and Mehta in addition to me, which would be a big deal for him. He must be getting stronger."

"How much stronger could he get?"

"Not sure. He's pretty much full-grown, as far as I can tell, but I have no idea what his ultimate limits will be. How much stronger are *you* going to get?" Aeron countered with a grin.

"Probably not much at this point. I'm only getting older, not stronger."

"Well, you'd better hop on before you keel over, then." Aeron extended his arm.

"You don't want to do that. I'd pull you right out of the saddle," Garrick said. "I'll manage on my own."

And Garrick did manage, albeit on his second try, to get onto Wafer's back. When Garrick was fully mounted, Wafer arched his back down and groaned.

Aeron whacked the side of Wafer's neck with his palm. "Quit being so dramatic."

"What am I supposed to hold onto?"

"My waist, or the back of the saddle," Aeron replied.

"No offense, kid, but again, if I hold onto you, and I go down, you're coming with me."

"Nonsense. Wafer would catch me before I hit the ground," Aeron said. "He'd probably let you fall to your death, though."

"How comforting," Garrick muttered. "I'll hold the back of the saddle."

"Don't worry about his wings. It'll look like they'll flap up and might hit you, but they won't, even with as tall as you are."

"Got it." Garrick shifted his position on Wafer's back and took hold of the leather saddle. It wasn't the surest grip he'd ever had, but the trip up should be short enough—he hoped.

The smooth, scaly hide between Garrick's legs seemed to tighten as Wafer's whole body tensed. Garrick tensed in response, and then Wafer leaped into the air, furiously beating his wings and slowly gaining in altitude.

As the ground and the lake dropped away from him in jerky movements, Garrick decided to stop looking down for fear he might vomit or lose consciousness.

Watching the rock protrusion bob up and down with each labored flap of Wafer's wings wasn't any better, and closing his eyes made everything worse, so he stared out across the lake instead.

They'd risen about fifty feet above the highest trees now, but instead of ascending straight to the top, Wafer flew around the rock protrusion, arcing upward at a steady pace.

Chilly wind blasted Garrick in his face, but he gritted his teeth and endured.

Without question, the sensation of flying unnerved him, but he now fully understood its allure as well. He figured that if he could learn to relax up here, he might get used to it and even enjoy it.

But for the time being, he was just glad Aeron hadn't decided to make Wafer perform any aerial tricks with Garrick on his back.

They reached a landing about two minutes later, and Wafer set down in what appeared to be the temple's moonlit courtyard. It resembled the courtyard of the Crimson Flame temple in Etrijan—small and nothing more than a flat slab of rock framed in by two stone walls on either side.

The temple entrance, framed by stone pillars, awaited them at the far end, and Kent sat on the stone steps leading up to it, watching them land.

Wafer started wheezing as he lowered to the ground. When he touched down, his whole body shuddered.

Garrick wondered if that was normal or if his size had put too much strain on Wafer.

Aeron leaned forward and patted Wafer's scaly neck. "Good work, buddy. Good work."

Garrick took that as his cue to dismount, so he swung his right leg over and slid down Wafer's left side. As soon as Garrick's boots hit the ground, Wafer inhaled a deep, obnoxious breath.

Garrick glared at him.

Aeron just laughed. "I'm going to let him rest for a minute before we go get Mehta—that is, if I can find him in whatever shadow he's hiding in down there."

Garrick paid Wafer no mind. Instead, he enjoyed the sensation of solid ground—or rock—under his feet again. It felt safe. Secure.

He turned toward Kent, who stood up from his spot and started over toward them. "Think we can get in the front doors?"

"I can certainly get them open. As to how much noise it will make, that is another matter entirely."

"If it's loud, are you boys prepared for a fight?" Garrick rubbed his hands together, partially because of the cold, and partially because a fight would be a nice way to break up the monotony of all the traveling they'd been doing.

"Absolutely," Aeron said. "Any chance to carve some answers out of these cultists would make my day. If we lure them into this courtyard, maybe Wafer and I can drop down behind them and keep them from running back inside."

"I am prepared to fight as well," Kent said. "And Mehta is always ready for a fight, perhaps even when he should not be."

"Speaking of which…" Aeron and Wafer crawled toward the edge of the rock and dropped off the side.

Garrick heard a loud *whap*—the sound of Wafer's wings opening and catching the air.

"I envy them sometimes," Kent said. "The freedom that flight must bring them."

"I don't," Garrick said. And he meant it.

Moments later, they returned. Garrick noticed that Wafer wasn't breathing hard when he landed with Mehta on his back. He took personal offense to it, and Wafer made the effect worse by scowling—if wyverns could scowl—at Garrick after he landed.

Mehta dismounted and joined the others in the courtyard. He only said one word.

"Well?"

A question burned in Garrick's mind. He looked at Mehta. "You were in a cult. We know these bastards worship fire and sometimes use fire magic. Anything else you can tell us?"

Mehta replied, "If we were about to face a sect of Xyonates, I would advise against it altogether. In any case, we must be decisive when dealing with the Crimson Flame, as they will be decisive with us. Their minds, corrupted by lies or not, are already made up. Ours should be, too."

Garrick glanced at everyone in the group. "Anyone feel differently?"

They all shook their heads, but Aeron added, "Try not to kill all of them right away. One of them might know where Kallie is."

"Agreed," Garrick said. "Let's get these doors open and find us a dragon egg."

Aeron and Wafer took a position at the top of the temple, on the part of its roof that jutted out over the double-doors that served as its main entrance. Aeron's suggestion to drop down behind anyone who came out of the temple was a good one, so Garrick had sent them up to do just that.

Meanwhile, Garrick stood in the courtyard, holding his snow steel sword and shield, both of which glowed blue and teal in his hands. They gave off the same faint ringing sound as the first time he'd brandished them in a temple courtyard.

Garrick expected they would destroy any cultists just as quickly as last time, too.

Mehta crouched in the shadows of one of the walls, and Kent stood at the doors with his palms flat on them, awaiting Garrick's signal.

"Now," Garrick said.

Kent's hands flared with blue light, then it disappeared into the doors themselves. He bowed his head, and a moment later, the doors each split down their centers with two loud cracks.

Kent whipped his arms to the sides. Wood and metal screeched as one half of each door flew in opposite directions and struck the courtyard walls with two loud bangs. Then he drew his sword, stepped back into the courtyard, and stood next to Garrick.

No one came out.

They waited there for a few minutes, unmoving but ready. After a few more minutes of no reaction from anyone inside, Garrick grew impatient.

Tired of the cold wind blowing at him, he motioned toward Mehta, who crept toward the broken doors. Garrick didn't know how he did it, but even when Mehta moved, he looked more like a shadow than an actual person.

Whatever the case, Mehta peered into the temple entrance with his knives drawn and ready. Then he disappeared inside the temple's dark doorway.

From atop the temple, Aeron put his arms up and mouthed, "Well?"

Garrick shook his head and mouthed, "Not yet."

Mehta emerged from the temple about two minutes later and motioned them forward.

"Stay here for now," Garrick said to Kent, who nodded in return.

He headed over to Mehta and shook his head at Aeron again. They stayed put.

"What's happening?" Garrick asked.

"I don't see anyone inside," Mehta replied. "At least not immediately. But it's a big place. Looks like a lot of halls and rooms, potentially multiple floors."

Sounds a lot like the temple in Etrijan. Garrick asked, "Are we clear to go inside?"

Mehta nodded.

"Good enough for me. The dungeon's below the temple anyway. That's the real test."

Garrick turned back and motioned Kent over to them, and he looked up at Aeron and Wafer and brought them down as well.

"We're good to go inside," he told them. "Mehta didn't see anything."

"I guess Wafer stays out here, then," Aeron said. "I didn't see any entrances around that could've fit him inside."

"I doubt he'd fare well in the dungeon, anyway," Garrick said. "The last one had spaces barely large enough for me to fit through. All the same, I'd like to keep the map with him, if you don't mind."

"Not at all."

Garrick handed the parchment tube to him.

Aeron dismounted, removed his spear from its anchor point on Wafer's saddle, and slung a pack on his shoulders. In the spear's place, he anchored the parchment tube instead. Then he patted Wafer's neck a few times and muttered some words to him that Garrick couldn't make out, and then Wafer chirped and took to the sky.

"He's hungry anyway, and there's a herd of deer snoozing on one of the hills nearby, so he'll be fine," Aeron said. "Alright. I'm ready."

They headed toward the temple doors together.

Mehta went in first. He signaled an all-clear, and Garrick entered next, followed by Aeron and then Kent.

Though it was dark, the entryway resembled the one from the temple in Etrijan. If the same fanatics had designed both temples, then Garrick would know exactly which way to go to find the entrance to the dungeon below.

He took two steps forward, and a tile depressed beneath his foot.

That's not good.

Behind them, a huge piece of flat, forged iron dropped from the ceiling and crashed into the floor in front of the temple entrance, blocking their escape. The sound boomed in Garrick's ears, almost deafening him.

Could've been worse. The iron slab could've hit them on its way down.

Then a series of torches mounted to the walls around them ignited with crimson fire, casting the space in shades of red.

Garrick scowled. *Crimson Flame, indeed.*

Nothing else happened for a long moment, but the four mercs stayed on their guard anyway, unmoving.

Then the sound of several sets of footsteps, moving fast, approached them. The sound grew louder and louder until a dozen men clad in white robes emerged from two of the hallways that fed into the entryway.

Each of them wore a white hood that ended in a point between their eyes and crimson fabric over the lower halves of their faces.

In the center of each hood, over the cultists' foreheads, the Crimson Flame symbol was embroidered in gold.

From the left side, a man in crimson robes approached, but his hood was down. Red light glinted off his bald head, and black fabric covered the lower half of his face.

The cultists formed two lines of six men, staggered so they filled half of the space and left the other half to the four mercenaries. The cultist in red stood in front, centered. He stared at the four mercs, and they stared back at him.

Garrick expected some sort of speech or taunt, but no one said anything.

Instead, the lead cultist flung his robe off, revealing a lean, muscular chest with the Crimson Flame Emblem tattooed on over his sternum in red ink. The hilts of two long daggers protruded from his belt.

The cultists in white did the same, revealing comparable tattoos, daggers, and bald heads with the lower halves of their faces still covered.

The leader, who wore loose black pants instead of white, like the others, stepped forward and drew his daggers.

Garrick, standing at the front of the four mercs, started forward to meet him, but a hand grabbed his wrist from behind. He glanced back.

It was Mehta.

"He's mine," Mehta uttered.

Normally, Garrick would've balked at the idea, but from what he'd seen of Mehta thus far, he knew he could handle himself. In fact, Garrick enjoyed watching him work, so he stepped aside.

Mehta shed his cloak and drew the two knives from the sheaths in his belt. The lead cultist's eyes narrowed, and he launched forward.

CHAPTER SEVENTEEN

M ehta smiled when the lead cultist came at him.

The way the leader carried himself reminded Mehta of the Xyonates he'd left behind. His proud, upright stance had conveyed a sense of confidence and certainty in his skills.

But when he made the first move, he sealed his fate.

He'd had the advantage of reach due to his daggers being longer than Mehta's knives, and he was taller than Mehta and had longer arms as well.

By bolting forward, he'd closed too much of the distance.

And Mehta's knives were ideal for close-quarters engagement.

Now those daggers lashed at Mehta from the right side, as he'd predicted. The cultist was right-handed, so his left dagger came in first. It was a setup for the killing stroke following from his right hand.

Mehta watched the two blows and reacted with clean alacrity. As the left-hand dagger sliced at Mehta, he rolled under it and brought the knife in his left hand up to block the cultist's other dagger.

At the same time, Mehta slashed his other knife across the cultist's belly, opening a red line across his pale flesh. Mehta's thirst reveled in the cut and begged for more.

But the cultist staggered back before Mehta could land another strike. The cultist pressed his left forearm against his gut to stanch the blood pulsing out of the wound.

His right hand held the dagger out to regain some of the distance that he'd lost, but the fight was already over.

Mehta had learned early on in his training that blood loss could prove fatal in a fight, even if the wound itself wasn't. An opponent's energy and will to fight tended to ooze out with their blood.

The instinct of any living creature, sentient or otherwise, was to keep its blood in its body above all else. Without intense, drastic training, those instincts typically won out.

So for the cultist, given the severity of his wound, the best he could hope for now was to kill Mehta before he bled out or became too weak to fight. Mehta gave him the next best option instead.

He advanced, batted the cultist's dagger away, and slashed open his throat, his forearms, and his inner thighs in quick succession.

The cultist wilted to the floor, and blood from his numerous wounds quickly pooled underneath him.

Mehta's thirst still cried out for more.

He scanned the dozen remaining cultists, then he sheathed his knives, bent down, and took up the lead cultist's daggers. His knives were savage weapons, but against multiple opponents, leveling the reach disparity between them was a wise decision.

"Who's next?" Garrick asked from behind Mehta. Beside him, Aeron and Kent shed their cloaks.

The cultists all started forward at once, and the entryway descended into chaos.

❧

AERON COULDN'T REMEMBER THE LAST TIME HE'D FOUGHT MORE THAN TWO people at once—at least not without riding Wafer. So when all twelve of the cultists charged the four of them, it freaked him out.

But then he remembered that these bastards had taken Kallie, and his rage kicked in.

He jabbed his spear at the one nearest to him, but the cultist knocked the spearhead to the side and continued to press forward, his daggers primed to cleave Aeron into chunks.

Aeron knew he'd never get the spearhead back in time, but its blunt end would do just fine. He shifted his grip on the spear shaft and swung a follow-up blow at the cultist.

But the cultist avoided that, too and kept coming.

With no weapons left, Aeron shot a kick at the cultist while he was in mid-swing.

His boot slammed into the Crimson Flame tattoo on the cultist's chest and knocked him away, but another cultist immediately took his place.

Daggers flashed at Aeron, and he blocked a flurry of attacks with the ends and the center of his spear shaft, but the cultist continued advancing, pushing Aeron back.

The second cultist was smaller than Aeron, though. That almost never happened in fights, so Aeron pushed back—hard.

It worked. The second cultist regained his footing and pressed forward again, but this time Aeron blocked his attacks, picked his moment, and used timing and strength to shove him against a nearby wall. He pinned the cultist there with his spear and delivered a head-butt to his face that cracked his nose.

The second cultist grunted and clenched his eyes shut, but before Aeron could do any more damage, a third cultist came at him from the side.

Aeron released the pressure on the second cultist and whipped his spear-head down hard at the third, who parried the strike with his daggers.

He didn't want the cultist he'd pinned against the wall coming at him from behind, so Aeron threw his elbow back at him. It struck his jaw with a heavy thump, and the second cultist dropped to the floor next to Aeron.

The first cultist returned to face Aeron and joined with the third cultist in approaching Aeron again.

Aeron knew better than to just leave the second cultist lying there. His blow couldn't have killed him, so Aeron stepped back and stomped on the second cultist's head. A sickening crack cut through the battle, and Aeron struggled to refrain from shuddering at the sound.

His foes didn't allow him time to consider what he'd done. They attacked him in harmony, hurling attacks opposite of each other, trying to divide Aeron's attention.

Aeron's spear moved in a blur, but some of the attacks got through and clanged against his armor. They were barely giving him room to breathe, much less produce any sort of counterattack.

Then Aeron saw an opening. He ducked low, under a dagger, and cracked the shaft of his spear against the side of the first cultist's knee.

The knee buckled to the side, and the first cultist went down, but Aeron couldn't finish him because the third cultist attacked from the other side.

Aeron raised his spear to block, but a red fireball sizzled past him and drove the third cultist into a wall. He ignited with fire and shrieked as he frantically tried to pat out the flames.

But Aeron didn't waste the opportunity. He plunged his spear into the exposed chest of the first cultist beneath him, killing him.

When he looked back, Aeron saw Kent lighting another cultist on fire with yet another red fireball. Their eyes met for a moment, and they exchanged a brief nod.

Aeron skewered the third cultist, who was still running around and still on fire, mostly to put him out of his misery, then he rejoined the battle.

§

To Garrick's surprise, the cultists hadn't used magic even once throughout the whole fight. Perhaps it was because they were in Muroth. Even on an island in a secluded lake, they had to leave sometime, and the risk of expulsion or execution was too great.

But the idea that a fire-worshiping cult would voluntarily follow the laws of the country they operated in confused Garrick. Why bother following society's laws if they had no intention of interacting with that society?

Of course, none of that mattered right now. All that mattered were the half-dozen daggers lashing and stabbing at him from as many different angles.

But he'd gone into berserker mode, spinning and hacking and bashing anyone dumb enough to get in his way—which was most of them.

Their blades clanged off his sword and shield, and at times they struck his arms and legs as well. As usual, his thick skin repelled everything but the stabs, so he focused on parrying those.

His sword hissed whenever it hit one of these Crimson Flame cultists instead of freezing them like it had in the temple in Etrijan. Either his sword was reacting differently because of the room's warmth, or these fanatics ran hotter than normal humans.

By the time he'd felled three of the cultists, they'd stopped coming at him anymore. He glanced around, breathing quickly.

Kent had taken out at least three of them, two more lay near Aeron's feet, and three others, including the lead cultist, lay in pools of blood around Mehta, who was also looking around for someone else to kill.

When Mehta's eyes met Garrick's, an icy ball of steel dropped into Garrick's gut.

He looked away and immediately wished he hadn't.

Garrick never wanted to show weakness, but showing it in front of Mehta was especially bad. All of his partners were ferocious and formidable in their own ways, but Mehta was the only one who truly gave Garrick pause.

Fortunately, only one enemy remained, and when Garrick looked away, he ended up looking right at that lone cultist. Kent and Aeron were already heading toward him, and he'd backed up against a wall made of dark wooden beams.

Kent threw a blast of fire from his right hand, but the cultist dodged to the right, and the fireball exploded against the wall instead. But Aeron hurled his spear and pinned the cultist to the wall, through his shoulder, under his collarbone.

The cultist's eyes widened, then he bared his teeth. The daggers slipped from his hands and clanked onto the floor as he groped at the spear protruding from his upper chest.

Aeron took hold of his spear with both hands. "Grab him."

Kent and Garrick took hold of the cultist's arms and pulled them apart, holding him in place against the wall.

Aeron yanked his spear free, and blood streamed from the wound down the front of the cultist's chest and from the exit wound on his back. The cultist yelped and tried to resist Kent and Garrick's hold on him, but he couldn't do anything against their strength.

Garrick had grabbed the cultist's good arm, just in case he tried something. He didn't trust Kent to hold the cultist in place properly, so he'd handled it himself.

Aeron whacked the side of the cultist's knee with the blunt end of his spear, and his knee buckled. He dropped to his knees, and Aeron put his three-pointed spear under his chin.

Garrick approved wholeheartedly. These flamejobs deserved whatever they got.

"Your cult took my sister," Aeron said. "Her name is Kallie. She has blonde hair and blue eyes. She has a mark on the back of her neck—sort of a bronzy-gold flame, but not like your usual emblem. Where is she?"

The cultist laughed, but it turned into a cough. "I don't know anything about any girl with a mark."

"Then there's no reason to keep you alive," Aeron said.

The cultist tensed, wide-eyed again as Aeron urged the spear closer to his neck. He blurted, "Wait!"

"Changed your mind?" Aeron asked.

The cultist's wide eyes narrowed. "No. But if we took her, she's already dead."

Aeron's face hardened to steel, and he drove the spear into the cultist's throat so hard that it burst out the back of his neck.

He wrenched the spear out of the cultist's neck, and then Garrick and Kent let him slump to the floor. Aeron stood there, facing them. A few new scratches tainted his teal armor and his gauntlets, but otherwise he looked fine.

"Do not let his words trouble you," Kent said. "I suspect it was more bluster than anything. He likely knew we would kill him anyway. We *will* find her, Aeron."

"I know." Aeron's face remained stern, and he sighed. "So what's next?"

"We need to clear this place out. I don't want anyone lurking in the shadows behind us." Garrick looked at his fellow mercs and said, "Follow me."

It took them close to two hours to navigate the temple's network of halls and rooms, which ended up being laid out in the mirror image of the Crimson Flame temple Garrick had visited in Etrijan. In that time, they rooted out several more cultists, all of whom tried to fight back, and all of whom eventually perished because of it.

Unfortunately, none of them provided any useful information about Aeron's sister. Garrick felt for the guy; were someone close to him in that situation, he would've been equally as frustrated and desperate to help.

Except Garrick wasn't that close to anyone—not anymore.

Disappointed but resigned to continue the job, they finished scouring the temple, and then Garrick led them to the grand hall. Inside, he recognized the ornate etchings of huge, scaled beasts along the hall's stone walls.

Dragons.

The etchings weren't identical, but they conveyed the same idea. Fearsome dragons rampaging, breathing fire, and obliterating entire cities.

Garrick hadn't given them much thought the first time around, but seeing them here, as well as the map indicating there was a dragon egg somewhere beneath their feet, made him wonder.

Perhaps the Crimson Flame wasn't a fire-worshiping cult after all. Maybe they worshiped dragons instead.

Kind of a dumb thing to worship, since dragons were long dead.

Like in the other temple, black tapestries hung from the walls, all bearing the Crimson Flame emblem. Black granite pillars supported the hall's lofted ceiling, and a matching granite altar stood in the center of a platform.

The altar in the temple in Etrijan had moved, albeit not easily, to reveal a lever underneath that opened a secret room hidden behind the far wall. Without a map of the temple itself, Garrick had nothing else to go by, so he directed the others to help him move the altar.

They inched it aside, and sure enough, a lever like the one at the previous temple rested in a metal apparatus beneath it. With all four of them standing on the platform, Garrick reached down and pulled it.

But instead of a room opening along the wall, the floor dropped out from under them.

§

KENT HADN'T EXPECTED TO FALL THE INSTANT AFTER GARRICK PULLED THE lever, but it happened nonetheless.

The stone blocks that made up the floor plummeted, and he went right along with them, as did Aeron and Garrick. Even Mehta, who was always so light on his feet, got caught off-guard.

The dark hole swallowed them, and moments later, a series of heavy splashes sounded beneath them. Then Kent's boots hit the water as well, followed by the rest of his body.

Icy water tried to rush into his nose and mouth, and he couldn't see anything for a moment.

It jarred him, but he was still alive. The fall hadn't killed him, and as far as he could tell he wasn't hurt, either. For now, that would have to be enough.

He clawed toward the surface, broke through, and inhaled a deep breath. The air was stagnant and musty and stank of mildew, but he could breathe. The crimson torches in the grand hall above them cast just enough light down into the space for Kent to see.

Kent looked around and saw three more heads pop through the water. Aeron splashed nearby him, frantic.

Could he not swim?

His armor. It was weighing him down. Practically a death sentence in water.

Kent swam over to him as Aeron's head and gauntleted hand slipped under the water again.

Kent dug into the water and grabbed Aeron's wrist. Mehta was there as well, also reaching down for Aeron.

As they hauled Aeron back to the surface, all of them kicked hard to stay up. Kent wondered why Garrick wasn't helping.

Aeron's head broke the surface again, and he gasped for air, still flailing in the water, but somehow still holding his spear. Kent supposed wyvern knights trained hard to never drop their weapons—something he imagined they were prone to do in midair battles.

Together, they swam toward what appeared to be the edge of some land or stone, and the bottom of the pool gradually rose to meet their feet until they could walk out.

Barely visible in the low red light, Garrick was already out of the pool, sitting on the stone, panting and breathing. His snow steel sword and shield lay beside him.

"Thank you," Aeron said to Mehta and Kent. He crawled onto the stone, and his armor scraped against it as he rolled onto his back and exhaled relief. He reached for his lower back and started to rub it.

Kent and Mehta got out of the pool and stood. Kent hadn't done a lot of swimming in his lifetime, but he'd learned enough to survive. Mehta had doubtless trained to kill people in the water, so it hadn't surprised Kent to see him swimming skillfully the moment he hit the pool.

Even Aeron, he understood. Why bother learning to swim if you were going to wear armor and fight on the back of a wyvern?

But Garrick...

"What are you staring at?" Garrick growled.

Kent didn't stop looking at him. "I thought you grew up in the islands north of Etrijan, raiding villages along the coast and guiding ships across the water. During all of that time, did you not learn how to swim?"

Garrick stood to his full height, but he left his sword and shield where they lay. "I did, but I weigh 400 pounds. I don't like swimming. I prefer to be on top of the water, not in it. You got a problem with that?"

"I am merely making an observation."

"Why don't you *observe* a way for us to get out of here instead?" Garrick countered.

Kent shivered as he searched the darkness around them. Far above them, a red, rectangular-shaped hole showed where they'd fallen through. But as the only source of light in the space, it didn't afford Kent the chance to see beyond where they were standing.

As such, he had no sense of how large this place was, or what lay beyond his range of sight, in the darkness.

But Mehta could probably see just fine, thanks to his enhanced vision.

"It's too dark, and now that I am all wet, I don't have any dry kindling I can spark into flame." Kent turned to Mehta, trying to keep his teeth from chattering. "What do you see?"

"A lot," Mehta replied. "This cavern is huge."

"Are we in imminent danger?" Kent asked.

"I don't think so. We're the only ones in here, from what I can tell. But I don't see any way to get back up there, either."

Kent frowned. They'd only brought limited provisions into the temple with them. If they were to be stuck down here indefinitely, that would prove troublesome.

"Do you see any other ways out of here?" Garrick asked.

"It's hard to tell," Mehta replied. "We're up against a flat wall of stone, here. There are a bunch of boulders and rock formations spread as far as I can see. There may be tunnels or paths throughout the space that lead deeper into the dungeon, but I won't know for sure until we get closer."

"*This* is the dungeon?" Aeron asked, still lying on his back on the stone floor.

"It is beneath the Crimson Flame temple, so I would hazard to guess that it is," Kent replied.

"I've never been in one, so I don't have anything to compare it to," Aeron said. "But this… it's just not what I expected."

"So you're telling me we have to wander around in the dark until we find something important?" Garrick asked.

"We'll have a guide, at least," Aeron said. "And we can't just stay here forever."

"Fine." Garrick snatched up his sword and shield, but the runes along them no longer glowed when he held them. "Which way do we go, then?"

"Garrick," Kent said. "Your weapons…"

"What?" Garrick looked at them. Then he cursed. "What's wrong with them?"

Kent shook his head. "I do not know. Does water harm snow steel?"

"It had better not." Garrick cursed again. "Wait…" He held the sword up closer to his face. "I can see a bit of light coming from some of the runes. Maybe it just needs to dry."

It wasn't exactly warm in the cavern, but it wasn't freezing, either, so the cold wouldn't affect the snow steel's runes much, if at all.

They would've made for a useful light source down here, though. If nothing else, they would've made Garrick easier to keep track of.

Aeron pushed himself to his feet and set the butt of his spear on the floor. He pulled a mushroom out of his pack and stuffed it into his mouth.

While chewing, he said, "If it's all the same to you guys, I'd rather not sit around and wait for something to find us and eat us."

"I agree," Kent said. "Mehta, would you please choose a direction you feel is viable and show us the way?"

Kent smirked at the changeup in their roles. Mehta, who usually kept to himself and hid at the back of the party, now had to lead them.

Mehta replied, simply, "Yes."

He led them through a maze of rocky stalagmites, around boulders, and through smaller, shallower pools of water. He announced each new potential hazard with a warning and a description, but it didn't keep the rest of them from stumbling here and there.

It took close to an hour, but they made it halfway around the cavern and to a tunnel set into the cavern wall.

When they did, Kent wished he had chosen to swim across the pool to the other side when they'd fallen through the temple floor. They would've been right at its mouth, and even in the low light, they could've seen it yawning open at them.

But they'd gotten there all the same, and they entered the opening.

The tunnel started as little more than a narrow path through stone, so they walked single-file with Mehta leading the way. The deeper into the dungeon they progressed, the more the tunnel widened and angled down. They also drew closer to a distant source of green light.

The constant dripping of water sounded from random spots all around them. Kent had felt cool droplets of water hit his shoulders and head a few times, but due to the low light, he had yet to see any actual water droplets falling.

Worse than the incessant noise was the smell. Though not overwhelming, the scent of death and feces accompanied their every step.

Before long, the tunnel widened to where they could've walked four across. Soon after that, the tunnel transitioned from uneven rock walls to a proper corridor with walls made of stone blocks, a tiled floor, and unlit torches hanging from the walls and vaulted ceiling.

But the green light still served as the only real light in the space. The runes on Garrick's sword and shield had started to give off a faint yet noticeable glow, but it was only enough to mark his location in relation to the rest of the group, not enough to light their way.

As they progressed through the corridors, they passed several alternate paths branching off both to the right and to the left. They ignored all of them and continued to head toward the green light.

"Aletians," Garrick muttered.

"What about them?" Kent asked.

"This place…" Garrick motioned to the corridors and toward the green light ahead. "They built it. They built the last one, too."

"What's that mean for us?" Aeron asked.

"It means tread carefully."

Aside from having studied the language of the ancient Aletians, Kent didn't know much about them. They had founded the continent, and some said they were descended from the gods themselves, but it had all happened so long ago that Kent couldn't decipher fact from legend.

Whatever the case, they were an extinct race now. Dungeons like this one were among the last remnants of their civilization that hadn't yet been overrun by humans or other races.

As such, Garrick's warning made sense—who knew what kind of dangers they would encounter in a place like this?

Several minutes later, they emerged from the corridors into a vast cavern, perhaps even larger than the one they'd fallen into. Green light permeated the space, and Kent finally saw its source: veins of green crystal glowed throughout the cavern, casting everything in a vivid green hue.

It was scorallite. Tons of it. More than the entire Murothian Army could ever possibly use.

But it was glowing. Whenever Kent had used or seen scorallite before, it didn't glow.

"What is that stuff?" Aeron stared at the walls and ceilings with wide eyes.

"It is a type of crystal called scorallite," Kent said. "When I was the heir to House Etheridge, we would use it to identify mages. If a mage touches scorallite, the crystal draws out their magic by force."

"And then what?" Garrick asked. "You'd kill them?"

"We would try to extract information from them first," Kent replied. He preferred not to think of all of the people like him whom he'd killed or ordered killed over the years. After all, the past was in the past. "And then, yes, we would execute them."

To Kent's relief, Garrick didn't inquire further.

"Must've been quite the shock when you found out you were one of them, huh?" Aeron said.

Kent nodded as he took in the sprawling cavern. "You have no idea."

As enticing as the scorallite looked, Kent decided against touching any of it right from the start. The glow especially set him on edge—if non-glowing scorallite drew magic out of mages, what would the glowing kind do?

It wasn't worth the risk to find out. Not now, anyway. Perhaps some other time.

Water had pooled along a good portion of the floor, all in one spot except for a few sporadic puddles here and there. But thanks to the glowing scorallite in the walls, Kent could see the large pool was shallow.

Upon reflection, it made sense that the place had a lot of water inside. After all, an entire lake lay just beyond the cavern's walls. They had descended pretty far into the dungeon at this point, so the lake could have been *above* them, for all Kent knew.

Whatever the case, the foul smell wasn't as strong in this room. Kent silently thanked the gods for that.

Before them, three gigantic statues carved out of pillars of rock towered over them. Two of them were surprisingly distinct and detailed for having been stuck under a lake for several thousand years.

One was clearly a man—strong, clad in armor with a grandiose helmet on top, and raising what had probably been a sword as if leading a charge. The sword had broken off at the hilt, but the pommel and the lower portion of the hilt still protruded from the bottom of his hand.

The second statue was a woman, also clad in ornately carved armor and extending a spear or a staff into the air. Like the man's sword, most of the spear had broken off. The woman was also missing her left arm at the elbow.

The carving on their faces was intricate and precise to the point that Kent could even see their eyes. Their pupils resembled those of a reptile's eyes, only they lay horizontally instead of vertically.

Kent had to squint to make sure he wasn't imagining it at first, but sure enough, their eyes had been carved that way intentionally.

"Aletians?" Aeron asked.

Garrick nodded. "Probably. From what I've seen, they were an arrogant race of meta-humans. Makes sense that they'd make statues of themselves."

Kent raised an eyebrow. *So do humans.*

Aeron gawked at the statues. "You think they were that big in real life?"

"No idea. If they were, it didn't do them much good when it came time for their race to die out." Garrick pointed toward the statues. "I think I see something between the man and the woman. Let's go."

As they headed deeper into the cavern, Kent got a better look at the third statue.

Where the first two had been incredibly detailed, the third one had been reduced to little more than legs and the lower half of a torso with a huge, smooth gash in the center. A steady drip of water from the ceiling trickled onto that gash, rolled down the front of the statue, and landed in a shallow pool at the base of the rock.

The statue's arms protruded from the pool, broken into several chunks. Over time, the dripping water had worn the stone down.

By the size of the statue's legs, compared to the statue of the woman, Kent figured the eroded statue must've been another male. He briefly wondered what kind of weapon the eroded man might have wielded.

Between the first and second statues, they found a pair of massive doors constructed of blue metal and set into a wall of stone. The metal was etched with swirling vines and leaves and other delicate images, but from the look of it, there was nothing delicate about the doors themselves.

Kent recognized the blue metal immediately—the Inothians had used that same type of metal for shackles.

Unlike scorallite, which drew magic out, this blue metal suppressed it, preventing mages from using magic whatsoever. If these doors were locked, Kent's magic could do nothing to help open them.

As they got closer, Kent noticed a thin slot cut into the two doors at about head height, perpendicular to the line where the two doors met and just above two thick handles made of spiraling blue metal.

Some sort of keyhole, perhaps? But what kind of key was shaped like that?

Aeron stared at them. "That's a pretty awesome set of doors."

"Can you get us inside?" Garrick asked Kent.

Kent shook his head. "These are made of a strange blue metal. I have seen it before, but I never learned what it was called. The scorallite draws magic out, but this blue metal nullifies it. We will need a proper key to access whatever is inside."

"Unless they're already unlocked," Mehta said from the back of the group. The closer they'd come to the light, the farther back he'd slipped until he'd resumed his spot at the rear once again.

Garrick and Kent looked at each other, then Garrick sheathed his sword and strapped his shield to his back. They both headed over and took hold of one of the doors' blue handles. They pulled and hauled, but the doors didn't budge.

When Kent let go, Garrick tried Kent's side. Perhaps he'd thought Kent wouldn't be strong enough to open it, but sure enough, it didn't move for Garrick, either.

"Satisfied?" Kent asked, his voice flat.

"I had to be sure. Don't be so sensitive." He turned to Mehta. "They're locked."

Mehta just shrugged.

"So where's the key?" Aeron asked.

They all looked around as if it might just be lying nearby. It wasn't.

"We passed several alternate paths on our way into this cavern," Kent said. "Perhaps the key may be found down one of those routes? In another room of some sort?"

Garrick inhaled a long breath and exhaled it in a sharp sigh. "The last dungeon was a big runaround. Half of it was fighting bugs and monsters, and the other half was a jaunt across a bunch of platforms over a river of lava and then a climb up a towering rock face. Then there was a rock golem after that."

Kent and Aeron glanced at each other.

Garrick sighed again. "This isn't going to be easy. These sorts of things never are. We're gonna have to do a lot of looking around to find this key. I just hope it's actually in here."

"Why wouldn't it be in here?" Aeron asked.

"Think about it," Garrick said. "When you leave your house, how else do you lock up without a key? And then what do you do with that key when you're done locking up?"

Aeron shrugged. "We didn't really ever lock our house in Govalia. We lived in a pretty safe neighborhood."

"My servants handled the keys at House Etheridge," Kent said.

"I've never had a house of my own," Mehta said. "But I've gotten into plenty of houses without ever using a key."

Garrick rubbed his forehead with his hand. "The point is, they might've taken the key with them. It could be on the other side of the continent, for all we know. And it certainly won't be lying on the floor or in one of these pools, waiting for us to stumble over it. That would be too easy, and the gods have never favored me like that."

"Then let us go look for it," Kent said, "rather than standing around here wasting time."

Garrick stared at him. "We're in Muroth now. By all means, lead the way."

So Kent did.

GARRICK DIDN'T LIKE THIS HELLHOLE AT ALL.

Falling into it had been bad. Landing in the water was worse.

And finding another locked door that needed another key in another dark dungeon probably teeming with more horrific things that wanted to kill him made it nearly unbearable.

The stink of those corridors hadn't helped anything, either.

It wasn't that he wanted to shy away from a fight. Garrick didn't mind facing down any number of weapon-wielding foes that came at him. He could control most of those types of situations easily enough.

No, it was the thought of encountering something like those scorpion-spider hybrids again—scorpers, he'd called them—back in the Etrijan dungeon, or having to fight another foe like the duotaur, or being swallowed whole by the slime monster in the water.

A straight fight was no problem. Anything else drove him close to madness.

But as far as he knew, they were trapped in here anyway. They couldn't get back out the way they'd entered—it was too far up and impossible to climb.

Perhaps he should've insisted that Wafer come along after all. Then they could've flown back up to the temple's grand hall without issue.

At the very least, walking around meant they might also find a way out. If they found Lord Valdis's dragon egg and the tome of rituals, but they couldn't get out, it wouldn't matter.

So Garrick brandished his snow steel sword and shield and followed Kent back toward the tunnel where they'd entered this green cavern.

They backtracked all the way to the first corridor that branched off from the main path, and they started down it. It made sense, strategically, but it still annoyed Garrick anyway.

Without the light from the rocks in the green cavern, the first corridor was dark and foreboding. But Garrick had an answer for that.

He strapped his shield to his back, sheathed his sword, and pulled the red vial from his pack—the last one from Irwin's original stash. They'd been using it to help light campfires on these cold winter nights, and now only a few drops remained.

Irwin's legacy, reduced to a few drops. Garrick shook his head. He couldn't wait to get out of here and find Noraff and Phesnos. Neither could the mage steel knife in his belt.

He grabbed for a torch from the wall, but the one he grabbed was mounted there and not a separate torch sitting in a bracket. So he grunted and ripped it out of the wall, spraying the others with rocks and dust.

Garrick didn't apologize. They would survive.

He anchored his teeth around the cork and popped it out of the vial. Then he poured a single drop of the red liquid onto the torch. It ignited the ancient pitch which immediately burned hot and bright.

Garrick handed the torch to Aeron, then he replaced the cork, tucked the vial away in his pack, and drew his weapons once again.

Kent reached into Aeron's fire and took some into his hand, and they walked side-by-side, lighting the other torches mounted along the walls as they advanced.

Before long, they'd traversed the entire corridor, entered all of the rooms adjacent to it, and found nothing of note beyond a few rats that quickly scurried away into the shadows or into holes in the walls or floors.

It both pleased and unsettled Garrick that they hadn't found anything of consequence. He hoped it meant they were closing in on something of importance.

But it might've also meant his fears were valid—perhaps there wasn't a key in here at all. Perhaps there wasn't a dragon egg beyond those blue doors, either.

The corridor ended at an intersection that led two different directions: left or right. Kent took them to the right.

Garrick wanted to remind him to keep track of where they were heading, but he reasoned that the torches they'd lit along the way would serve that purpose well enough. Even so, torches could go out, so Garrick tracked their progress as well.

Deeper and deeper into the dungeon they delved, and Garrick began to worry if they'd wandered into an actual Aletian labyrinth. Growing up, he'd heard myths about labyrinths, about men entering with the hopes of finding priceless treasures and never again finding their way out.

Along with tales of sea monsters and bloodthirsty beasts of the land, labyrinths made frequent appearances in the bedtime stories Garrick's father had told him. He later realized they were all born of cruelty rather than love, so he'd written most of them off as fables and legends designed to inspire nightmares.

But now that he was down here, he wasn't so sure anymore.

They turned another corner and lit several more torches, and as they advanced, the wretched smell of the place intensified. Whatever they were approaching, it stank of filth and death many times over.

Garrick wanted to vomit, but he held back. It had been so long since he'd eaten anything that nothing would've come up anyway.

Kent started to lead them into a room off that corridor, but he and Aeron stopped short and covered their mouths and noses with their forearms. They both moaned.

Garrick and Mehta approached quickly, and they both reacted in kind when the smell hit them. They'd certainly found the source of the odor.

Inside the room lay several piles of excrement, piles of bones, and piles of both of them mixed together. Filth and death, many times over.

Garrick wished he'd brought his cloak down, or something—anything—to cover his face. Anything to block out the smell.

"This is revolting," Kent said.

"I doubt the key's in there." And even if it was, he didn't want to go looking for it. Garrick's eyes had actually started watering, and he could even taste the smell when he spoke. His stomach flipped in his belly, and he almost puked. "Let's get out of here."

They moved past the room in a hurry.

The smell had been abhorrent, but what alarmed Garrick more was that something within this dungeon had piled those bones and had left excrement specifically in that room. Whatever had done it had demonstrated a degree of intelligence and forethought.

And it ate meat.

Garrick kept his sword and shield ready.

The farther away from that room they moved, the less the smell bothered them, but when they reached the next intersection, Kent stopped their progress.

He turned back to face them, and the light from the orange-and-blue fire burning on his hand illuminated the side of his face. "We have encountered this intersection before."

Garrick caught up and stared down the two paths available to them. Neither one had any torches lit. "There's no light in either direction."

"Kent is right," Mehta said. "I've been tracking our progress. We came from the right, but now those torches are no longer burning."

Garrick peered down the dark corridor. If it were just Kent saying it, Garrick would've continued to doubt his assessment.

But with Mehta saying it too, as precise as he was, he couldn't be wrong. Garrick must've lost track somewhere along the line. Maybe the smell had thrown him off.

From their location in these corridors, they couldn't see the green light from the large cavern anymore. So Garrick wasn't sure where they'd ended up in relation to it.

His father's old labyrinth stories resurfaced in his memory, but he pushed them aside. He refused to get lost in an abyss like this place.

"Did someone put them out?" Aeron asked.

"It could've been wind," Garrick said, though he didn't really believe that. Not after the bones and the dung heaps they'd just seen. "Or maybe the pitch burned up."

"In *all* of the torches?" Kent said. "Unlikely. And Aeron's torch is still burning."

"It's not good, whatever it is," Mehta said.

"I believe we are being followed," Kent said. "Or worse, something or someone is trying to trap us down here. Trying to confuse us."

"Should we even bother lighting torches along the way anymore?" Aeron asked.

"It would be safer to mark the walls instead," Kent held up his burning hand. "I can do it."

He blasted the wall with a concentrated stream of fire and seared an arrow pointing to the right.

"So you're marking the way out?" Garrick guessed.

"Precisely."

"As long as you get it right."

"If he doesn't, I will," Mehta said.

"Shouldn't we be more concerned that something is following us?" Aeron asked.

"I've got the rear," Mehta said. "Nothing's going to sneak up on me."

Despite the creepy vibe Mehta tended to exude, he never seemed to lack confidence. Better yet, in practice, Mehta had actually measured up to it. Garrick rarely saw such consistent capability in anyone, let alone personal awareness of it.

"Should we double back and see if we can catch whoever or whatever is behind us instead?" Aeron suggested. "Then we don't have to worry about looking over our shoulders."

As if in response, something scraped at the opposite end of the corridor they'd just come down. They turned to look.

All the torches in that corridor were still lit, and Garrick saw nothing in it at all.

Then the scraping happened again.

Garrick raised his sword. He was tired of wandering around in the dark with nothing to kill. It was time for some action. "I'm going for it."

"Wait," Kent said. "It may just be another rat."

"Rats don't put out torches." A wretched thought hit Garrick's mind, one of a huge rat scurrying after them, snuffing the torches with its wiggling haunches. He decided not to entertain that as a possibility.

He started down the corridor.

As he approached the room with the bones and the excrement, he inhaled a quick breath and held it as he stormed past.

Then something hit him from the side and slammed him into the wall.

CHAPTER EIGHTEEN

When the dark green blur launched out of the side room and collided with Garrick, it actually startled Mehta—something that didn't happen often. He hadn't examined the room closely enough because of its horrible smell, and he had clearly missed something.

Mehta had been the first one to follow Garrick, and he was the first one to reach him and the beast attacking him. He leaped onto the beast's back and jammed his knives into its neck and back repeatedly.

Its scaly skin was hard, and if Mehta hadn't stabbed with full force, his knives wouldn't have pierced through. The blood that came out was dark— maybe even black.

The beast writhed and grabbed back at him with talon-tipped, webbed fingers. Mehta dodged its reaches and kept stabbing, driven by his thirst.

Garrick had recovered and now looked at the beast with rage-filled eyes. He drew his sword back to skewer the beast.

If Mehta hadn't seen it, Garrick might've run him through as well, but he slid off the beast's back and dropped low to the floor.

Garrick's sword burst through the beast's thick hide the next instant, and the beast tumbled backward, tripped over Mehta's crouched body, and hit the floor.

Mehta mounted the beast and drove his knives into its chest and throat, flinging dark blood on the walls. When it stopped moving, Mehta stood up and faced the room with the bones, his knives ready for more.

Nothing else came out except the rancid stink of death.

"What was that?" Aeron asked as he and Kent approached.

Mehta didn't look away. The smell threatened to suffocate him, but his thirst was stronger. If more of them appeared, he would sift them.

"Garrick..." Aeron said. "You're bleeding."

Mehta glanced back.

Red lines streaked from Garrick's forehead, through his eyebrow, and down the left side of his face. Matching lines marked the skin on Garrick's right arm.

Had it... scratched him?

More importantly, how had its claws managed to pierce Garrick's skin?

Garrick dropped his shield and dabbed at his face. Blood came back on his fingers. He snarled at the sight of it, stormed past Mehta, and hauled the beast up by one arm.

For the first time, Mehta got a good look at its face. Though it was human in shape and had a scale-covered hide, its face looked halfway between that of a fish and a lizard, with bulbous white eyes, an underbite, and prickly, narrow teeth jutting out of its wide, lipless mouth.

Two tiny nostrils marked either side of its snout, and what looked like gills gaped open in its neck, distinct against the various stab wounds Mehta had inflicted. More wounds punctuated its yellow underbelly and chest, and bloody ice crystals had formed in the single large wound in its gut where Garrick had impaled it.

It had reversed knee joints and webbing between its toes, which spread wide and were also tipped with talons. The same dark green scales covered its shins and thighs as everywhere else, except for its chest and stomach.

Garrick held its wrist and hacked its arm off at the elbow, and the beast's body slumped back down to the floor. Instead of its severed arm bleeding, more ice crystals sealed up both exposed ends.

Garrick studied the beast's talons. "I don't know how or why these can cut me, but they can."

He flung it aside, stepped forward, and slammed his sword down onto the beast's head. It split open like a melon, and its frozen brain rolled out of its skull in two halves.

"Gods, I hope there are more of them," Garrick said.

Mehta didn't mind the idea of more foes to sift. It would help to occupy his thirst, which had awakened after helping to bring down this thing.

"What is it?" Aeron asked.

"The last time I encountered something and didn't know what it was, I gave it a name," Garrick said. "So these things are fishcrocs."

Kent shook his head. "That is a terrible name."

"It's clearly part fish, part crocodile." Garrick motioned toward it. "There is no better name for it."

"I can think of a half-dozen right off the top of my head," Kent countered.

"Doubtful."

Kent started counting them on his fingers. "Darkfish. Lurktiles. Gatorfish. Reptides. Gillfangs—"

"Alright, alright." Garrick picked up his shield. "Point taken."

"You did not allow me to say my best one."

Garrick sighed. "Fine. What is it?"

Kent smirked. "Crocfish."

"I hate you." Garrick reluctantly added, "Reptides is a better name, though."

The scrape sounded at the far end of the hall again, and Mehta turned to look. So did everyone else.

Then the dead beast's body jerked into the room of bones.

᪥

AERON ALMOST DROPPED HIS TORCH. HE FUMBLED IT WHEN THE REPTIDE'S BODY lurched into the room, but he managed to catch it one-handed, as he still had his spear out, too.

But when two more reptides sprung at him from within the putrid darkness, he went ahead and dropped the torch anyway. Aeron backed up and impaled one with his spear, but the other one soared at him uninhibited—

Until a blast of fire knocked it aside and sent it tumbling down the corridor away from them. Aeron watched it until the reptide he'd skewered started squirming and trying to reach for him.

He slammed it onto the floor, and Garrick's heavy boot crushed its head with a wet *crack*. Kent ran past them both, his hand still pumping fire at the other reptide.

Mehta ran the other way, facing yet another reptide that had emerged from the other end of the corridor.

Aeron was going to follow Mehta, but then Garrick's sword fell from his hand and clattered onto the stone floor. Aeron looked over at him, and Garrick teetered toward him with a dazed look in his eyes.

"Oh, no..." Aeron dropped his spear, grabbed Garrick's torso, and tried to pin him against the wall to keep him upright. "Kent? Mehta?"

Gods, he's heavy... Aeron shifted his legs to try to better stabilize Garrick.

"Feel... weak..." Garrick said. "Poison."

Aeron cursed. He called, "Guys... their talons are poisoned!"

As Aeron started to shift again, his lower back erupted in brutal, white-hot pain from the added weight of trying to hold Garrick up. Aeron's knees buckled, and they both went down.

The impact didn't hurt much, but only because Aeron's back was already killing him and because Garrick somehow didn't land on him when they fell. They both lay there, Garrick unable to move and Aeron unwilling to try.

But if Aeron didn't get a shroom for his back, he didn't know when he'd be able to get back up again. And if he couldn't get up, he couldn't fight. He couldn't help.

He glanced up at Kent, who had charred the first reptile to a crisp and now held off two others with a wall of fire he'd ignited from the floor to the ceiling. The reptiles were shielding their eyes from the light or from the heat —or maybe both—but there was no guarantee the fire would keep them at bay.

In the other direction, Mehta had already slain two more of them, but a third was giving him trouble.

With great pain, Aeron pulled the pack off his back, reached in, and removed a shroom. It wasn't the right kind, so he put it back and fished around again. He found another one—with yellow spots—and devoured it.

Garrick moaned next to him. "Must... get up."

He tried to get his arms under himself, but he slumped onto his side.

Aeron wanted to tell him to take it easy, but based on the increasing threat around them, having Garrick up and fighting would make a huge difference. Besides, wasn't Garrick supposed to heal faster? Did that apply to poison, or whatever this was, as well?

Aeron's shroom wouldn't kick in for another few minutes at least, and by then, they might be overrun. But he'd fought through pain before—many times. And he'd survived life itself without Wafer at his side for a time.

If he could do it then, he could do it again now. His friends needed his help, and he needed to help them.

He rolled onto his stomach and pushed himself up to his knees. The pain in his back flared, but he resisted it and reached for his spear.

KENT'S FLAMES HAD FELLED TWO OF THE REPTIDES, BUT MORE OF THEM HAD gathered at his wall of fire and started advancing toward him, forcing him backward down the corridor. He'd already directed magic through both of his hands, flooding the space in front of him with an inferno, but it wouldn't be enough.

He'd passed Mehta on his way to confront the reptides on this end, but where were Aeron and Garrick? Did Mehta need so much help on the other end of the corridor that they'd both rushed to his aid?

When Kent glanced back for a look, he saw Aeron and Garrick both lying on the floor. He cursed. What had happened?

Aeron had yelled something at him about poison talons. Kent hadn't processed the words at the time—he'd relegated them to the back of his mind and instead focused on the threat at hand.

But now it registered. If they could break Garrick's skin, and their talons secreted some sort of venom, it would explain why Garrick went down. Had Aeron been scratched as well?

The reptides ahead of Kent burst through the flames and lurched toward him. He redirected all of his magic into one, and its hide ignited with fire. It wailed, but the next one made it past and swiped at Kent.

He stepped back, but the reptide kept coming, kept swiping. He shifted his focus and poured his magic out, trying to incinerate the one nearest to him instead. Fire ate into its chest, and it squealed as the first one had.

Pain raked across his right forearm, and the fire billowing from that hand stopped. One of the reptides had clawed through the fabric of Kent's tunic and into his flesh.

The wounds weren't deep, but blood oozed from his open skin. If these things were venomous, then they had already afflicted Kent.

He resolved that if he was going to die, he would die fighting.

Kent continued to back up to avoid further damage, and as he did, he drew his sword.

The reptide that had scratched him lunged forward again, and Kent slashed at its head. The sword cut through its face and into the bone beneath, and the reptide went down.

Another one leaped at him, and Kent sidestepped and split its gut open with his blade. The reptide's steaming innards splattered onto the stone floor, and it lay there, writhing in its own blood.

Then Kent's vision went hazy, and his legs weakened. His next step faltered, and he stumbled to one knee. Exhaustion racked his entire body as he tried not to lose focus on the fire magic in his hand. If the fire went out, he could no longer use it until he found another source.

Another reptide barreled toward Kent, but he couldn't raise his sword to defend. His arm refused to obey. The reptide was going to overtake him, and there was nothing he could do about it.

Then Aeron's spear pierced through the thing's chest, and it hit the floor.

Kent hit the floor right after it, and he struggled to keep his eyes open. Was he really going to perish here? He hadn't killed Fane yet. Or Kymil. Would he die so unfulfilled?

Aeron fended off two more of them before they overpowered him as well, clawing at the gaps between his armor and at his face. Before long, he went down as well.

The last thing Kent saw before his eyes closed was a half-dozen more reptides entering the hall beyond Aeron.

❦

WHEN GARRICK WOKE UP, HE COULDN'T MOVE HIS ARMS OR HIS LEGS. HIS HEAD lolled forward and back, and his stomach swirled with bile. It was even hard to breathe, and he couldn't see anything but dark blurs intermixed with a lot of green light.

Somehow he was upright—something was holding him in place, but he wasn't quite standing. He was anchored there, somehow suspended by his arms and legs.

He kept blinking, and the blurriness gradually sharpened. His head stopped bobbing on its own, and his neck regained some strength. He looked around.

Garrick was in a cavern like the one with the blue-doored vault—or whatever it was—only smaller and without a vault. Instead, he stared up at a rock formation with a flat top maybe six feet above his head.

Rough, uneven stairs carved into the rock led up one side, and some sort of misshapen stone chair sat atop the formation. Maybe some sort of throne?

When he looked down, he saw the edge of a ledge, and then a massive pit full of darkness below him. It had to spread twenty feet across, and it stank of death and decay.

A stone path led around the pit to the stairs along the rock formation on one end. On the other end, he saw an opening in the cavern, but he couldn't make out much more than that.

The path was wide enough for several people to stand shoulder to shoulder, but on the side opposite of the pit, it dropped off into what looked like a chasm. Garrick didn't want to think about what was at the bottom on the other side.

He tried to move his arms, but they were restrained. Metal clamped his wrists to a pair of boards jutting out at opposite diagonals. When he looked down at his feet, he saw similar clamps locking his ankles to the same two boards.

By some miracle, he still wore his leather breastplate, his boots, and the rest of his clothes, but his sword and shield were gone. He suspected they'd taken the green-handled mage steel knife that Noraff had stabbed him with as well. It wasn't in his belt anymore.

Someone had affixed him to an X-shaped cross, which explained why his head had kept bobbing back and forth when he'd awakened. There was nothing to rest his head against.

It also explained why it was harder to breathe. With his arms raised above his head, he had to pull himself up to draw a full breath.

Had the reptiles done this to him?

He looked to the left and saw Kent hanging from another X, and beyond him, Aeron hung from yet another. Both of them were still unconscious. Their X-crosses also stood on the stone ledge overlooking the pit below.

Would they wake up like Garrick had? Or had the troll blood in his veins spared his life?

Whatever the case, *he* was awake, and *he* needed to find a way out of this. He couldn't count on anyone but himself.

But when Garrick looked beyond Aeron, he didn't see a fourth X, nor did he see one to the right. He didn't see Mehta.

Had Mehta escaped? Had he left them to die?

Or was he already dead?

Mehta didn't seem like the type to ever stop fighting. Perhaps he'd resisted until the end, and they'd killed him for it.

Whatever the case, he wasn't there, but Garrick, Kent, and Aeron were. And the reptiles purposely hadn't killed them—they'd secured them to X-crosses and positioned them over a pit of death.

It made very little sense. Why not just kill them?

Garrick looked down again. The pit was darker than the rest of the cavern, but he could see well enough to realize it had some sort of bottom.

And he could see something down in it—or rather many somethings. Maybe they were bones? Whatever they were, they lay scattered along the pit floor, unmoving.

As far as Garrick could tell, they were alone in the cavern. He pulled at his restraints, but they wouldn't move.

He braced his butt against the center of the boards, where they intersected, and tried to pull with his arms and legs. The boards bent, and the clamps groaned, but he couldn't achieve much beyond that.

Worse still, when he released the tension, the boards wobbled and rocked, creeping him closer to the edge of the ledge. He held his breath and stiffened, hoping he wouldn't topple over into the pit.

The boards stopped rocking and went still, and Garrick exhaled a shaky breath. The board on his left leg was only inches away from the edge.

He still wasn't back to full strength—he felt weaker than usual. He felt like… a normal human. It was miserable. How did all the other men in Aletia cope with being so weak all the time?

He looked over at Kent. No wonder he had worked so hard at mastering magic. If his strength was this pitiful all the time, he needed *something* to give him an edge in combat.

But it was, perhaps, Kent's magic that could set them free from their bonds now, if Garrick's strength didn't return soon enough.

"Kent," he hissed, and the cavern echoed his voice back to him.

That was bad. He hadn't been loud at all, but the cavern had sent his word back to him at nearly the same volume.

Still, if Kent were alive, he could probably magic his way out of his irons in no time. It was worth the risk to try again.

"Kent!" Garrick called, even louder. Again, the cavern echoed him, but Kent didn't even stir. Garrick called Aeron's name next, but he didn't move, either.

A low growl sounded below them.

Garrick didn't move. That sound hadn't come from one of the reptiles. He slowly peered over the ledge and into the pit, but he didn't see anything in the darkness below.

Then something moved, quick and sudden, a shadow within a shadow. And then it was gone.

Garrick shuddered, albeit involuntarily. If he could've stopped himself from doing it, he would have, but the sensation had snuck up on him. Besides, no one had seen him do it anyway.

He needed to get out of there. Garrick grunted and strained against his bonds again, pulling even harder this time than he had before. The boards bent, and the metal clamps issued another faint groan.

His muscles burned, still weak, yet stronger than a few moments earlier. When he felt like he was running out of energy, he slowly released the tension on the boards instead of just letting them snap back into place. As a result, the X didn't wobble, and he didn't end up any closer to the ledge.

"*Kent!*" he outright shouted this time. His voice hollered back at him from the cavern walls, but Kent still didn't awaken.

Garrick really would have to do this alone.

The low growl sounded again from below.

Maybe if Garrick just waited, he'd regain enough of his strength to break out. If he kept shouting, then the thing below him might wake up or realize he was there. It wasn't worth the risk.

But just when he'd decided to shut up, a new sound filled the cavern—a sort of rumble from somewhere beyond the cavern. It swelled into a rhythmic slapping like the patter of rain on a rooftop. It was getting closer.

Garrick looked down. About ten feet below him, a column of reptiles padded into the cavern from an opening in the wall below.

Their webbed feet smacked the floor at random intervals, and they swayed with each step. There had to be at least three or four dozen of them.

The reptiles followed the path around the pit toward the rock formation with the throne on top, but none of them ascended the stairs. Some continued to shuffle around the edge of the pit, and they stood there, looking up at Garrick and the others and then looking down into the pit again.

At least, it seemed like that's what they were doing. With their cloudy, bulbous eyes, Garrick couldn't tell where they were actually looking.

They chattered and screeched like a bunch of chickens, with some gurgles and slurps mixed in as well. Another low growl sounded from the pit, and they all quieted momentarily, then they resumed their dialogue as before.

A loud whoop split the cavern's foul air, and the reptiles fell silent once more. They all turned toward the rock formation and looked up.

Garrick looked up at it as well.

Heavy webbed feet smacked the top of the platform, and a hulking figure approached the edge. It was another reptile but nearly double the size of any of the ones down below.

It had a round, yellow belly, a thicker neck, and broad, muscled shoulders, but otherwise it looked identical to the others. It also dragged some sort of sword behind it.

The weapon was huge—easily big enough that Garrick would have to wield it with two hands because of its length and girth. Perhaps it had been forged for an Aletian who would've only needed one hand to wield it.

Red gemstones glinted from its hilt, which was a greenish color. Its blade was dingy metal, but it might've just been dirty or tarnished from a lack of care. As far away as Garrick was, he couldn't tell for sure.

A weapon like that didn't deserve to be dragged along the floor or held by a dirty, webbed hand. Garrick couldn't see much detail on it from that distance, but if it had originated in this dungeon, he'd find a way to get ahold of it.

That is, if he survived whatever these small-brained jackasses had in store for him.

The big reptide sat in the rocky throne and leaned back, still holding the sword. He gurgled and squawked, and the reptides below answered with a series of chirps.

Was Garrick looking at the reptide version of a king?

He scoffed at the idea that even wretched beasts like these followed a hierarchy of some sort.

The reptides turned back toward the pit and started stomping their feet, first in unison. Then the stomping broke into a free-for-all trample. They added in screeches and warbles, and over it all, another low growl sounded.

But this time, it only grew louder.

The reptides kept up their concert until the king bellowed something in their language—if Garrick could call it that—and then they all fell silent.

Then several of the reptides pushed one of their own into the pit.

The victim reptide tumbled down into the pit, screeching and scraping for purchase but finding none. It hit the bottom, from what Garrick could tell from the low light, and it immediately scraped and scratched against the rocks, trying to find a way out. All the while, it loosed desperate squeals.

The low growl sounded anew, and Garrick saw something shadowy in the pit move again. Then the reptide shrieked, and its scraping intensified.

The low growl became a low roar, and the pit floor started moving.

A gaping mouth opened, glowing with pale, orange light and revealing dozens of rows of sharp teeth, curved inward, along the roof of its mouth.

The pit floor was *alive*.

Tendrils on either side of its mouth extended out and coiled around the reptide's ankles first, then up its legs to its waist. Though the reptide struggled and strained and screeched, the tendrils continued to reel it in closer.

Finally, it dumped the reptide into its gaping mouth and chomped down on it. The reptide got out one final screech before the pit beast's teeth shredded it beyond recognition.

Garrick frowned. He'd imagined his death dozens of times, but he'd never pictured anything like *this*. He'd always hoped he'd die quickly and painlessly, or at worst, with very abrupt, very temporary pain.

But the combination of those teeth and his extra durable skin meant he'd survive longer than anything else this pit beast had ever eaten. It would hurt for far longer, and far worse, than anything Garrick could've conceived of.

He envied Kent and Aeron. If they were already dead, or at least asleep, from the reptides' toxins, they would go to their deaths in violent ignorance.

He envied Mehta even more. Whether he'd escaped or perished in that foul-smelling corridor, he was better off than Garrick, too.

With the reptide now devoured, the pit beast's mouth gaped open once more, and its tendrils lashed back and forth, searching for more prey.

The bulky reptide king motioned toward Garrick, and the dozens of reptides below all turned to look up at him as well.

Then Garrick heard the familiar sounds of scraping talons and smacking feet approaching him from behind.

CHAPTER NINETEEN

Mehta wasn't dead, but neither had he entirely escaped.

When Garrick went down, Mehta had taken one side to try to fend off the reptides approaching from that end of the corridor. He'd felled two of them before he heard Aeron's warning of poisoned talons.

The warning itself hadn't shifted his tactics all that much, but Mehta took extra care to make sure he wouldn't sustain so much as a prick from their talons. His thirst and his training had taken care of the rest.

But then the reptides had broken through Kent's wall of fire and overpowered him, and when Aeron rushed over to help, they took him down as well. It became clear that there were too many for Mehta to defeat, so he abandoned the fight and fled, much to his thirst's dismay.

He found a hiding place in one of the rooms off the corridor and waited until he no longer heard any reptide-like sounds, and then he quietly emerged from his secret nook. Sure enough, they were all gone.

Mehta crept back to the corridor where they'd been battling. He'd expected to find his comrades torn apart and possibly devoured down to the bone, based on what he'd seen in that wretched-smelling room.

But instead, he only found the bodies of the reptides they had slain, stacked into a new pile in that same refuse room.

Without any light, Mehta couldn't distinguish between the colors of the blood on the stone floors, so he didn't know if they'd killed his comrades before taking them away or not, but their bodies were nowhere in sight.

Perhaps less strangely, the reptides had ignored their weapons and their packs and left those behind. They'd even left behind the green-handled knife Garrick always wore in his belt.

So Mehta gathered up their weapons and stashed them all back in his hiding spot. If they were still alive, they'd need them later.

Mehta intended to learn their fates, one way or another. If they were dead, he would try to complete the quest without them. And if they were alive and could be saved, he would try to save them. Getting out of this place would be easier if he wasn't alone.

He considered wielding Garrick's sword and shield, but they were too large for him to use effectively. Even if he'd used the sword with two hands, he doubted he'd be as efficient as with his knives. The same went for Kent's sword and Aeron's spear.

In the end, he stuck with his knives. Compared to the reptides' talons, he still had a slight reach advantage, and without switching to larger weapons, he could more easily outmaneuver them in fights.

They were fast, but he was faster. They fought out of instinct, but he had been relentlessly trained. Their only advantage was in their numbers. If Mehta could defend against getting overwhelmed, he could sift every last one of them.

And his thirst welcomed the opportunity.

Mehta crept through the dungeon's corridors for close to an hour, listening and trying to pursue the reptides. In that time, he learned to distinguish between the skittering of rats and the scrape of reptide talons against stone.

Along the way, he noticed a bit of green light coming from a path that curved upward, away from the rest of the corridors. He followed it and found a chunk of scorallite in the wall, casting light onto another set of doors made of familiar blue metal.

In the center of the doors was a slot that matched the slot in the other doors exactly. Similar markings of leaves and branches adorned the doors as well.

Mehta made note of these doors and their location. Of all the rooms he'd seen within these corridors, hidden or otherwise, only this spot had doors like that. It had to mean something.

His search for the reptides eventually brought him through a tunnel to another large cavern illuminated by veins of glowing green scorallite. Through the cavern entryway, he saw a hunk of stone sitting atop a rock platform.

And from inside the cavern, he heard Garrick calling for Kent.

Mehta waited. Had Garrick somehow escaped? Or was he trapped somewhere and calling for Kent's help?

Mehta started to advance into the cavern, but at the sound of the approaching reptides below, he stopped. Instead, he waited inside the entryway and watched as they entered the cavern.

They pattered along the wide stone pathway, staying clear of the edge closest to Mehta, which dropped off into some sort of chasm.

A whoop sounded behind Mehta, and he recoiled. He'd been so focused on the gathering of reptides below that he hadn't considered something might be coming through this entryway.

He quickly receded into the shadows of the tunnel and prayed to Laeri that whatever was coming couldn't smell him.

Meanwhile, his thirst prayed that it *would* smell him so he'd have the chance to sift it.

Heavy, wet smacks filled the tunnel, accompanied by the sound of clicking talons and some sort of metal scraping along stone. Then a much larger version of a reptide clomped up the tunnel, right past Mehta, and into the cavern, dragging some sort of massive sword behind it.

Mehta caught sight of a green handle adorned with rubies or garnets, but some sort of grime covered its huge blade, so Mehta couldn't tell whether it would make an effective weapon or not. It was certainly too big for Mehta to wield it with any skill.

The large reptide took a seat on the hunk of rock in the center of the platform, which Mehta now realized was supposed to be some sort of throne. It gargled some gibberish, and the reptides below started stomping and screeching.

What happened next, Mehta couldn't be sure, but with the reptides occupied, he darted out the entryway hid behind the hunk of rock, directly behind the large reptide seated there. A series of desperate screeches and shrieks cut off abruptly.

Mehta peered out from behind the rock and saw Garrick mounted to two boards in an X shape. Beside him were Kent and Aeron, both of whom were either unconscious or dead and also mounted to boards. But Garrick was awake and looking around the room.

And the reptides were all looking up at him.

Below them all lay a gaping pit. Mehta couldn't see what was in it, but whatever it was had clearly killed one of the reptides. Worse yet, another reptide had emerged from a tunnel behind Garrick and to his left.

Mehta put it all together—the reptide was going to push Garrick into the pit next.

Not if I can help it.

He emerged from his cover behind the throne, ran past the large reptide seated on it, and leaped off the edge of the rock platform down toward Garrick's ledge.

The reptides chattered below, and Mehta caught sight of something orange glowing within the pit, but his focus didn't stray from the reptide standing near Garrick's X.

He slammed into the reptide, leading with his knees and his knives, and both hit their intended targets.

They went down together, into the tunnel behind Garrick, and Mehta dragged his knives from the reptide's neck down into its chest in a harsh, vicious motion. Blood sprayed out from the wounds and onto Mehta's face and chest, but he didn't care.

Then he sprung up and darted back out to Garrick's X. But before he could get there, Garrick jerked his arms forward and snapped both of the boards in half against his backside.

"Why didn't you do that in the first place?" Mehta asked as he emerged from the tunnel.

Garrick tore the metal shackles holding his wrists in place from the boards. "I was still weak from their toxins. I'm still not back to normal, but I wasn't about to let that thing eat me."

As Garrick set to work on the shackles around his ankles, Mehta peered into the pit below. The light was coming from a hellish orange mouth lined with innumerable curved teeth.

Mehta didn't blame Garrick for not wanting to end up down there.

"Where's my sword?"

"Safe." Mehta kept his focus on the swirling mass of reptides below.

They'd started heading back into the tunnel they'd used to enter the cavern, all while trying not to topple into the pit. Mehta didn't know for sure, but he guessed they would head straight up to the ledge.

Atop the platform, the large reptide hissed and clawed at the air with one hand. It stalked back and forth along the platform, full of rage, pulling the sword along with each step but still scraping it across the floor.

But it didn't look like it wanted to make the jump. If Mehta had been its size, he wouldn't have gone for it, either—especially not with that pit beast below.

"Kent and Aeron still aren't awake," Garrick said.

"Are they alive?" Mehta asked.

Garrick nodded. "They're breathing, so I think they'll wake up eventually."

"We have to get off this ledge." Mehta was facing the tunnel with the dead reptide in it. "They're coming, and we can't hold that many off for long."

"Are they *all* coming?"

"All except our friend on the platform." Mehta nodded toward the large reptide, who hissed at them again.

"I'd like a piece of him," Garrick said. "We need to jump down to that walkway below. It's the only way."

Mehta faced the tunnel again with his knives ready. "How? Kent and Aeron are asleep."

"I'll carry them and jump."

Mehta gawked at him. "You said you weren't at full strength."

"Whether I am or not, this is our only chance. There's no other way down."

"If you miss, you'll fall into the pit, or you'll fall into that chasm. I couldn't even tell if it had a bottom or not."

"Like I said, this is our only chance," Garrick repeated. "Another scratch from one of those things, and we go right back to sleep. And then we'll get thrown into the pit anyway. Might as well expedite the process."

Mehta wanted to disagree, but Garrick was right—there was no other way.

"Can you hold the others off until I get these two situated?" Garrick had already started pulling on Kent's restraints.

The thirst wanted him to sift every single one of the reptides.

Mehta replied, "Yes, but hurry."

"Obviously," Garrick fired back.

Mehta stole another glance at the large reptide on the platform.

He was still there, fuming and hissing and probably cursing them in whatever tongue he was speaking. He moved as if he meant to wave the sword at them, but he only managed to get it a couple of inches off the ground.

Then a screech sounded from the tunnel leading to the ledge.

Mehta raised his knives as the first of the reptides set upon him.

It lunged for him, and he sidestepped and let it go careening off the ledge on its own, directly into the gaping orange maw of the pit beast. It shrieked all the way down.

Mehta glanced at Garrick. He'd gotten Kent free, hefted him onto his shoulders, and then moved down to Aeron, whose X sat on a narrower part of the ledge. If Garrick lost his step, they would all drop into the pit.

But Mehta couldn't focus on that now. His job was to keep the reptides from reaching Garrick, and that's what he intended to do.

Two more of them scampered down the tunnel toward him, but one of them stumbled over the body of the reptide Mehta had sifted on his way down from the platform. It spaced them out some, which worked in Mehta's favor.

The first one leaped at him, but from farther back. If Mehta had simply moved aside like he had for the last one, it would've still landed on the ledge.

So instead, Mehta timed his reaction and let the reptide fly directly at him. At the last second, he dropped to his back, planted his right foot in the reptide's chest, and helped guide it the rest of the way over his head.

Mehta didn't see it, but based on its trajectory and its shrieks cutting off abruptly, he guessed it fell into the pit beast's mouth as well. He couldn't look because as he stood back up, the other reptide lurched toward him.

Unlike the first two, it didn't jump at all. Instead, it swiped at his head.

Mehta rolled his head under the swipe and slashed his knife across the reptide's belly. Dark blood pulsed out of the wound, and the reptide's hands clutched at his gut, just as the lead cultist had done when Mehta had wounded him.

It was instinct.

But that instinct, combined with a lack of training, had left the reptide exposed, just as Mehta had anticipated.

As soon as Mehta's knife finished slashing open the reptide's belly, his other knife was already thrusting up, under the reptide's exposed chin. The knife plunged deep into the soft tissue.

The blow was probably fatal as it was, but Mehta ducked low and forced his knife to follow. It caught on the inside of the reptide's jaw and Mehta yanked him over his shoulders.

As the reptide's legs tumbled over his body, Mehta pulled his knife free. The reptide fell into the pit, not screeching like the two that had gone before him.

The screeches and scrapes from the tunnel were getting louder, closer, and more numerous. Mehta turned toward Garrick.

He'd gotten Aeron free and was hefting him onto his other shoulder, opposite of Kent.

"Hurry!" Mehta shouted. "They're coming!"

"I know!" Garrick yelled back.

"I mean now!" Mehta waved him forward. "We're about to be overrun. Make your jump now!"

Garrick roared and charged toward him, and Mehta stood with his back flat against the wall to give him space to pass. Garrick stuttered his last few steps, but he jumped anyway.

Mehta jumped immediately after, watching Garrick fall all the way down.

GARRICK LET GO OF AERON ABOUT TWO SECONDS BEFORE THEY HIT THE STONE path below. Aeron's armor clanked against the floor, and he tumbled once, but then he skidded to a halt along the stone.

Garrick's feet hit first, and he cupped the back of Kent's head with his hand, tucked his own chin, and rolled. They came to a stop next to Aeron, and he let go of Kent and laid him flat on his back. All of them lay sprawled out along the stone path.

Garrick looked up in time to see Aeron's torso tipping into the chasm on the side opposite of the pit.

He lashed his hand out and grabbed Aeron's ankle, stopping his descent into the Underworld. Then he got to his knees and hauled Aeron back onto flat ground.

Aeron's teal armor had plenty of new scratches and scrapes, and he was still thoroughly unconscious thanks to the scratch lines on his face, but he seemed fine, otherwise.

Then again, Garrick wondered how Aeron's back would feel once he woke up from all of this. Hopefully when Mehta had stashed their weapons, he'd stashed their packs, too. Aeron would need a magic mushroom to cope, most likely.

Mehta landed just behind Garrick, and he executed a perfect roll into a standing position with his knives still in his hands.

"Showoff," Garrick muttered.

"*You're* the showoff," Mehta countered with a smirk. "I didn't have two grown men on my back."

A heavy, repetitive smacking noise sounded, and Garrick looked up the carved stairs. The reptide king hissed down at them and paced back and forth at the top of the rock formation, still dragging that monstrous sword behind him.

Mehta tossed Garrick one of his knives, and he caught it. "Go claim your piece."

Garrick looked at the knife. Compared to the size of his hand, it was more like a toothpick than a knife. "No thanks. I'm going to crush his ugly skull instead."

Mehta caught the knife. "Suit yourself."

Before Garrick could start climbing the stairs, a series of screeches and shrieks sounded from the ledge they'd just left. He looked up at it.

The reptides had emerged from the tunnel en masse. The ledge couldn't have possibly held them all, and they were in such a rush to get up there that they'd started knocking each other off the ledge and into the pit—and it kept happening.

Garrick loosed a hearty laugh. "Bunch of morons."

"If any of them get back down here, I'll handle them," Mehta said. "Give my regards to your new friend."

Garrick cracked his knuckles. "Oh, I will."

As he started to ascend the stairs toward the reptide king, Garrick tried to think of the last time he'd had a straight-up fistfight with someone.

It had been years since someone had been dumb enough to challenge him to one. Even then, Garrick had just let the guy break his fist against his jaw, and then Garrick finished him off with a single punch of his own.

But he couldn't be so lax with the reptide king. He couldn't let those talons cut him again.

He touched his face where the reptide in the corridor had scratched him. The wounds had already closed, but the skin was still raised as if it had scarred over. By morning, they'd be gone entirely.

When Garrick crested the final step, the reptide king was standing ten feet behind the throne with the sword still at its side, its tip still on the ground. Up close, the beast looked to be right around Garrick's size—height and width included.

Garrick motioned the reptide king forward.

It took two lumbering steps, easily as long as Garrick's stride, and whipped the sword at his midsection. Garrick hopped back, and the sword slashed just beyond his leather armor.

But the swing had left the reptide king exposed, so Garrick closed the gap in two quick steps of his own and slammed his right fist into its face.

Garrick had expected to take it down with one massive punch. A blow like that could've felled a horse, but it hardly fazed the reptide king.

Apparently, it was going to take more than a single well-placed punch.

Its head turned with the blow, and one of its needle-like teeth popped out of its mouth with a spurt of dark blood. Then it screeched at him, tensed its shoulders, and swung the sword again.

Garrick braced his hands against the reptide king's arm to stop his momentum, but a hand tipped with vicious talons reached over the top and slashed at Garrick. He shoved the reptide king back, and the talons swiped through the air, missing Garrick's shoulder by inches.

The reptide king stumbled, and Garrick pressed the advantage. He charged forward and delivered three stunning blows to the reptide king's face before he could get the sword back around.

When the reptide king slashed at him again this time, Garrick caught its right wrist with both hands, stepped under its arm, and wrenched it up hard, the wrong way, behind its back.

Snap.

The reptide king shrieked and struggled, but Garrick didn't let go.

Normally, Garrick would've kicked the back of its knee to drop it lower, but its knees were reverse-jointed. So instead, he stepped forward, positioned his left leg in front of the reptide king's right leg, and yanked its arm farther up along its back.

A series of cracks sounded, and the reptide king tripped over Garrick's leg. It hit the stone floor face first, and the sword clattered out of its left hand.

He pressed down on its broken arm, keeping it locked against its back. Then he pinned it down with his knee, took hold of the reptide king's head with his other hand, and knocked its head against the floor repeatedly until it stopped moving and stopped squealing.

Then he stood to his full height and crushed its head with the heel of his boot.

Dark blood and brains splattered across the stone floor. The reptide king's body twitched once more, then it went still forever.

Garrick stepped over it and picked up the sword. Grime and dust covered the blade, so Garrick ran its flat sides along his pant leg to clean it off.

Absent the grime, the blade gleamed with mirror-bright steel, reflecting green light from the scorallite deposits all around them.

Like his snow steel blade, this sword weighed less than it looked. To his surprise, the blade wasn't worn down or even dull, despite being dragged around by the reptide king. Its edge was perfectly sharp, and the blade didn't have a scratch on it.

Dark-green metal formed the sword's hilt and cross-guard in a series of layered sections that resembled scales, and red gemstones accented the pommel and the center of the cross-guard. Black, scaly leather wrapped the sword's long handle in a series of X shapes, providing Garrick with an excellent grip despite the sword's huge size.

It was a dragon sword. Garrick didn't know if a "dragon sword" was a real thing or not, but that's what it looked like.

He was itching to try it out. Given its weight, he could wield it with one hand if necessary, but it was heavy enough and long enough that it made more sense to use two hands instead.

Garrick rushed down the carved staircase and hurried toward Mehta, who was fending off a trio of reptides that had either found their way back down or managed to jump off the ledge and land on the path.

"Move, Mehta!" Garrick yelled.

Mehta stole a glance back, met Garrick's eyes, and dove aside.

The reptides turned their attention toward Garrick, screeching and hissing at him. He answered with a mighty swing that cut through all three of them in one clean sweep.

The reptiles fell to the stone floor in multiple pieces with a series of wet plops.

Garrick swore. "This thing is amazing!"

Mehta stood up next to him, staring at the blade. "What is it?"

Garrick shook his head. "Some sort of dragon sword. I don't really know, but it's mine."

"I'm glad you like it," Mehta said. "Because we aren't out of this yet."

"Good." Garrick grinned. "Let them come."

⚡

WHEN AERON'S EYES OPENED, ALL HE SAW AT FIRST WAS A BLUR OF GREEN LIGHT. His mind immediately associated it with the scorallite from the cavern with the blue doors, but he didn't understand how he'd ended up back there.

Or perhaps he'd died, and the Underworld was also filled with scorallite?

He blinked, and as his vision slowly came into focus, Aeron realized this wasn't the same cavern they'd found before.

Garrick grunted somewhere nearby, and the sounds of wet chops and stabs mingled with screeches and squeals from the reptiles. A fight? Had he somehow survived the battle in the corridor?

As he tried to sit up for a look, his back protested, and he groaned. He was used to the back pain, but his shoulders and knees felt tender as well, as if they'd been banged or bruised while he was asleep. It made him yearn for a shroom all the more, but his pack wasn't anywhere to be found.

He looked up and saw Mehta and Garrick fending off several reptiles along a stone path. Between the two of them, they were carving through the reptiles at a breakneck speed.

Aeron didn't recognize the sword in Garrick's hands. Perhaps that had something to do with it.

He groped for his spear. Aeron had to help Garrick and Mehta, even if they didn't need it. He was part of the team. He had to contribute.

Kent groaned next to him, and it reminded Aeron of his aching back, knees, and shoulders.

Maybe Aeron could help by checking on Kent instead.

Aeron crawled over to him, still weakened from the reptides' poison. "You alright?"

Kent groaned again, and his eyes opened. "I cannot see."

"It'll come back. It just takes some time," Aeron said.

"I cannot move, either."

"Same thing. I don't think I can stand yet, but I couldn't move a few seconds ago, and now I can."

"Where are we?"

"Some sort of cavern. Not the one with the doors." Aeron looked around again. "I'm not sure."

"How...?"

"I don't have a lot of answers right now. Garrick and Mehta are fighting off a bunch of reptiles over there. I don't know what else to expect."

Aeron managed to get up to his knees. Were it not for the armor on his kneecaps, he didn't think he could tolerate the pain. He might end up taking two shrooms—if he ever saw his pack again.

"Can you help me sit up?" Kent asked.

"Yeah." Aeron reached for him, and they clasped each other's wrists. Aeron leaned back and pulled, and Kent managed to get up into a sitting position.

"I am starting to be able to see," Kent said.

"What about your magic?" Aeron asked. "Do you feel that?"

Kent slowly raised his right hand. Blue light sparked from it. "Seems to be working."

"Good." There was no telling when they might need it again, but it was bound to be soon. Aeron's legs felt stronger, so he tried to stand. He wobbled at first, but he managed to stay upright despite his back pain.

"Help me up?" Kent asked.

"I need a moment." Aeron's head had started to swim, and he had to hold out his arms to regain his balance.

He glanced at Garrick and Mehta again. They were still holding their own against the approaching reptiles, and now, from what Aeron could see, only a few remained.

"Alright." He reached down toward Kent. "Ready?"

Kent took hold of his wrist again, and Aeron hauled him to his feet. He, too, wobbled a bit, but he steadied himself and stood firm. "Thank you."

Ahead of them, Mehta jammed one of his knives into the side of a reptide's head, then he kicked it into the chasm to the left of the stone path. At the same time, Garrick cleaved another one in half from his head down to the bottom of his torso.

Now only one remained, and it stood between Mehta and Garrick, glancing between them with its arms up, ready to strike.

Something whizzed past Aeron's cheek. Before he could turn back to look, a pointed rock embedded in the center of the reptide's face, caving in its skull. Its arms slumped to its sides, and it fell straight back onto the stone path.

Garrick and Mehta looked back, and so did Aeron.

Kent stood there, holding a stone in his hand and grinning. "I hope you will forgive my interruption. I wanted to settle a score with at least one of these abominations before you killed them all."

"Nice of you to help out," Garrick quipped.

"I suppose we have missed quite a bit." Kent started toward them, and Aeron joined him.

"We'd all be dead if it weren't for Mehta." Garrick motioned toward a pit to the right of the path. "Have a look down there."

Aeron glanced at the glowing orange mouth and the tendrils below again. "Thanks for coming back. Big time."

Mehta just nodded.

"It appears you have found something of value." Kent nodded toward Garrick's sword.

Garrick grinned. "Took this off their leader. He's up there, on that platform."

"May I?" Kent held out his right hand.

Garrick extended it toward Kent, pommel-first. "It's some sort of dragon sword, by the look of it."

Kent took it and held it in front of his face. Aeron could see Kent's reflection in it as if he were holding up a mirror.

Aeron had never been much of a sword guy, but that one looked fantastic. Though it was too large for him to properly wield it, as a blacksmith's son, he still admired its craftsmanship.

Pa could've never made something like this.

"It was forged with magic," Kent said. "I can feel it trying to pull at my power, as if it wants me to infuse it with more."

"Yeah, no thanks." Garrick held out his hand. "It's mine."

Kent handed it back to him without any argument. "Fascinating."

Aeron surveyed the dead reptides lying along the path. "Did you get all of them?"

"Only one way to find out." Garrick hefted the dragon sword onto his shoulder and let it rest there.

"Should we check the cavern for anything else of interest?" Kent asked.

Garrick looked at Mehta. "There's a tunnel at the top of the platform. Anything important up there?"

Mehta shook his head. "No. I came into the cavern through that tunnel. It just leads to another set of dungeon corridors."

"Then let's go get our stuff back," Garrick said.

Mehta led them out of the cavern, through the dark corridors, and to a chamber where he'd concealed all of their gear. Aeron snatched up his pack and scarfed down a shroom for his back pain, then he picked up his spear.

Garrick had opted to keep the dragon sword in his hands, so he strapped his snow steel sword and shield to his back. He also tucked his green-handled knife back into his belt. Then Kent sheathed his sword and donned his pack, and they were ready to go.

"Where to?" Aeron asked.

"We pick up where we left off," Garrick said. "Keep roaming through this labyrinth until we find what we need."

Kent stood there, staring at Garrick. Or was he staring at Garrick's new sword?

Garrick noticed. "What? It was *your* idea to canvass these corridors in the first place."

"I wonder if…" Kent started.

"What?"

"I wonder what kind of key is narrow one way and wide the other."

Garrick squinted at him. "What are you talking about? Those toxins still messing with your head?"

"Not remotely," Kent replied. "But I am suggesting that the sword in your hand may be the key itself."

It all made sense to Aeron in that moment. The dragon sword *did* look like it might fit into the strangely shaped keyhole in the two doors.

Garrick looked down at the dragon sword. "You may actually be right about that."

"If nothing else," Kent suggested, "it will give us a chance to rest and reassess our plans going forward."

"You don't have to convince me," Garrick said. "We're going. Come on."

With Mehta's guidance through the darkness yet again, they made their way back to the first cavern.

The ancient statues heralded their return with utter silence, but the persistent dripping of water still sounded all throughout the cavern. All of it was a welcome change of pace from fighting off reptides and avoiding pits with monsters in them.

They splashed through the puddles and made their way to the blue doors. Once they got there, Garrick lined up the dragon sword with the keyhole and slid it inside.

It fit perfectly. Garrick pushed it all the way to its hilt, and it clicked into place.

Garrick didn't bother waiting for Kent. He just grabbed both door handles and pulled.

CHAPTER TWENTY

Nothing happened.

Kent had fully expected the doors to fling wide open and let them inside, but they didn't budge. It was as if nothing had changed, except that they had clearly found a key that fit the lock but wouldn't open the door.

Garrick tried again, and the doors still refused to move. He shifted his full attention to one door, and he pulled and yanked and jerked at it, all to no avail.

Finally, he stood back and studied the door. "I don't understand. This must not be the key."

He reached for the dragon sword and tried to pull it out, but it didn't budge.

"I don't believe this." Garrick cursed and rubbed his eyes with both hands. "What more do the gods want from me?"

"Let me try." Aeron stepped forward and started pulling on the door handles and on the sword. His results matched Garrick's identically.

Mehta went up next to try his luck, and then the three of them began discussing the problem at hand, with Aeron and Garrick doing the majority of the talking.

Kent stood there, observing it all. When he had held the dragon sword for a brief moment, he'd felt it trying to draw magic out of him.

It reminded him of when Fane had placed the scorallite crystal in his hands at their home back in Etheridge, on the day Fane had framed him for their father's murder. The scorallite had forced his magic to manifest, and blue flames had ignited from his hands as a result.

The dragon sword had given him a comparable experience, only not as strongly. It made him wonder if the sword *needed* magic for some reason.

Kent stepped up to the dragon sword's hilt, which extended out toward him at eye level. The Aletians had been taller than humans, so it made sense that their keyholes and handles would be higher up as well.

He reached for it, but he hesitated. He'd tried to use magic with Garrick's snow steel sword, and though it had sent a blast of ice magic into a nearby tree branch, Kent had nearly frozen his hand off in the process.

If this sword was indeed the key to opening these doors—doors that potentially contained a dragon egg inside—what would happen to Kent when he used his magic on it?

"What are you doing?" Garrick asked him.

Well, now Kent had to move forward. He couldn't hesitate with Garrick watching. His pride wouldn't allow it.

So he took hold of the dragon sword's handle with both hands and opened the flow of his magic.

The sword inhaled Kent's magic as if gasping for air, and instead of trying to take of the sword's essence, Kent simply let the magic flow out of him. The red gemstones on the dragon sword's pommel and at the cross-guard glowed crimson, and then the inside of the lock began to shine with golden light.

The light filled the crack between the doors until it both touched the floor and ascended up to the top of the doors. Inside, metal clanked and churned until it finally stopped with a heavy *clunk*. Then the light emanating from within the door darkened to nothing.

The dragon sword pulled out of the lock with ease, and Kent held it in both of his hands. Its blade glowed with golden light so brilliant, it made it difficult for Kent to see past it.

Kent slowed the flow of his magic, and the light gradually faded until the blade radiated a warm, golden glow.

Garrick, Aeron, and Mehta had all been shielding their eyes with their hands, but as the light faded, they lowered their hands and stared at him.

"I guess it likes you better," Garrick said.

"Not necessarily." Kent tossed the sword back to him, and Garrick caught it one-handed. The residual glow faded from it immediately. "But it did like my magic better."

Then Kent turned, pulled the doors open, and led them inside.

⚜

MEHTA HAD NEVER SEEN ANYTHING LIKE IT.

The interior of the room resembled a sort of arena-like space, illuminated by veins of scorallite running through the walls. But these scorallite veins followed a noticeable diagonal pattern—they each streaked down the upper walls in regular intervals.

The scorallite terminated at a circular wall of stone blocks that formed the lower third of the arena's perimeter. It looked to be about equal to Kent's height, or perhaps a bit shorter.

The doors slammed shut behind them, and the same heavy *clunk* sounded again, sealing them inside.

Mehta scanned the arena and found no other exits. The blue doors were the only obvious way in or out.

"I take it we're stuck in here, now?" Garrick asked no one in particular.

"I believe so," Kent replied. "There is no keyhole on this side, and the doors..." He shoved against them, and nothing happened. "...refuse to move. And my magic cannot do anything against this blue metal."

"Great," Garrick said. "Then we need to find a way to get them open."

"*If* they open," Aeron muttered.

Garrick shot him a glare.

"What?" Aeron held out his open palm. "For all we know, this was just an elaborate trap, and now we'll be stuck in here forever."

Somehow, Mehta doubted that, but he didn't speak up. Why would anyone lock them in an arena-like room as a prison cell?

No. They were clearly meant to battle someone—or something—in here. But there was no one else in the room.

Then a thought occurred to Mehta. *Are we supposed to fight each other?*

It didn't make sense why that would be the case, but if it came down to it, Mehta would be ready. Based on the others' behavior, they hadn't yet considered that as a possibility. It gave him an edge, should he need one.

Tiny rocks and sand covered the stone floor, almost like those at a shoreline or a riverbed. In the center of the floor stood a pyramid of sorts, but only about the size of Garrick and with a flat top instead of a point.

It was made of the same blue metal as the doors, and it bore the insignia of a four-pointed star with an eye in the center. But the eye's pupil was elongated and stretched horizontally like that of a goat's eye, or a lizard's eye turned sideways, just like the eyes of the statues of the Aletians outside this room.

Mehta could've been fine with the understanding that rooms shaped like arenas probably were arenas, and they were about to walk into some sort of battle.

He could've been fine with knowing there weren't any other ways out.

And he could've been fine if the room's weirdness had stopped there.

But it didn't.

Instead of a stone ceiling, a shallow pool of water rippled above their heads. Mehta could see the actual ceiling through the water between ripples.

"What in the third hell...?" Aeron saw him looking and gawked up at it. "That's not... that doesn't make any sense."

"Magic." Garrick spat into the sand.

Kent eyed him, and Garrick frowned.

"No offense," he said.

"I do not like the look of that water," Kent said.

Garrick shrugged. "It's just water."

"...suspended on the ceiling."

"Yeah. Means we're not getting wet." As Garrick said it, a drop of water hit the end of his nose. He wiped it off. "That doesn't count."

"It does not at all concern you that a pool of water is hovering over our heads?" Kent asked.

"As long as we get what we came for, I don't care if a bear strolls in and pisses into it from the side." Garrick nodded toward the blue pyramid in the center. "I'm guessing that's where we'll find our quarry. If you're scared, you can stay here."

"Your attempts to mischaracterize my concern are as unfounded as usual." Kent started toward the pyramid first, leaving Garrick trailing behind him.

Aeron followed next, and Mehta brought up the rear like he preferred to do. And in a room this well lit thanks to the scorallite, they didn't have to rely on his enhanced vision to get them around.

Mehta made a mental note to make sure they brought their own torches if they planned on entering any more dungeons in the future.

The top of the pyramid contained a slot comparable to the one in the blue doors, so Garrick inserted the dragon sword into the slot and pushed it all the way in until it clicked. Then he stepped aside and motioned to it.

"Go ahead," he said to Kent. "Do your thing."

Kent stepped forward and wrapped both hands around the dragon sword's hilt. And the instant he did, every ounce of the water hovering along the ceiling fell.

It drenched them, and the sand-and-rock mix on the floor absorbed some of it, but there had been enough that it filled the arena floor up to their ankles.

It was cold water, too—nearly ice cold—and the sensation shocked Mehta for an instant. Then he shook his head and shook out his arms, allowed himself to shiver hard, and his body temperature began to recover.

Mehta had expected the others' reactions to vary as to their personalities, but instead, they all just started swearing and cursing. Apparently, frigid water was a great equalizer of men.

But as the others slung profanity around like fishing nets, Mehta noticed the water moving. It wasn't just rippling the way water usually did. It was *moving*. Shifting. Consolidating.

"Guys?" he said, wide-eyed. "The water is—"

Something pulled Mehta's feet out from under him, and he barely managed to tuck his chin to keep from slamming the back of his head on the stone floor. But as soon as he hit the floor, the water rushed over his face and began to smother him.

It felt as if the tide had come in, full force, on top of him. Mehta struggled and swam and clawed against the water, but it was somehow holding him down and trying to drown him at the same time. No matter what he did, he couldn't get his head to break through the surface.

Through the swirling, frothing water pinning him to the floor, he could see Kent, Aeron, and Garrick reaching down toward him, trying to pull him up. It took all three of them to manage it, but they got him up to his feet.

Yet somehow, the water stayed with him. It covered him from head to toe, encasing him in a standing liquid coffin, keeping him from breathing. His comrades tried to pull him out, but the water shifted and moved to counter each pull.

Mehta was running out of air. His lungs burned, begging to breathe, but if he inhaled now, he'd only be sucking in icy water. Just when he thought he couldn't take it anymore, Garrick kicked him in the chest.

Mehta flew backward from the kick, clear out of the watery coffin, and he landed on his back. He was still wet, but he was surrounded by air. Sweet, precious, musty, miserable air.

His lungs consumed a full, deep breath, and he felt the water on his body pulling at him, back toward the tidal wave now rushing toward him.

He'd wanted to draw his knives and fight, but how could he fight water? He couldn't stab it. Couldn't cut it. Couldn't punch it or kick it or bite it or choke it.

So how could he fight?

The water on his body consolidated around his ankle in the form of a tentacle-like arm, and it hauled him toward a cascade of white-foamed rapids. The water crashed down on him once again, pummeling his face and chest with the entirety of its weight.

He'd gotten a full breath this time, and he had an idea of what the water might do, so he held his breath and thrashed against it. It didn't take his comrades long to get over to him again, and once again they pulled him up to his feet by force and tried to reach in for him.

Again the water repelled their attempts to aid Mehta, and the air in his lungs started to turn toxic. Garrick readied another kick, and Mehta braced himself.

But as Garrick threw the kick, the water intercepted the blow and coiled around his leg. Then it rushed away from Mehta and enveloped Garrick instead.

Mehta inhaled air anew and immediately set out to help Garrick.

"What's happening?" he shouted at Kent and Aeron.

"I don't know!" Aeron shouted back as they dug into the water to try to get ahold of Garrick.

"Stand back!" Kent ordered. He let blue magic flare from his hands, and then he dug them both into the water itself.

The water swirled away from his hands as if to avoid touching it, and it abandoned its intention to drown Garrick. This time, instead of going after Kent or Aeron or Mehta again, it dashed away from Garrick, flowed across the arena floor, and collected into a furious, roiling mass.

Garrick dropped to his knees, coughing and sputtering, but he stood up, drew his snow steel sword and shield, and snarled.

The mass took the shape of a man, albeit indistinct and fluid. Its head and chest resembled oval-shaped waterfalls with dark holes in the center, only the water seemed to flow in reverse—up from the dark centers and cresting at the tops of the waterfalls.

As it drew more water to itself, the watery form increased in size. Mehta noticed droplets of water that were clinging to him being drawn off his body —and even out of his clothes—and flying toward the watery form.

"What is it?" Aeron held up his spear, and Mehta couldn't help thinking that neither that spear nor his knives would do anything to harm it.

"A golem," Garrick replied.

"Golems are made of stone," Kent said.

"Then it's a water golem," Garrick said. "Same principle. It's made of one element, and it tries to kill by using that element with brute force. You got to name the reptiles. I'm calling this a water golem."

"How do we beat it?" Aeron asked.

"No clue," Garrick said, "Just try not to drown until we figure it out."

The water golem dove forward and splashed across the floor. It washed toward them and reformed into four smaller water golems, one for each of them.

Mehta drew his knives.

When Aeron slashed his spearhead through the water golem's arm, the part he'd cut off splattered on the arena floor and quickly rejoined its legs. But when he struck the water golem's head with the spear, its whole body broke apart and smacked to the floor, and it took longer to regain its humanlike form again.

"I don't know if this means anything," he called to the others, "but whenever I hit it in the head, the whole thing goes down. At least, it does for a little bit."

No one answered him. They were all battling person-sized versions of the water golem themselves.

Aeron didn't know what else to do, so he just kept aiming for the head whenever it would re-form. And it just kept re-forming, no matter how many times he hit it.

Of course the creature trying to keep Garrick from obtaining Lord Valdis's dragon egg had to be made of water, and it had to be trying to drown him.

Garrick cursed his own ignorance earlier in life. He should've taken the time to learn how to swim better, how to hold his breath longer.

But he hadn't, and now he had to deal with the weirdest possible consequence for his lax attitude about it.

On the plus side, the snow steel was working quite well against the Aeron-sized water golem that had formed in front of him. Whenever it lashed its watery tentacles at Garrick, he sliced through them with ease or blocked them with his shield.

The snow steel froze some of the water into chunks, and the water golem either couldn't or didn't summon the ice back to it. Whether or not it was a permanent solution, Garrick didn't know, but at least he felt like he was making tangible progress.

When Aeron shouted something about aiming for the water golem's head, Garrick took it to heart. He stepped forward and jammed the tip of his sword into the dark hole in the center of the water golem's head.

Ice rippled through its whole body, freezing it solid all the way down. It stopped moving and stood there.

Garrick was about to start celebrating his victory when the other three water golems abandoned his partners and rushed over to the frozen one.

They swept it away, across the arena, and morphed into a watery cyclone around it.

As the water swirled, the ice golem broke apart and melted fast, and it all reformed into the one large water golem again.

Garrick cursed. He thought he'd been making progress, but it turned out he hadn't even harmed it.

How were they going to defeat this thing?

The water golem dove at them from the far side of the arena and transformed into a torrent that rushed toward them. Garrick tried to hold his ground, but the water battered his legs, and he fell forward.

Then it swept him backward and slammed him into the arena wall. The impact forced the air out of his lungs, and then the water itself tried to drown him. But his shield and sword kept turning it to ice wherever the water touched it.

When they'd fallen into the pool under the temple, his snow steel weapons had lost their glow. But here, amid this watery assault, the runes continued to give off light and the weapons continued to freeze the water as long as they stayed in his hands.

Eventually, Garrick managed to get his head out of the surf and take a breath. As he did, the water pried its way between his fingers and tore the sword from his hand. It washed away in a block of ice, no longer freezing any of the water around it.

Garrick couldn't believe he'd lost it. No one had disarmed him in at least a decade—made of water or otherwise.

The water dug at Garrick's shield next, but he refused to let go of it. The shield was strapped to his forearm, which helped him keep it in his possession. So he hunkered down and braced himself against the cascade of water plowing into him.

<hr />

KENT SAW THE SNOW STEEL SWORD SQUIRT FROM GARRICK'S GRASP AND FLOAT away on the current. Then he watched as a maelstrom tried to overwhelm Garrick, only for it to break against his shield, freezing and then unfreezing and repeating the cycle as the water golem thrashed against him.

Meanwhile, the snow steel sword rose up twenty feet to the ceiling on a pillar of water, well out of reach. But the water golem had intentionally taken it from Garrick. Why would it do that unless the weapon had been harming it?

Kent was perhaps the only one of them who could get it back. Ever since

Kent had tried to use his magic on the water golem, it had avoided him. Rather than actually trying to fight him, it had only thrown half-hearted attacks at Kent while trying to full-on drown the others.

That meant his magic could hurt it.

So while it focused the majority of its attention on Garrick and kept the others busy, Kent sent a blast of raw, blue magic at the man-sized water golem swirling between him and the pillar of water.

The water golem parted to avoid getting hit by the blast, and Kent seized the opportunity. He leaped between the halves of the water golem's body and landed in a sprint toward the pillar.

The water roared behind him, chasing after him, but he just kept running, all the way to the pillar. Then he jammed his hands into it and loosed his magic.

The pillar shuddered and broke apart, splashing down on Kent and releasing the snow steel sword. Kent caught it and turned back in time to see the water from the pillar shooting back toward the center of the arena—back to the water golem, which had abandoned its battle against Garrick, Aeron, and Mehta entirely.

Now it launched toward him alone, gathering its strength as it rode along a tidal wave of liquid power. It thundered across the arena floor with outstretched arms and watery chasms in its face and chest. It grew larger with each passing second, and it would soon slam Kent into the arena wall with the full force of its power.

But Kent had Garrick's snow steel sword.

When he had held it the first time, back when Garrick had threatened him among the trees, Kent had tried to take the sword's essence. Doing so had almost frozen Kent's hand, but in the process, it had also shot out a beam of ice.

When he'd held the dragon sword, it had yearned for his magic. Instead of trying to take of the dragon sword's essence, Kent had simply let his magic flow into it, and it had activated. So this time, he tried the same approach with the snow steel sword.

He pointed its blade square at the water golem's furious waterfall of a chest, and instead of trying to cycle his magic through the sword's essence, Kent loosed his magic into the sword itself.

The snow steel blade glowed with blue-white light and shot a beam of the same color at the water golem's chest. The beam struck true, and ice spread up the waterfall in its chest, throughout its arms, head, and torso, and it froze everything all the way down to the raging surf where its legs would've been.

Kent continued the flow of his magic until the water golem coasted to a halt along the sand and gravel, no less than three feet from the tip of the snow steel sword. It sat there, frozen solid, reaching for Kent with icy tentacles.

Kent exhaled the breath he'd been holding in just in case his plan had failed. The amount of magic he'd dumped into the sword had left him feeling exhausted, but as far as he knew, the water golem wasn't dead yet—and if it melted, it could keep coming after them.

So he let the sword drop from his tired hands, and he walked up to the frozen water golem. It was a marvelous creation, to be sure. Intricate in appearance, yet made of one simple element, and wildly powerful and unpredictable, just like water itself could be.

But no matter how incredible it was, he couldn't allow it to live—not after how hard they'd had to work just to fend it off until now.

So Kent put his hands into the center of the water golem's chest. The ice chilled his fingertips, palms, and knuckles, but he didn't pay it any mind. Instead, he pumped magic into the water golem's chest.

The ice turned a brilliant blue color, and it spread throughout the water golem's entire form. Darker blue fissures formed in its icy chest, arms, head, torso, and base, but Kent didn't stop. He pushed more and more raw magic into the water golem, to the point where he felt like he might pass out.

Then the fissures crackled, and the ice golem shattered into a huge pile of vivid blue ice chips. As Kent watched, the pile quickly disintegrated into nothing. By the time it was all gone, the arena looked like it hadn't seen a drop of water in a millennium.

Garrick, Aeron, and Mehta stood twenty feet from Kent, staring at him with raised eyebrows and open mouths.

Kent had squeezed the majority of his magic into the sword and then into the water golem afterward. It would replenish quickly, but at the moment, he felt slow and sluggish, worse than when he'd awakened from the reptiles' venom.

He sat on the arena floor, rested his elbows on his knees, and let his head hang down.

"Are you alright?" Aeron's voice asked from above him.

Kent blinked and looked up. All three of them stood around him, but he hadn't heard them walk over.

"Yes, thank you," he replied. "I ought to be able to activate the key momentarily. I just need a moment to breathe so my magic can regenerate."

No one said anything.

"If you require your sword, Garrick," Kent continued, "you may claim it at your leisure. I do not believe I will need to use it again unless we discover another water golem or some other liquid-based creature intent on doing us harm."

Garrick picked up the snow steel sword and sheathed it. "I don't usually give compliments, but that was one of the most powerful displays I've ever seen."

Kent looked up at him and smirked. "As I said to you the first time I held that sword, I am capable of violence on a scale the likes of which you have never seen. Now you have seen it. Some of it, anyway."

They continued to stare down at him, and even Mehta looked impressed.

Finally, Kent raised his arms. "Will someone kindly help an old man up, please?"

Garrick and Aeron each took hold of one wrist and pulled Kent to his feet.

Once he was up, Kent felt better. He walked of his own accord over to the blue pyramid and to the dragon sword embedded in the top of it.

His magic had returned almost fully, but the normal kind of fatigue—plain old tiredness—still afflicted his body. Kent needed a hot meal and a good night's rest.

He would get neither of those things down here.

So he took hold of the dragon sword and let it call forth his magic once again.

§

GARRICK WATCHED AS THE GEMSTONES IN THE DRAGON SWORD'S HILT GLOWED crimson. Again, the blade shined with golden light, just as it had when Kent had opened the doors.

Two lines, one stretching from each end of the keyhole down the sides of the pyramid, began to glow with golden light as well. The pyramid gave off a popping noise, and it split into two halves along those lines.

Then the light from the sword faded, and a cloud of dust billowed out from within the center of the pyramid.

A recognizable *clunk* sounded from the arena doors. They'd unlocked again.

Garrick smirked. This was working out well.

Kent stepped back, but the dragon sword stayed in the lock, which went with half of the pyramid to one side.

As the dust cleared, Garrick approached the pyramid and reached for one of the objects inside.

CHAPTER TWENTY-ONE

M ehta had never seen a dragon egg before, but when Garrick pulled one out of the blue pyramid and held it up, he wasn't impressed.

It just looked like an egg-shaped rock. The only eye-catching aspect of it was that it glimmered green from the scorallite thanks to a few granules of crystal or glass embedded along its surface.

Garrick was smiling as if he'd just laid eyes on the love of his life. He looked at each of them in turn and then said, "We're rich."

Either Garrick was right, and they had found a legendary dragon egg, or this was all an elaborate hoax by a bunch of long-dead Aletians, meant to fool whoever stumbled upon the ruins they'd left behind. But Aeron and Kent were both smiling, so perhaps Mehta was being too pessimistic.

Garrick unslung the pack from his shoulders and carefully placed the egg inside. Next, he pulled a huge tome from the open half of the pyramid and set it inside his pack. It was easily twice the size of the largest book Mehta had ever seen, but then again, the Aletians had been larger than humans as well.

Mehta caught sight of some sort of gold or bronze image stamped on the tome's cover, but it was too dusty for him to make out exactly what it was. Perhaps it was the Crimson Flame emblem.

As Garrick started to pry at the metal that covered the closed half of the pyramid, a loud crack above them split the silence. Everyone looked up.

A long fissure ran from one edge of the ceiling toward the center, and water started trickling in from above.

Another crack sounded, and another fissure opened next to the first one. More water sprayed inside the arena.

"Uh... I think we need to go," Aeron said.

The lake must've been directly above them, and it was going to break through and drown them all. It explained the sound of constantly dripping water they'd heard in the green cavern.

Whether they had somehow triggered it or whether it was just a freak chance, it didn't matter. They had to get out now, like Aeron had said.

And Mehta knew one possible way out. He'd seen it in the maze of corridors—another pair of blue doors with another key slot.

He didn't waste any time. If they had any chance of escaping, and if those doors were the way out, Mehta would need to be the one to lead them to it. "Come on. Follow me."

"Where?" Kent asked.

"I think I know a way out," Mehta replied.

The ceiling cracked again, this time on the opposite side, and water poured in.

"Hurry!" Mehta yelled.

Aeron and Kent followed immediately, but Garrick was still hunched over in front of the other half of the pyramid, which he'd managed to get open. Though Garrick's body was blocking Mehta's view, he saw Garrick stuff something else into his pack.

"Garrick!" Mehta, Kent, and Aeron all shouted in unison.

"What are you doing?" Kent hollered.

"Grabbing some insurance!" Garrick slung his pack over his shoulder and stood to his full height.

"Bring the sword!" Mehta shouted. Without it, they might never escape this place.

A chunk of the ceiling plummeted to the floor, and hundreds of gallons of water flooded the arena.

Garrick yanked the dragon sword out of the pyramid, turned, and ran hard toward the arena doors.

Behind him, the rest of the ceiling collapsed, and the entire lake emptied into the arena.

AERON WOULD'VE RATHER DONE ALMOST ANYTHING ELSE THAN RUN FOR HIS LIFE while wearing full-body armor, but at the moment, he didn't have a choice. So he ran through the green-lit cavern, past the Aletian statues, and into a series of dark corridors, all while praying the water wouldn't catch up to him.

The instant they got out of the arena, Mehta took a hard right turn toward the corridors. Aeron followed, running nearly as fast as Mehta, though he couldn't quite catch him. His armor was definitely slowing him down—that had to be it.

Or maybe he just didn't run enough. Then again, why run at all when he had a wyvern he could ride?

Kent followed behind Aeron, and Garrick brought up the rear.

More accurately, the *lake* brought up the rear.

It burst through the arena doorway, furious and raging and violent as it slammed into the rocky cavern. The water pulverized the base of the female Aletian statue, and she toppled into the torrent behind them.

Aeron kept running, kept breathing hard. They'd just made it past the male Aletian statue when the water took it down, too, but the corridor was in sight. They could reach it.

By now, Kent had caught up to Aeron, and so had Garrick. As they bolted into the corridor, most of the water slammed into the cavern walls, but some of it shot after them. Aeron felt its cold spray on the back of his neck and head.

He stole a look back at the water and saw a wall of froth and fury barreling forward, only about twenty feet behind them. He hoped that as they passed the corridors to the left and right that some of it would disperse.

Sure enough, as they ran, the wall of water veered left and right, picking up the bodies of several slain reptides. But it only slowed slightly, and it didn't stop pursuing them.

Mehta took them to the left, then right, and then right again. Aeron didn't know if he was simply trying to avoid the water or actually taking them somewhere. Whatever he was doing, they were running out of time.

Then Mehta took another hard right turn into—a corridor with a bit of green light in it? Aeron followed and found himself running along a narrow path that curved upward, away from the roaring rapids below.

Kent and Garrick made it onto the path as well, and the water screamed past them below and splashed onto the bottom of the path. The water slowly poured in and started to rise. If this path didn't lead somewhere, it would eventually rise up enough to drown them.

But Mehta soon brought them to a chunk of scorallite in the wall. It radiated green light onto another set of blue metal doors with a familiar sword-sized slot in the center.

"I don't know what lies beyond these doors, but I also don't know of any other way to escape from this place," he said.

Garrick passed Kent the sword, and Kent pushed it into the keyhole with a click and activated it. Familiar golden light shined from the keyhole and between the doors.

The water had risen halfway up the path and was drawing steadily closer to their position, churning and frothing as it did.

"Be quick, guys," Aeron muttered.

The doors unlocked with several clanks. Kent removed the dragon sword, and Garrick hauled the doors open.

Aeron exhaled a relieved sigh.

Everyone rushed inside, and then Aeron tried to pull them shut behind him, but they didn't close entirely.

"Don't bother," Garrick said. "Just keep moving."

Aeron didn't want the water to continue following them, but it was rising slowly enough now that perhaps it wouldn't be an issue. He abandoned his efforts and followed the others.

The path continued to curve upward and around, gradually ascending. Most of it was shrouded in darkness, so they relied on Kent, who still held the dragon sword, to cast its golden light around them.

The fighting and the running had messed up Aeron's back again, so with the danger now behind them, Aeron opened his pack and devoured another shroom. He was running low and would need to stock up as soon as he could find an apothecary who sold them.

But it wouldn't be anywhere in Muroth. That was for sure. From what Kent had described, he might get killed just for inquiring.

As he walked, the shroom started to kick in. He would've taken one for his anxiety as well, but the thought of the real danger being behind him made him decide against it for the time being. Better to stay more alert as they tried to navigate their way out of this place.

Furthermore, the more aware he was of his surroundings, the more likely he might notice something that would lead him to Kallie. In an ancient place like this, the odds were long that he'd find anything, but if something were there, he didn't want to risk missing it.

After about thirty minutes, the path gradually shifted from stone to dirt and terminated at another door—really more of a hatch above them. None of them could reach it on their own thanks to a steep incline leading up to it.

Unlike the blue metal doors, it was made of old, weathered slats of wood, and they couldn't see anything through the slats. It barely moved when they tried to open it, but that had been with Garrick holding Mehta on his shoulders.

As Mehta pushed on the hatch, bits of dirt sprinkled down onto Aeron's head. At first, he just brushed it off, but then he realized what it meant—they might've finally reached the surface.

Kent realized it, too. He passed the dragon sword off to Aeron. He said to Garrick, "Put me on your shoulders instead. I can clear it off."

Garrick grunted and grumbled, but he managed to get Kent onto his shoulders. Kent was taller than Mehta, so it was easier to reach the hatch in the first place. He gave it a few sturdy shoves, and when dirt trickled through the slats, he caught it and collected it in his left hand.

Then both of his hands ignited with blue energy. He raised his right hand toward the hatch. The ground above them rumbled for a moment, and when it stopped, Kent wiped the last few flecks of dirt in his hand on his trousers.

Then he pushed the hatch open with ease, stepped on Garrick's head, eliciting a grunt from him, and climbed out. Moonlight streamed in through the opening, and Aeron welcomed the sight. Anything was better than what they'd just endured.

Mehta went next, and then Aeron passed the dragon sword and his spear up to them, and then Garrick hefted him onto his shoulders. Aeron grabbed the snowy edges of the opening and pulled himself up with only a hint of pain in his back thanks to the shroom he'd taken.

As Aeron emerged from the hatch, a chilly wind blew in his face—but it smelled fresh, not like the musty air he'd been inhaling since they'd fallen through the temple floor. It both invigorated and exhausted him at the same time.

The air got cold really fast, and he shivered. They'd shed their cloaks in the Crimson Flame temple to fight the cultists, so they either had to go back for them or they'd have to do without and buy new ones later.

But right now, they had to haul Garrick out of the tunnel before they could move on, and they had to move on so they could find a safe, warm place to camp for the night.

Together with Kent, Aeron lay prone in dirt-covered snow next to the hatch, reached down into the tunnel, and helped Garrick up. Thanks to Garrick's weight, the strain agitated Aeron's back, but the shroom was still in his system, still working its literal magic, and it dulled the sensation quickly enough.

With Garrick safely out, they all took a moment to rest and revel in their success—though Mehta's idea of resting was standing watch.

They'd emerged from the dungeon under a cluster of trees, and Aeron wondered how far away Wafer was at the moment. If he blew the Wafer whistle, would Wafer be able to hear it?

He probably would. Wafer was pretty good about flying around the area whenever their connection started feeling too faint. It felt faint now, so Aeron guessed Wafer was already in the air, flying in wide arcs to reestablish a stronger sense of closeness, even though Aeron hadn't yet called for him.

Garrick got them up and moving around, trying to find their bearings.

Under the moonlight and clouds, and partially because of the trees around them, Aeron couldn't see the lake—or perhaps, what had *been* the lake. If it had indeed emptied into the dungeon beneath the temple, then Aeron wasn't sure what it would be considered at that point. A crater? A valley? The imprint of a giant, misshapen doughnut?

"I think we ended up north of the lake," Garrick said. What he was basing that conclusion on, Aeron didn't know.

"If we are, then the horses may be southeast of here, as we were approaching the temple from the southwest when we entered Muroth." Kent nodded in that direction.

"If you want, I can call Wafer and do some scouting," Aeron said.

"That's a good idea," Garrick said. "Go ahea—"

"Someone's coming," Mehta blurted. His knives jumped into his hands, and he faced a grouping of trees nearby.

They all readied their weapons and faced the forest as a group of men, armed with swords, spears, axes, and bows, emerged from the trees.

THE SIGHT OF HIS FORMER COUNTRYMEN APPROACHING, CLAD IN MUROTH'S white and bronze armor with black trim, stirred a wide range of emotions within Kent.

Part of him wanted to fight them, to use his "curse" and show them the breadth of the power he'd awakened to once they'd expelled him from his homeland. He still held the dragon sword, and between it and his magic, he would certainly wreak havoc among these men who had come for him.

Part of him wanted to flee, to make his way through the trees, mount his horse, and ride back to Urthia. There, he would be safe, and he could complete his journey north to Xenthan to deliver Lord Valdis's prize to him.

Part of him wanted to surrender to whatever punishment they had in store for him. It was a sentiment born of a misplaced sense of loyalty to the country that had cast him out. An empty suggestion that perhaps, if he acquiesced, they might take him back and restore him to his old life.

But Kent did none of those things. Instead, he stood his ground along with Garrick, Aeron, and Mehta.

The men approaching bore two standards. The first was the national flag of Muroth, half-white and half-black with a bronze lion in the center. The other was the flag of the Frostsong province, blue with a regal-looking, silvery snow leopard.

Kent had always admired the Frostsong province's flag and colors. They suited the name of the province, which was of course named after the noble family that had founded and still controlled it.

But he preferred the standard of House Etheridge even more—a bold red and green flag with a bronze gryphon in the center.

Of course, he could no longer claim it as his own. Fane had seen to that.

The Murothians outnumbered Kent and the other mercs by more than a dozen. At least, that's what Kent thought until a voice called his name from behind.

He turned back and stared into the ice-blue eyes of Lord Aurelius Frostsong.

"Welcome back to Muroth," Lord Frostsong said, his voice level, despite the frigid weather.

Lord Frostsong's thinning hair was as white as the snow on the ground all around them, and it appeared to glow under the moonlight. He wore a thick bearskin cloak overtop of his royal blue armor, which was trimmed with silver and bore his house's snow leopard emblem on his chest.

Unlike many of the other provincial lords in Muroth, Lord Frostsong did not wear a beard. Kent had seen him many times throughout his life and never once saw Lord Frostsong with so much as a hint of stubble. During better times, he'd joked with Fane that Lord Frostsong shaved thrice daily to maintain his clean-cut appearance.

Lord Frostsong asked, "What brings you to the land of your birth?"

Kent noted he hadn't said "homeland" or "home country." He'd been stripped of his titles, birthright, and citizenship by his own father. Then Fane had decided it wasn't enough of a punishment, so he'd murdered Lord Etheridge and seized control of the province.

But Lord Frostsong didn't ask the question with an accusatory tone, either. It came across as more of a casual question rather than a loaded inquiry that Kent might've had to answer with great caution.

Then again, he couldn't exactly reveal that they'd come to Muroth in search of a fabled dragon egg on behalf of a dark lord from Xenthan who wanted it for... whatever he wanted it for. So Kent had to answer carefully anyway.

"Just passing through," he replied. "If Your Lordship will allow us to do so."

"Passing through the dungeon beneath the temple in the lake, you mean?"

Kent had no idea how Lord Frostsong knew, but it didn't matter. He could either be honest about it and hope to gain some trust, fleeting as it might be, or he could lie and probably achieve nothing at all.

"Yes," he replied. Being honest didn't mean he had to explain every detail of their journey and their plans.

To Kent's surprise, Garrick didn't make so much as a sound at the admission of their foray into the dungeon. But Kent *had* made him promise to keep quiet when it came to communicating with Murothian locals. Perhaps he was just living up to his word.

Lord Frostsong studied Kent and then took in each of the other mercs. "What strange company you keep these days."

"I would introduce you, but I suspect you are not interested in discussion."

"On the contrary," Lord Frostsong said, "that is precisely what has drawn me out of my warm bed in these early hours of the morning."

Kent squinted at him. "Forgive me, Your Lordship, but I do not understand."

"If you will permit me to take you into custody without incident, I will gladly explain."

Kent glanced at Garrick, whose eyes conveyed both warnings and threats at the same time.

Aeron stood there, motionless, unwilling to contribute anything either way—probably because he was high on magic mushrooms to one degree or another.

And Mehta stood exactly where he'd been standing, holding his knives, ready in case Lord Frostsong's men got too close.

Kent was indeed surrounded by strange company, but he'd grown to trust and admire each of them for different reasons. They'd truly started to form a team rather than just a group of four individuals working toward a common goal.

But did they trust Kent enough to let him make a decision they probably didn't want him to make? Even if Kent believed it was the best option?

"Perhaps we can negotiate terms?" Kent offered. It was a reach, but he had to try.

"Kent, you are outnumbered, tired, cold, probably hungry, and are generally in no condition to resist," Lord Frostsong said calmly. "There will be no negotiation because I have no reason to negotiate. Surely you did not lose your tactical intelligence when you were stripped of your nobility."

Lord Frostsong's words stung, more at the reminder of Kent's painful past than as an insult. Lord Frostsong probably hadn't even meant any insult in saying them—he was just making an observation.

"I did not, Your Lordship," Kent replied.

"So what choice will you make?" Lord Frostsong pressed.

Something within Kent told him to trust Lord Frostsong. They had been as close as nonrelatives could be—Kent considered Lord Frostsong to be the uncle he'd never had.

But if he surrendered, he would put everything they had worked for at risk —and that included far more than the dragon egg in Garrick's pack and Aeron's chances to find Kallie.

If Lord Frostsong was luring him with calm words, only to later escort Kent to his execution, then Kent could never deliver the reckoning to Fane that he deserved. He could never avenge their father's murder.

"Kent, it is cold outside," Lord Frostsong said. "You must choose now or the decision will be made for you."

Kent looked into Lord Frostsong's eyes, then he looked at the dragon sword in his hands. And he made his choice.

⚡

It had taken some convincing on Kent's part to get Garrick and Mehta to lay down their arms—Mehta, more surprisingly, had held out longer than Garrick.

Meanwhile, Kent only had to convince Aeron not to call Wafer to them. The arrival of a full-grown wyvern, while they were in the process of surrendering, would destroy every last shred of the goodwill Kent had bought—or *hoped* he had bought—by cooperating with Lord Frostsong and his men.

In the end, the other mercs elected to trust Kent's judgment, though they all remained wary of Lord Frostsong's designs for them.

Within an hour of their surrender, the four mercs arrived at Lord Frostsong's estate along with Lord Frostsong and his men, much farther south than they'd ever intended to travel on their own.

Kent guessed it must've been close to sunrise by the time they arrived. They'd entered the temple only a couple of hours after nightfall, and with winter bringing longer nights as it dragged on, they had spent the majority of the night in the dungeon.

Kent hadn't expected a grand welcome, but he also hadn't expected Lord Frostsong's men to throw them behind bars. The actual response landed somewhere in between: rather than a jail cell, they'd locked Garrick, Aeron, and Mehta in a grand bedroom within the manse.

Lord Frostsong had personally asked them not to damage anything, and he'd offered to have some food sent in to them. Aeron had looked like he'd wanted to say "yes," but Garrick answered first and declined for all of them.

"Very well," Lord Frostsong said. "Kent and I are going to have a conversation. If he is honest with me, I promise you will see him again."

Those words noticeably set everyone on edge, but Kent held up his hand to reassure them. The last thing he needed was one of them doing something to change Lord Frostsong's mind about how he was treating his "guests."

The guards locked Garrick, Aeron, and Mehta inside, and Lord Frostsong and Kent headed toward his study, followed by armed guards.

Along the way, Kent re-acclimated himself to the interior of Lord Frostsong's manse. He'd been inside dozens of times and remembered many of its features. Blue tapestries trimmed with silver hung along the wood-paneled walls, and plush blue rugs ran along the fine wood floors.

The lumber trade. Every inch of wood in the manse had doubtless originated directly from the forests owned and logged by Lord Frostsong's family. Silver fixtures punctuated the walls, and silver doorknobs protruded from the various doors they passed by.

They stopped at a set of grand double-doors that reminded Kent of the study at Lord Glavan's manse in Govalia. And when they went inside, Kent found plenty of additional similarities.

Bookshelves, a fire roaring in the hearth, a sprawling desk with comfortable sitting furniture—the only main differences were the room's layout and the silver fixtures. Lord Glavan's had been bronze.

Lord Frostsong sat in one of two stuffed leather chairs before the hearth, and for a moment, the sight reminded Kent of his father. He pushed away the thought and the associated feelings of loss and regret.

He sat in the other chair. It felt incredible, sitting in such a fine piece of furniture, especially given all they'd endured. Kent probably could've fallen asleep right then and there, but he couldn't grant himself the luxury—not with Lord Frostsong expecting answers.

They sat there in silence, staring at the flames flickering in the hearth and letting the fire warm them.

Finally, Lord Frostsong turned back to his guards and said, "Leave us."

The guards complied without hesitation. Kent admired their obedience, but he wondered at the wisdom of Lord Frostsong's decision. If Kent had meant him harm, he could certainly do so without anyone to stop him.

Lord Frostsong had been a cunning warrior once, but age slowed everyone down eventually. And even if Lord Frostsong had been young and spry, Kent's magic still would've overwhelmed him.

When the study doors closed, Lord Frostsong faced the fire again. "I must confess, it is good to see you again, Kent."

"It is good to see you as well, Your Lordship."

"Please dispense with the pleasantries." Lord Frostsong continued to stare into the fire. "Refer to me by my first name."

"If that is your wish," Kent said.

"As you know, your father and I were lifelong friends. It grieved me deeply to hear of his passing."

"It grieved me as well," Kent said.

"Did it?" Lord Frostsong smiled at the flames. "What a strange sentiment for his supposed murderer to express."

Kent's voice hardened. "You said it yourself. *Supposed*."

"I will hear your version of the events that transpired, but before we move any further, there is a matter of singular importance that we must first resolve."

Kent waited for Lord Frostsong to continue.

Lord Frostsong dug into his bearskin cloak—which he still wore over his armor—and produced a chunk of green crystal about the size of his fist.

Scorallite.

"Open your hand, Kent." Lord Frostsong held it as if to drop the scorallite into Kent's palm, just as Fane had done that fateful day nearly a year ago.

Kent had hoped they might find common ground apart from his "cursed" nature of being a mage, but that didn't seem to be an option anymore.

What would Lord Frostsong do when Kent took the scorallite into his hand and ignited his magic? Did he also have a dagger tucked into his cloak, ready to strike Kent down—or try to—the next instant? Would his guards somehow know and come rushing in to finish Kent off?

"Please, Kent," Lord Frostsong said. "I must know who I am dealing with."

Kent stared at the scorallite. It amazed him how he'd been around so much of it in the dungeon only hours before, and it hadn't bothered him in the least. But now, the sight of one small chunk of it set him on edge.

Of course, he hadn't dared touch it. That much scorallite in one place, and glowing, too—Kent had no idea what it would do to him, so he'd left it alone.

Perhaps his aversion to it was because Fane had used it to prove to their father that Kent was a mage. After that, as Kent was attempting to escape the country, General Calarook had tried to get him to hold a piece of it as well. That hadn't gone well for either of them.

But now, Kent didn't have much of a choice. Short of jumping through Lord Frostsong's study window and fleeing into the trees surrounding his estate, Kent had few other options. And that would mean leaving his companions behind to fend for themselves.

Kent decided he'd jumped through enough Murothian windows by this point in his life. He'd come this far. He'd chosen to trust Lord Frostsong up until this point. He also knew Muroth's laws and what it would mean.

But he reached toward Lord Frostsong nonetheless and opened his hand.

CHAPTER TWENTY-TWO

G arrick was livid that Kent chose to surrender instead of fighting when
Lord Frostsong's men had surrounded them. He thought he had
conveyed his concerns to Kent through his eyes and expressions in that
moment, but Kent apparently either hadn't cared or hadn't realized what
Garrick was trying to say.

In any other circumstance, Garrick would've spoken up and taken charge,
but he'd promised he wouldn't interfere with any of Kent's interactions with
his own countrymen.

And now they were locked in a big room in a manse owned by one of the
very Murothian lords Kent had expressed specific concerns about.

That's the last time I let anyone else lead my expeditions.

They'd found the dragon egg. They'd found the ritual tome. Garrick had
found a bit of insurance as well, and even more impressive, they'd managed to
escape the dungeon despite it nearly collapsing on top of them.

And then Kent had stymied their momentum by allowing them to be
captured.

It made Garrick wonder if Kent had somehow been planning this all along,
but he couldn't conceive of how Kent could've planned everything to line up
so perfectly. Nor did he know what Kent stood to gain from bringing a
dragon egg and a tome of ancient magic rituals into anti-magic Muroth, of all
places.

Garrick looked at Aeron and Mehta, both of whom appeared to be asleep,
though their slumber manifested in drastically different ways. Aeron had

sprawled out on the bed in the room, on his stomach, while Mehta sat in a chair with his arms folded and his eyes closed.

If Garrick had so much as coughed, Mehta's eyes would've popped open to survey the room for potential threats, and then they'd close again. But if Garrick wanted to wake Aeron, he'd probably have to outright smack him in the face.

Exhaustion plagued Garrick, too, but he couldn't sleep. Not with his quarry in his possession, while under lock-and-key within Lord Frostsong's purview. He didn't want to let the pack out of his sight, much less leave it lying around for anyone who felt obliged to peer inside.

So he'd kept the pack in his arms and sat facing the door. Every so often, he would check it occasionally, just to make sure its contents hadn't fallen out or somehow vanished from inside.

But it was growing tiresome. The sooner they got out of there, the sooner he could get the dragon egg back to Lord Valdis and get paid. So if Lord Frostsong was going to execute Kent, Garrick preferred he'd just get on with it already so the rest of them could leave.

He didn't *want* Kent to get executed—he'd actually started to like and trust Kent, up until the moment he'd surrendered them to Lord Frostsong—but if Kent had to die, sooner was better.

Until someone told him otherwise, he would just have to wait. So he continued to sit in the chair, holding the pack, while he waited.

Then he checked it one more time, just to make sure.

❧

To Kent's surprise, Lord Frostsong never placed the scorallite in his hand.

Instead, he pulled it away and tucked it back into his bearskin cloak.

"I have never agreed with Muroth's treatment of the accursed among us, but the law is clear," Lord Frostsong said.

Kent bristled at his use of the word "accursed" to describe him. He was a person, just as much as Lord Frostsong was, just as much as other mages were. And magic wasn't a curse. If anything, it was a blessing.

"If I have incontrovertible proof that someone is cursed with the scourge of magic, the law states that I must act swiftly and decisively. You know this as well as I do. You once enforced it with even more vehemence than I ever have. You were a shield to us all from the Inothians to the south."

Indeed, Kent did know the law, through and through. That's why he'd hidden his magic from the moment it awakened in him, at the age of forty.

"And I am oathbound to uphold that law. I swore I would do so upon my very life." Lord Frostsong turned his head toward Kent. "So until I *see* otherwise, I have no reason to suspect you are cursed. And thus, I cannot be derelict in my duty to Muroth if I cannot prove your condition."

His reasoning was frail, but if Lord Frostsong needed to rationalize why he was keeping Kent alive, then Kent would abide it—even if he had to endure comments about being cursed along the way.

"The scorallite crystal was a test—not of your condition, but of your composition," Lord Frostsong said. "I needed to reaffirm the kind of man you were, and are. I needed you to earn my trust in this small but important way before I could hear your story with truly open ears and an open heart. Please do not fault me for putting you in such a difficult position."

"I understand," Kent said. "I hold no ill will toward you for it."

"Good. Then, by all means, explain to me what happened the day your father died. And remember, anything that might indicate you are anything other than a perfectly normal son of Muroth will force me to act upon what knowledge I might glean from hearing you out."

Kent understood his warning. He explained the entire sequence of events that day, but he intentionally avoided any mention of magic or Fane placing the scorallite in his hand. He didn't lie about it—he just didn't bring it up.

"So Fane is single-handedly responsible for your father's murder?" Lord Frostsong asked.

"Yes," Kent replied. "And I long for nothing more than to deal Fane the reckoning he deserves for it."

"Fane claims that your father stripped you of your lands, titles, rights, and privileges before he died. Is that true?"

Kent needed to tread carefully around this subject. "For reasons I cannot discuss... yes, he did. That is the truth."

"I see." Lord Frostsong rubbed his bare chin. "Did he order your execution?"

"No. He banished me from the country."

"If a certain son, shall we say, were cursed with magic, and his father loved him dearly, is it conceivable his father would have banished his son from the country instead of executing him?"

Kent smiled ironically. "That would be a reasonable assumption in such a situation."

Lord Frostsong nodded. "I am inclined to believe you, though I do not believe I can provide aid to you, should you endeavor to take House Etheridge back from your brother. He holds the lordship, and unfortunately, he has branded you as a traitor and an enemy of the state far too well for you to overcome his word."

"The reckoning I intend to bring him does not mean I will regain my birthright. I believe that is forever lost to me because the laws of Muroth are what they are, and I cannot change them."

"Careful, Kent." Lord Frostsong raised his finger. "Do not reveal too much."

"Then I will leave it at that."

Lord Frostsong nodded again. "Your brother is a cad. He has always been a wretched little imp, jealous of what he could not have and yet all too eager to take more than he deserved or needed. I fear the personality defects so evident in his youth have endured in our trade dealings since your father perished."

"I am not surprised." Kent couldn't think of a single time where Fane had ever dealt with anyone fairly, including their own father. Why should he start behaving properly now, when he actually had real power within his grasp?

"Likewise, it was never in your character to rebel against Muroth or do as Fane claims you have done to your father. I do not see any reason why you would have turned against your family and your country of your own volition."

"I would never have done anything of the sort."

"Yet I am told you took up with Inoth—specifically with the late Inothian queen herself. If you were truly a patriot, why join Muroth's sworn enemy against your homeland?"

He'd referred to Muroth as Kent's homeland. Lord Frostsong must've believed him.

"A dead patriot may still be a patriot, but he is also still dead. Rather than be unjustly executed by a country I loved, I chose to flee to a country I hated. It was the last place Muroth would think to look for me."

"That much is for certain. Yet Fane found you nonetheless."

"That is another story entirely."

Lord Frostsong waved his hand. "To be frank, I do not wish to hear it. The less I know, the better. I am too old to worry about the affairs of the provinces around me, except insofar as they intersect with the affairs of Frostsong. Since you are not petitioning me for aid, I am not obligated to provide any, and thus, I shall not.

"But likewise, I cannot harbor you for very long. You are welcome to rest for a day or so under my protection, and then you must leave," Lord Frostsong continued. "I hope you understand that when I learned you were in my province, I had to act. If for no other reason, so that I might tell Fane, truly, that I saw no evidence that you were cursed."

"I understand, and thank you," Kent said. Morning light had begun to creep over the distant horizon. "We will take you up on your offer, and we will leave by sunrise tomorrow morning."

"Very good."

"May I inquire as to the status of our belongings?" Kent asked. "Specifically, our weapons? Simply put, I know my companions would feel more at ease if they were armed."

"If you can assure me that your friends will mind themselves and my men, and if they will respect my hospitality, then I see no reason why they ought to go without."

"They will behave. I assure you."

"Then their weapons will be returned to them in short order."

"Thank you." Kent asked, "Did your men happen to find some horses tied to tree branches near the lake? They would have been saddled."

"They have already been boarded for the night in my stables. I assure you they are well cared-for."

Kent grinned. "It seems you have thought of everything."

"I took care to ensure that it would be incredibly difficult for you to flee the country a second time if you chose not to be honest with me," Lord Frostsong said. "But it appears my old friend, your father, raised you quite well."

"That, he did."

"He was so proud of you, you know." Lord Frostsong stared at Kent with those ice-blue eyes of his. "He often told me so. Especially in his final years, when you started running Etheridge on his behalf. It was such a relief to him. You brought great honor and respect to your family."

"Until the day he died." Kent's heart ached with regret. Lord Frostsong had torn into his deepest emotions, whether he'd realized it or not. "His final words wiped all of that away, once and for all."

Kent had loved his father, but the last words his father had ever said to him were his proclamation of Kent's banishment and the stripping of his family name and birthright. He had often considered how those few words, spoken within mere seconds, had poisoned every good moment they'd ever shared for all forty-eight years of Kent's life.

"I beg to differ," Lord Frostsong said. "As a Lord of the Realm of Muroth, he exercised the only power available to him to save your life. His act of banishment was his final act of love for you, even if it seemed at that time that it was not."

Kent had given that idea serious consideration since it had happened, but he'd never been able to make the jump to seeing it from that sort of optimistic angle. Now, hearing Lord Frostsong say it, from a definitively objective point of view, shifted Kent's perception of his father's final moments.

"And I know he would be proud of the man you are today, in spite of all that has transpired," Lord Frostsong continued. "And, above all else, I know that he would endorse your drive to bring a reckoning to his murderer. Lord Oswin Etheridge was certainly a lot of things, but meek was not one of them."

Now *that*, Kent could get behind. His father had loved Fane as well, but had he survived Fane's assassination attempt, he would have put Fane to death that very day.

Kent closed his eyes. *I promise, Father, that Fane will pay for his crimes against you and against our family. It just may take me some time to bring you the justice you deserve.*

"Now if you do not mind, I would prefer to take some time on my own to ponder everything you have told me. If you knock on the study doors, the guards have been instructed to let you wander the grounds freely, though I advise you not to leave the manse until you are ready to leave for good."

"Thank you, Lord Frostsong."

He smiled at Kent. "I asked you to call me by my first name, Kent."

"I would never dare to show such disrespect to one of my oldest, truest friends."

Lord Frostsong chuckled. "You certainly have the 'old' part right. Please, get some rest. I hope to join you and your friends for dinner this evening."

"It will be our pleasure. Thank you again."

With that, Kent headed over to the study doors and knocked.

⸙

GARRICK'S EYES POPPED OPEN WHEN THE DOOR TO THE BEDROOM UNLATCHED. He must've drifted off to sleep, and he chided himself for it.

He checked the contents of his pack and verified they were undisturbed. Everything was as he'd left it.

The door swung open, and Kent walked in with all of his limbs and his head still attached to his body.

Garrick took it as a good sign. "Well?"

"It was a challenging conversation," Kent whispered, "but we are welcome to stay until tomorrow morning at sunrise as Lord Frostsong's guests."

Garrick shook his head. He realized he should keep his voice down as well. Even if he refused to sleep, it didn't mean that he had to wake Aeron up in the process.

The first rays of early-morning sunlight shined through the room's large windows, which reached nearly to its high ceiling.

Garrick said, "We should leave now, before it gets any lighter outside."

"We are all exhausted. Your eyes are bloodshot and red. We need rest."

Kent was right, but Garrick refused to acknowledge it. "What we *need* is to get back to Xenthan and deliver our findings to Lord Valdis."

"We have time to rest," Kent whispered. "It is a two-week journey back to Xenthan, at minimum. We are on good terms with Lord Frostsong, and his men are notoriously obedient. We are safe here."

Garrick glanced at Mehta, who still sat in the exact same spot, in the same chair, with his eyes cracked open just enough to watch their conversation.

Garrick raised his chin in a gesture toward him. "What do you think?"

"A night in a secure location with real beds, or even just a fine rug on the floor, would be a welcome change of pace." Mehta added, "Especially after the dungeon we just endured."

"Traitor," Garrick muttered.

"Even the most loyal comrades need rest," Mehta said.

Garrick didn't want to admit it, but Mehta had a point. Ultimately, he did admit it by caving. He was tired, too, after all.

"Fine. Have your rest," Garrick grumbled. "Good luck getting any space on that bed with Aeron laying on it like that."

"I am sure we could each have our own room if we would simply make an inquiry of the guards posted outside," Kent said. "Lord Frostsong has been most accommodating thus far. I doubt such a request would stretch the bounds of his hospitality."

A bed—an actual bed, not the sorry excuses for beds in ramshackle inns scattered across the continent—sounded like a fantasy to Garrick. He couldn't remember the last time he'd slept in a nice bed. He certainly hadn't since he'd taken the job to recover the map the first time around.

"Alright. You convinced me," Garrick said. "But what about our weapons? If I'm sleeping in my own room, I want the means to defend myself in case someone gets the idea to snoop around my pack."

"You hardly require weapons to defend yourself," Kent said, "but Lord Frostsong is ordering his guards to return all of our property to us immediately, so you can expect to sleep easily. And if that still is not enough, I believe the doors can be locked from the inside."

"I'm sure," Garrick said. "But if you knew what we possessed, would you let a locked door stop you from obtaining it?"

"No, but a mammoth green man with dark blue hair and a set of snow steel weapons might deter me." Kent tilted his head and smirked. "Then again, perhaps it would not, if I knew that man were you."

The mention of Garrick's blue hair stirred a measure of rage within his chest, but he pushed it back down. In certain light, it looked black, but most of the time it was clearly blue, and there was nothing he could do to change it.

Mehta chuckled once, just enough that Garrick might've thought it was a cough if he hadn't caught a smile fading from Mehta's lips as well.

"Very funny." Garrick sneered at them. "We'll see if you laugh and make jokes when Lord Valdis pays us enough gold to buy a small village, all because *I* got us this job."

"I have no doubt that I will laugh all the more with that much coin in my possession," Kent said. "But as much as I enjoy verbally sparring with you, I, too, am fatigued and would prefer to retire. Perhaps we can discuss the finer points of humor at your expense this evening, at dinner, with Lord Frostsong."

Garrick sighed. "We have to eat with the guy, too?"

"It is customary to not refuse the invitation of someone who wishes to show you hospitality, especially one so generous as Lord Frostsong. He could have just executed us instead, you know."

"He could've executed *you*, maybe. But not me." Garrick sighed. "Fine. I'll be there." Garrick glanced at Mehta. "Hopefully that one doesn't kill anyone between now and then."

"Hopefully I do," Mehta responded, deadpan.

Kent and Garrick stared at him.

"It was a joke." His face shifted to wide-eyed horror. "Did I do it wrong?"

"I will let the guards know of our plans for sleeping arrangements." Kent nodded toward the large windows in the room. "You ought to close the curtains so the sun does not wake poor Aeron from his slumber."

"Do it yourself."

"Then you may go articulate our requests to the guards."

Garrick stood.

And then he headed over to the curtains and pulled them shut.

§

When Aeron woke up, he found himself in a bed that didn't belong to him, in a room he didn't recognize, and he was still wearing his armor. Stranger still, it was a *nice* bed in a *nice* room.

Then he remembered where he was, and he jerked upright. His lower back spiked with familiar pain.

Why do I keep doing that? He rubbed at the spot and dug his knuckles into it. *You'd think I'd know better by now.*

He lay back down for a moment in the silence as he tried to remember where he'd left his pack with the shrooms in it.

Aeron sensed Wafer nearby. As he'd expected, Wafer had caught on to where Aeron was headed and had flown to somewhere in the vicinity, waiting for Aeron to summon him. It reassured Aeron to know they hadn't been separated again.

Then he realized that he was alone in the room.

When he'd gone to sleep, the guards had locked him in with Garrick and Mehta, but they weren't anywhere to be found.

The room was mostly dark, aside from a few embers still burning in the hearth and the sunlight rimming the edges of the curtains over the room's large windows. There were plenty of deep shadows within the room where Mehta could've hidden if he'd wanted to, but Garrick could never have pulled that off.

So where had they gone?

At first, Aeron thought they'd been taken. But why take them and let him continue to sleep? He hadn't been *that* tired.

If Garrick had called out for him while the guards were taking him away, Aeron would've heard him. Garrick could be remarkably loud when he wanted to be. In that way—and in several others, Garrick reminded Aeron of Pa.

And if they'd tried to take Mehta, there'd be bloodstains everywhere. That was unquestionable.

And where was Kent? Had Lord Frostsong executed him?

Aeron's back pain flared again, and he resigned himself to find his pack before solving the conundrum of his missing friends. He rolled out of the bed, plucked it off the floor, and dug out one of only three painkilling mushrooms remaining.

He stuffed it into his mouth, and as he ate it, he realized how famished he was. A single mushroom wouldn't do anything to satisfy him, either. Maybe the Frostsongs would give him a final meal, at least, before they killed him—if they intended to kill him at all.

Then Aeron noticed his spear lying beside the bed. Why would they return his spear to him if they wanted to kill him? Was this some sort of twisted game of survival?

As he weighed options in his head, the door to his room opened.

Mehta stood in the doorway, perfectly still and bathed in shadows.

It was creepy as hell.

"What's going on?" Aeron asked.

"Meeting in Garrick's room."

Garrick's room? Things had either gone really well or really weirdly. "How long was I asleep?"

"Most of the day. It's almost the evening," Mehta said. "Dinnertime soon. Follow me."

With that, Mehta turned and walked away from the door.

Aeron scrambled to shut his pack, sling it onto his shoulder, and pick up his spear in time to follow Mehta. He didn't want to risk leaving any of it behind.

Inside Garrick's room, which dwarfed Aeron's, the four mercs reconvened. Aeron was glad to see everyone still alive—Kent especially—and well-rested, too. Kent and Garrick rehashed the plan to leave the next morning to Aeron, and he agreed. Then again, they probably would've left whether he'd agreed or not.

It was all fine with him. The Crimson Flame temple here in Muroth hadn't yielded anything usable in terms of information on Kallie's whereabouts, so he was anxious to get back to Xenthan, get paid, and get back to searching for his sister.

"Lord Frostsong has provided us with new cloaks to replace the ones we left behind in the temple." Kent started passing them out. "And last night, his men recovered our horses and stabled them until we are ready to leave."

Aeron accepted his new cloak with a nod. It was heavy wool and would go a long way toward keeping him warm on the return trip north. "I felt Wafer through our bond, too. He's nearby enough that he should be able to hear when I blow the Wafer whistle."

"Good," Kent said. "Following dinner, we will make inquiries about the purchase of supplies for our journey home. There is a town in this province called Craneridge, and I am certain Lord Frostsong's men could be persuaded to purchase whatever we require for the journey home, as long as we reimburse them for costs."

Kent warned them not to mention anything about his magic use whatsoever—he emphasized that they shouldn't even hint at it. They all agreed, and before long, they headed off to dinner, though Aeron wondered what kind of bargain Kent had struck with Lord Frostsong to get him to overlook his magical abilities.

They all left their weapons behind, except for Mehta, who refused to be parted from his knives.

Aeron wondered about that decision. The knives weren't anything special—just two simple iron knives with hilts wrapped in black fabric.

Mehta was a nearly unstoppable force, but what difference would two knives make?

Furthermore, it was pretty clear Lord Frostsong didn't intend to do them any harm. If he'd wanted to, he could've had Aeron killed in his sleep. Aeron doubted he was just waiting to feed them a good meal before he slew them.

But if having his knives made Mehta feel more comfortable then who was Aeron to say anything about it? After all, Aeron took shrooms for his back pain and anxiety when he needed to. No one had their life totally together.

Well, maybe Kent had at one point, before his brother betrayed him. But Aeron couldn't think of anyone else who even came close. Everyone needed something to give them reassurance. It just manifested differently from person to person.

Dinner that night was flame-roasted venison, cooked with garlic and herbs and served with a hearty helping of potatoes and greens. Aeron ate his fill and drank probably more mead than he should have, but they had ample reason to celebrate.

After all, they'd found and recovered something that wasn't even supposed to exist, and they would soon get paid handsomely for bringing it to Lord Valdis. And then Aeron would have more than enough coin to move his family out of Govalia before Commander Brove could do them any more harm and continue searching for Kallie.

Dinner came and went, and no one got murdered, much to Aeron's slightly inebriated delight. Back in Garrick's room, they gathered once more and agreed to take shifts through the night to keep watch on the pack containing the dragon egg and the tome, always two at a time.

"Do you mind if I examine the tome while we are here, where it is safe and dry?" Kent asked. "I would very much like to try to glean any secrets regarding magic that it may contain."

Garrick eyed him. "I'd rather you didn't touch it at all."

"I assure you that I will handle it with the utmost care," Kent said. "If it can provide me new insight into how my own magic could function, that will be a benefit to us all going forward."

Garrick sighed, but he reached into his pack and handed the huge tome to Kent. "Whatever. Go ahead. But don't damage it."

Aeron didn't see what the big deal was. It was already old and dusty. A few more creases in its spine wouldn't make a difference.

As Kent opened the gigantic tome atop the desk in Garrick's room and started studying it, Aeron caught sight of the emblem on its cover. He couldn't see the whole thing because dust was still caked on the cover, but what little he saw looked vaguely familiar.

But emblems and symbols didn't concern him much. Instead, he headed over to Mehta with his spear in hand and asked to swap blade-sharpening techniques.

"I still find it amusing that a dragon egg, a sword powered by magic, and a tome of magic rituals were hidden in Muroth, of all places." Kent shook his head and grinned. "I wonder what other magic artifacts are buried within Muroth's borders, ready to condemn Muroth's leadership just by existing."

No one replied. Garrick had already settled in to take a nap, and Mehta had already started his sharpening demonstration. But Kent didn't seem to mind. Perhaps he'd just been talking out loud.

A couple of hours later, Kent was still studying at the desk, while Garrick snoozed in the chair before the fire. Thanks to Mehta's sharpening skills, Aeron's spear was as sharp as it had ever been—at least, since the day he'd stolen it from Commander Brove and reclaimed Wafer.

"This is incredible," Kent said. "If I am interpreting the ancient Aletian correctly, then this tome is claiming that the entirety of the dungeon we were in very well could have been formed by magic rather than by hand, including the external structure rising from the water."

Aeron glanced over at him. "Someone made that rock rise out of the lake?"

"I mean the ancient Aletians might have used magic to not only draw the rock out of the lake, but they also might have shaped the rock formation itself, inside and outside. It is an entirely different task than just drawing the rock up from beneath the surface."

Aeron's eyebrows rose. "That's... possible?"

"I do not see any reason to doubt the text," Kent said. "A great many things are possible with magic. And no one really knows what the ancient Aletians were truly capable of. It may also be the reason why the cavern flooded so easily."

"Crazy." Aeron shook his head. It was way beyond his comprehension, and he'd started to tune Kent's explanation out.

"There is more," Kent added. "Evidently, there is a ritual in this tome that can 'awaken' the dragon egg. But it requires a sacrifice of someone bearing the mark of the dragon's soul."

Aeron lowered his voice. "You think he'd actually try that?"

"I have no doubt that awakening the egg is his intention, given the ritual described within this tome and that he specifically requested that we retrieve it for him."

Aeron shook his head. "I definitely don't like the sound of that. What good is a dragon going to do anyone?"

"I do not believe 'good' is what Lord Valdis has in mind."

If Lord Valdis had to sacrifice someone, Aeron figured Commander Brove would be perfect for the task.

"According to this text," Kent flipped a few pages back, "the worshipers of dragons appoint a young woman to serve in that capacity with each new generation."

A young woman? Aeron leaned forward. "What else does it say?"

"Apparently, this young woman is branded with a unique mark that identifies her as the chosen sacrifice." Kent looked up at Aeron with horror etched on his face. "On the back of her neck."

It can't be. Aeron sprung to his feet and darted over to the tome. He nudged past Kent, took hold of the huge tome, and shut it.

Dust billowed off the cover, and Aeron wiped the rest of it off with his hand, revealing the entirety of the golden-bronze emblem stamped on the front of the tome.

He'd seen it before, and it filled him with more dread now than it had the first time.

It was the same mark that Kallie had on the back of her neck.

CHAPTER TWENTY-THREE

At first, Aeron couldn't believe what he was seeing. But the more he considered it, the more all the pieces came together. His sister—*his little sister*—had been chosen to be the sacrifice for a dragon-worshiping cult.

And now Lord Valdis was involved. Did that mean Lord Valdis had Kallie?

Aeron glanced at Garrick, who was still sleeping in his chair. Then he looked at Mehta, who sat with his back to them, totally still.

Aeron needed to talk through this with Kent, but he didn't want to risk it with both Garrick and Mehta in earshot. He turned toward Kent.

"Would you, uh…" Aeron started. "Help me find something in my room? I think something fell out of my pack."

Kent nodded slowly. "Yes. I would not want you to go without."

He'd gotten the message. "Thanks."

They stood and headed out of the room, leaving Garrick and Mehta behind. Once they made it to Aeron's room, he shut and locked the door behind them. "Does Lord Valdis have my sister? Is he a member of the Crimson Flame, too, and we just don't know it? Is he going to sacrifice Kallie to awaken a dragon?"

"Be calm." Kent held up his hands. "We do not know anything for certain."

"Kallie has that mark, the one on the cover of that tome, tattooed on the back of her neck." Aeron's heart raced. This was the first real lead they'd found since Kallie had been taken—but it horrified Aeron to consider what it meant. "She's the sacrifice this tome is talking about."

"Your sister *does* have the mark," Kent confirmed. "But who is to say she is the only one who bears it?"

"What did the tome say?" Before Kent could answer, Aeron said, "It said a young woman from each new generation is chosen. One. Not many. *One.*"

"Think about it," Aeron continued. "Kallie was taken by the Crimson Flame. We found the tome and the dragon egg in a dungeon under a Crimson Flame temple. Lord Valdis wants the tome and the egg so he can hatch a dragon. It's all connected."

"I pray that it isn't so," Kent said, "but I think we must assume that it is."

"It's the best lead we've found so far."

"The *only* lead," Kent added. "Is Kallie a member of the Crimson Flame?"

The question stunned Aeron. "No. There's no way my sister is a member of the Crimson Flame. Absolutely not."

But even as he said it, he couldn't be sure.

After Aeron had been discharged from the Govalian Army and returned home, he'd gone back to work at Pa's forge. And every night after work, he'd spent a fair portion of his evenings catching up with Kallie.

One night, Kallie told him she'd earned some coin and wanted to contribute it to his efforts to buy Wafer back at an upcoming auction. Aeron had told her she ought to save it for her dowry for when she got married. She'd said she had no interest in getting married.

At the time, it had struck Aeron as strange. He'd figured most little girls looked forward to getting married, having children, and living their lives accordingly. But he hadn't given it a second thought because Kallie was a different sort of girl in a lot of ways.

Then, at the auction itself, Mum had asked her where she'd gotten all that coin. At first, Mum had outright suggested that Kallie might be selling herself, but Kallie had emphatically denied it. But she'd just as emphatically refused to reveal the source of her coin, too.

That, coupled with her comment about not wanting to marry, made Aeron seriously reconsider his certainty about Kallie's involvement, but it hardly constituted proof.

But coupled with her unexplained visit to Urthia, the mark on the back of her neck, and the fact that she hadn't resisted when that fire-wielding woman showed up at Mum and Pa's house...

"She might be," Aeron amended his statement. "Gods... she might be."

"What if the Crimson Flame is a dragon-worshiping cult and not a fire-worshiping cult?" Kent asked. "The tome used the term 'dragon-worshipers,' at least as far as my understanding of the language goes.

"Dragons are gone, but fire has endured. Perhaps this whole time, we have just assumed they worshiped fire, when they're actually a dragon cult instead."

Aeron rubbed his forehead. "It would explain the dragon-like etchings on the inner walls of the temples."

"I noticed those as well," Kent said. "And now the egg, the tome, and the sword. But if that is the case, there is a cognitive dissonance within their organization. More than one, in fact."

"What do you mean?" Aeron asked.

"Why would the Crimson Flame continue to designate a sacrifice every generation if they also guarded the only dragon egg in existence, this tome, and the map showing their location?"

"Maybe it's some sort of sick challenge," Aeron said. "Only someone who's worthy of figuring it out is worthy to hatch a dragon."

"In that case, Garrick would be the only one worthy, as he is the only person on the continent who has survived both dungeons," Kent said. "Not Lord Valdis."

"I doubt the egg will care who hatches it," Aeron muttered.

Part of Aeron didn't want to sit around and keep talking. At the moment, he was debating whether or not he ought to mount Wafer and just fly to Xenthan on his own to find out if Lord Valdis had Kallie. Whether Lord Valdis had her or not, Aeron couldn't let her be sacrificed.

"There is yet a second inconsistency we must consider," Kent replied. "Lord Glavan."

"What do you mean?"

"He was also a member of the Crimson Flame, by his own admission. So why would he seek to keep the map from falling into Lord Valdis's hands? If the Crimson Flame truly does worship dragons, then why not just let Lord Valdis have it, if he intends to bring them back?"

Aeron shrugged. "Could be internal politics. Every religion has sects. Every one of the gods and goddesses has different factions that worship them in different ways. I mean, Mehta came out of a death cult that worshiped Xyon by assassinating people."

"It is possible."

"What does all of this mean for my sister?" he asked. "Does Lord Valdis have her or not?"

"I cannot say for sure," Kent replied. "Given that Lord Glavan sought to keep the map from Lord Valdis, it is possible that the Crimson Flame captured Kallie to keep her out of Lord Valdis's reach."

"Or it's possible that Lord Valdis is also a Crimson Flame cultist and sent that woman to take her."

Kent nodded. "Yes."

Aeron sighed and sat on the corner of the bed. "So the only way to find out is to try to get Lord Valdis to tell us."

"And either way, I expect he will be looking for her if he does not already have her."

"Great." Aeron buried his head in his hands. *Kallie, what did you get yourself into?*

"The tome said the ritual must be performed under the new moon," Kent said. "Which would be about two and a half weeks from now."

That didn't give Aeron any sense of relief whatsoever. "If Lord Valdis already has her, then we'll be bringing him everything he needs just in time for the ritual. Xenthan is roughly a two-week journey from here."

"But he does not know when to expect our return," Kent said. "We have not sent word of our success, so it is unlikely he would base his plans off our progress."

Aeron shook his head. "I don't know what to do, Kent."

Kent took a seat next to him on the bed. "First, you must not reveal any of this to Garrick. If he learns of the connection, there is a good chance he will bar you from entering Valdis Keep, that is, if Lord Valdis allows us to enter this time. It is imperative that we maintain our secrecy for now."

"Agreed." Aeron normally didn't like to keep secrets from his friends, but where Kallie was concerned, he had no qualms about it whatsoever.

"We now know what the mark means, and that may reveal new paths for us in our search for Kallie. If she is not in Lord Valdis's possession, we will have more time."

"We'd have even more time if we could delay the journey back to Xenthan," Aeron said. "If we can stretch it out by another week, we'd miss the new moon entirely."

Kent shook his head. "I would not risk raising Garrick's suspicions. He will be all the more eager to return to Xenthan now that we have succeeded."

It prickled at Aeron, but Kent was right. Garrick was smart enough to figure out that something was wrong if they weren't careful. The last thing they needed was to ruin their chances of learning the truth before they even reached Xenthan.

"So we just... go with it for now?"

"I am afraid we do not have any better options," Kent said. "Time will tell what our next move must be, but for now, we need to obtain more information before we can act."

In other words, we're waiting until the last minute to figure out whether Lord

Valdis has Kallie or not. Aeron frowned and looked at Kent. "You're still with me, right?"

"To the end." Kent put his hand on Aeron's shoulder. "I vowed I would help you save her, and I will not rest until we have done just that."

MUCH LATER THAT NIGHT, MEHTA OPENED AERON'S DOOR. EARLIER, HE'D stood just outside of Aeron's room, eavesdropping on Aeron's conversation with Kent. What he'd heard was beyond troubling.

And it might interfere with his plans to sift Lord Valdis.

Mehta shut the door in perfect silence and glided across the paneled floor over to Aeron's bed. The room was dark except for a bit of wintry moonlight glowing around the edges of the curtains.

Now he stood over Aeron's bed, staring down at him while he slept. The thirst begged for a taste of Aeron's blood, but that wasn't why Mehta was there. At least, he didn't intend for things to go that way.

If they did, he'd reach his knives long before Aeron could get to his spear, which Mehta could see leaning in the corner on the far side of the bed, well out of grabbing distance. Aeron must've felt safe here, so he'd been lax with his precautions.

Even so, Aeron still wore his armor while he slept. One of his arms was exposed up to his shoulder over the bedcovers, and teal plating covered it down to his gauntlet. Mehta supposed that if something were to befall them, Aeron wouldn't have to waste time donning his armor before joining the fray.

Aeron stirred, and his eyes slowly opened. He blinked a few times and squinted at Mehta, dazed, either from the lingering influence of sleep, magic mushrooms, or both.

Then he jerked upright, terror etched into his face. Immediately after, he grabbed at his lower back, and his terror shifted to anguish.

Mehta didn't move. He just stood there.

When Aeron realized Mehta wasn't moving, his demeanor began to calm. He hissed, "What in the third hell are you doing here?"

"We have to talk."

Aeron's eyes widened slightly, then he squinted again, still rubbing his back. "Talk about what? It's the middle of the night."

"About your sister," Mehta said. "And Lord Valdis."

Aeron froze, and terror reclaimed his face. "I... I don't know what you mean."

Mehta just stood there, watching him. Aeron wasn't a good liar, so Mehta doubted he'd keep up the charade for long.

Sure enough, it only took five seconds for Aeron to cave.

"What do you know?" he asked.

"Enough," Mehta replied.

Aeron sighed and continued rubbing his back. "Do you mind if I take a shroom first? My back is killing me."

Mehta gave a slight nod, and Aeron rolled across the bed, toward his pack, which lay on a small reading table next to the bed. It was also the direction of his spear, so Mehta watched him closely.

Mehta's mind calculated a half-dozen ways to quickly disarm Aeron, sift Aeron, or both, if he reached for the spear.

In order to wield it effectively, Aeron would need to get both hands on his spear. In the time it would take Aeron to recover it, Mehta could draw one of his knives, bound over the bed, and lodge it in Aeron's throat or in any number of fatal weak points between his armor.

The thirst urged him to do it anyway.

But his calculations dissipated when Aeron turned back with only his pack in his hands.

Aeron nodded toward the curtains. "If this is gonna be a long talk, can you open the curtains? I can't see you, and I can't see what shrooms I'm digging out of my pack."

Mehta obliged, but he did so while keeping one eye on Aeron at all times. With the curtains open, silver moonlight washed over the bed and Aeron on top of it.

Aeron pulled out a shroom and devoured it, then he adjusted the pillows behind his back and sat upright. "Do you understand the situation I'm in?" Aeron said. "And do you understand why I can't tell Garrick?"

Mehta nodded.

"Are you going to tell him?" Aeron asked.

Mehta considered the question. He liked Garrick and Aeron more or less equally. Garrick was his employer, so Mehta probably had some obligation to tell him what he knew.

But neither of those things had any bearing on what he needed to do as far as Lord Valdis was concerned. That was the only question that mattered now, so close to the end of their journey.

Telling Garrick might endear Mehta to him further. It might ensure he would get into Valdis Keep this time instead of being forced to wait outside.

But it might not change anything at all, except to drive a wedge between Mehta and Aeron. And Kent, too, since he was obviously on Aeron's side.

It made no sense for Mehta to create tension where none currently existed. None of them knew his true intentions for Lord Valdis, and none of them needed to know until it was done, so he wasn't risking anything by not telling Garrick.

"No," he finally replied.

Aeron hesitated. "You sure?"

Mehta briefly reconsidered his answer. "Yes."

"You don't sound sure."

"Your perception of me is your business."

Aeron frowned. "That's not helping."

"I know what you're risking by not telling Garrick what you know," Mehta said. "If your sister is there, it will mean conflict and possibly bloodshed."

The thirst reveled at the suggestion, and Mehta had to push it to the back of his mind yet again.

"And I understand that you will not stop until your sister is found and freed," Mehta continued. "I gain nothing by telling Garrick, so I won't tell him."

"Alright." Aeron paused. "Why not?"

Mehta paused for a moment to collect his words. He had to make sure he conveyed the correct sentiment without giving away his intentions regarding Lord Valdis.

"I have a sister, too, and I would do anything to protect her as well." Mehta's voice broke the tranquility of the room. "That's why I sent my earnings from the map job to her and my grandfather."

He touched the triangle-shaped pendant around his neck—the symbol of Laeri.

"Did she give that to you?" Aeron asked.

Mehta hadn't discussed any of this with Aeron, although he'd told Garrick a little bit about it.

"No," he said. "This came from Ferne. She's a little girl I saved from the Xyonates back in Sefera. She gave it to me as a way to remember her and to remember to ask Laeri for guidance. I would do anything for her as well, just as I would for my sister."

"So you really *do* understand." Aeron sighed and looked at the ceiling for a long moment, then he refocused on Mehta. "I don't want to wreck everything for you, Kent, or Garrick, but I can't let him sacrifice my sister."

The more Mehta considered it, the more this whole situation might work out in his favor. If conflict transpired, it could leave Lord Valdis exposed, and then Mehta would strike.

A tinge of guilt hit Mehta's gut at the prospect of leveraging Aeron and his sister to get a shot at sifting Lord Valdis, but he rationalized it away. After all, if he succeeded, and Lord Valdis perished, he couldn't sacrifice Aeron's sister —if that was truly his intent.

"Don't worry about me," Mehta said. "Just do what you need to do."

Aeron rubbed the back of his neck. "I'm really sorry about this."

"There's no reason to apologize," Mehta said. "The Crimson Flame took your sister. They're an evil cult, and you are right to do everything you can to rescue her, regardless of what anyone else thinks."

"Believe me, I will." Aeron nodded. "Nothing is more important to me than saving Kallie."

"Then see to it that you do so," Mehta said. "I will not stand in your way."

৬

LESS THAN TWO WEEKS LATER

MEHTA RECOGNIZED THE MOUNTAIN PATH THEY'D TAKEN SOUTH FROM XENTHAN into northwestern Urthia about a month earlier. They were close to the border now, and soon after crossing over, they'd arrive at Valdis Keep—a full two days before the new moon.

They made their way through the mountains on horseback amid blustery winter winds and icy air, both much colder than when last Mehta had been in Xenthan. As such, he was all the more thankful for the cloaks Lord Frostsong had given them. His cloak was a bit baggier than he was accustomed to, but in weather like this, he wouldn't complain.

Before long, they crested the mountains along the border, and Valdis Keep yet again rose in the distance, a black spike amid the endless white snow covering the surrounding terrain. Mehta caught sight of Aeron and Wafer flying through the brooding red skies above them, weaving in and out of dark clouds.

Within a few more hours, they'd descended the slopes to the flatlands, and their horses slogged through the snow toward Valdis Keep.

Mehta's anticipation burgeoned with every stamp of the horses' hooves. His travels were finally coming to an end. Soon he would sift Lord Valdis, take his coin, and return to his home in the mountains to the east.

As long as they let him into the castle this time.

At the castle's outer gates, the same soldiers who'd banned Mehta, Kent, and Aeron from entering last time still stood guard. Aeron and Wafer landed farther away so as not to spook them again, and Aeron dismounted and joined the others. Together, they approached the courtyard gates on foot.

With each new step, Mehta's thirst swirled to life more and more. If the soldiers refused to let him in this time, he wouldn't restrain his thirst from controlling his actions. He'd nearly died several times in Lord Valdis's service, and he refused to risk his life further for a man whom he intended to sift the first good chance he got.

But the involvement of Aeron's sister had complicated things. Throughout the journey back to Xenthan, Mehta had entertained a variety of scenarios about how the next few hours could go.

If possible, he wanted to sift Lord Valdis without Aeron, Kallie, Kent, or even Garrick being harmed. But there was a realistic possibility that if Mehta sifted Lord Valdis before Aeron got Kallie back, it might lead to Kallie's death anyway. And if Aeron unknowingly got in the way, he could ruin Mehta's chances to sift Lord Valdis at all.

Mehta couldn't explain any of that to Aeron, of course. But neither did he want to fail his final commission. He needed to put an end to Lord Valdis's abuses of his village, of his grandfather and sister.

Aeron had his family to take care of, but Mehta had one of his own now as well. He'd just gotten them back, and he didn't want to lose them again.

One question had continually gnawed at Mehta's mind: if Aeron got in the way, what was he prepared to do?

The thirst's answer was always the same: *sift him, too.* But the thirst couldn't be trusted. It gave the same answer in every situation, whether it was practical or not.

It always wanted him to take more lives. As such, at times it was easy to ignore because he already knew what to expect. But in situations where sifting was an actual, viable option, its voice threatened to drown out Mehta's own sense of reason.

He didn't want to sift Aeron. He'd told him he wouldn't interfere if Aeron had to fight to save Kallie. And over the last few months of traveling together, Mehta had developed an affinity toward him. He liked Aeron, and Mehta didn't want to sift him in order to get to Lord Valdis.

But even so, Aeron wasn't Mehta's chief concern. If he absolutely had to, Mehta could sift Aeron with relative ease—especially without Wafer around to defend him.

Garrick, on the other hand, would make for a monstrous foe, and based on everything Mehta had observed, he seemed to still be steadfastly loyal to Lord Valdis. If he got in the way...

Mehta had given plenty of thought as to how he could sift Garrick, and every solution involved surprise, speed, or some combination of both. With Garrick's durable skin, his advanced healing, and his incredible strength,

Mehta would have to land some devastating stabs to vital spots, and quickly.

It would prove exceptionally difficult, but Mehta could do it if he needed to. The problem was, what would Kent be doing during that time? Would he try to defend Garrick, or would he stay out of it?

Given his closeness with Aeron, Kent could go either way. Mehta didn't know what to expect if it came to blows aside from remaining aligned with Aeron through everything. That, he could count on as a certainty. So if they interfered with Mehta's attempts to sift Lord Valdis, they would interfere together.

As with Garrick, dealing with Kent would require quickness and an outright betrayal of the trust they'd forged thus far. If Kent saw an attack coming, Mehta would have to totally revamp his plans. And with the unpredictability of Kent's magic, Mehta's certainty of success diminished greatly.

Perhaps even worse, Garrick had also bequeathed the dragon sword to Kent. Aside from unlocking dungeon doors, the sword might have additional magical properties that Mehta wasn't yet aware of. And in Kent's capable hands, who knew how it could alter the direction of a fight?

And if for some reason Mehta had to fight all three of them, he doubted he would be able to triumph. If Lord Valdis didn't have Aeron's sister and the other mercs meant to leave, they might directly oppose Mehta if he attempted to sift Lord Valdis.

He'd seen how they could work together if they so wished, and the prospect of facing all of them at once and then trying to bring down Lord Valdis didn't appeal to Mehta at all. He couldn't possibly win in that scenario.

Worse yet, they would likely all be in the same room together when Mehta sifted Lord Valdis. If Mehta succeeded and they tried to attack him after the deed was done, he could flee. But if he failed... he wasn't sure what he would do.

He resigned himself not to fail. Lord Valdis was a dark lord, a sorcerer, but he was made of flesh and blood just like Lord Glavan was. Although it had been difficult, Mehta had managed to sift him.

And Lord Valdis didn't know Mehta was coming for him.

If he could get inside the castle.

"Back again?" the lead soldier at the gate asked.

Mehta recognized the scar running on a diagonal across the soldier's forehead, and he gripped his knives under his cloak.

"Yes," Garrick replied. "And this time, we're all going up. We have what Lord Valdis requested."

The scarred soldier stepped aside and motioned for them to enter the courtyard. "He's expecting you all. Everyone except the wyvern, of course."

Mehta blinked, and his grips on his knives relaxed, but he didn't fully release them. That was it? The last time, they'd refused to let anyone but Garrick pass. Now everyone could go inside, without question?

If your enemy gives you an advantage, don't ignore it. Exploit it. The words of Lament, one of Mehta's combat-training instructors from his time in the Xyonates, resonated within his memory.

Ironically, Lament had perished because of an advantage Mehta had exploited in their final confrontation.

If Lord Valdis meant to let him inside this time, Mehta would gladly exploit that advantage.

Mehta forced his thirst into its box with the reassurance that it would be released soon. Then he followed Garrick and Kent into the castle's main doors, careful not to let his eagerness get the better of him.

Mehta had trained for these types of situations for nearly two decades of his life.

He would be ready.

CHAPTER TWENTY-FOUR

As a former noble, Kent had visited his fair share of castles and fine mansions throughout his lifetime. While he didn't love the dark aesthetic of Valdis Keep, either inside or out, he couldn't deny that it was well done and perfect for a sorcerer living in the dismal country of Xenthan.

The fearsome, obsidian gargoyles mounted overhead, watching their every move with lifeless eyes, were an especially nice touch. He wondered if they were considered "art" or if they existed solely to intimidate passersby.

Or perhaps Lord Valdis was so powerful, he could make them come to life and do his bidding. Kent had given it serious consideration, but in the end, he didn't see how it was possible, based on what he knew of magic.

They passed through a set of black double-doors, held open by two soldiers guarding them, and entered a throne room of sorts. Compared to the brightness of the last throne room he'd been inside—Hunera Palace in Inoth—this one felt dark and oppressive.

But Aveyna had been a practitioner of light magic, whereas Lord Valdis practiced dark magic. Kent wasn't well-versed in either discipline, but he'd seen Aveyna do magic that had only worked because of her access to light. Perhaps some aspects of dark magic functioned the same way.

The throne room's gray walls arched toward its cathedral-style ceiling, and huge, iron bowls of fire hung from charcoal-colored granite pillars spaced at even intervals. Beneath them all, a floor made of dark granite tiles stretched from one end to the other.

And at the far end, on the wall, hung the sigil of the three-horned ram, barely visible in the darkness.

Beneath the sigil sat a man in dark robes on a throne made of twisted black bones, and his hands rested on twin black skulls. Given Kent's previous experiences with dark magic, particularly the way Lord Glavan harvested the bones of his fallen guards in battle, the sight of the chair unnerved him.

But as they approached, the look of Lord Valdis's eyes set Kent on edge even more. They seemed to exude darkness itself. None of the other dark mages he'd encountered—not Eusephus, Kymil, or Lord Glavan, whose eyes had transformed into insect-like black orbs—had eyes like that.

Kent didn't want to think about what Lord Valdis had done to earn such eyes—about the price he, and likely many others, had paid for them.

"Come forth," Lord Valdis said.

They approached the throne, and Lord Valdis stood.

He might've been as tall as Aeron. His dark hair was slicked back, and Kent couldn't have guessed his exact age if he'd been threatened with execution. It could have ranged anywhere from thirty to fifty, or perhaps even older.

"You have brought what I requested?" Lord Valdis asked.

"Yes, Lord Valdis," Garrick replied.

Lord Valdis raised both of his arms, and three pairs of guards emerged from the shadows behind the pillars. Kent hadn't even realized they were there until they'd started moving.

Was he slipping now that he was pushing fifty? He *should've* noticed them. If something had gone wrong, they would have caught him totally unaware— and with Aeron's sister's fate in the mix, his lack of awareness could've proven fatal.

The guards wore black robes and had dark skin comparable to Mehta's. Each wore a gleaming scimitar at his waist, and each pair of guards carried a wooden chest just like the one Garrick had brought into the pub weeks earlier.

They set the chests before Lord Valdis and opened the chests in unison, displaying the mountains of perfectly stacked gold coins within.

Lord Valdis held out his hand. "The egg."

One of Lord Valdis's guards stepped forward to receive it in his stead, also holding out his hand.

As Garrick reached into his bag, Aeron stepped forward.

"Lord Valdis, sir," he said.

In unison, each of the guards stepped back with one leg and grasped the hilts of their scimitars, but they didn't draw them.

"Whoa, whoa." Aeron held up his hands and took a half-step back. "Sorry."

He wore his spear across his back on a diagonal. It somehow made him look taller, but as Kent had guessed, he was about the same height as Lord Valdis.

"What are you doing?" Garrick growled.

Aeron glanced back at him and held his hands up. "It's fine. Just give me a minute, here."

Kent tensed, but Aeron had to do what he was about to do.

"*Aeron,*" Garrick snapped.

Aeron ignored him. "Please, Lord Valdis. I promise I'll be brief."

Lord Valdis stared at Garrick with those haunting eyes, and then his threatening gaze shifted to Aeron. Kent didn't envy either of them for it.

"My time is precious, so state your business quickly." Despite the interruption, Lord Valdis's voice remained smooth and calm. He pulled his hand back, sat down on his twisted throne, and rested both hands on the skulls once again. The guard in front of him also retracted his hand.

"I've come to learn that you may have a certain young woman in your possession who's supposed to play a pivotal role in a ritual," Aeron said. "On the night of the new moon."

If Garrick could've burned holes in the back of Aeron's head with his stare, he would've done it by now. "What in the third hell is going on?"

Lord Valdis held up his hand to Garrick, who promptly went silent. Then he turned his head slightly, almost imperceptibly, and focused his insidious eyes on Kent. "I assume you are the scholar of the group?"

Kent had stared down a variety of intimidating men in his day, but he'd never encountered someone as quietly menacing as Lord Valdis. He inhaled a steady breath to calm the uneasiness growing in his chest.

"It is over-generous to call me a scholar, but I deciphered the ritual."

Now Garrick was glaring at Kent instead.

Lord Valdis's expression remained dark and stony. "I suppose I didn't order you not to *read* the tome. I also didn't think that someone who could read ancient Aletian would deign to live his life as a mercenary."

"It is a recent occupation, Lord Valdis," Kent admitted. "As is my comprehension of the ancient Aletian language."

Now Aeron was looking back at Kent as well.

All of the pressure had shifted to Kent. Normally, he didn't eschew pressure; he often welcomed it as it forced him to become better, more capable. But now a large part of him wished he hadn't spoken up.

Lord Valdis said, "A certain young woman bears a unique mark and a status conferred upon her by an ancient order of dragon-worshipers—"

"And she will be sacrificed as part of the ritual to awaken the dragon within the egg," Kent finished for him. As soon as he said it, he wondered if he should have refrained from interrupting Lord Valdis.

"That is incorrect," Lord Valdis said.

The room fell silent, and Kent and Aeron glanced at each other, and then Kent found Garrick's cold stare once again.

"Your comprehension of ancient Aletian is inadequate," Lord Valdis said. "The ritual does not *hatch* a dragon egg. It is advanced, dark magic that enables the ritualist to harvest the essence of the dragon itself."

Kent's eyebrows rose. *He means to take the essence of a dragon?*

"The result is the ritualist obtaining godlike power." Lord Valdis's stoic mouth curled into a wicked smile. Again, he extended his hand. "The egg."

"Do you have her or not?" Aeron blurted.

Lord Valdis pulled his hand back once again. His smile faded, and now his stare burrowed into Aeron even more than Garrick's. "She is in my possession, as you supposed. What of it?"

Kent's heart rate doubled. Lord Valdis had Kallie.

His mind swirled with questions, connections, and the new information that emerged as a result. But he relegated it all to the recesses of his mind for the time being. The only thing that mattered now was getting Kallie back.

"The girl you took is my sister," Aeron said. "I don't want her sacrificed. I'm sure you can understand. I want her back, please. I'm willing to forgo my portion of the fee for bringing back the egg if you'll release her to me."

Lord Valdis tilted his head slightly. "Your sister?"

"That's right." Aeron nodded. "Her name is Kallie."

Lord Valdis rubbed his chin. Then, to no one in particular, he said, "Bring me the girl."

Kent couldn't believe it. It was working. They'd not only found Kallie, but it looked like Lord Valdis was going to give her up. He couldn't have hoped for a better outcome—if it did, in fact, play out that way.

He looked at Garrick again, who now wore a mix of anger and confusion on his face rather than outright rage. The revelation that Lord Valdis had Aeron's sister must've made an impact. But Garrick's behavior thus far had also reinforced Kent's admonishment to Aeron not to tell him anything.

Kent stole a glance back at Mehta, who, according to Aeron, also knew about all of this. Mehta met Kent's eyes for a moment, gave him a subtle nod, then they both refocused on Lord Valdis. So far, so good.

A tall, burly soldier emerged from the darkness behind the throne. He wore black armor that bore Lord Valdis's three-horned ram sigil on his chest and tugged a young woman with blonde hair behind him.

He escorted the girl to the space between Lord Valdis and the mercs and helped position her, not gently but not forcefully, either, so they could see her and she could see them.

The girl brushed her hair away from her face.

It was Kallie.

CHAPTER TWENTY-FIVE

Aeron had found her. At last, he had found his sister.

At first, he couldn't believe it. Everything was going so well—nothing about this journey had been easy, and he'd made so little progress in finding her until the ancient Aletian tome had revealed everything.

And if Kent hadn't known some ancient Aletian, they never would've realized Kallie's connection to all of this. It was a miracle, and Aeron silently thanked all the gods and goddesses at once for providing it.

Aside from being barefoot and looking somewhat dazed—though no more than Aeron probably did when he'd had an extra magic mushroom or two—Kallie appeared to be unharmed. She wore a red robe with the emblem of the Crimson Flame on the chest, embroidered in gold.

It reminded Aeron of the one worn by the woman who had taken her so many months before, and the sight of it threatened to boil his blood. After all, that woman had burned down his parents' house and nearly killed his entire family—and Kent.

Aeron started toward her, but the guards resumed their stance, ready to draw their swords, and he stopped mid-step. He hesitated—that was a bad sign, but maybe they were just hyper-vigilant guards.

He locked eyes with his little sister and said, "Kallie, are you alright?"

Kallie gave him a familiar, crooked-toothed smile. But as wide as Kallie's crooked smile was, there was something thoroughly wrong about it. It seemed… disingenuous somehow. Fake. Artificial.

Forced.

"I'm fine, Aeron." She approached him, gave him her usual kiss on his cheek, and took his hands in hers. "Why are you all the way up in Xenthan?"

Aeron recoiled a bit. She'd been taken from her family... her question didn't make any sense. "I'm here to bring you home. Mum and Pa are worried sick, and so am I."

"Nonsense." Kallie shook her head in big, side-to-side lolls. "You know how they like to exaggerate things."

Something was definitely off. Aeron glanced at Lord Valdis, who continued staring at him with those freaky eyes of his, and then he looked at Kallie again. "Do you remember being taken from our home and brought here?"

"Of course, silly," she replied. "But that was just a misunderstanding. I wanted to come here."

Aeron's eyes widened. *What is she saying?*

He surveyed the guards once again. They still stood there, ready to draw their swords if he moved forward even another inch. Very bad.

He caught Garrick's eyes again, too. His fury had dissipated some, but there was no doubt he was still pissed at Aeron for interfering with his job. Aeron knew he'd been betrayed before by other partners, but this was way different. This was Aeron's sister.

"Do you..." he started to ask her, "...do you know what they're planning to do to you?"

She shrugged. "More or less. I know I've been chosen for a great honor, yeah? I'm gonna help bring about real change on this continent, Aeron."

"But Kallie," Aeron's voice lowered, "they're going to *sacrifice* you. They're going to kill you as part of some ritual involving a dragon's essence."

"Yes, and I'll live forever within that essence. My soul will be eternally tied to the dragon's soul. My spirit will be immortal!" She sounded vaguely excited about it, but at the same time, her words lacked any substantive emotion.

It all felt wrong to Aeron. Something was influencing her, either directly or surreptitiously. This wasn't normal.

"Kallie, I can't let you do this."

"It's my choice, Aeron," she said. "It's my honor, and you can't take it away from me."

Aeron shook his head as she finished talking. "You're confused. You need to come home. You're not yourself."

"I feel fine."

"I've been searching for you for *months*. You wouldn't believe the mayhem I've gone through in order to find you." Aeron held his hands out. "You can't just expect me to leave you here to die."

"That is exactly what she expects, Aeron." Lord Valdis's attention shifted to her. "Kallie, my child, you wish to stay, do you not?"

Kallie turned back toward him slowly, lazily. "I do, my lord."

Aeron's world swirled into confusion. *What is happening?*

"Then the matter is settled."

The big soldier grabbed Kallie by her wrist and pulled her away, out of Aeron's reach.

"No!" Aeron turned his attention toward Lord Valdis. "You can't do this. She's my sister!"

"She has made her choice, Aeron. You must let her go."

Aeron shook his head again. He couldn't believe this was happening. "No… she's not right. *None* of this is right."

Was Lord Valdis wielding some power over her? It seemed as if he were controlling her, somehow, but Aeron didn't know if such a thing was even possible.

"You have heard it with your own ears. The matter is closed." Lord Valdis and his guard both extended their hands in unison. "Now, the egg."

Garrick hesitated for a moment, but he pulled the egg out of his pack and started to step toward the guard.

Aeron only had an instant to make a choice, and only one choice would give him a chance to save Kallie. If he hesitated, she'd be lost forever, and he refused to let that happen.

So Aeron did the only thing he could do.

He snatched the egg out of Garrick's hands and scampered away with it held high over his head.

❦

KENT TENSED, GLANCING BETWEEN AERON AND THE GUARDS AND GARRICK AND Lord Valdis, all while planning his response to any number of potential outcomes. None of them played out well in his head—for any of them.

The guards drew their scimitars and immediately started toward Aeron.

"Don't come any closer!" Aeron shifted the egg to one hand, and it wobbled wildly. He pointed at them with his free hand. "Or I'll shatter this thing, right here, right now."

The guards halted in place, glancing between each other.

"Aeron!" Garrick dropped his pack to the floor with a *thunk* and stormed toward Aeron with his fists clenched.

"I said *stay put!*" Aeron shouted. He reared back like he meant to slam the egg against the floor.

Garrick's progress faltered, and he stood there, seething at Aeron. "Give it to me."

"No. He releases Kallie to me first, and then I'll hand it over."

Several more guards appeared from the shadows of the pillars, surrounding Aeron and Garrick, although they'd done well to stay back as Aeron had ordered.

Kent slowly dug into one of the pouches on his belt and pulled a stone into his fingers. He didn't want to have to use it, but he would if he had to.

"She does not wish to go with you, Aeron," Lord Valdis said.

"You're lying!" he yelled. "You've bewitched her, or messed with her head somehow. She needs to come home. I'm *not* going to let you hurt her."

"Aeron, you're going to get us all killed," Garrick growled. "Now give me the egg, and maybe I can still save our lives."

"No chance." Aeron cupped the egg with both hands again. "Make a choice, Lord Valdis. The dragon egg, or my sister. What's it gonna be?"

Kent held his breath.

❦

It was definitely the stupidest thing Aeron had ever done, but he'd gone too far to give up now. He was hopelessly outnumbered, and he didn't really have a plan. But he needed to do something to save Kallie, and this was the only thing he could think of.

Truth be told, he was astounded that he'd managed to steal the egg out of Garrick's grasp in the first place. Even if he died as a result, that was a pretty incredible way to kick off the last few moments of his life.

"I'm waiting, Lord Valdis," he said. Perhaps it wasn't a great idea to taunt and threaten a stupidly rich and powerful dark lord, but, again, he'd already come this far, so why not keep going?

"What assurance do I have that you will leave the egg unharmed if I give her to you?" Lord Valdis asked.

Aeron's eyes widened. *He's actually considering making the trade?*

Aeron hadn't accounted for that. He'd just planned to smash the egg and then try to kill as many of them on his way to dying heroically while trying to save Kallie. But this had opened up a whole new world of possibilities for him.

"Uh... I promise?" he said. "I promise I won't smash it if you give her to me. Unharmed." He quickly added, "And you let us out of here. Out of the castle, I mean. I'll leave the egg with the soldiers at your front gate. And both of us have to be unharmed, not just her."

Lord Valdis didn't so much as move. "Anything else?"

It unnerved Aeron how calm Lord Valdis was being this entire time, especially compared to the murder-eyes Aeron was still getting from Garrick.

"Yeah," Aeron said. "You can never bother us again. You don't follow us, you don't send people after us, and you forget we ever existed in the first place. And if I'm forgetting anything else important, that applies too. Just find a new sacrifice for your ritual."

Lord Valdis exhaled a long, loud sigh. "Very well, Aeron. You have me at a disadvantage. I agree to your terms."

He lifted his right hand off the skull on his chair and made a slight motion with his fingers. The huge soldier—he was almost Garrick's size—who'd been holding onto Kallie walked her halfway over to Aeron.

The huge soldier stopped just inside the perimeter of the scimitar guards and released his grip on Kallie. She didn't move at first, so he gave her a nudge with his armored knuckles, and she started toward Aeron.

She passed Garrick, who stared at her with the same rage that he'd been staring at Aeron with, and then he refocused that gaze on Aeron.

As Kallie approached, Aeron glanced at Kent, who hadn't moved. His face remained neutral, and Aeron hoped he could still count on Kent for help if it came to it. After all, he'd promised to help Aeron do whatever it took to bring Kallie back safely.

Then again, Aeron's actions had now directly threatened all of their lives in an impossible situation. If Kent helped, he would almost certainly die along with Aeron, so perhaps Kent might not intervene. Aeron had no problem dying for his sister, but he couldn't expect to hold Kent to that standard as well.

A part of Aeron withered when he met Kent's eyes. He'd finally found Kallie, but doing so had thrown his life into disarray. To save her, he would lose his new friends one way or another.

But Kallie was more important. He had to protect her. She meant more to him than a band of mercs ever could.

Aeron would've looked at Mehta next to try to read him, but it would mean looking too far away from Kallie, and Aeron didn't want to risk it.

Mehta definitely wouldn't help. He was too smart to risk his life in this sort of situation, especially when he had a sister of his own to care for back in some village in the mountains somewhere.

So Aeron was alone. But if no one tried to sneak up on him from behind, they might have a chance to make it out alive.

Kallie drew in close enough that Aeron could take her by her wrist, so he shifted the dragon egg to one hand again and took hold of her. The egg wobbled in his hand, and Garrick tensed, but Aeron found his balance and kept it from falling.

If it fell, he wouldn't have any bargaining leverage anymore, and they'd all be dead. Or at least he would, and then they'd do whatever they wanted with Kallie afterward.

Aeron glanced down and remembered Kallie was barefoot, but he wasn't about to demand they find her some boots. Once he got her onto Wafer's back, it wouldn't matter anyway. She could wear his cloak if she got too cold while they were flying.

Then again, the cold might do her fever some serious good. He could feel how hot she was running even through the leather of his gauntlets.

Focus, Aeron. None of it would matter if he couldn't get her out of there alive. *One step at a time.*

"You really shouldn't be doing this," Kallie muttered. She had a dazed look in her eyes, and she quivered and wobbled like the egg in his other hand.

She was definitely not right, but at least she wasn't outright resisting him. He hadn't been too sure she'd comply once he took hold of her.

"You'll thank me later," Aeron muttered back. "You know, when you're still alive."

With that, they started walking backward toward the throne room's double-doors.

But as he walked backward, something shot at him out of the corner of his eye.

It was one of the scimitars, gleaming as it flashed toward his neck.

Aeron gasped.

But the scimitar clanged to a halt against two simple, iron knives, both held by a pair of dark-skinned hands.

Mehta.

He moved in a savage blur, and the next instant, the guard who'd attacked Aeron slumped to the floor, bleeding out from deep lacerations in his throat, stomach, arms, and one of his legs.

CRASH.

The sound of stone shattering against stone ripped into Aeron's ears, and he looked around for another guard coming toward him.

But it wasn't another guard.

Then Aeron looked down and saw the fractured remains of the dragon egg scattered across the throne room floor.

CHAPTER TWENTY-SIX

Mehta watched as Lord Valdis rose to his full height with his fists clenched and baring his teeth at the sight of the shattered egg. Anger exuded from every inch of his body, and his eyes flared with dark power.

But despite his evident rage, Lord Valdis didn't move beyond that, nor did he use any magic that Mehta could discern. Instead, as his guards approached to continue the fight, Lord Valdis sat down on his throne again, still obviously furious and attentive to the happenings in his throne room but not engaging in any of it himself.

That was fine with Mehta. Better to work his way over to Lord Valdis if that's how this was going to play out. Fighting off a bunch of guards and potentially several of Lord Valdis's soldiers would consume most of Mehta's attention, and dealing with the power of a dark lord amid all of that would pull his focus in too many directions at once.

As Aeron ushered Kallie into a corner, Mehta stared down the two nearest guards.

When the first guard had attacked Aeron, instinct had propelled Mehta forward to intervene. He didn't know exactly why he'd done it, but he'd chosen his side, and now he needed to make sure he survived long enough to sift Lord Valdis in spite of his choice.

The two guards hurtled toward him in a flurry of fast, arcing scimitar attacks.

Mehta ducked under the first cut, closed his distance, and slashed his knife across the guard's inner thigh. The knife split his trousers and his flesh wide open, and he went down, clutching at the bloody, gaping wound.

The next guard also swung high, but from Mehta's other side. Mehta slipped under that attack and drove his knife hard into the guard's gut. Then he wrenched it through the guard's flesh and innards and back out again, flinging blood and soft tissue across the floor.

Mehta's thirst reveled in every single drop of blood spilled.

As the second guard fell, Mehta tucked his knives into his sheaths, reached down, and picked up the guards' fallen scimitars. Aeron joined him with his spear at the ready, and they faced the approaching guards together.

Then Garrick shoved past the guards, wielding his snow steel sword and shield. A fury the likes of which Mehta had never seen burned in his dark eyes.

⚘

As Kent watched the situation unfold, he realized he had to make a choice, and quickly. A portion of the guards surrounding the four mercs had turned their attention toward him, despite his silence and stillness since Aeron had taken the egg.

The throne room was a large space, and it would've afforded him ample ability to move around to engage the approaching guards. And with all the granite in the throne room, he'd have an ample supply of fodder for rock-based magic, even if it meant possibly bringing down the castle in the process.

But when Garrick pushed past the guards and charged toward Aeron and Mehta, Kent recognized only a handful of possible outcomes.

Factoring in Garrick's choice to side against Aeron and Mehta, the number of guards, the inevitable arrival of Lord Valdis's soldiers, and Lord Valdis's untold power, only one outcome ended with a high probability of Kent staying alive.

So as the guards approached him, he released the rock in his hand, bent down, placed his palms flat on the stone floor, and cycled his magic into it. The technique worked as it had back in Lord Glavan's study, and he started to become a living statue.

It pained him to do so, but not physically. He'd sworn to help Aeron find Kallie and bring her back, but the way the situation had deteriorated, there was no chance Aeron would survive, even with Kent intervening.

The end result would mean certain death for Aeron and now Mehta, and ultimately nothing would change. Kallie would still be sacrificed, and they'd

278

all be dead. So it made no sense to sacrifice himself along with Aeron if they couldn't succeed.

Kent was a man of honor, but when sworn oaths conflicted with each other, he had to choose between them. The oath he'd sworn to avenge his father's murder trumped his oath regarding Kallie. It was a hard choice, but he'd made hard choices his entire life. And this wouldn't be the last hard choice he would have to make.

As his body fully turned to stone, Kent took one glance at Lord Valdis, who again sat in his chair, wearing a mask of anger as he surveyed the fracas —or perhaps he was just focused. If Lord Valdis joined the battle, everything would end much sooner.

The large soldier who'd brought in Kallie stood at Lord Valdis's side, apathetic. The black helmet on his head concealed his face, so Kent couldn't discern his reaction to any of it.

But despite it all, Kent's mind was already made up. If he wanted to live, he had to do this. And he had to live if he intended to bring Fane his reckoning one day.

Now totally made of stone, Kent removed the dragon sword from his back and his other sword from his hip, and he laid them both on the floor before the guards. In the past, when he'd turned to stone, he couldn't talk. Likewise, he couldn't speak now.

In order to show submission, Kent bowed his head, touched it to the floor, and continued to cycle magic into the stone through his forehead as he raised his hands in surrender.

❧

AERON COULDN'T BELIEVE THIS WAS HAPPENING. HE'D HAD EVERYTHING UNDER control until that guard had attacked him. If Mehta hadn't intervened, he'd be dead, and Kallie would've soon followed.

Now they stood toe-to-toe with Garrick, who attacked them with reckless abandon. Aeron jabbed his spear at Garrick multiple times, but Garrick's shield had deflected it each time.

Meanwhile, Mehta darted around, dodging and swinging his scimitars at Garrick like a demon from the Underworld. He leaped and lashed and flipped and even slid across the floor while trying to attack, but Garrick defended each strike with precision and great timing.

Aeron noticed a handful of guards circling around Garrick and Mehta's fight toward Kallie, who still hid in the corner, curled up with her hands covering her head. He rushed to engage them.

The first guard swung his scimitar, but Aeron had the reach advantage and jabbed the guard in his gut before he could get in a follow-up swing. It wasn't a fatal blow, but it had drawn blood, and the guard staggered back with his free hand pressed against his stomach.

Another guard took his place, more cautious than the first, and unwilling to attack first. Aeron swung at him, and the second guard parried the strike away. Aeron leaned into the momentum of his strike being batted away, and he brought his spear around his head high and hard at the guard.

It clanged against the guard's scimitar, but it knocked the guard off-balance. By that point, Aeron was already in motion. He leaped at a nearby pillar off his right leg, planted his left foot against the pillar, pushed off it, and delivered a stunning kick to the guard's head.

When Aeron landed, his back pain spiked, but the guard went down hard, unconscious. Aeron wanted to take a moment to breathe, but two more guards took the first one's place. No time to rest.

Aeron didn't know why Lord Valdis hadn't jumped into the fray with his guards, but right then, it didn't matter. He was just glad he didn't have to fight a dark lord in addition to Garrick and all of these guards.

He could handle the guards well enough... probably... and once he did, he could get Kallie out of there.

Aeron regained his footing and then engaged them next.

❧

GARRICK WAS MOVING FASTER THAN HE'D EVER THOUGHT POSSIBLE—FASTER than he had against the guards at Lord Glavan's manse and the cultists in the Crimson Flame temples. But he had to in order to block Mehta's attacks and still manage some sort of counterattack.

The way Mehta moved baffled Garrick. It was unlike any fighting style he'd ever seen, full of acrobatic evasions and attacks, punctuated by insanely fast strikes and combinations, and glancing parries and blocks only when necessary. Mehta was absolutely relentless.

As they fought, Garrick recalled the few instances where Mehta had made him uneasy. This was Garrick's chance to show that he wouldn't be intimidated, that he wouldn't back down.

If Garrick had been fighting Aeron alone, the fight would've ended within seconds. But now, fighting Mehta, he wondered if he could even land a single blow.

No, he couldn't think like that. Mehta was talented and skilled, but he was no match for someone like Garrick. And Garrick aimed to prove it to him.

He parried two quick strikes from Mehta's scimitars with his sword, then he blocked another three with his shield. The runes on both of his weapons glowed with blue and teal light.

What was it with the mercs he'd recruited lately? First Noraff and Phesnos had betrayed him, and now Mehta and Aeron. He wanted to kill them all.

Noraff and Phesnos had done it for the coin, while Aeron was just trying to save his sister. On some level, Garrick couldn't fault him for it; if he'd been in Aeron's situation, he would've fought for her, too.

But that didn't change the fact that Aeron had nearly ruined everything in the process.

Mehta, on the other hand... Garrick wasn't sure why he'd chosen to fight alongside Aeron. Perhaps he'd simply made a different choice.

Or perhaps he'd had some sort of ulterior motive all along. It hadn't made sense when he'd refused to take gold from Lord Glavan's vault. Maybe it had something to do with his betrayal here and now. Garrick didn't know for sure, and he probably never would.

Kent had proven little better. He'd known about the situation with Aeron's sister, and he hadn't said anything to Garrick. They'd finally started getting along, too, but in the end, he'd chosen loyalty to Aeron over Garrick.

Then again, maybe he hadn't. Once the fight broke out, he'd turned himself to stone and surrendered his weapons. Kent hadn't outright sided with Aeron in this battle, but if he'd wanted to regain a measure of favor with Garrick, he should've helped take down Mehta and Aeron instead.

But he'd been close with Aeron since the beginning, so perhaps Kent choosing to remain neutral, in this case, was the best Garrick could've hoped for. It would've been far worse if he'd sided with them *against* Garrick.

Ultimately, Kent's decision had been a shrewd one, even if Garrick didn't like it.

He could ignore Kent... for now. But in light of what had happened, Garrick would need to re-prove his loyalty to Lord Valdis by bringing him their heads. He just hoped it would be enough to save his own life.

And he had to do it before Lord Valdis decided to join the battle. If that happened, it would be too late for Garrick.

No. He would prove he could handle this.

If he could find a way to defeat Mehta. Any attack Garrick threw, Mehta countered three-fold.

If Garrick couldn't find an opening, how would he end the fight?

WITH THE OTHER GUARDS DEAD OR DISABLED, AERON TURNED HIS ATTENTION back to Kallie, who still recoiled in the corner. Above all else, Aeron had to get her out of there.

If Mehta came with them, they'd have a better chance of escaping the castle. And if they could get outside, Wafer would do the rest.

Somehow, Mehta knocked Garrick's shield to the side with his scimitars, ducked low, and spun around with a kick that swept Garrick off his feet.

With Garrick down, it was their best chance to escape.

"Mehta!" Aeron cried as he pulled Kallie up to her feet. "Let's go!"

❧

MEHTA WHIRLED TOWARD THE SOUND OF AERON'S VOICE. HE STOOD AT THE double-doors leading into the throne room with his spear in one hand and Kallie in the other.

Then Mehta glanced back at Lord Valdis and the scene before him.

Garrick lay on the ground, but he was starting to get up. Lord Valdis still sat in his throne, unmoving, with the big soldier standing next to him.

Why hadn't Lord Valdis attacked? Was he really that unconcerned with the four mercenaries dueling each other in the middle of his throne room? Did he consider them to be just a nuisance and not a real threat?

Halfway between Mehta and Lord Valdis, Kent had knelt down with his forehead to the floor, laid his swords in front of him, put his hands up as if in surrender. Somewhere along the way, he'd turned himself into stone.

Several guards still stood between Mehta and Lord Valdis. They were spread out enough that he'd have time between each one if he had to engage them, but they were close enough that they might manage to overwhelm him, especially if Garrick continued to fight as well.

And thus far, he hadn't broken through Garrick's defenses except for that one leg sweep. With Garrick's snow steel sword and shield in play, coupled with his durable skin, enormous strength, and fighting prowess, how would Mehta even get close to defeating him?

And if Lord Valdis found a reason to join the fight with his untold power, what then?

But a hard truth gnawed at Mehta's core: if he didn't find a way to sift Lord Valdis now, he would never get another chance.

If Mehta went with Aeron and Kallie, he could save them. They would need his help to get out of Valdis Keep alive.

Yet in doing so, he would leave his final commission unfulfilled. Lord

Valdis would continue to live, and the deaths of Mehta's parents would remain unavenged.

He would let down his grandfather, his sister, and Ferne. He would return to them a failure.

The Xyonate within him refused to fail. His thirst urged him to take on the remainder of Lord Valdis's guards, to find a way to overcome Garrick, and to send Lord Valdis to the Underworld where he belonged.

And that's how Mehta knew it wasn't the right decision.

His thirst only wanted blood, death, and destruction. It didn't care what consequences his actions might trigger. It didn't care about the people he loved. And it didn't care whether he lived or died.

It just wanted what it wanted.

So Mehta chose to follow Aeron and Kallie.

But first, he had to get rid of the scimitars in his hands. So Mehta lined up his throw, pulled both scimitars over his head, and hurled them at Lord Valdis.

They arced through the air, two gleaming blades of death that reflected firelight onto the dark walls and pillars around them as they spiraled. It was a perfect throw—Mehta's aim had been true.

But the huge soldier ripped his sword from its scabbard and smacked both of the scimitars out of the air the instant before they could reach Lord Valdis. Then the soldier sheathed his sword and stood at Lord Valdis's side as if nothing had happened.

The three-horned ram sigil on his chest mocked Mehta's failure.

And Lord Valdis hadn't so much as flinched.

There was nothing else to be done, so Mehta drew his knives and ran after Aeron and Kallie, trying to ignore his disappointment.

Outside the throne room, the two soldiers who'd opened the double-doors for them on their way in attacked. Mehta sifted one with his knives, and Aeron skewered the other with his spear.

Then Mehta led Aeron and Kallie through the castle's dark halls and toward the way out.

By the time Garrick made it to his feet, Mehta, Aeron, and Kallie were gone. Mehta's kick had taken him by surprise, but it hadn't hurt him any more than landing on his back had.

He rushed toward the door, eager to pursue them.

"Garrick." Lord Valdis's voice pierced into Garrick's ears, and he stopped.

He watched the doorway for a moment, pondering what his response should be if Lord Valdis or his men attacked. Would he fight back? Try to remain alive for as long as possible? What would they do to him? What would they do to Kent?

Hopefully nothing. After all, Garrick still had one last card to play—one final effort to nullify Lord Valdis's ire.

So he turned around and faced his employer.

"You have failed me yet again," Lord Valdis said.

Garrick looked down at the remains of the shattered dragon egg on the floor. Then he started walking toward his pack, which still lay on the floor near the chests of gold where he'd dropped it.

"With all due respect, Lord Valdis..." Garrick stopped at Kent's position and nudged his stony form with the toe of his boot. Whatever was about to happen, Kent was going to endure it right along with Garrick, whether he wanted to or not. "...no, I haven't."

Garrick let his snow steel sword slip from his fingers, and it clattered onto the floor. Then he pulled the shield off his arm and let that drop as well. It hit the granite tiles with a *clank*.

As Kent rose to his feet next to him, his stony visage began to shift back into that of human skin. He stared at Garrick with curiosity and confusion in his eyes.

Garrick just gave him a small nod. They would have words later on, for sure. But first, Garrick had to save their lives from Lord Valdis's wrath.

He approached his pack slowly, and Kent followed him by several tentative steps.

While the guards, the big soldier, and Lord Valdis watched his every move, Garrick picked up the pack, opened it, and pulled out the bit of insurance he'd taken from the blue pyramid.

CHAPTER TWENTY-SEVEN

By some miracle—mostly thanks to Mehta's ability to see in the dark and his unbelievable fighting prowess—Aeron and Kallie had escaped Valdis Keep. They never would've made it out without Mehta's help. Aeron owed him more than he could probably ever repay.

Aeron had helped along the way, but it was hard to keep track of a confused Kallie, wield a spear, and not lose his bearings, so Mehta had done most of the work when it came to Lord Valdis's men.

The moment they emerged from the castle's doors into the snow-covered courtyard, Aeron blew his Wafer whistle with every ounce of air in his lungs. He prayed that Wafer would hear it over Xenthan's howling, bitter winds.

Poor Kallie was still barefoot, but when she stepped into the snow, it hissed and steamed around her. She was running unnaturally hot thanks to her fever, but weather like this might kill her anyway, regardless of her temperature.

So Aeron tossed his spear to Mehta, who used it to fend off the approaching guards while Aeron scooped Kallie into his arms and carried her through the snow. He alternated glances between the crimson skies and the castle doors to make sure no one was following them.

Meanwhile, Mehta painted the snow red with the blood of the soldiers rushing toward them. The sight made Aeron wonder why he'd even bothered to learn to use a spear in the first place. By comparison, Mehta's proficiency made Aeron feel like a boy with a long stick.

Wafer still hadn't come, but Aeron could feel him approaching through their bond. He was close.

Aeron continued to trudge through the snow, and Kallie whimpered in his arms, shivering and dazed. She wasn't heavy, but his back was starting to ache. He couldn't carry her forever. Wafer needed to get there fast.

Hurry, he sent to Wafer through their bond.

Soon, Wafer sent back.

Aeron just hoped it would be soon enough.

Mehta felled the last of the soldiers approaching him from the courtyard gate, then he started heading back toward Aeron and Kallie—or rather, toward the soldiers now pursuing them from inside the castle.

As Mehta passed them by, Aeron saw Wafer descending from the skies. He landed hard in the snowy courtyard, snarling and growling. Aeron got Kallie over to him and helped her onto Wafer's back, just behind the saddle. Mehta would have to ride behind her, and Wafer would have to make do with the extra weight.

Aeron turned back and called for Mehta, who'd already slain two more soldiers and was now taking on three others. As he did, Aeron noticed movement along the battlements of Valdis Keep.

Archers. And... catapults? And ballistae?

Soldiers in black armor rushed along the walls, taking up various positions and readying large-scale weaponry.

All to bring down Wafer? All to stop Aeron from escaping with Kallie?

"Mehta!" Aeron screamed again. "We have to go *now!*"

Mehta felled one of the three guards coming for him and abruptly turned and hurried toward Aeron and Wafer. As Aeron rushed back to mount Wafer, arrows began landing in the snow around him. One even glanced off the armor on his left shoulder.

He cursed and leaped onto Wafer's back.

Then the arrows started to hit Wafer.

Most of them pinged off his scales, but every so often, one stuck into his hide. Each time, he grunted. Arrows wouldn't kill Wafer or even do significant damage thanks to his scales, but if enough of them hit true, they might make it harder for him to fly. And they could certainly hit Aeron, Mehta, and Kallie.

Worse yet, the ballistae and the catapults were moving. The cranking and clinking of their metal chains broke through the vicious wind and reached Aeron's ears.

Mehta wasn't going to make it in time. They needed to come to him, or the heavy weapons would take Wafer out. Plus, Wafer would have an easier time lifting off with only two people rather than three, especially in this snow.

"Hold on!" Aeron yelled to Kallie, and she wrapped her arms around his waist. He could feel her shivering, but she gave off heat like a fiery furnace against the back of his armor.

Amid the dozens of arrows zipping down at them, Wafer loosed a roar and jumped into the air, and his wings slapped against the frigid winter winds. Aeron directed him toward Mehta, who still hurried toward them as fast as the snow would allow.

A heavy *thunk* sounded from above. Aeron looked up in time to see a rock the size of Wafer's head careening toward them.

Dive! he sent to Wafer, who complied instantly. The dip sent a rush into Aeron's gut, and the rock sailed over them by at least ten feet.

Ahead of them, Mehta lifted the spear horizontally over his head, holding it with two hands, and he kept running. Arrows chased his footsteps and dug into the snow-covered ground all around him.

Perfect. Smart. Aeron told Wafer to grab the spear, and they swooped even lower toward Mehta.

His talons opened, and he snatched up the spear, taking Mehta with him. Wafer's wings beat harder and faster with the added weight, but he continued to ascend into the crimson sky.

Two-hundred feet. Three hundred. The arrows weren't even coming close anymore.

Another *thunk* sounded, and then another, both different than the first two.

Two iron bolts, each nearly the length of Aeron's spear, shot toward them.

Wafer evaded them, but in doing so, he flung Mehta off the spear. To Aeron's surprise, Mehta didn't scream or yell—or maybe the relentless wind was drowning him out.

But Wafer dipped and dove after him. He must've shifted Aeron's spear to a single set of talons because he grabbed Mehta by his leg about twenty feet from impact. Then Wafer flew parallel with the ground for a good fifty feet before he started to ascend again.

Arrows pinged off Wafer's scales once more, and a few narrowly missed Aeron. He couldn't tell from atop Wafer whether Mehta had been hit or not, so he just kept Wafer flying away.

Eventually, the arrows fell short once again, and before long, they'd flown far beyond the reach of even the most advanced battlement weapons Aeron knew of. They landed ahead of the nearest mountains, with Wafer setting Mehta down on a patch of virgin snow, upside down.

Mehta bounced up, took hold of Aeron's spear from Wafer's talons, and tossed it to Aeron, who anchored it in its spot on Wafer's back. Then Aeron extended his hand down toward Mehta to help him up.

Mehta brushed the snow off of his cloak and out of his dark hair. He took Aeron's hand and climbed onto Wafer behind Kallie.

"Thank you," he said.

Aeron wanted to laugh. Mehta was thanking him when he had singlehandedly saved both Aeron's and Kallie's lives.

"No," Aeron said. "Thank you."

Wafer's head bobbed in agreement. Then Wafer chomped his jaw open and closed.

"We'll get you something to eat once we're out of here," Aeron said. "As soon as I figure out where we're going."

Thanks to an apothecary in western Urthia, he'd been able to restock on shrooms before they'd returned to Xenthan. So before they took off again, Aeron popped another one. Carrying Kallie had aggravated his back, and he didn't want to fly while in pain.

But even if he'd run out of shrooms and had to live with constant pain the rest of his life, it wouldn't have mattered. Kallie was safe—as long as Aeron got her somewhere out of this weather in a reasonable amount of time—and they'd escaped Lord Valdis's clutches.

Aeron commanded Wafer to fly again, and he leaped into the air and started flapping his wings. Within a minute, they'd ascended a thousand feet into the sky.

Kallie still clung to Aeron, and Mehta held onto Kallie while Wafer did the heavy lifting. Kallie still burned behind Aeron. It made flying through these harsh winter conditions both better because of the added warmth and worse because of Aeron's concern for her. But as an added bonus, her heat helped to soothe his back a bit.

"Head south," Mehta called.

Aeron shook his head. "We can't go back to Govalia. That's what they'll expect."

"That's why you should head south," Mehta yelled over the wind. "Let them see you flying that way. It'll confirm their suspicions. Then, when we're far out of range, cut to the west and head north along the mountains that run between Xenthan and Etrijan."

"The Thornback Mountains?" Aeron asked as he directed Wafer to the south.

"Yes," Mehta shouted.

"Why? What's up there?"

"A safe, secret place," Mehta yelled. "My home."

Kent didn't know what to expect when Garrick reached into his pack. And when he saw what Garrick pulled out, he marveled at the sight of it.

Another dragon egg.

There had been two all along? And Garrick hadn't told anyone?

Like the first one, it looked like an egg-shaped stone, gray and simple, but flecks of crystal across its surface glinted in the firelight as Garrick held it out toward the guards.

At the sight of the egg, Lord Valdis smiled, although his horrible eyes did not change whatsoever. They continued to burn with that same dark, arcane energy.

He extended his hand, and one of his scimitar-wielding guards extended his hand as well.

Garrick stepped forward and placed the egg in the guard's open hand, then he returned to his position next to Kent. He dug into his pack again and produced the huge tome of rituals with the emblem that matched Kallie's mark on its cover.

"I have this, too." He held it up for Lord Valdis to see. "Just like you requested."

Lord Valdis's hand was still extended, and a second guard's scimitar lowered, and he opened his hand.

Garrick walked over to him and placed the tome in that guard's hand. When he'd returned to his spot, he looked at Lord Valdis and waited, silent.

"I must say, Garrick," Lord Valdis began, "your former partner gave me great cause for concern. With his theft of the young lady who had committed herself to the forthcoming ritual, I must now postpone it until she is returned to me.

"I suspect that will not happen before the new moon in two days, so I must postpone the ritual yet again until the lunar cycle catches up to my ambitions." Lord Valdis shook his head slightly. "To say that I am displeased would be a drastic understatement."

"I apologize, Lord Valdis." Garrick lowered his head and shot a glare at Kent. "I couldn't have foreseen that he'd behave in such a way. I didn't know any of this would happen."

Kent didn't respond one way or another. Garrick hadn't told him or any of the others about the extra egg, so he didn't feel nearly as bad about withholding the truth about Aeron's sister from him. Besides, it wasn't Kent's fault that Garrick had fallen asleep during the beginning of that conversation.

And besides that, Lord Valdis already knew Kent's role as the tome's translator, so he understood Kent's role in Aeron's plot—if it could even be called that—as well. He just prayed he'd found the right mixture of loyalty and restraint to justify his continued existence.

"I suppose you would tell me that you should not be punished since you succeeded in delivering that which I requested of you," Lord Valdis said.

Garrick remained silent for a long moment.

Kent didn't blame him. In the face of such power, and given the entrapping quality of the question, he wasn't even sure how he would've answered.

Finally, with his head still bowed, Garrick said, "Lord Valdis, I ask only that you give me a chance to undo the damage I've done. I brought you what you requested, but in doing so I've interrupted your plans thanks to my poor judgment regarding my partners. If you'll allow me the opportunity, I *will* make this right."

Kent admired Garrick's resolve and loyalty, but he couldn't fathom why Garrick would remain steadfast and true to someone like Lord Valdis. The dark lord was saturated with dark magic. The cost for attaining such power meant he'd done horrific, unconscionable things, and he'd done them repeatedly over many years.

How many people had died to fuel Lord Valdis's "ambitions?" How many more would perish if he recovered Kallie, performed his ritual, and managed to absorb the essence of a *living dragon?*

And yet, despite having so much power already, Lord Valdis hadn't joined the fight. *But why not? If he could have just ended it...*

Kent didn't even want to think about it, yet Garrick stood next to him, offering to continue to play a pivotal role in Lord Valdis's plans. Maybe he felt as if he didn't have a choice.

Or maybe he actually *didn't* have a choice.

Lord Valdis had every advantage over Garrick. He had all the leverage.

And here, now, Kent worried that Lord Valdis had all the leverage over him as well, by virtue of his association with Garrick and his complicity in Aeron's plot. The question facing Kent might very well be, *what am I willing to do to stay alive?*

Lord Valdis stared down at Garrick, who was still bowing. "Rise."

Garrick straightened up, and Kent was once again reminded how much taller he was.

"I do not often give second chances," Lord Valdis said. "You have proven exceptionally useful to me over these last few years when I have called upon you. And it is not directly your fault that I now lack all of the elements I need to complete the ritual."

He paused. Kent and Garrick remained silent before him, unmoving and unwilling to speak.

"But you know your quarry better than anyone else I could hire, and you are far more motivated to succeed, so I will accept your offer."

Lord Valdis motioned with his hand, and two pairs of guards closed the lids on two of the three chests, picked them up, and carried them into the shadows beyond the pillars. One chest still remained.

"And when you return," he continued, "I will pay you the balance owed for bringing me the egg and the tome."

Garrick bowed to him again. "That is most generous and fair. Thank you."

"And what of your friend, here?" Lord Valdis's wicked eyes focused on Kent, and he had to try not to shudder.

It took a lot to make Kent uneasy, to strip him of his confidence, but Lord Valdis's gaze did that in an instant.

Garrick stood upright again and looked down at Kent, but he didn't say anything.

"Will he be joining you?" Lord Valdis asked.

Kent's concerns had come to fruition. He had no leverage. Lord Valdis had it all.

If he said no, Lord Valdis would probably just kill him.

But Kent hadn't surrendered earlier only to be killed now, at the end.

Yet if he said yes, was he tethering himself to Lord Valdis's will indefinitely, just as Garrick had?

Or was he already tethered anyway?

There was only one choice to make, and Kent made it.

"If Garrick will permit me to accompany him," Kent said, "then I will go."

Lord Valdis's menacing gaze shifted to Garrick, who studied Kent for a long, tense moment. Kent's fate was in Garrick's hands, and if he was mad enough about Kent withholding the information about Kallie, then Kent would perish sooner rather than later.

"I'll take him," Garrick finally said.

Kent exhaled a silent breath of relief. He was fully prepared to go down fighting, but he was all the more glad he didn't have to.

"And together, we'll bring back that which is rightfully yours."

"Yes," Lord Valdis said. "You will."

The certainty in Lord Valdis's voice sickened Kent to his core, but what else could he do?

Lord Valdis extended his hand, and the guard holding the egg approached him and placed it into his palm. "Before you go, I want you to bear witness to this."

He cupped the egg with both of his hands, one on each side. Then his hands began to glow with violet light, similar in color to when Lord Glavan had stolen the life from his own guards. Only this light was different—brighter, yet still born of darkness.

The flecks of crystal within the egg glowed with the same violet light, and the egg's appearance gradually transformed from bland gray stone to a fiery orange shell spattered with burgundy and light-blue spots. It expanded to nearly double its original size.

Then it moved in Lord Valdis's hands—on its own.

Kent wasn't sure he'd actually seen it at first, but then it happened again.

The egg jerked one way, then it jerked another.

A *crack* split the quiet of the throne room, and a jagged fissure ran down the front of the egg from near the top.

Until that moment, a large part of Kent hadn't believed any of this would actually work. But now he stood in Lord Valdis's throne room, watching an egg formerly made of stone begin to hatch.

If that egg indeed contained a dragon then Lord Valdis would take its essence and use it to obtain unimaginable power.

And if Lord Valdis had already claimed the lives of countless others to obtain the terrible power he already possessed, what would he do once he took the dragon's essence?

The egg cracked again, and this time a trio of talons attached to black, scaly fingers poked out.

Upon seeing them, Kent made another choice, even though this time, he knew it would absolutely get him killed eventually, and even though it meant forsaking his oath of vengeance against Fane.

This decision was far, far more important.

Kent had chosen to stop Lord Valdis once and for all.

The three talons cracked away another piece of the egg, revealing a glowing red eye.

It blinked.

And then it stared directly at Kent.

THIS BOOK IS OVER, BUT THE MAYHEM DOESN'T STOP HERE!
The story continues in *PATH OF SHADOWS*,
Book 2 of the Blood Mercenaries series, now available for preorder!

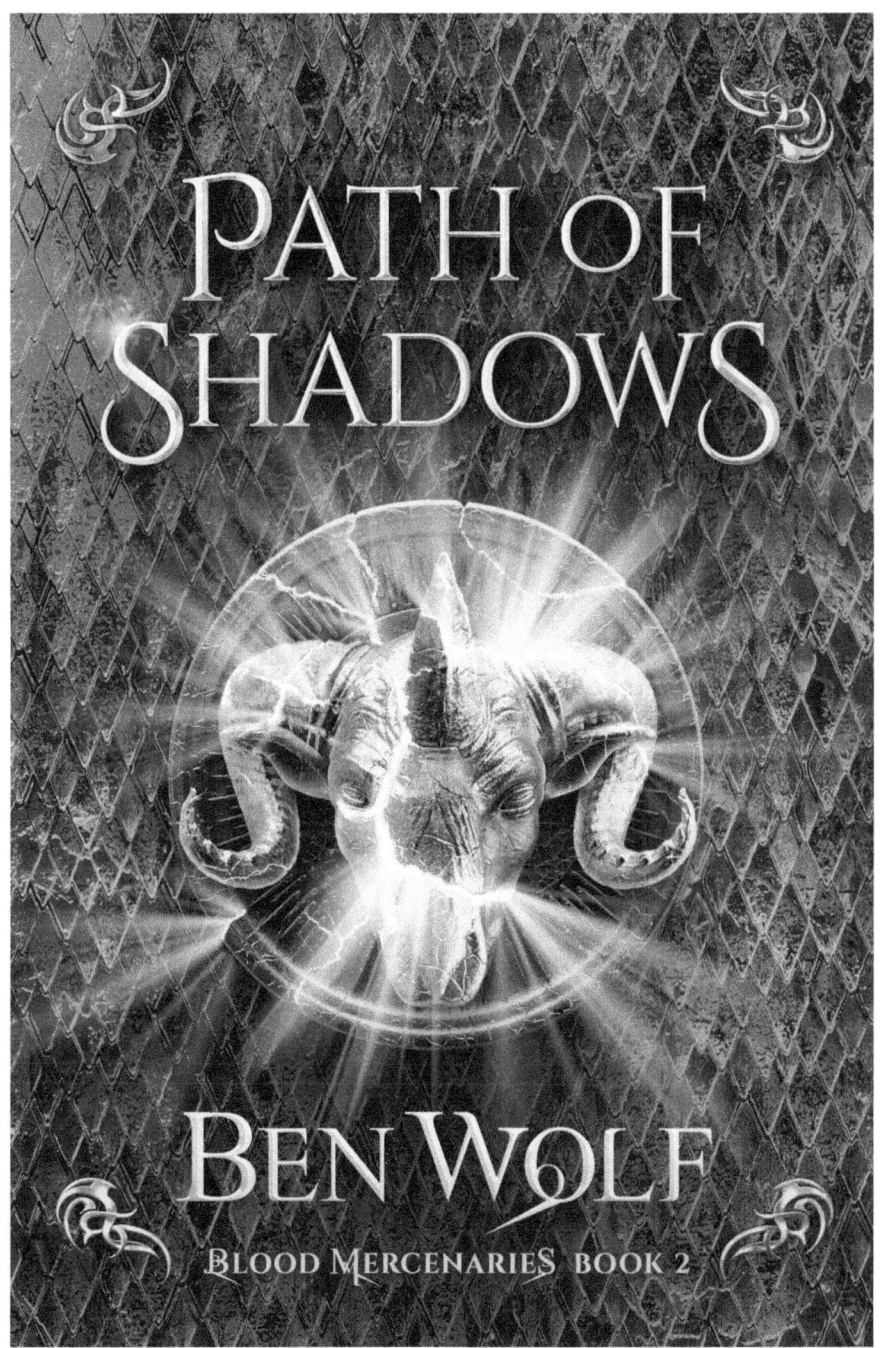

PATH OF SHADOWS

BEN WOLF

BLOOD MERCENARIES BOOK 2

WANT FOUR FREE BOOKS?
Sign up now at WWW.SUBSCRIBEPAGE.COM/FANTASY-READERS

WANT TO KNOW HOW AERON GOT WAFER BACK?
WANT TO KNOW HOW KENT ESCAPED MUROTH?
WANT TO KNOW HOW MEHTA SURVIVED THE XYONATES?
WANT TO KNOW HOW GARRICK WAS BETRAYED?

Then sign up for my newsletter. I'll give you FREE access to four prequel stories (a full novel's-worth of reading) in the Blood Mercenaries series.

Sign up now at WWW.SUBSCRIBEPAGE.COM/FANTASY-READERS

If you enjoyed this book, please leave a review on Amazon and/or Goodreads. Reviews are integral to the success of this book and my other books. Even a short review is helpful!

I love talking with my readers about my stories, so send me your thoughts at ben@benwolf.com.

Lastly, I invite you to interact with me and hang out with fellow readers who have enjoyed my books. Check out my Facebook group for readers: www.facebook.com/groups/benwolfpack/

ABOVE ALL ELSE, **THANK YOU** FOR READING *THE CRIMSON FLAME*!

WWW.BENWOLF.COM | @1BENWOLF

ACKNOWLEDGMENTS

Every published book is the culmination of a lot of hard work, dedication, and support. The author writes the book, but everything that comes after is equally essential to the success of the book.

First and foremost, I want to thank my Lord and Savior Jesus Christ.

Second, thanks to my parents for always encouraging me and for funding my early writing endeavors, trips to writers conferences, etc. You guys believed in me at an early age and continued as I grew older. Thank you.

Thank you also to my sister, Lauren, who is always a ray of sunshine.

Thanks to my all-star beta readers, Daniel Kuhnley, Chris Hall, Paige Guido, Peter Younghusband, and Michael LaBorn for your excellent feedback, encouragement, and for having my back as intelligent readers.

Thanks also to my mastermind group. It's a secret group, but you all know who you are. (insert evil laugh)

Kirk DouPonce, you are a genius. The cover is breathtaking, and I can't wait to do the rest of the series with you.

Will Wight, you are a titan. You singlehandedly helped me see the many ways the initial "finished" version of this book could be improved. Thank you for pointing me in the right direction and for being one of the catalysts that got me going on the right path. You've been so generous with your time—I am forever grateful.

Dakota Krout, thank you for your incredible generosity and time that you invested in answering my newbie questions on so many topics. I can't express how crucial your feedback and input has been to me. Thank you.

Spencer Fisher, UFC veteran and friend, thanks for being a mentor to me and for singlehandedly taught me 90% of what I know about fighting. Thanks also to Dirty Mike Hueser and the boys at jiu-jitsu for encouraging me and teaching me while simultaneously beating me up. I'll see you knuckleheads at practice, and I've got loop chokes for all of you.

Thank you to all of my readers. Without you, I wouldn't be doing this.

Thanks especially to my haters and to the people who have treated me like garbage over the years. Your behavior has made me a better person (as in, not terrible like you) and to succeed so hard that you all get jealous of me. If you're not jealous yet, you will be. Give it time. I'm just getting started.

If I neglected to thank someone, please forgive me. I still love you.

Thanks also to my kids, Liam and Violet, who at the time this book was initially published were nowhere near old enough to read it. But you're still great kids, and I love you very much.

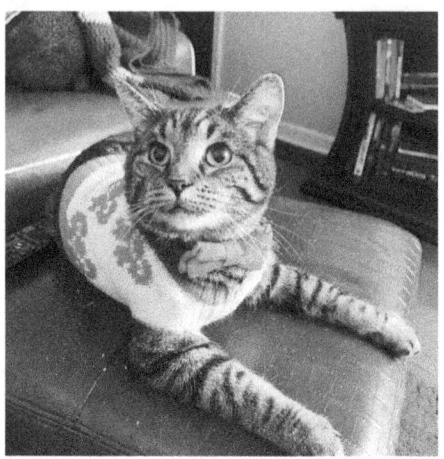

Marco, you're my fluffiest little friend, and I love you. Thanks for distracting me from working whether I need the distraction or not.

Last of all, thank you especially to my intelligent, beautiful, thoughtful, and ultra-supportive wife, Charis. The mere thought of you fills me with joy, and I am so blessed to have you in my life. None of this would be possible without your hard work and sacrifices over the years. I love you.

About Ben Wolf

In 7th grade, I saw the movie "Congo." It was so bad, I wrote a parody of it set in Australia that featured killer kangaroos. So began my writing career.

I endeavor to produce stories that question the boundaries of morality, faith, justice, and interpersonal relationships. And I do it with lots of action, explosions, gunshots, sword-fights, and battles.

Because I love to hear myself talk, I've taught at 40+ writers conferences nationwide. I'm also the owner and founder of Splickety Publishing Group.

When not writing, I occasionally choke people in Brazilian jiujitsu. I live in the midwest with my gorgeous wife, our kids, and our cat, Marco.

Did you enjoy this story? Check out my other books on Amazon.com:

If you enjoyed this book and want updates on future projects, join my author email newsletter for occasional updates on forthcoming stories. **Sign up now!**

WWW.SUBSCRIBEPAGE.COM/FANTASY-READERS

WANT TO CONNECT WITH ME DIRECTLY? FIND ME ON SOCIAL MEDIA!

facebook.com/1benwolf

twitter.com/1benwolf

instagram.com/1benwolf

amazon.com/author/benwolf

MAP of Alethia

Elrijon

Xenthaa

Sefern

Qeburyx

Urthia

Mureth

Firstborn Province

Strecton

Drijon

Elucidor Province

manse
SEF

Govalia Shire

Govaliston

Inoth

csnal

Zindax
Ocean

Veldmoor

Tahn
Sea

pushufen

Cacles

Bonon Ocean

meow.